ALL THIS BY CHANCE

All This by Chance

Vincent O'Sullivan

INTERNATIONAL
DUBLIN
LITERARY
AWARD
2020

Victoria University Press

TE WHARE WĀNANGA O TE ŪPOKO O TE IKA A MĀUI

VICTORIA UNIVERSITY PRESS
Victoria University of Wellington
PO Box 600 Wellington
vup.victoria.ac.nz

ISBN 9781776561797

A catalogue record for this book is available from the
National Library of New Zealand.

Published with the assistance of a grant from

ARTS COUNCIL OF NEW ZEALAND *TOI AOTEAROA*

Printed by 1010 Printing International, China

For Fiona

Some of the people

Ruth (Babcia): b. 1903.
Sarah: b. 1907. Eva's mother.
Ellen McGovern: b. 1912.
Eva: b. 1927.
Stephen: b. 1925.
Lisa: b. 1947. Stephen and Eva's daughter.
David: b. 1951. Stephen and Eva's son.
Esther: b. 1975. David's daughter.
Fergus: b. 1944.
Milan: b. 1969.

Breslau was a German city close to the Polish border, largely destroyed by the Soviet army towards the end of World War II. The Potsdam conference in 1945 assigned the city to Poland, when it was renamed Wrocław.

ALL THIS BY CHANCE

1947

_____

When as a youngster David asked his father what was it like then, when they had met, what did she tell him about the train for instance, or before the train, his answers, as his grown-up son would tell him, slipped away as though he were the one being looked for, hunted down. And as the boy grew to the man who demanded more aggressively, Stephen told him how so little of the past was there, could he not see that? It was not a tide that went out and then returned. It became a sea that did not exist. But at the time he had used an image that he thought the boy with his grasping for what was gone might understand. He said you must imagine what it would be like if you took fragments chipped from a mosaic and handed them to someone, and expected him to know what it was, the picture it had been taken from.

'Or *her*,' the boy insisted. 'Expected *her*.'

'And in any case, David, you are asking me to give you what isn't mine to give.'

The boy understood little of what was said to him, any more than did the man he became and forty years later pestered still, watching as his father's hands no longer trusted themselves to raise a cup without carefully attending. Yet even then, he would say to the alert but frail man, 'Love. You shy away from saying that as if it would scald you.' And the old man would tell him simply, 'Very likely,' thinking how those as close as he and David might like to be, pass without comprehension.

In the beach house out on the coast, with the long constant haul of the surf coming up to them, David rose from the chair facing his father, angry as he so easily became, to stand at the big window, his forehead against the pane, fists in his jacket pocket. His father looking past the middle-aged man to the strident green of the hills and the patches of black bush. The strain that would never end between them. It saddened him, as did the silence so often in the room with them, as if a third person who could no more leave than he and his son might walk through the glass into the afternoon's late glittering light. He did not say, because the truth of it would rile David even more, 'You want more than any child can ever have. You cannot become your parents. Let alone the parents before them.'

He did not especially care for the successful impetuous man he had fathered. A fact of life that one accepted. He watched him at the window there a few feet in front of him, David's resenting the room he stood in, perhaps as resentful, his father supposed, of so much that lay beyond it. They said little to each other for several minutes. Then David turned and crossed the room and leaned above the old man to press his lips to his forehead. 'I know I should let things rest,' he said.

His father's hand rose to brush at David's wrist. He hoped that at least might please him.

When the boy used to insist, 'But you must remember something when you first arrived,' his father had laughed and said, 'It stank. England stank.' It shocked the boy that he had come out and said so, and thought his father teased him. But that was it all right. How it had first struck him. The old world with its reek of ash.

Unlike the fellow passengers he had nodded to, and the handful he found he could speak to without too much shyness by the journey's end, he had expected nothing, and so was neither surprised nor disappointed. On the long weeks sailing across there had been so much chatter in the dining room, then in the big lounge with its leather chairs where some passengers played bridge or dominoes or sat and ordered another round from the white-jacketed stewards. Those last few evenings, the talk of places with names like King's Lynn and Saffron Walden, and jokes about the East End and snatches of songs as someone went and sat at the piano, songs about the Old Kent Road, or following the van, lines that amused or saddened those who stood round the pianist with glasses in their hands, but none of it meaning much to him beyond the strangeness, and his own sense of loneliness, even as they kindly drew him into the sense of fun. The older men offering to buy him a stout, for good luck's sake. And that curious feeling, the apprehension he had woken with each morning since the hot green encroaching banks of the canal at Panama, and the brightly painted houses and the church where the far wall glittered with cascading gold, where they had gone ashore for six hours and his first proof that there was somewhere else. But now it was 'the home stretch' for most of them, or others who called it home even though they had not been there before. Each morning as he woke and lay watching the grey dipping sky through the porthole with its thick brass fitting, he thought, I am further away, further each day, rather than I am closer, closer to whatever it is we are coming to. But that word *further* carrying no more regret for him than did *closer* move him to much sense of excitement. From a place that at times he hated, to a place he knew nothing of.

Then through the stillness of the fog in these last two days when they had taken on trust the announcements over the loudspeaker that the coast was out there, the Lizard if only they might see it, and Land's End, as it might be told to a man whose sight had failed. And into the greyness of the estuary, the fall of flattening light on water the same colour as the air. The shape of England there in cranes and the spread of wharf sheds and the first small figures of men working heavy ropes, and the flung uncoiling thud of the loops hurled out from the ship, and the call of voices from the crew to the men running and placing them across the bollards at the wharf's edge. The ship's slow swing across the narrowing strip of churning water. But it was not this first swift taking-in of what the other side came down to after six weeks of sailing towards it, this mesh of what seemed already descending dark, although it could not be that, not yet; nor the men's high voices calling above the engines' thrum that most struck him, nor the toy scale everything seemed to take on from where he stood on the deck, and London disappearing off into haze. 'There's no end to it,' the quietly spoken Cornishman who had shared his cabin for those long waiting weeks had remarked that morning.

Not size nor the meagre light nor the strange voices that so came home to him, the narrow streets with their identical houses almost right up to underneath the ship.

'It stinks,' he had said, to a stout woman with tears in her eyes who stood beside him and moved away when he spoke. He meant not even the soft odour of rot coming up to him as the ship drew in, the debris and flotsam on the scud of water beneath them. He realised his words were more a question than a definition. It was not decay nor squalor that came in on him, but something not yet defined. A soft nudging wind now carried a drift of rain across the deck. Stephen drew the collar of his gabardine coat closer against his throat. Ah, that was it, he thought. It was the heaviness of ash pungent with rain. The smell clawed the back of his throat. He feared that he might retch at the clogging press of it, so close it seemed as if a cloth drenched with it were held against his face. And the realisation surprising him, almost as if a physical shove thrust in on him what was so obvious, and yet had not occurred to him until now. He had come to a city where war still trailed in the air. That was what he smelled.

He was glad to leave the ship, and the bonhomie he had never felt at ease with. He carried his one suitcase and followed directions a steward who was also a Londoner had given him when they talked together a few nights before. These were written for him on the folded square of ship's stationery he carried in his pocket. The streets, the buses, the Tube stations he might look out for. To walk on land again, even that felt strange. The lights from shops and the big streets tipped into a brightness that was like something on a stage rather than for real, although he had never seen a stage if it came to that, except as they

13

sometimes came up when they were part of a story at the pictures. Yet that is what so much was like, looking out from the bus window. As everyone on the ship had said, London was like nothing else. It was the centre. It was where whatever happened was bound to be new to you. That is what Will the Cornishman had warned him of. Just let things happen, he had said, just keep a sharp eye.

He had waited with other people at a bus stop, watching for the number written on his piece of paper to arrive. He saw the lights stretch out like ribbons and jog across the river, and the first buildings that he thought he recognised from photos he had seen. From the lids of cake tins even. Or ones like them anyway, because London was like itself, over and over again. And what struck him most, the buildings that were only partly there, the snapped walls and broken angles and piled brick, and the smell of ash that must be there, although he knew that might just be in his mind. You see dead broken buildings, great burned-out chunks, you imagine ash. It came in on him that this is what winning must look like. To make it like this and make it worse for someone else until they stop, and so you've won.

He changed buses twice. People were helpful if you asked them, although not easy to understand. And in a hurry. You expected that. The way you expected the sky to be glowing right across, because London was the capital, even its sky. It cheered you up, Will had said, you knew a city was safe if its sky reflected like that. He looked forward to the sky as much as anything, going back after years away. London at night, he said again. Although he didn't mind the stars, once he was down back home. Don't get him wrong.

Stephen rubbed at the window with his sleeve. The rain began again, but lightly. It was more a veil trailing across the traffic than what you would call rain. But the wetness on things shone. The branches of trees slicked and shining with it. And the brightness of the buses slipping past. All so good to look at. The circles of mist around the street lights, softening them. Then the road the bus was on became a bridge, and a long train slid beneath, the rails running between rows of houses banked on either side.

The conductor touched his shoulder. 'It's a long walk back,' he said, 'if you don't get off here, lad.' It was the street he had asked for nearly half an hour back. The short jolly man's hand in the bag he wore across his shoulder, stirring its coins as he called out stops and joked with passengers. 'Keep your curls dry,' he said, as Stephen stepped down with his suitcase into the sad attempt at rain. Then a quick moment of regret, which was hard to explain, as he watched the bus move off into the night, the lights from the shops smearing streaks along its sides.

He walked back twenty yards. He saw a clock that confirmed it was not quite six o'clock. It felt as though it might be ten. He knew the number of the shop he was looking for, in fact he had known it before the ship pulled out weeks ago on a blustery morning and the dome of the post office at the top of College Hill and a church spire that must have been Ponsonby Road, the last things he recognised before the city fell away, and the departed coast thinned out. There was the number now on a strip of glass above the doorway to the shop. So this was where he was meant to be, where Mr Lewis in his blue bow tie, his black Homburg hat, had promised him he would arrive at, as they talked in Shortland Street months before. Mr Lewis with his great eyebrows, like a joke someone wore to a party, his passion that his students get things not simply right but *exactly* right, because lives depend on that, never forget, on measurement, on precision, on following exactly what they had learned. Pharmacy is not a trade, gentlemen, it is a calling. There are people, Mr Lewis assured his evening class in the wooden annexe in Symonds Street, people who will come into the premises you hope one day to work in, who will never afford a doctor. They will trust you to listen carefully. Listen with patience and courtesy but most of all with skill. As he also would tell them while they looked back with incredulity, there is nothing to fear in examinations, it was the privilege of knowledge to be tested, that even potassium, say, to take an element at random, was a wonder in itself, as was every other word he instructed them on. He was easy to make fun of, with his accent that was like a comedian's waiting to make them laugh, and the finicky care of his dress, the thick black-framed glasses above a nose that could have come with the exaggerated eyebrows from the Joke Emporium in Karangahape Road. Mr Lewis who had no notion of the kindly mockery when at the end of one term his class gave him a large Cuban cigar as a present, for he never went to the cinema, nor knew how his dignity, which meant much to him, teetered on the edge of ridicule. But Stephen liked him, and Mr Lewis liked him back. Without assuming more closeness than was proper between teacher and pupil they would at times talk a little after class, and the pupil sometimes helped to tidy the room where a dozen other young men, and one middle-aged woman, two evenings a week, learned the privileged mysteries of the ancient craft of pharmacy, as he so insisted they call it. 'Chemist' was a misnomer they were wise to avoid. At least Stephen and Miss Clifford understood. Theirs would be an ageless gift, to make the world a better place.

'So, London?' Mr Lewis said. 'So soon as next month?'

Stephen told him, 'I fight with my father every time I see him. Better to get out of it altogether.'

'The war's hardly over. It won't be beer and skittles.'

'I have to go somewhere. I don't know anywhere else.' Even to himself, as he said it, the curious sadness of what his life must sound like putting it like that, the thinness of it, which was not what he meant. He meant a place to learn about other things.

Mr Lewis stood silent a moment, as though surprised that he might be confided in. He tapped at his glasses. Then 'Away is sometimes the best,' he said. He wrote a name and address on a piece of paper, an old and good friend he said from when he was his best pupil's own age. Before that, even. A friend to whom he would write. 'It is always good to have a contact,' Mr Lewis said. 'It is an easy place to get lost.' And Stephen knew without it needing to be explained that the man in front of him, with the kind of tie you saw no one wear except in photographs of Winston Churchill, with a face people sometimes smiled at, was the kindest person he had met. They shook hands and Mr Lewis did an unexpected thing. He put his other hand on Stephen's arm and drew him towards him, so slightly that their shoulders barely touched, and he then turned and walked up the hill, each of them too embarrassed to have known what to say. The number he had written for him there in front of Stephen now. In gold, on glass that was black like tar. And swirly, dragony, so old-fashioned it must have been up there a hundred years.

17

This then was where he was meant to be. In the window in front of him there was a huge glass bottle, almost the size of a man, full of lime-coloured liquid. The stopper was as big as a head. The door Stephen opened was divided into squares of orange-tinted glass, and along one wall of the space he entered were shelves cluttered with an array of differently shaped cardboard boxes. Below them were rows of wooden drawers, with handwritten cards set in metal slots, and brass clasps to slide them in and out. The names on the cards were abbreviated Latin words. The mysteries of the craft, Mr Lewis had liked calling them, the words he insisted to his students they must become as familiar with as with their own names.

A man seated behind the counter looked up as he entered, a wire running from above the door tripping off a tinny ringing. As he moved, a dot of reflected light slid across his balding head. He stood, both hands pressing on the counter as though to help him rise. He wore a white smock and a plain dark tie, and gave the impression of formal tidiness, although within those few seconds Stephen took in how the shop could do with a thorough tidying up. Then as the man walked towards him, he saw that he was not as old as he had supposed, although his face was hatched with deep lines, as though a fine net pulled back against the skin. There was a name for that condition, Stephen thought, I should remember that. He would look it up.

'Mr Golson?' Stephen asked.

The man looked at him without speaking, and nodded to his suitcase, meaning him to set it down. Then after what seemed a long time, he said, 'You must be the boy.'

'What boy's that?' An edge of truculence in Stephen's

voice, which embarrassed him. But he disliked the man saying that to him.

The man surprised him then by laughing, shaking his head as if to say, We're off to a bad start here then, aren't we just? 'I don't know what I expected. What kind of native old Nat had sent me.' And noticing his visitor seemed more disconcerted still, he rubbed the back of his neck, as if pondering where he might go from here. 'So,' he said. A finger tapped at the bridge of his spectacles. He was a man who fidgeted. The light continued to slip across his moist baldness at each move. 'So this is what they look like out there, is it? If they grow up eating decent food?' He continued to laugh, a curious almost soundless opening of his mouth, a slight tilting back of his head.

I seem to strike him as a joke, Stephen thought. He felt himself warm with confusion. The man's accent alone was puzzling for him, the kind he had heard only in the pictures, odder even than Mr Lewis's. Yet so obviously there was kindness in his speaking too, even the sense that he was pleased the young fellow had arrived. And now that Mr Golson raised his hand to run it along the length of his tie, Stephen saw he wore a ring with a small black stone on his little finger, a ring which in time he would see so often removed and placed on a square cloth in the small dispensary out the back, as though to work while wearing jewellery was not the thing a professional ought do. But out here, in the shop, it was always there, the ring with the black stone.

Then out of the blue Mr Golson was assuming Mr Lewis and the young man he had sent must surely have been friends. 'And Nat?' he was asking. 'I don't expect he'll ever come back, not now?'

19

Stephen again embarrassed, at his having to say Nat Lewis had been his teacher, that he himself was just one among other pupils, he hardly knew him well enough to talk about anything other than what they were there for, to become pharmacists. 'Mr Lewis never talked about himself.'

'I suppose not,' Mr Golson said. He was disappointed. He turned and nodded at the shelves, while his hand indicated beyond where they stood, to the counter with its slew of papers, to whatever lay there beyond the counter, behind the curtain made from dozens of long beaded strings. Two lights in round white semi-transparent globes, set above curled iron brackets, lit the entire shop. Mr Golson said, 'Different when my assistant was here. She believed in lighting up the street until the blackouts. Now it's only me I get by on half.' And laughing his almost silent laugh, as though there was a joke there somewhere Stephen failed to catch, 'You'll get used to it all. If you've a mind to.'

And so it was done, as quickly as that. There was no further mention of the letter from his old friend, his fellow apothecary across there on what he imagined the world's bright side to be, for it would become a habit, in the months ahead, even when the stream of traffic in the road outside glittered in sunlight, and people moved about in summer clothes, for David Golson to remark that his assistant must be missing it, surely, missing the grand weather he was used to over there, back home? The Pacific. The word itself was a flaring lamp.

'It's the end of winter there now, mind,' Stephen had said at first, 'it's cold and slush just like winter anywhere,' but his boss was not to be deceived. He knew it was a land of sun his assistant had come from, anything said to the contrary a mere modest disclaimer. At times when he looked at the young man whose shyness in the shop was less of a problem with the passing months, and was something indeed the ladies rather warmed to, it was palms and beaches and a flawless sky Mr Golson hung behind him, colourful as a stage set. Although what it had made him think of too were photographs his nephew had sent him from Haifa when he trained there for Special Ops a few years before. His nephew who did not return but Haifa, the beach and the beauty of it, must be there still. The Mediterranean and the Pacific had a lot in common, imagined from here.

On that first late afternoon then Stephen was invited to the back of the shop, to the small room with space for not much more than two chairs set to either side of a bright yellow table, with a square of plain linoleum cut to fit its top and tacked down at each corner, and three shelves above it with folded papers, reference volumes and professional journals, and paper flags for the Allies pinned above those again. Two cups hung from screws at the edge of the middle shelf, and against one wall there stood a small metal sink, and a bench to hold no more than a kettle and a few plates. One bright naked bulb descended from a flex above the table. And oddly everything out here neat and tidily arranged, so unlike the clutter of the shop. As if saying, here is where life matters, out there is where so much else steps in. But Stephen already aware that you could not go round putting your labels on what you observed, or imagined things to mean. A courteous puzzlement at so much, already establishing itself as his way with the world.

And the further embarrassment that first day in England, after Mr Golson made him tea and took biscuits from a tin, and explained the mess out front by telling him of Mrs Garnett, who had worked for him for years, and how there was no question of replacing her, although that was three years back now. Until the end of the war, that had been his excuse, everyone's excuse for putting things off, once it's over we'll attend to things. 'Now we can't,' he smiled, 'can't come at that one anymore. But I still say so. You'll have to make what you can of it. Pick up the traces, isn't that what they say, from where Mrs Garnett put them down?'

Stephen would find in the months ahead that of Mr Golson's many stories Mrs Garnett was the one he most came back to. Mrs Garnett whose name was Phoebe. She was not of the faith, he explained, but that had not mattered to him then any more than it did now, with Stephen. She had worked here four days each week; her husband was afflicted, a man in a chair who seldom spoke. She learned to read scripts, to make up prescriptions, as though she were born to it. A finely gifted woman. She learned things first as a surprise for him, she said he had given her another life. And then Mrs Garnett coming back one evening after playing bridge with her sister on the other side of the High Street because her house keys she had left in the storeroom. It does not seem logical, he said, that women can be so confused about something so important as keys, but there we are. This was in '42, when things were at their worst. Her sister had said, Stay the night why don't you, it's late enough, you never know. Know when they'll start that racket flying over and the rest of it. Well I need to get the ration book too in any case, she told her sister, it's in the purse and what if anything happened to that? So that held her up, her coming back here to the shop, and then walking home when she might have stayed at her sister's, and the sirens starting and instead of going to the shelter she just kept on walking back, that was what Mrs Garnett was like. And that was the night three houses copped it down in Fellows Avenue. There is no particular drama in the way Mr Golson tells it. But that is the reason, he says, why the place is not as it might be if Mrs Garnett had kept coming in. Mrs Garnett kept it neater than a pin. Then one month becomes a year and he thinks as soon as all this is over, the raids stopped so surely it is only time, a matter of time, until it's back to how things were and there'll be so many looking for work, women with their men back, he would wait till then to replace her. 'But you're here now, Stephen, so we can tidy up.'

This first time he told the story he said something in another language Stephen of course did not understand and Mr Golson did not explain. He would come to understand that it was something the older man always said when one of his stories meant, So that is how it is, we can do nothing about it, it was meant to be. Phrases that in time Stephen would recognise and come to know and so much later use himself to make some of the older women laugh on the counter's other side. Each day there would be other stories so that Stephen smiled and said to him, 'I know as much about round here as if I lived here. Thanks to you.' But this first day Mr Golson so strangely moved by what was he was saying so casually that he removed his spectacles and rubbed them with the handkerchief he took from his pocket. 'You did not know Mrs Garnett,' he said. 'If I told you about her you would know everything.'

23

Everything settled so quickly, then, on that afternoon when he arrived, a young man not able to explain why he had left a place where there were beaches and shops with more food than they could sell, and more work than there were men for, left what was there in fact and what Mr Golson imagined to be there, to come to this, where for weeks that smell of ash would come at Stephen when he did not expect it, when no one else remarked on it. And the sense of shame that same early evening, after the tea they drank at the yellow table at the back of the shop and the tentative conversing until at last there was a pause and Mr Golson turned to look up at the clock with its Coronation emblem and said as they stood together, 'You have somewhere to go now? You know how to get there?' Stephen's dreadful moment of awkwardness, how it must seem he assumed so much, coming directly from the wharves, as though the end of his journey was here, as though he had never considered beyond that. His first shaming at his own naïveté, a word he would not at that stage of his life have known and still less used for the sense of dumb emptiness, the feeling that his clothes were canvas against his skin. A shame sharpened by the memory flooding back to him of the man he had so hoped to forget, his father leaning forward, shouting at him, Go to bloody London then, find out what's so grand about those doss houses he and his cobbers put up at on leave, what a bloody lie it was, all that London caper! His father shouting at him, jabbing with the poker at the opened door of the range, spit jumping onto his son's sleeve, 'Mix your bloody cough mixtures over there then if that's all you want from life!' And as the door to the range clanged shut his stepmother moving in front of them both, between his father's anger and his own resentful silence, to place on the hob the big pot whose handles she held in her raised sacking apron. An image so sudden and searing in his mind that the sting of it seemed more real than where he now stood, the suitcase held against his side. The remarkable thing that Mr Golson seemed in some way to understand, as he looked at the confused young man in front of him.

'These things are not impossible,' he said. He raised his palm as if patting the air, and Stephen again put down his suitcase while the man went to the telephone at the end of the counter. He spoke quickly, quietly, and came back to stand in front of the boy with his lowered eyes, one raw hand drawing together the sides of his coat, fastening a button, unloosening it.

'I cannot,' Stephen began to say, but Mr Golson raised his hand for the second time. Then the old man asking him, with what even at that moment Stephen knew was said with a curious kind of humour, 'I gather you have no strong feelings about Jews?'

Stephen smiled, as if even that was a kind of awkwardness, as he looked to the strangely creased face, the glasses with a smudge mark where a finger had adjusted them. 'I have never known any,' he said. He could think of nothing else to say.

'Don't let our friend Nat hear you saying that!' Stephen knowing then it would be all right to grin. He said, 'I didn't know. It didn't matter.'

'Lucky Nat, then.'

Mr Golson fetched his coat from the tearoom. They walked for five minutes down a sloping street, and then along a road that levelled off. There were big trees on the edge of the pavement, tall gloomy houses behind low brick walls, the sharp angles of their roofs black against the tinted sky. They walked without speaking, as if the past hour had used up whatever might be important for their first meeting. Mr Golson hummed softly. The only other sound was the flat impact of their steps, and the bump of the suitcase brushing against Stephen's coat. He was glad for the silence. He thought, Mr Golson mustn't mind being with me or he'd not be making that half-singing sound.

They stopped at a high house with steps rising from inside its gate to a porch at the side. There were lights showing on one floor, and when the gate clicked and then grated as it swung back, the curtains in the next house moved slightly, as though a breeze had stirred them. Mr Golson said, as if making a joke, 'The English look out for each other.' And then, 'You will be all right here until you're sorted out.' He touched the brim of the black hat he had taken from the peg in the storeroom before they left the shop. 'Sam will look after you. He is my good friend.'

The door's brass knocker was the shape of a horseshoe. The man who opened the house to them was short and balder than Mr Golson, and harder to understand. 'Everyone is from somewhere else,' he said. And that was almost all. He went ahead upstairs, nodded to where the bathroom was, and said only, 'You must sleep as long as you need. I am always in the kitchen. If you are hungry you must tell me.' And he too remarking something in another language, as he closed the bedroom door.

It was on the top level of the house, a small room with bare walls and an ornate blue cover on the single bed against the wall, rucked and looped like the curtains in a picture theatre. A table and an empty glass, and a chair pushed in against the table. The room was musty.

Stephen guessed no one had slept in here for a long time. He opened the window and the cooler air was damp, but good to let in. There was the slightest misting still of rain that fell across the street lights, a drift of trailed gauze. He saw now what he had not been aware of when he walked down the street with Mr Golson. From the window he looked across to the jagged fragments of what remained of a house across the road, most of which had fallen while the hedge in front of it, taller than a man, had survived and continued to grow. There was also in the air the scent of something neither bitter nor sweet, and yet distinctive, the slight fall of rain perhaps sharpening it. He thought, I am here, at last. I am alone in a room in England for the first time. It will be all right. He left the window slightly opened on its latch. Then the man was at the door again, to say he must come down. Not a feast, he said. But there is bread. There are sausages. He puffed out his cheeks. To keep the wolf on its lead, is that what one says? On its lead. From the door. To keep the wolf.

Sam Abrams liked to talk. 'I ask nothing,' he said on the first morning after he had done his friend a favour and taken in the young stranger who had crossed oceans, now of all times, to live here, where he supposed half the world must like to live as well. Crazy, he thought as he watched the quiet young man at the kitchen table, crazy whichever way you look at it. And that first morning too, saying the visitor could use the room another night if he liked, which in turn became another night after that and then another, and it was a week later when Stephen asked, 'Am I your boarder then, Sam?', and he was looked at with surprise, as if why would he have thought anything else, was he sleeping across the road Sam asked, and only pretending

27

to be here? You would never miss Sam's jokes because his own laughing told you. And as Mr Golson liked to say, sometimes several times a day, 'Things will be fine.' *Zorg zich nisht.*

Mr Golson liked to explain with care, believing it the first step to accepting his own point of view. Each day they talked as they drank tea in the storeroom, until the bell sounded as a customer entered from the street, or Stephen reminded him, 'If I'm to get on with things,' and Mr Golson would look at the clock and tell him, 'One day you will be a hard man to work for,' and tap the young man's shoulder as he walked through to the shop. Mr Golson also liked to think he was helping the boy from so far away, from his place of sun and ignorance, to understand what the true world was. 'Your chance to start over,' he would say. And Stephen began to pity him a little, suspecting there was a sadness which he could only guess at behind the code of what he said.

With Sam his landlord it was so much more open, more direct, this facing the business of how things were, how life turned out. In his quick tumble of words that seemed at times as though he were talking in a language that was only partly the one he shared with his young friend, Sam would tell him, 'David Golson, God be good to him, believes we must hold on to ropes that are not there. Not now. Not anymore. But he will not believe the world is bad, as we know, you and I, Stephen, as we know it is, eh? Of course we know that.' But saying so without rancour, as if to face the grimness of things, could be said lightly enough, for Sam so openly enjoyed what he called 'the business of getting on'. 'You got that,' he told Stephen. 'I see it just the way you walk up the street. You get on.'

'I don't know with what,' Stephen said.

'You get on,' Sam repeated. 'You listen to me.'

Wednesday nights, especially, Sam liked to talk. Wednesday nights he would come in late, and Stephen knew the old man was pleased if he was still there in the sitting room, pretending to study the most recent book Mr Golson told him he would be the smarter for getting on top of. Sam flushed from the entertainment, the glasses of schnapps, coming in from the club up in Finchley Road. 'That Herz! That Viennese! He makes everyone forget, can you imagine a gift so big as that? Everyone in the room close to everything bad and he has us laughing before we know we laugh. These Viennese!' He insisted Stephen join him with a glass before he went up to bed. 'He is something I can tell you. Laugh!' Holding the small blue glass with its gold rim, the liquor Stephen disliked the taste of, but it was Sam's mood that warmed him, Sam raising his own glass as he says, 'Because we are here together, my friend. Because we can do this,' and leans across to tip the rim of their glasses against each other.

'And Mrs Einhorn,' he liked to say, 'Ah, we drink to Mrs Einhorn.' His repeating 'Ah' but drawing it out halfway to a song rather than just a sigh, their drinking to a woman who could not be put into words. 'Impossible in English,' Sam regretted, thinking of what surely must be said to do justice to the figure, the presence, the *shaina maidel* they raised their glasses to.

Sam drank only that one night of the week, at the cabaret as he called it, and Stephen having no more idea of what that might be other than a room where only Jewish people went, and heard performers, and where stricter people would keep away from, the cabaret was no place for

29

them. You will not see hair locks there, Stephen, I tell you that. Not even our friend David. At home with books. Do I not tell him, 'You cannot be serious every day,' but will he listen? You work with him. When does David listen? But sorrowful then as he thinks of it, of his friend David who is never the same after the night of the bomb, when the lady who worked in the shop died. He raises both his hands, and lets them fall on his knees. 'I know nothing about that, Stephen. I tell you nothing because I know nothing.'

The first glass would become a second but never more, as Sam talked on, slipping away from English, coming back to it, and even there Stephen losing much of what he was being told, until at times it was as though Sam spoke not to him so much as aloud to himself, finding the words to make clear to himself what needed to be told. 'Livandowski,' he would say, when he guessed he may have been drifting towards darker things, talking now of the music at the synagogue in Belsize Park, his palms coming together as though he were about to sing. 'What a voice can do to you.' And Stephen would again lose the drift of what he said, how much good it would do his friend David to come with him, It is not your English go there, Sam said. But no, David could not be cheerful without being sad, the boy must know what he meant? Sam saying how he was not the first man, David, not the last man either, not to have the wife he deserved, that there are women who leave the kindest of husbands for a man not worth that, not worth so much as that, snapping his fingers. 'For a man with dogs out Walthamstow.' His disgust was intense. 'It is when the war is on and people do crazy things. David will tell you the shop goes wrong when that lady who works for him dies in the air-raid. That is not the whole story, Stephen. Not the only story.' Then Sam stands and takes the glasses, and says as he leaves the room, 'Not that you say a word. You know nothing, Stephen.'

'Nothing,' Stephen assured him.

Most Wednesdays he waited until Sam finished in the kitchen, washing the glasses, moving plates that have something to do with what they will eat tomorrow, quietly singing snatches of song in a voice that has little tune to it, and that at times may be broken into by a laugh, and as he said one evening, pausing at the door before taking to the stairs, 'I think we must get a cat one day, eh? A cat from Vienna. I have a name for her but I keep that to myself. Until we get the cat.' He taps the side of his nose. 'She will never know unless we tell her.' Sam thinking it a better joke than did his young friend, his laughter keeping on as he makes his way up to his bedroom. And so much later Stephen saying to his children, who at times will think only how often have we heard him tell us this, 'I owe everything to them, the man whose house I boarded in, the one I worked for in the shop. Everything. Like the name you have now, David.' And once this button was pressed, as the children said behind his back, they waited for the other sentences to follow, and might almost have mouthed with him, 'So little I even understood. I had no idea what to say to almost everything, or why things happened as they did.'

There were fragments he still failed to understand. One week when Sam Abrams ceases to speak of Mrs Einhorn, any more than Mr Golson mentioned his own wife so much as once, who left him but that did not matter, and

Mrs Garnett who died, and took his heart with her, in one of Sam's phrases. 'And you never got the cat,' young Lisa will say. While thirty years on again, in the bach on the coast, and with only the boy left to tell, 'All of us were ghosts,' Stephen says, 'only they were real ones and I was still waiting my turn.'

'That's bullshit,' David will tell his father. 'No one can have so little to say about back then.'

His father contradicting him. 'I must be one of those who can.'

'Your rambling on about old men. My mother wasn't even there. That has still to come. Even you can't make her a ghost that early?' He clattered the tumbler he drank from on the low glass-topped table between them, in the bright room with the hard breaking of the surf coming up to them as it did on those afternoons when the westerly picked up. At other times the old man seldom hears it, although the younger people do. The girl who was married to a road worker further down the beach, who came in two mornings a week and cooked for him when he was alone, told him she could not imagine not having it there, that sound. It has been there all her life, she told him, except when she was in town, and hated it there at night, the other sounds, but not that, not being able to hear the sea.

He wished as always there was more he might tell his son, as he had been able to write about to Lisa, a little of it anyway, years back, when she too had begun to ask him questions. But there was nothing new to be said, no dredged incidents, no anecdotes, any more for Lisa then than David now, nothing they had not heard in pieces from him before, or from their mother, and she too had come back to half a dozen things, so much of what they had wanted her to tell them not there to tell.

Six months had passed since Stephen arrived, and then almost a year, and it was December when he sent his one card home, but never knew if it had arrived, or if his father had read it or as likely burned it unread. 'A farm,' he would say, when Mr Golson asked him more about his home, about where he had grown up. 'Cows and mud and half a day by bus from anywhere. That's enough to remember. My father who was in the other war was mad.' And as a joke to make his boss who was now his friend smile quietly at him, and shake his head as if his way of saying, Now I know you are having me on, you are making fun of me, Stephen, he said, 'It was less like Finchley Road than you might think.' Then they would talk of other things that mattered more than the past. Mr Golson said it was too late now for people like himself and Sam Abrams and most of their friends ever to be free of, but you are the lucky ones. The young. The ones from so far away you don't need to know what we mean. He began to give Stephen papers and pamphlets to read, the kind of thing he said that the English, good people that they are, are always afraid of, a world that starts again. He explained what the important words meant. Proletariat and capital and commodity exchange, and not so much the need for another world but the certainty that it would arrive. One must believe that.

'There are rich and clever people who think as we do,' he said, and sometimes they would read a weekly newspaper together, and a man called Mr Laski at times came into the shop, and said, 'You must come along with

David. There are so many young people at the meetings you would feel at home.' But the thought of being with those his own age who spoke of things he found vague, even when explained, intimidated him. He found excuses until Mr Golson understood his reticence, and although they continued to speak of such things he no longer pressed him. 'We find our own time,' he said. 'I was forty before I read a page of any of this.' Yet even so Stephen came to understand more clearly the lies that history made up about itself, and the nets that were spread for working people, and at another and distant time enraged his son by saying he would have joined, almost certainly he would have gone to meetings as Mr Golson so waited for him to do, had he not met their mother, and life became so immediate and demanding, so vivid it was as though until then he had only heard of colour but never seen it. Anything other than her seemed not to matter. And his son's anger not simply at the politics, which he detested, but that even when speaking of back then, his father did not say 'love' when he spoke about their mother but found a dozen others ways. 'When we met', he would say, or 'when we became close', or 'once we had decided', or, 'There is so much in that saying, swept off your feet.' His son even shouting at him, 'You never bloody say "love" ever, you must know that!'

'It's not a word, David, just to be used in chatting about things.' But 'Sam Abrams,' he will say, 'I owe him everything for that. For seeing the advertisement outside the church, and forcing me to go. Otherwise I might still be there.' Sam had told him he was too young to be a hermit, to sit and read, to not realise women withered without attention, it was his duty to attend. He saw the advertisement for the dance. He insisted the boy attend. 'David will never tell you these things. You must listen to me. Sam knows these things.'

The young woman was taller than Stephen by several inches, pale and tall and shining, the way the dark green satin of her blouse took the light and gave it back. The parish hall they stood in, each so obviously alone, was too large for the number of young people attending. With the coloured paper decorations along the walls, the smiling older woman who played the upright piano on the low stage at the hall's end, the kindly young cleric in his collar and grey suit, not much older than the fifty or so young people who watched him from the floor or from the benches that ran along the walls as he assured them, 'You are all so welcome here.' But there was the chill of space and social stiffness, as the parish determined to 'get things back to normal', as indeed it almost was, for only one of the young men wore a military uniform, a cadet of some sort. A year or two ago, as the woman at the piano could have told you, the crowded hall seethed like a parade ground, and the girls the prettier for it, she would tell that too, the edge always of uncertainty at that time that made the dances poignant, as now they were likely only to be dull. This was the first of its kind in months. The young vicar smiled as he spoke to them and opened his clasped hands as though he released something none of them would have expected, the quiet unruffled fun of peacetime. That is what he would like them to think. Each fortnight from now on, and numbers would surely swell when the word got round. The fun is back. After his few words he nodded to the woman at the piano who began to play the Lancers, which perhaps half of the young people knew the steps for. The one older man who had stood with the rest and listened, who must have been thirty, and held a cigarette in his hand although a notice at the entrance requested that you smoke only outside the hall, turned and left. He had seemed an adult come to the wrong event. But then the vicar himself, who had asked everyone to call him Robin, broke the ice and was the first to enter the spirit of things, by mock-bowing to a girl who in fact was his fiancée. How strange all this seems, Stephen thought, close and strange together, the sudden sense of so many girls in colourful dresses, their bright slashes of lipstick and that English way of laughing. And yet how distant too, in that way so much about living here still seemed to him, that feeling so often with him in the shop, his own smiling and nodding in the talk of ration books and rebuilding and the shame, what else was it, of kicking Mr Churchill out, after all that he had done. And yet not really being here, that feeling too almost always with him. He wondered if there was anywhere he would not feel that. He supposed now that this was what 'parish' meant, people who liked to be together, who sounded the same as those they talked with, so much shared between them they might take for granted. It was hard to imagine what these people were like when they were not here, within a few yards of him. It was hard to say that about anyone, really. Although he guessed that the tall girl in the green blouse, the dark pleated skirt, was no more parish than he himself. She was the only one he noticed who was dressed like that, as if she had come from an office, and not especially for this, the church's 'Let's Get Back to Peacetime' special dance. The other girls were in frocks, two of them even

36

in sort of gowns as if they too had not quite understood.

He had found a space on one of the benches far enough from anyone else that he would not be obliged to talk. When he put his head back for a moment against the wall it crinkled against a big rosette of blue and red and white paper, and he again leaned forward. He watched across the hall, through the hopping of the dancers, as the vicar nodded to a boy in a suit, who went up to the girl in green and leaned to speak to her, and her quick firm shaking of her head. As though this was the last thing she expected, to be asked to dance, here of all places! Stephen smiled across at her, knowing how they must be in the same boat, exactly, but if she noticed him she did not acknowledge it. The light across the shininess of her blouse now on the fall of her fair hair as well, as she lowered her head and her face was obscured, and she looked down on her hands as they lay on her lap. He wondered if maybe she was afraid, her stillness that of an animal whose defence was not to move. But his attention suddenly interrupted by the young woman who broke off her dancing with the vicar and came across to him, laughing as she drew close, demanding—she used that word, *demand*—that he dance with her, they were all friends here. 'No piking,' she teased him, taking his hand, drawing him towards her.

'I've never,' his telling her, 'I don't know. Really.'

'Where we all begin, then,' she said. 'Where else can we?' She held him firmly and accepted his shuffle and he scarcely took in what she said as she prattled to put him at his ease, telling him her name was Lorna, 'Robin's Lorna', floating her hand in front of him, the ring with its glinty stone for him to see. And stupidly he asked, 'Are there other Lornas?', which she thought a droll thing to say, and steering him, directing him, not noticing that he bumped her, confiding that the beat, the beat was the thing to follow, the rhythm and the beat were everything, kind and firm and welcoming as she told him how Robin so wanted to get the parish up and running at the youth level especially, youth and a little older, it was so much harder here mind than it was in Surrey. 'But you go where you're put,' she said, 'do what you can. You marry into where they send you.'

He felt a rush of relief as Lorna thanked him when the piano paused. This, it seemed, was when the dancers clapped for a moment, and found other partners, before the elderly lady with her big smiling teeth launched into a foxtrot. Lorna said, spotting another man sitting by himself, 'Thought he could get away!', and left Stephen as he most wanted to be, alone again, no one trying to be kind to him. He went back to the bench against the wall. He wondered how long he must stay before he might leave without it looking rude to walk out on so much kindness. He saw another older woman, so thin and a little hunched that he supposed she might be related to the pianist, who fussed about at a long table at the far corner of the hall, arranging plates, setting out tall jugs of coloured drinks. But the dancing had barely started, they would not be expected to eat and talk together so soon as that? The new fear that he must dredge for things to say, that the words would not be there for him. No, he must go before then. He must make a break for it.

There was a new buzz in the room as couples laughed together when again the dancing stopped, and Robin called out to the pianist, who showed her teeth and smiled back, and someone whooped as the notes banged out for a reel. Stephen felt a kind of panic as a girl came close to him, and he shook his head. Why was time stretching out like this—was it ten minutes or half an hour since Lorna had told him, 'There, I'll be keeping an eye on you, Stephen, making sure you join in.' He could tell the dark girl disliked his saying no to her like that, his not so much as thanking her for asking. He closed his eyes and once more leaned his head against the soft crush of paper. Then the decision made for him, the rescue, he would joke with her about it, remembering the day each year from now on as exactly that, the rescue. The tall girl's voice, clear and precise and urgent, 'We must leave here now.'

Seconds later they stood in the porch to the hall, a darkly varnished space that smelled of wax and damp coats, and with a tiny Gothic red-paned window that the lights from a passing car smeared into a quick flare. The piano still pelted out its reel, there was the fun of changing partners and stooping beneath the raised meeting hands, but all that already part of another life they had dipped into briefly and were free from. The girl took a coat from one of the hooks and draped it across her arm, while Stephen sought out his, and the scarf Mr Golson had insisted he borrow, this time of year you only had to listen to all that hawking in the shop. Then only outside, past the wall at the end of the church grounds, they stopped to help each other with their coats, their breathing as though forced to make a run for it, their laughing before they even spoke, the camaraderie of those who get away.

'Your scarf,' she said, quickly taking it up from where it had fallen from his arm. Her first real words to him. And his own, a joke that he did not intend but that amused her, 'It doesn't belong to me. You had better wear it.' He raised

39

it and put it over her head because, as he was saying now, the night was so bitter and the coat she wore so thin. Then 'Eva,' she said, as they walked back towards the main road that glittered in patches through the naked branches of the trees on the rise leading up to it. No more than that, and she already knew his name was Stephen, she must have heard the vicar's fiancée call him that, for she thanked him with his name when he gifted her the scarf that belonged to Mr Golson.

Tall and quiet and calm, the words first occurring to him as he walked beside her, the words others would most often say of her as well, at the beginning, at the end, although the last becoming that touch more insistent, as one life changed to another, and then another again. All this *by chance*, as they kept saying to each other in those first months together, and never ceased to wonder at even in the other times, the sheer chance of a church social both had felt so awkward at as to run away from. 'An Anglican dance you were sent to by a Jew who thought you a loner, that I was urged into going to by Quakers.' It amused Eva always to speak of it like that.

'I don't get the joke,' David would say to her in his teens, already angry, already humourless, that so much seemed so deliberately concealed from him.

'If you don't then it's not a joke,' his sister telling him. 'I wouldn't lose sleep over it.'

1948

———

'Now?' he said. 'You mean here?'

'Yes. Now. Yes.'

Her hands at his belt. The stretch of the sea, the colour of a pewter plate, across her shoulder. The grass slope from the stone walls behind him falling away from where they stood, towards a road beneath them. People with a spread rug perhaps a hundred yards away, a woman in a big hat calling to a dog that ran and then returned, excited, leaping, from here it was hard to say at what. A couple who had passed a few minutes back were now out of sight, beyond the huge corner of the castle that rode above the town.

'There's no one here,' Eva said. 'No one can see.'

'There's those down there.' The dog's exuberant barks coming up to them.

'As if they care!' Her hands now at him, once his belt fell loose. Her face not against his but drawn back, watching him, his attempting to make a game of it as she was doing, so calmly, in command, amused, while Stephen stood, his hands flat against the wall behind him, nervous and yet insisting, yes, keep on. The joke of it and the pleasure now the same thing.

'This belongs to the King. This whole place. It's against the law in castles.'

'You don't come from here,' she told him. She leaned forward and took the lobe of his ear between her teeth and bit. 'They don't arrest foreigners.'

'Hey!', drawing back.

'Then do as you're told.' Her hand moving quickly on him. His head flinging back against the wall, hurting him.

'Faster, then!'

Her hand tightening, slowing. Her other hand rising to her already undone blouse. Her commanding him, 'There, then.' Her fingers spread behind his head, drawing his mouth down on her.

'They're looking,' he tried to tell her. He saw a man stand from among the picnickers, slapping a white hat against his leg, calling at the dog now lolloping up the slope towards them that then halted and turned when the man took a schoolyard whistle that shrilled across the park. The man watched them for a moment before he went back to the women on the rug.

Stephen said, 'I know they've seen us.'

'No,' Eva said, 'no they haven't.' Her breathing warm at his neck. The man had thrown a yellow ball down towards the road, the women turning that way to watch their dog retrieve it. The man had put his white hat back on his head.

Eva leaning then to rub her hand across the coarse web of the grass, her laughing, telling him 'They might have liked it mightn't they?' as he turned towards the wall, settling his clothes. The excitement of it, the brazenness, still in his mind later in the afternoon as the train left the station and arced beneath the hill that rose up to the castle, each of them looking to it, Stephen saying nothing, Eva smiling. 'A history lesson too.'

How she could startle him with her sudden aggressive turns. And yet a game, it was that as much as satisfaction, such certainty between them. The frankness of what they did so beyond anything they said, or referred to later on. 'The freedom' was the closest she came to speaking of it. The delight they took in each other was as if naming another world.

She liked the habit and routine and always too the discovery as they made love in the room they rented in Sam Abrams's house. She insisted they leave the curtain drawn back, the fall of the streetlight across them. When they gasped back from each other and lay regaining their breath, You are like a fish, Stephen wanted to tell her, the length of her glistening and turning beside him. Yet his knowing when she said nothing could bring them closer, she was beyond him still, that it was *there*, as much as what they shared, she meant as she stood beside the bed at times and let her dressing gown fall from her in a way that she must have known startled with its suddenness, and said, as she came down to him, 'the freedom'.

Eva knew how she pleased and shocked him, taking his hand at unexpected times and placing it against her, even as they sat up on the Heath where he first told her she was like a furnace to him, and she laughed and said people would never imagine what a romantic he was, so solemn, so much the polite young man in the shop. It was

43

the contradiction in her that 'so got to him', as he tried to tell her, and her laughing at him again as he failed to find the words and settled for, 'All right then, you'll just never know'; know how whatever they did as lovers, as a married couple, 'demure' stayed with him as so singularly marking her, as much as it had that first evening when he watched her through the tinkle and make-believe of the parish dance they ran away from. 'There is only us,' she would say to him, quietly, when their hands moved across each other.

Yet how she hit it off with 'old Sam', as she called him, so liking his affection for the young man who had crossed the world and whom he would have taken into the business like a shot, if only the boy settled to a trade the older man might have taught him, had he not been content to stand in the darkness of a shop and smile at old ladies, selling them stuff to rub on their sore legs.

'He will be a rich man in ten years,' Sam promised Eva as he instructed her in his kitchen, the recipes and meals that he assured her would hold any man. Things he knew from his own mother. 'You maybe lose everything else from your people,' he chided her, 'but your children will know at least what they like to eat. They will not have lost everything.'

There was an easiness between them as each overplayed how they saw each other. Mr Golson she came to like as well, but he was not a man to take things lightly. He was disappointed that she had no gift, as he called it, to prepare herself for the better world that was there for the taking, the new Israel where if he were only ten years younger he would go to, oh she might smile, but indeed he would, and teased her just a little. 'Stephen would go if you asked him.

You tell him Zion is there for all of us, he would go. A good man does what a good woman says. But I am a realist above all,' he would also say. 'It is no more your fault what has happened with you, what you have lost, than with any of us.' He settled for giving her pamphlets and magazines to read so that when he said Bevan and Atlee and Arthur Isaacs, she knew who and what he meant. While Sam in his sharp-tongued way told her, as they stood at the table in his kitchen, 'David is happy so long as he talks, because he believes you cannot listen to him without thinking David, my friend, you are right again. He is a socialist when he begins to talk and when he finishes he believes you are one as well.' Making a popping noise with his lips, making a joke of himself as well, the bewildered foreigner. But it is good windows, he tells her as they chat over the *knish* he instructs her in, the windows that he crosses London to get from a friend in Stepney, a friend who makes new frames from broken buildings, and that Sam then installs in so many places there will never be an end to it. What is it people want most in life? Windows that open and shut. Windows that fit their frames. 'Mr Bevan will tell you that but not David.' He claps his hands and holds them open towards her. What can one do with a man who paints a shop without asking the advice of a friend who has painted a hundred houses? This very week a lady in Holland Park whose father is an artist, but who did she ask about the colour on her walls? Yet his loving Mr Golson like a brother, he insisted, ridiculing him slightly, envying that Stephen was close to him as a son.

The old man took a bagel from the plate that was cooling between them. 'One day they will give you work in the Cosmo,' he flatters her, the one place he swears to her where the food is good, the *only* one, this side of Golders Green. 'David will talk about the Dorice but I tell you, and I am the one to know, it is the Cosmo.' He liked to look at his new young friend, who reminded him of girls he once had known before he was even here, but they were gone like so much else. The girls. The town even, not even its name there if you looked for it. Although Sam hated it, had he not told her this more than once, hated this business some people come at of *cry, cry* whenever there is the chance, as if we cry things back? Yet when the mood is on him doing that himself, and Eva listened to him in silence, touching his hand, when he goes to find a photograph to show her, young people in those old swimming costumes on the edge of what he said was a lake, and another of a man in a uniform, his cheeks smooth as a woman's, his cap with an elaborate badge on his crossed knee. He takes another slice of what she has just baked and tells her, 'You will be the first person in the world to take these to Stephen's country.'

It was now a matter of weeks until they sailed, until they left for whatever 'home' in another place might turn out to be. Once summer came, or the first watery weeks that stood in for it, she thought of places she and Stephen should visit together. There was that day at Hastings and then another in Wales, a wide estuary whose tides and glintings altered as they stood above them, the cries of the wheeling birds, so much louder in the lull of a wind dabbing at them from the west. Her freedom there as well, their standing together above the village they had walked up from, Eva half-clothed as she leaned in towards him, the distant speck of walkers across a broad sweep of sand. He later told her

46

in the room they had taken for the weekend how this is what he would never quite make out about her, her ease and shamelessness, her certainty which he knew he was unlikely ever to have himself. And yet what he so puzzled at, telling her, 'A room is somehow quieter when you sit in it than when there is no one there.' For they could go for hours without speaking more than a few sentences, just as at other times they chatted on to each other, the gossip from the Whitehall office where she worked as a typist, the stories of its dozens of women, its remote commanding male figures, and he told her of the less spectacular but oddly detailed lives of those who came through the shop. After doctors and vicars, Stephen guessed, chemists must be near the top of those who people confide in? Hadn't Mr Golson said that to him, in utter seriousness, way back in his first weeks? How if a customer knew you stopped the ache in her elbow, she was ready to receive a political idea?

'There is not a thing,' Eva assured him, 'that I know about myself that you don't know as well.'

'I've so much less to tell,' he said. 'So much less has happened to me.' Thinking how uneventful his own life seemed as he recalled it, as remote and simple as though it were another person's rather than his own. His conviction too that for Eva to love him was a gift that must come entirely from her own expansive kindness. It could not relate to anything he might deserve or be.

'But there must be more to tell,' she sometimes said to him. 'More about the farm. When you were young. I want to know about that.'

His wanting to say back to her, 'You cannot describe a wall even if you've lived against it.' But no one says things like that. So 'If you could understand the dreariness,' he was content to tell her. 'Not so much a memory even as just the feeling of it. The years when time did not seem divided to this day and then the next nor even one year followed by another, but a massive block that nothing might change or dissolve. That is how I remember it.'

He answered her quiet questioning but was unable to give her what she hoped to hear, some privileged understanding of what made him the man she loved. You must imagine, he tried to convey to her, a place along a flat road where there is not another house for half a mile on either side, a wooden house that you might mistake for a shed if you drove along the road with its low row of hills behind scrappy paddocks and on the other side the always huge and changeable sky, where the land slid towards the gradual seep of the tide at the end of an inlet, where the shallow water slid among mangroves and mud. And not waves as you usually think of them but as close to inert as water might get, a creeping fringe of scummed advancing tide, and hours later its drawing back. One of his persistent images, the emptiness of standing in the last paddock before the sea and land gracelessly came together, the boy's sense of loneliness, and in the silence, or what seemed the dregs of silence between the shriek of gulls and the intermittent raking bellow of cattle back closer to the house, the sound that seemed below such silence rather than merely part of it, the hiss and suck of the mud beneath the roots and branches of the mangroves. 'That must seem strange to you,' Stephen said, 'but that's the sound that defines so much of what my memory now makes of it.' Where he was the only child, where the woman who was his father's second wife disliked him as she inevitably must. He had understood that by the time he was five, yet her not liking him was a secondary thing to her. The first was that she hated the man she had to sleep beside each night and feed through the day, and the quiet in the house as another tide they lived beneath. That feeling too. Of always *under* something else. But no, he said when Eva questioned him, no cruelty, like beatings and stuff, at least not that. Or, as he tried to joke, only that rarer kind of beating which never being touched with affection almost becomes. His father a tall memory of a shape in oilskins moving against persistent rain, although that of course is how one simplifies the past. And the sound not of his father's voice so much as his grunts, his strained breathing, as he moved among the reeking but marvellously warm and stolid herd, and what seemed to the boy the cattle's endless and unendurable patience as they waited for their turn in the stalls, their udders swollen and corded with veins, their plod back through the paddocks and the rain. Which is nonsense of course, Stephen laughed with Eva, pressing her fingers where they stroked against his arm. There were months of summer and I liked school because it was somewhere else, and the school bus that picked me up and dropped me off each morning and afternoon at the wooden stand at the gateway onto the road, where the great cans were left for the milk truck to pick up. He might tell her of the long summers and good things like eeling in the creek and building forts in the trees and the satisfaction of being good at what the school, with its war-memorial gate and its corrugated cricket pitch, expected of him, and the school footy jersey you got to wear if you stayed at school that long. Yet how packed Eva's early life seemed when she spoke of it, compared with what little he offered in return.

'And then she wasn't there,' he said. 'All that and then so suddenly not there.' One day his father came in from the rain, the mud from his boots leaving smears across the kitchen lino so the woman shouted at him before he stretched out his arm to take a pot from the kitchen range with its flicker of fire at the narrow bars of its grate, and flung it to where it rang and clattered to the floor and a clot of stew slid down the yellow wall. The woman's screaming stopped and she and the boy stood unmoving as his father went through to the bedroom and the sound coming through to them as he not only yanked back the wardrobe door but cracked it from its hinges. There was the split of ripping wood and the falling of a chair and he was back in the kitchen with them, carrying the gun the boy had been told he was never to touch. His father walked back between his wife and son and flung back the door onto the veranda and they heard him step down into the yard and then again a silence that seemed as much a physical force as the mere absence of sound, the rain now pelting on the iron roof and when the woman raised her fist towards her mouth there was the beginning of a whimpering dribble that the two gunshots from the shed cut across and stopped. The boy felt a fear that was different from anything else he had known. Stephen touched the fall of Eva's hair as he watched her troubled look. 'It's all right,' he said. 'He had done no more than go out and shoot the two cows that enraged him because their milk had dried off earlier than the rest of the herd. That was the straw that broke him.'

'There must be more.'

'He stayed on at the farm until just before I left to come over here. Then some men came soon after that and my father went off to a hospital in Auckland, and the wife who had come to the house after my mother I never saw again. When I left secondary school I went to the city and found a job with a pharmacist in Ponsonby who had troubles of his own and went to prison for them, although he attempted none of what he was convicted for with me. I was supposed to be there to deliver things and help tidy up and he paid me next to nothing but I fell in love with coloured bottles and wanted to have my own. And here we are!' And lying in their narrow bed he tried at times to tell her what he knew was her experience even more than his, the feeling that you are really two people and yet there is only one you know about, even though the other never leaves you.

'So there are really four of us in bed together all the time?' Eva teased him.

'At the very least.'

She had laughed when he told her how his life was decided the moment a shy smart boy looked into a shop window with its outsize flasks of coloured liquid. Red and green, which had struck him as pure enchantment.

'A good thing you didn't look at a butcher's window first. You might have fallen in love with hams and we'd never have met.'

'The butcher in the town I grew up in was what they called a snappy dresser and danced like Fred Astaire. I remember my aunt going on about that. So I might have asked you to dance that night at St Aiden's and we wouldn't be here now.'

They joked and made love and talked until they fell asleep as he was telling her, yet again, how he envied her that family who had brought her up, how they had passed on to her, they must have, so much that he admired in her. I was lucky, she had told him, I was lucky they were Quakers. Not that Stephen had ever met one. 'Then take my word for it,' Eva said.

Yet she had never thought of them, not really, as her only family, for all their goodness. In their honesty, in their thinking of her rather than just themselves, they insisted she know there was another world that might have been hers, at another time. In a different country. 'But it was all so English, and polite, and I never knew much about the uglier things. Even the stories I read edged me away from life rather than closer to it.' It was romantic stuff she had liked to read about, but that was part of England too in its curious way. She had gone through a stage at school when for a year she read nothing for fun that was not in some way about India. 'Elephants meant more to me than the family car. The war was going on round us and I lived in rooms with punkahs and servants with turbans! There was a Walter Scott story I read over and over and at the end a bad man's head was stood on by an elephant.'

When she came to London for her job and met two girls at a social who like herself had come to England as children, they had seemed as English as she was. And then the shock, for it came as strongly that. The shock of meeting another girl, a little older than herself, who had been taken by a family of their own people, Eva said, a girl called Becky who spoke in a London accent that seemed almost foreign to her. Becky had told her, 'But you must come and meet the people we are,' an invitation she had never taken up.

'It was all as if I began on the other side of a wall,' Eva once said, 'and yet further off than ever, once I knew about it. You understand what I mean?' Meeting up with people like Mr Golson, with Sam, that was the closest she had come. She liked them—how could you not like them?—but they were still strangers who had become her friends. That phrase Becky kept returning to, 'our people'. Nothing like that was there for her to feel.

Stephen was surprised at how firmly she insisted on it. 'But you don't feel drawn to them at all? I mean to what they *are*?'

'Are you?'

'I know nothing about Jewish things. Apart from here. I can hardly be drawn.'

'There you are then,' she said. Her English family had told her the little they knew, how her mother had been a journalist and disappeared, her father a journalist too, both of them socialists, but he was not a Jew. That was all she knew. He was in touch with important people and she had gone to an orphanage to be safe, and already she had another name by the time she came to the people who loved her here, when she was five. Earlier than those other children, the *kindertransport*, who came later. She had been brought across with a family who believed the same things as her English parents. Another boy and his sister who sat by her in the carriage. All too far now to remember. She had been given an orange that she held until they arrived.

How much more it meant to her that they were soon to leave for Stephen's country, a place that was as real to him as the creaking wooden peaceful house in High Wycombe had been to her. Never mind those awful stories about his father, the mud, the farm, the woman whose name he never said, only 'the woman my father married'. There was so much more than that. There had to be. And for her, the newness of it. The fact it would be *theirs*, that was the thing, as nowhere else might be. The place they made together.

In her lunch hours Eva walked up from the typing pool in Whitehall to New Zealand House in the Strand. A friendly middle-aged woman gave her books and brought out newspapers, most of which Eva made little of but liked to read the social pages, the columns that gave her some idea of the country that would be hers. She sat at the reading table with a pink-covered weekly, turning its shiny enticing photographs. So much forest. So many beaches. So much sport. The dark native people in some of them, although mostly the women and men in the photos looked as though they might have arrived that morning from where she was now. But people she supposed who would talk like Stephen. Who would take the same things for granted. Page after page told her how everything there was getting better, which more than anything the pages of the *Free Lance* and the *Weekly News* so wanted you to believe. While in the tea breaks in the little room behind the shop, Stephen heard Mr Golson's own message that he came back to daily, that carried even for England the kind of optimism Eva read of, looked at, on the other side of the world. 'A new age,' he insisted to Stephen. He spoke of the health service Labour was on the verge of, the pensions the government declared as the right of every citizen, the opening doors of education, the trimming down of privilege. Mr Golson rejoiced—'That is the word I must use, Stephen, *rejoice*'—in the workers' country England was about to become. Just as Israel, distantly and yet with even greater promise, was about to make the deserts bloom. 'It is a privileged time to live.' And how closely, in David Golson's mind, one future flourished beside the other, however much his friend Sam taunted him with his question of how could people who have lived so long as we have, David, who have seen what happened to us, play at optimism like that? 'This time,' Mr Golson assured him, 'this time we know what to do, that is why.'

He liked to remind Stephen not only that Marx had been Jewish, one must not forget that, but that his own grandfather's brother, who already had come across, that far back, to live here, had seen the great man walking in Green Park with his clever daughter, the one whose own life turned out so badly. A moral to us all, he added at this point in his reminiscing, how great intelligence is no defence against our glands. Yes, he would see them, his uncle, as they turned in at the entrance not far from his own shop that was famous for its Italian-made umbrellas. They were talking, always talking, the father so often listening to the girl, that is what had struck him in those stories, Marx attending to the girl. That is the sign of a great and humble man. While Stephen listened, amused, when it was Eva rather than himself who liked to tell Mr Golson that such things as the Government now planned to do in England had been done years before in her husband's country, that Marx's daughter most certainly would have approved her own decision to marry a man from such a place. Stephen asked was that woman who put things aside for her at the High Commission also paying her to advertise? And a few days after her boasting, after Mr Golson had time to visit the library and verify with his own research, he informed his young friends that a prime minister in that distant place had himself been Jewish, Stephen of course did not know that? Not a specially enlightened one perhaps by Marx's standards, but he had written a book about a future place where good things would evolve.

'Thus truth slowly prevails, worldwide.' Mr Golson liked to use phrases with such touches of eloquence. Stephen raising his brows behind his boss's shoulders, Eva smiling and agreeing with the older man who regretted only one thing, the fact of what she herself had lost, the girl who had been one of themselves and had been deprived. And Sam reprimanding him, provoking him that the entire future of the world need not fit the requirements of a Hampstead Zionist.

'Then so much the worse for that,' Mr Golson said. 'I know you disagree with me, my friend, but that I tell you as a fact. So much the worse.'

Then the change, when the vane spun in sudden contrary winds. So often that is the image she will come back to. There had been a weather vane shaped like a whale on the gabled house in High Wycombe where Eva grew up. She could see it from her own bedroom window, the clipped tin shape and the swollen metal blob soldering it to the stem that allowed it to pivot and turn. Her English father explained to her how it was a useful lesson the tin whale with its mountainy back could teach us, that what seemed so certain might change so quickly as that, the blunt head pointing this moment to the hills, an hour later to the town. The whale knows that nothing lasts long enough to be sure of forever.

How simply her kindly stepfather saw things, how wise she had thought him, how much he imparted to her. At first where rivers ran and what to call them, the capitals of distant countries, the music he showed her how to play, sitting beside her on the long piano stool, always showing her, never just instructing. As later on the mathematics that puzzled her at school became clear to her because of how he talked. All that he said and passed on to her beneath this great cone, as she had sometimes thought of it as a girl, where God and silence came together.

She and Stephen were back from one of what they called their adventure weekends. They would choose a town they may not even have heard of, or knew about only because of something famous so far back it was now a different world, and take a train on Saturdays once the shop had closed. They stayed overnight in small country pubs, or took a room in a house with an advertisement in the front window, a written card propped against the curtains. The women who let an upstairs room and asked them about breakfast were mostly widows, women who sometimes wanted to talk more than did their young guests, who discreetly checked Eva's hand for its ring. She and Stephen liked to walk a long way from a village and once they made love in a flare of wild flowers near Ascott-under-Wychwood. 'There must be people who know the names of all of these,' Stephen said. 'You won't see them like this back home.' At times there was a story-book enchantment to where they found themselves spending the night. On the border of Wales once they came on a house that said 'Guests Invited', where the patterned wood around the windows and under the eaves was cut in scoops and painted red against the drab colour of the stone. It was as if a child had drawn it, wayward and attractive together, a house unlike any other they had seen. Their upstairs ceiling was a narrow inverted V, where only one of them could stand upright at a time.

It was here Stephen asked was she certain, utterly? 'I

57

don't think you'd ever guess how different things might be.'

She repeated, 'Second thoughts?' She pushed gently at him and both knocked their heads against the angle of the roof as they fell towards the bed. She told him, 'I think of it all the time. Because it will be *our* place as nowhere else can be.'

'Even if you can't stand it?'

'Then we'll find somewhere else.'

Another weekend they walked to a church whose arched stone doorway was nicked round with a pattern of triangles like teeth. There was a panel in the porch that told you how old the building was. There was a carving of an angel on a side wall, beside a tablet for a writer who had been born here and baptised in the church and died in the Great War. In the quiet there was that burring of flies on a high sill that so seemed the sound of such places. Stephen waited outside, as Eva sat for several minutes in the back pew. Any church was foreign to him, he supposed that was it. She told him as they walked back to the main road how it had never meant all that much to her. Not as it did to many people.

'Churches?'

'Praying. Those meetings when I was a girl. My parents. Other families like ours who did not attend the church where most people went. We sat in rooms without anyone preaching, without choirs or altars or whatever. I never knew what to pray *about*.'

'You mean believing?'

'Oh, that didn't really come into it. You don't think about that as you pray. And yet I loved the silence of it. The silence you get in an empty church like the one we've just been to. The way it has to take you in. If you want it to. That's what my father used to say. It lets anything in except unimportant things.'

It was that evening, after the afternoon in the church. As Eva sometimes thought of it, amused that it came to her like this and yet knowing that even Stephen would think it strange should she say it to him, 'The day the whale turned, remember that?'

Back at Sam's, friends from the social club sat in the sitting room. Two elderly men in black suits and tieless white shirts who formally shook hands and smiled when it was explained to them that these were the young married people who lived upstairs, who were soon to leave the country. The men were drinking from the blue glasses that Stephen knew must mean a special occasion, but they spoke too little English for Sam to press the young ones to join with them as he otherwise would have done. The men looked almost shyly at the tall handsome Englishwoman and Stephen guessed Sam already had told them the story of what, alone with them, he called 'the lost girl'.

'We'll take our tea upstairs,' Eva said, 'in case you're using the kitchen.' As she went back across the hall she saw the white envelope addressed to Mrs S. Ross, aware that Sam watched her from the doorway to the sitting room. 'May it be good news,' he said to her. An odd thing for him to say, although later, once she had read the letter, and again took in the address stamped on the envelope's back, she understood why he had said it, and the expression on his face.

She did not recognise the name of the group it came from. The letter asked her to attend an appointment at a building near Russell Square. She sat with the letter still in her hand until Stephen brought up the tray with the toast and the poached eggs he had prepared for them, and the brown china pot of tea, and placed them on the small table she had drawn between where she sat on the edge of their bed and the chair her husband took across from her. She passed him the letter to read. He looked across at her, at the steady clarity of her looking back.

'I don't quite get what it's about. What woman?'

Eva told him simply. 'It's a relative they have found from over there.'

It took a moment before he answered. 'From before?'

'Before all this.' One hand lifting slightly from her lap, and then again resting on the palm of her other hand. So small a gesture as that to take in 'all this', the room they sat in, the husband facing her, the street outside and all the streets of London, the years from the time a train had drawn in beneath the high black roof of Liverpool Street and through the rise of steam and the high echoing noise a child was lifted down from the doorway of the carriage and swung onto the flickering movements of the platform, and she had looked up to a yapping dog a lady held at a lowered window high above her. The day memories began. 'From then.'

A blur, as the next few weeks would always seem for them, with 'life'—Eva's word for so much that could not have been guessed at—so suddenly catching up. Yes, she had said when the next morning she telephoned the number at the head of her letter, when the man asked her would she be alone, or who would be with her? She would like her husband to come with her, there was nothing which might happen now that did not concern them both. At eleven in the morning, then, two days from now?

Eva knew the street behind the British Museum, where she had gone to children's Christmas meetings at Penn House. There were flowers in the foyer of the building they entered, and what came across as a mix of efficiency with a not quite convincing attempt to make all this seem an occasion, this 'coming together', as a man with a strangely narrow face described it as he first spoke to them across his desk. He introduced himself as Henry Scherr. He looked at the address on the sheet of paper in front of him. 'Belsize Park?' he asked, meaning one of the synagogues they might attend. 'There may be other affiliations?'

'No,' Eva said, 'no affiliations.' It was not a word she had ever used. If her answer disappointed him, Mr Scherr was too well trained to let her see. He looked at them, benignly, Stephen thought, that is what he is intending us to think. He was here to help, he said, and to say the important things first. He quite understood if the news had come as more than a surprise to them. As a shock even, perhaps?

'Perhaps,' Eva said.

The great reward of his work, if he might mention that, was to play some small part in occasions such as this. When you felt history did not always have the last word. Or as you might even say, when we begin to make our own. When lives reconnect. Take up where they left off. Stephen supposed what they heard was a necessary preliminary, a little set speech. He admired his wife's almost icy calm. He knew the effort it cost her. At the moment she seemed a woman he scarcely knew. When Stephen spoke it was to answer the man on their financial position, for Mr Scherr had said it was, they would appreciate, a matter he must touch on? Stephen explained that they were very soon to leave, and where for.

'The outer reaches,' the man said, as though quoting something he had heard before.

'Not for us,' Eva cut across him.

'But you are living here? For the moment?', pointedly directing his question to her husband.

'No.' Eva again was the one to speak. 'We are living there.'

The official looked at her more carefully. He was that in both her mind and in Stephen's too, rather than Mr Scherr. The functionary whose opened folder with its neatly clipped papers struck them as about to throw his shadow across their lives. He would always remain to them simply 'the man'. He explained the facts to them clearly, concisely. The family connections, the reasons for only now informing them, the parts of the story that were still obscure. 'You might be surprised,' he said, 'how loose ends from so many places are resolved every day. So many families brought together.' The merest hint, perhaps, of reprimand in the way he told them, noting the absence of obvious joy which, as he also told them, was the deepest satisfaction of his work, the joy of bringing people together, when hope so often had been given up.

As though for the man's sake, Stephen said, 'We had no idea of any of this. You'll appreciate that.' Even his wife's real name, or the fact there was an aunt she had never imagined, or details of how the child was brought here.

'So much was done against the clock,' the man reminded them. 'It had to be. The miracle is what we can still retrieve.'

'But you are certain now, though?' Eva asked.

'The paperwork, now we have the names sorted, was exemplary at the other end. A case of a deliberate mistake being made. Earlier along the line.'

'For Eva?'

'For Lisabet,' the man said, glancing at his folder. 'Then a girl with another name,' he smiled, checking the dates in front of him. 'To help you get away. And now of course your own. As you've now become.' He said the three names together. Lisabet, Gerda, Eva.

'I was called that from the start,' Eva smiled back, reminding him that in so far as her memory went, she was Eva to begin with.

'To begin with *here*.' The man meant England.

'Three names, then,' he went on. 'The first on this,' he said, again laying a finger on a paper he turned to. 'Then the one the institution who first took you, back there, used to protect you. Before the one you were given here. There are cases more confused than this, I assure you.' He did not say how rare it was to see those his work brought him in touch with seem so unmoved. It was not for Mr Scherr to guess. He then asked if they would like tea? He tapped a bell on his desk which must have been for that alone, for no one responded until a few minutes later a girl carried in a tray, placed it on a table without looking at those it was intended for, and the man told her, 'Thank you. I'll take over there.'

He knows we are nervous, Stephen thought, he knows it is an ordeal and he is disappointed in both of us. Even when the photographs had been handed across to them, Eva had taken them, looked at them for perhaps a full minute, then passed them on to her husband without speaking. One was of a young child, unmistakably her, the hair much lighter, almost white, but the steady gaze, the distinctive eyebrows, straight as if drawn with a ruler, the slight dip to one side of her mouth. It moved Stephen to look at it. The child who had no notion of what her world was, or would come to be. A lucky one. The man said, 'As you can see from the table it was some kind of event. Perhaps your birthday?' He told them other things important for them to know. Her mother had died of what then was simply called anaemia, which nowadays would cover other possibilities as well. He shrugged. There were some questions not possible to ask. Her father was later with a workforce in a camp to the north of Berlin. He had represented workers on some committee so one should not be surprised. He had written for magazines, although not always political ones. He was a man with contacts, obviously. The people who cared for her before the train to England were of quite a different kind from those one might expect him to know. 'There were good people everywhere.'

Mr Scherr handed her another photograph, the kind you might think had been taken for a passport, were it not for what the woman looking out at you wore. Unmarried, the man said, thirty-two at the time of the photograph, presumably resilient and in good health or this morning would not be taking place. Eva held it for no more than a few seconds and passed it on to Stephen, who gave it more attention. An ordinary-looking woman, he thought, with close-cropped hair, part of another world impossible to imagine, there was nothing one could think beyond that. And older, her looking so much older, than the official had said. There would be thousands, tens of thousands, of photographs not so dissimilar. A blank, guarded stare. A few seconds of one life. He wondered what Eva thought as she turned the cup on the saucer she held. She told him afterwards she was thinking still about the photo of herself, a plate of food blurred at its edge. It was not the same but very like the image her English mother had been given when the train brought their new daughter, when she and her husband decided on the girl's new name, rather than accept the one the back of the photograph bore. The name which was wrong already, because of the confusion the man had just explained to them, her real father in another country rightly thinking a lie would serve her more than the truth, and called her what no one else had thought of, until that moment of losing her, saving her. The child named at birth as Lisabet and then renamed Gerda, which did not sound Jewish, and then Eva, as she has always thought herself to be. And how close she now was to the older woman who may have held her as a child, or perhaps did not, but was her mother's sister, and wore a prison smock as she looked towards the camera in the other photograph the man returned to the file opened on his desk. The aunt whose name at least had remained the same from one life to another, and was on the front of the file, written in blue ink: *Ruth Hannah Friedmann.*

'There are other names here,' Mr Scherr said. 'Relatives.' Names he began to read. 'Chaim. His wife, of course. Her sister Sarah.' Others from the same address. 'A German city at that stage, with its different name.'

'What happened to those? The ones listed there?'

He looked at the handsome woman who questioned him. The effort her calm cost her. 'You know nothing of them?'

'How could I?'

'I can have a copy made of what we have. Date of transport. Destinations.'

Stephen could not imagine what was coming in on Eva, dawning on her. He wanted to press her against him and tell her none of this was taking place. Deny that their lives already were somewhere else, where there was no going back from. He watched her fingers on one hand crush against the ring on the other, her stillness as she repeated, 'Destinations?'

'Camps,' the man said.

'The same place? They were together?'

'So it seems. One did not arrive. One of the older ones.'

Eva surprising her husband yet again. She stood abruptly, making it clear that nothing else Mr Scherr might say was essential to her. She said, 'The one you brought us here for? Can we see her now?'

They walked through to another part of the building, to a room meant to be more welcoming than an office. A bowl of flowers stood on a table against a wall, and a large reproduction of a painting hung above it. An English countryside with a tall-spired church and bunched-up clouds. Stephen looked at it while he and Eva waited for another door to open on the room's other side, and thought how pictures and photos can be like what they represent, and yet there is always, even in the seemingly accurate, something that makes you say, No, this is not quite so. Life-like is not the same as life. He had no notion of what his wife might be thinking as they waited. How beautiful she was, just to look at as she sat there, her hands still in her lap, her profile against the big window onto the street. Eva. Those other names he had just heard that were hers as well.

'From then on,' as he would tell their daughter a long time ahead, at the back of the Westmere pharmacy. 'From then on I suppose things were never quite as we had hoped.' And what he did not say to her, but so searingly remembered, the first hint of how already their lives had begun to change that evening as he and Eva lay together without speaking, until his asking what was it that she was thinking and her telling him, 'Nothing,' repeating it when he said, 'It's this morning, then?' And for the first time, her not seeming to mind whether he touched her or not. She turned towards him as he wanted her to do, but it was not the same.

This morning when the door across from where they stood had opened and two women came in. The final thing the man had said to them as they left his office, 'Some people find this part a challenge, Mrs Ross. This part.' After his also saying it might encourage them to hear that a situation like this was what healing the past came down to. It was not uncommon, a situation like this.

'It is for us,' Eva had said.

The door opening and a smart woman walking towards them, telling them her name was Mrs Bland. Her hair was arranged in a plait that crossed the top of her forehead. One hand held that of the older woman who followed a little behind her. She said, briskly and yet warmly, 'This is a happy time,' and spoke to the woman in what Stephen guessed was German. Then letting go the woman's hand, she stepped aside, and Eva and the woman stood a few feet apart. 'So here you are,' Mrs Bland said. 'It has been a long time.'

A few minutes before, as they waited on the other side of the door, she had joked to the older woman, 'There. We must look the part,' and lightly touched her lips with the tube in her hand, and rubbed at her cheeks. 'She will be nervous too.' She had raised her hand to touch the coil of her own wheat-coloured hair. And now, facing her niece, the woman said, '*Ach, schön*,' at the instant Eva stepped towards her, and their faces touched, and their hands moved across each other's arms, and Stephen's strange thought that it was almost as if they were blind people he was watching, the flicker and movement of their hands confirming yes, this is what they were. And then for half an hour the three women and Stephen sat on leather chairs arranged in the middle of the room, an air of such unreality about it. That is what I was thinking, Eva would say later to her husband, it was as if somehow this was not happening even as it was, none of us knowing what was real and how much we acted parts we could not escape from. We had been free for the last time.

Mrs Bland was the one everything had to pass through. The older woman rested her hand on the translator's arm, as if claiming her. After their drawing apart from that long minute of holding and touching and bewilderment, she and Eva then sat as if in some sudden shyness, watching each other, each finding words inadequate, the simplest things lost to them as they were taken and put into another tongue. Eva took in the blunt broad nose, the frank grey eyes that watched her as though somehow expecting her to stand and leave the room, the distorted left hand partly concealed by a leather mitten. Her aunt and Mrs Bland again speaking in the language she and Stephen did not comprehend.

'You remember her?' Mrs Bland asked. 'You remember Lisabet? The girl who was given your mother's name?'

'No,' the woman said. 'I remember there was a child a long time ago and I see this Englishwoman now and you tell me they are the same. So we hold each other and that is important. We are the same whether we think we are or not. Although I might be wrong. I might not have seen her before. I don't remember that.'

'You mustn't think—' Mrs Bland began to say, and Ruth cut across whatever it was she intended. 'No,' she said. 'No. There is time for all that.' She put the practical question. 'How will we talk?'

The older woman saying something close to her friend's ear, and Mrs Bland, smiling as though there were something even amusing in what she passed on, 'Why not begin again where you may have left off?'

Eva too smiling slightly, the older woman relaxing for the first time. But Stephen saw the sharpness of what his wife then said, at the logic beyond its apparent lightness: 'So I will be a child and my aunt young again and we will pretend nothing much happened in between?'

Mrs Bland did not translate. She said simply, 'I understand you will be together because you feel you have no choice, no more than Ruth has, and that it's asking a great deal. But anything you say to each other is better than nothing. And however you say it.'

'But it will not be like adults speaking,' Stephen said. Until now he had been silent.

'No,' Mrs Bland said. 'But there is so much more to it than that.' Her inviting this stiff distant couple to consider what she had hoped it would not be necessary for her to spell out, that distress and awkwardness and the unpleasant press of inevitability were small enough things, against what had gone before. 'Nothing makes up for anything,' she said, almost coldly. 'But you decide to try, or you do not.'

'We understand that,' Eva said. 'We are not avoiding what we know we have to do.'

Yet the frankness seemed to add to the ease in the room. Stephen spoke again. 'Names are a good place to begin,' he said. He smiled at the drab older woman with her short grey hair, the heavy shoulders beneath her plain dark frock. He felt pity surge through him as a physical force, pity for his wife, for the woman, for everything that made this meeting what it was, with its reluctance and apprehension and fear, and the hope each knew they must have faith in, must persist with, or the darkness had taken them as well.

There was almost levity as they moved from one to the other, now that the matter of names had been raised, and the older woman said it must be left to them, to the young ones, surely, what they felt at ease with? Stephen said remember this would be the name that in time their children would know their relative by, and Eva added it must be a word to bring and keep us together, the best word for that, and why not grandmother, why not that? For the sake of the children. Wouldn't it be good if they knew her as that? For that is what she would be to them. Ruth said, *Babcia,* why not? What her own grandparents would have said, at another time, in Poland. And while Mrs Bland was there to advise with her directness and common sense, Stephen asked again about how they might talk together? 'Neither of us knows another language and I doubt that we'd be much good at it. I know I wouldn't be.'

The young woman said Babcia—why not start with that at once?—Babcia and Eva would find a way, there was no point in being programmatic. Perhaps English lessons later on, but for the moment their being together was what mattered. But it made sense, German, at least for a start, for the old woman was telling them they had spoken little else at home but the language that would later oppress them, that their status, among their own people even, so depended on that. They were cultured. They were educated. Their father was a businessman. She will not say, or not for now, how that had so defined them, their preference for something other than what, a generation before, they so accepted without question, the Polish spoken so naturally with neighbours, the Yiddish among themselves at home, a time which Babcia's mother so liked to insist was further back than that, oh so far back, while her father, with his socialism, his sense of humour, teased his wife was only round the corner after all, demanding as he touched her hair with affection, 'What do you think we were back East? Berliners?'

It was messy from the start, Stephen will always believe. There was hardly a way it could not have been, messy and never really to be resolved, and the life they believed they would have grew instead into the one they found themselves with. A fact which one of their children will understand, and the other be too angry to accept, until the story had gone on for so much longer and by then had become another story. But for now they are on the journey back home, as Stephen naturally calls it, to what Eva also already calls it, for 'home', that is the word that has come to stand for everything she hopes for, rather than what she knows. While Babcia calls it nothing, it is so far distant and so long a journey to get there, it cannot mean anything other than a place to arrive at that will be different from anything she had known or thought of. And in the meantime she and her new family, her old family, begin to find and use the words that in fact will never run to more than a few hundred, and even less than that, if one means words used with precision or certainty or ease. David, who will not be born for another six years, one day will write, 'Talk for us at home, if "us" means anything like the five people who lived in the same house, was not much more than a way of pointing. And we expected it to do so much. The jumble of words we tried to use, which were never enough.' It bothers his sister Lisa far less, whose view of life is more generous.

Lisa, which will be short for Lisabet, once her mother's name for a short time, and her great-grandmother's for a lifetime. Unlike her brother, she will have the gift of standing a little to the side of almost everything, not by choice, but because the centre, if such a thing exists, is not so easy to locate as most assume. And she will be the one to understand as well how her parents did not take in, as they might have done, the warning already there when the man with his file and copies of documents and the papers that linked them into a story as defining as closing the door on a cell, said, 'Your aunt perhaps is not so clear-minded as a woman of her age might be. There's no wonder of course at that. But her contentment comes at a price. At a certain loss.'

They sailed from Southampton in late summer, the weather as placid and clear as the day of Stephen's arrival almost two years before had been one of murk and rain. To save on the fares, Eva and her aunt shared a cabin, while Stephen was with three other men a deck lower down. His memory of the voyage will fade to a general mêlée of women and young children, brides moving to the world's far side, men who it seemed preferred for the most part not to talk more than they were obliged, the evenings in the lounge when a pianist played and stewards delivered glasses to the tables, the languor of the last days before the harbour with its scatter of islands, its low rim of hills. There were times at the beginning of the voyage when he and Eva would go below and have the women's cabin to themselves, but there now seemed such awkwardness in doing so, while their relative sat on deck in a canvas chair and looked out to the sea, that neither suggested it as eagerly as they might have done a month before. And whatever the advice Mrs Bland with her corn-coloured hair may have given them, Eva repeated the German words for 'blue' and 'yellow' and 'ship' which Babcia taught her, and the old lady attempted to return the English words she smiled at, rather than remembered, or cared to use. 'The old lady' as the married couple always thought of her, who a week before the end of the voyage would turn forty-five.

The extraordinary event, as Stephen will always think of it, on their second day on open sea, the land already dropped beyond the hard dark line one now looked out to, is an overweight woman with her confining scarf, her shapeless dress, her shoes heavy as a man's, approaching Stephen as he sits in the ship's small library while Eva and Babcia walk arm in arm on the deck, their crossing between the thick window in front of him and the ship's rail across the narrow stretch of white-scrubbed wood, and five minutes later their passing again, in the opposite direction.

The stolid woman announcing simply, 'I am Miss McGovern.' A harsh, grating accent Stephen tried to place from those he had sometimes heard in the shop. Irish of some sort. Scottish, even. Yet for all her severity and squatness and the curt pulling-back of her hair beneath the tight brown scarf, there is an oppressive warmth he instinctively dislikes. A too-blunt intrusion.

'Your friend out there,' the woman called Miss McGovern told him. 'The older one. I know her.'

Eva and Babcia for a moment at the window, and then past, and only the stiff lines of the railing, the grey stretch of sea.

'I don't think so,' Stephen said. He did not offer his name in return for the woman's.

'She does not speak English?'

'No.'

'May I ask where she is from, sir?' That last word so raising his irritation.

'That's something I don't know.'

'I would like to speak with her. To ask her.'

'I don't think you know her.' He is sharply aware of his own rudeness, but does not regret it. He guesses that the book she carries is a religious work of some kind, the edges of the pages a dull shiny old, a thin red ribbon attached to it as a bookmark. 'No, there is no way you could have known her.'

Miss McGovern smiled at him, amused even, was it, as though she can do nothing about his ignorance? She knows he does not like her, but she continues to stand in front of him, to demand that he look at her. Later he will know that whatever this grating woman means by God surrounds everything she knows or does or thinks, that she might no more be diverted from where she believes her certainty lies than the ship they are on is likely to change course. Yet he will never hear her say the word, or invoke his name. She does not need to.

Stephen silent as he watches her, as she too watches him, a disconcerting quiver, a jitter almost in her eyes, and her lips moving slightly, as though she were about to speak. He took in the hair which was neither brown nor not yet grey, from what he can see of the wisps worked free at the scarf's edge, the unattractive massing of her cheeks, her flesh the colour of dough. They both then look through the long deep window as the women pass, still arm in arm, as compelled to be together as though actually shackled. Then Miss McGovern explains that the Purser had told her his name was Mr Ross, and the tall handsome woman was his wife, but he had told her no more than that. She was certain, however, so the name was not the point. Certain she knew the woman whose arm his wife now held.

'She is my wife's aunt,' Stephen said.

The woman then telling him, as matter-of-factly as if she spoke of ordinary things, 'She was with my sister when she died. But there is more than that we have in common.' And of all things, her suddenly laughing. Stephen startled to hear the soft, throaty laugh, as though a woman is explaining something to a child, as she says, 'The unexpected joy of seeing her here!'

1968

———

Then barazei, wasn't that the phrase the Greeks used to say. Never mind, it meant. What the hell.

Just better bloody live with it. Among the few phrases Fergus remembered from the time they spent there. It was a rare and casual world, Greece in the Sixties, before the military camp. It was a simple enough matter to set up private English lessons, which needed to pay only moderately well to cover rent and getting by. There was no need to think beyond the day, and the weather, and the kind of immediacy that made them believe that the movie of *Zorba the Greek*, and the music that belted from tavernas and beach resorts and the ships between the islands, was the key to whatever stood against the puritanism New Zealanders loved to tax themselves with, believing they shucked off its long shadow as they danced and pissed it up and loved into the world of light. As Fergus had told her while they sat on the ferry's deck on the way back from several days in Samos, the sea glinting with the late sun tracking across to the Turkey they never visited yet talked so much of getting to, their skins and minds alive—'their souls' too, he even grandly said—as they had never been at home. 'You know, Lisa, if I ever had a tattoo, know what it would be? Right across my back, in big letters? *Fuck Westmere*, that's what it would be.'

When Lisa sometimes thought of it later, even out there at the Mission, what stayed with her was the inane simplicity of what they thought life might be. And how much they misunderstood of the country they lived in, reading their Penguin *Odysseys*, their *Alexandria Quartets*, diligently learning their words each day, even the word for 'revolution', which in a few weeks they would hear more often than any other.

The pupils they taught were from well-off families, pleasant youngsters who by twelve or fourteen carried the charm, the incipient panache, of the pampered adults their parents paid good money to ensure they became. 'That's only Kolonaki,' an Australian girl told them. 'That's the flash part of town, remember. Come out my way to Nea Smyrna it's a different story.' Lisa liked her. The girl talked about the linguistics course she would begin in Paris at the end of summer, and Lisa said there was a course in London she would love to do, but that was years off yet. It was nice to talk like this because mostly it was just herself and Fergus, who was generous and fun and for the moment there was no call to think past that. Soon, but not quite yet. She liked the fact that she enchanted him. She was excited by the idea as well as the fact of sensuality. At how she did not greatly care for the person she saw herself not becoming exactly, but heading towards, on the way towards being someone else. When she tried to say something of this to

Fergus, he laughed and told her, 'There we go, us puritans all over.' That was not what she had meant.

Lisa had no notion that she might enjoy teaching, and found that she did. She took her pupils seriously and did not follow Fergus's advice to joke along with them. They always liked you he said if you made them laugh. But she encouraged them to have a shot at saying things, to catch their interest enough for them to want to tell her what the words were not quite there for, and so want to grasp at more. She liked the quiet sitting rooms with their heavy furniture, their flashy lamps, the glimmer of ikons in one corner, the plush cover on the table they sat at, the small glass cup of coffee that was brought to her, the gold patterning around the blue or green glass, the matching plate with its loukoumi or baklava. The pupils seemed to like her. 'The boys can be little pricks,' Fergus said. 'If there's two of them together they'll try to have you on. Little capitalist shits.'

She considered it carefully when Vicky from Adelaide told her that 'bourgeois' was a word you could use here as you never could back home, the word for those families in the handsome white marble apartments, with the mothers gracious to you because they knew there was nothing to fear from a young foreign woman who would sit here with textbooks and someone else's children for seventy drachmae. Some liked to show off the English they knew. Sometimes the coffee was carried in by maids, who were always dressed soberly. Living here, she said to Vicky, was like getting very slowly into a story that was set in places you knew nothing about, so everything came as a surprise. Everything you are looking at, Vicky said, is built on the fact that the country exists because of its peasants. That is what these kind of people float on, the people whose children we teach. Lisa considered that too. 'I just don't know enough to take that in.' How unlike Fergus she was when it came to that. She joked with him that he would have made a good detective in some big store. The way his eyes flickered. Never missing a thing. He was so much quicker at taking things in, sizing them up. She was slower to decide, more attentive to what might lie behind what she saw.

She began to see that what Fergus and Vicky talked about had nothing immediately to do with themselves, but with an idea, a sense of structures and organisations, and yet they could miss a beat when it came to people.

He smiled as she dissected him. They sat in a taverna called the Dolphin, where you could eat well and for next to nothing. They had gone there often enough to be known by name, to call the waiters and the large woman on her stool behind the till by theirs. Sometimes two men would take instruments from battered cases and play, and customers dance. Always someone invited Lisa to join in. Fergus was happy to watch. She had no idea of course but quickly picked up on a few sufficient moves. He liked seeing what she was quite unconscious of, an innate gracefulness that people liked to watch. She quickly learned how to move to most advantage as she made her simple steps seem rather more than they were, to snap her fingers and yet all the time to hold a distance which offended no one, which the elderly woman at the till admired. There was nothing of the pushy tourist waiting to perform, to show how well she fitted in, none of what Fergus described as 'your average antipodean arse-trailing'.

He watched Lisa as he sat sipping at his retsina, into which the owner's wife slipped a sliver of apple. She danced with a handkerchief held high between herself and the man in a sharp jacket and a gold chain around his neck who moved through the steps with her. His name was Kostas and he had become a friend. He was frank and good-natured and a master of the kind of inaccuracy that Fergus admired and thought especially Greek. He was a teacher who supported his widowed mother, his father he said had been killed by the communists in the mountains beyond Karpinisi. His father had been a teacher like himself. He played with a key-ring from the moment he sat down. There was a leather and metal attachment that spelled out BMW. Unless you knew he walked back to a cheap room behind the station at Monasteraki when he left the taverna, as he confided to Fergus, a rented room where he slept with his trousers carefully laid beneath his mattress each night to keep them sharply creased, you might well think, as he intended you to, that he was perhaps in business and drove an English car. 'You have to love him for that,' Lisa said when she heard the story.

'What, the bullshit of it?' Fergus laughed.

'No, not that,' Lisa said, but left it there. She made a point that Kostas always sat by her. She knew he liked being marked, in front of everyone, as if a special friend. And it is so good for my English, he said. It is better than talking with Australians. And shamelessly, 'I tell my mother how my English teacher is a doctor. She is very proud of that.'

'Going to be,' she corrected him. 'That is a long way off.'

Fergus said that he liked places like Greece because people gave themselves away all the time. Everything, he said, is a performance, so there is always something to see through. 'There is always this space between the surface and the acting out, and both are real to them. I like that.'

Lisa said, 'I'm not quite with you. I don't know how we can know that.'

'Never mind,' he told her. And with a touch of conceit, as though this explained what she was unable to share: 'My mother used to warn me about it when I was a child. Don't watch people so intently.'

Fergus's mother at the other end of the Crescent, although Lisa had scarcely known her. A big busy pleasant woman, her son the only boy among several girls. She and Mrs Costello smiled at each other when they passed in the street, when her son worked for the shop after school and delivered prescriptions on the black clunky bike with the cane basket on the front, and its placard, 'Ross's Pharmacy'. When occasionally he called in home, delivering something her father asked him to drop off, her mother smiled but said no more than a few words as she thanked him, but Babcia made a fuss of him and plied him with treats, saying things he had no hope of understanding. Once she asked him to walk through with her to the sitting room to feel for a dead fish in the aquarium, and scoop it out. He and Lisa both lied for a year before their parents knew they were 'friends', and lied again, during her first year as a student at med school in Dunedin and his as a junior reporter on the *Evening Star,* as they planned for Greece. Ignorant and romantic and carried away by watching *Zorba* half a dozen times, and buying the soundtrack LP and reading Lawrence Durrell. 'A year off,' as they both said, a year that would force them to grow up. Take them into a bigger world than Westmere so much as dreamed of. One holiday weekend they went with a bus-

82

trip from the tennis club to the mountains at the centre of the island. Neither knew how to ski, but fumbled about on the learners' slopes, and became lovers, and were blind to pretty much anything else. *Head over heels*, her father said. He told her, 'I was the same in London so don't think I don't understand.' He had guessed and asked her and she had told him yes. 'Better not to bother your mother with this, perhaps.' She bluntly asked, 'You mean lie to her?' And Stephen said, without needing to explain, 'Do what's best for *her*.' His assuming Lisa understood why he told her that, and she admired him for it. She told him, 'I'll come back in a year's time and finish my degree. You needn't worry about that.' Her father replied, 'I know. I know you will.' There were things they felt no need to spell out. Her mother said little, and accepted the girl's saying she needed time to think, surely she would understand that? And Eva said, 'It saddens me your going, but yes I do. There is no real freedom until you have worked things out for yourself.' Lisa again struck, as so often, at how clearly she understood whatever Stephen said to her, but was puzzled, or taken by surprise, at her mother's remarks, by the train of thought she could only guess at that lay behind them.

Within a few weeks of flying in from Delhi, each had a roster of private students. Their lessons were taught from old-fashioned textbooks that used words like 'klaxon' rather than 'car horn', that taught 'may' and 'might' in ways that they themselves would seldom use with such precision. Other books were about Greek legends and the marvels of the ancient world. On the walls of the quiet rooms they taught in were hand-tinted formal photographs in thick gold frames, grandparents with granitely solid women and men with aggressive moustaches, ikons with a lamp burning before them, and all but the faces and hands of the saints, the Virgin, covered in hammered tin. Fergus quickly decided the children were spoiled and lied about their homework and were insincerely polite, and Lisa teased him that he was unable to cope with the rich, that he saw them through the simple-minded, watered-down socialism that New Zealanders thought it their right to inflict on the world. He came back that she had the political insight of a chook. The argument was good-natured but serious at heart. But they agreed their young pupils assumed that the good things in life were on call, and would come when whistled for.

He learned to say 'As God wills' in Greek to the aunts or the mothers who handed him cash at the end of the lessons and waited for the children to be praised. The saying from a foreigner delighted them. Some smiled as though he had attempted a joke. One older aunt patted his arm and told him New Zealanders were good people, she remembered them from the war—men with red faces but good hearts. She tapped her bosom and repeated for him, 'kali kardia'. He liked the feel of the folded drachmae in his hand, the pretence that to teach was not quite to be engaged in trade. One pupil was a girl of fifteen whom he suspected may have welcomed mild advances and then cried if he had done such a thing. He could be wrong, of course, but an Englishman he knew had told him of such things. Her name was Tasoula. She pushed her sleeves back to show the honey-colour of her arms to advantage. She leaned back with her hands clasped behind her head so her breasts in her ribbed sweater thrust towards him. She sometimes put her hand so close to his on the opened pages of a book that their fingers brushed above a picture of Odysseus tied to a mast, or Nausicaa girlishly tossing a ball. The less notice he took of her the more little tricks she employed. He knew she disliked the handsome thirty-year-old woman who had married her widowed father, a man related in some way, from what he gathered, to the Metaxas fortune. Every evening, last thing, he and Lisa drank a glass of the cheap brandy with the name on the label. The girl could afford to condescend a little. She knew Mr Costello, a name she liked saying, must be poor or he would not be teaching as he did, walking from street to street, hurrying once his lesson with her finished to his next hour with a very clever student—Fergus knew he riled her telling her that—in Amerikis Street. He guessed what she might be thinking, that if one day his hand brushed across hers, or his hand even paused against her breast, it would pay back her stepmother for so much. He guessed, but was wise enough to leave it be. He insisted they pay rather more attention to grammar than just the word-lists she asked him for, the words in pop songs, the slick talk she heard on the radio from the American base. But when he made love to Lisa he sometimes said, I am thinking of the brandy girl who would like me to grab her tits. Which Lisa knew was not in fact the truth, but as a game it was quite fun. One lie was worth another. She invented a pupil whose father was a banker, an unattractive boy who touched himself beneath the table while she explained to him the perfect tense. He knows that I know, Lisa said, he knows too that I shall never tell him to stop, which means he thinks I like his doing that, or I cannot be bothered caring, and it drives him crazy not knowing. Each invented more to goad the other.

Fergus had picked up on more than Lisa was aware of, the sense of lust that he sometimes thought pervaded the city. Because he had seen men on the prowl, he said, witnessed the cars pull up to the kerbs, inviting women to walk across. He was drawn not to that so much as the excitement of hypocrisy, the game that seemed to be played out wherever one looked. The men in the public lavatories below Omonoia Square, the rows of young and old who would have killed had their masculinity been questioned, standing at times for hours, glancing left and right, exposing, stroking. Or the middle-aged well-dressed women in the fashionable arcade near Syntagma Square, their hair expensively attended, gold glinting at their throats and wrists, casually passing and re-passing the fashionable shops, waiting their assignations, waiting the chance of something new.

How did he know, Lisa quizzed him, how could he know all that? They might just do it for a job.

They are not whores, he said, they are women who will go home and tell their families they have been shopping or meeting friends. Lisa said he was obsessed, that the obsessed always see what is not really there. Yet she told him yes, tell me more about what you see. It became as though Athens had turned them into different people. But at other times, her thinking it is not especially Athens, it is just our being in a place where the cages we lived in have had the bars removed.

Fergus told her he thought of those animals, he forgot their name, that exist for months in the constant reek of musk. He was in the street one afternoon that led down from Omonoia to the railway station, passing buildings pocked still by the spraying of bullets from twenty years before. He picked up the staleness of clothes, the seemingly idle drifting of those without work. He believed he could tell those who had come to the capital from the north, or up from the Mani, and were lost and fascinated by how vile yet commanding the city was. That afternoon there was a drama he never fully comprehended. At first he guessed that what he saw must be the making of a film, although he saw no cameras, no assistants with lights and clapboards. Yet there was a sense of reality so intense it could only be artificial. A woman with that heavy Mediterranean radiance movies made so much of, a woman in a short black leather skirt and a shiny golden blouse and black stockings whose edges did not quite reach the level of her skirt, waited at the corner of one of the grey bullet-scarred buildings. She walked a dozen paces in one direction or the other, then walked back. A crowd of thirty or forty men of all ages, most in the drab clothing of those who could not find work. The closest were standing several yards from her. She ignored them completely. None of the men spoke together yet there was an air of complicity, of a herd obsessed by the focus they could not break free from. There was a sense too among them of crude amusement, of undeclared contempt, yet these were subordinate to the enthralment gripping them as surely as if they had been trussed animals across a spit. There was nothing threatening in the scene, no sense that anything violent would occur, yet the word that strangely came to him was fury. A dark heavy resentment at something intolerably distant, yet the sense of the woman's magnetism pressing back to them, goading, mocking them, her searing reckless display as close as that, close enough to touch, to taste, yet no one moving closer, none crossing what seemed the boundary set between them implacably as razor wire. It held him too with its weird primitive force.

He waited for perhaps ten minutes, then walked back up to the square. He had no idea how long it would last, how it would end, no understanding of what exactly it was that he was witness to. He and Lisa talked of it while they sat in the flat late that evening, after their classes and a souvlaki at the corner stall. She took the Metaxa and two glasses from the tiny kitchen and brought it through to the couch that folded out to their bed. The window was opened to where it pressed against the metal grill, young voices calling across the street coming down to them. There was the sweet corroding smell of some vine from the balcony of the floor above. Already the evenings had become too hot to be at ease in. She scored her fingernails down the label of the bottle. She said, 'Tell me about the girl who wants you.'

Their corruption was a game. One morning Lisa said as she came back from the shower in the bathroom, a space little larger than a wardrobe, with its faint reek rising from the drain, 'I can't believe how I was last night and the person I am now are quite the same. I hope they never overlap completely.' She was dressed in a simple linen frock and ran a brush through her hair, standing in front of the circular mirror on the wall inside the door.

'I didn't think you people had hang-ups about sin. Not like us,' Fergus said to her. His saying so did not amuse her as he thought it would. She looked at him as he buttoned his shirt, ran his hand across his chin and said he thought he could get away with it, no one would think him scruffy if he gave one day a miss? She told him, 'There was nothing further from my mind. You miss the point at times, Fergus.' And then, 'No, I don't think you can get away with it. We're paid to look presentable as well as do a job.'

They were silent then until they left the flat and walked towards the bus stop in front of the public hospital. There was a café on the corner of Ravini Street where they ordered American coffees, and spread honey on the still warm rolls. Whatever the coolness had been about back there at the flat, things now seemed as on any morning. Fergus spelled out the headlines on a paper left on the next table. Politics was about all he could make out, the initials for the parties which meant nothing beyond one being Left, the other Right. Photos of men in military uniforms, slabbed expressionless faces. He smiled across at her, their fingers touching briefly. They seldom spoke in daylight of what they said to each other at night, beyond his sometimes, almost as a little ritual, quoting some lines or other, by a woman writer about 'wild nights'. At times he had no idea what Lisa might be thinking. If things were good why rock the boat?

Decades later, in the wide garden of the Home, beneath the tree where he insisted they sat, he told a young woman—young to him, certainly—with her black hair and her sober professional skirt, her fingers flicking across the keyboard, that if he made a lot of all that now, the physical side of their being together, it was because they had made a lot of it then. Not for the sex of it only, the old man told her, it was more than that. This whole business of what goes on in another mind. As if we ever know.

The flat was beneath street level. They saw only the legs of pedestrians when they looked through the sitting-room window. It was a posh street, Fergus said, the only reason they could afford it was that it was owned by a New Zealander they never saw, an archaeologist who was there only during the winter. It was a basement but of course it was fun. Hot as the summer came on, and crammed with the owner's bric-a-brac, his scraps from distant centuries, but who cared about that? It was an exciting time.

'You wouldn't believe,' he wrote home to his brother, 'the hatred for the Left, at least among the parents of the kids we teach. If you are even moderately socialist you are branded a communist.' It was clear-cut and absolute. Outside the rich, of course, it was different. You were waiting for revolution of a different kind. There was nothing much else to wait for. It will come, a fat Cretan in a shop in the next street told them. He meant the day of reckoning. The day the bastards went to the wall. But we knew few workers, Fergus will remember. We didn't live in an area where you heard much talk like that. When a man in a neighbouring flat quietly asked, so what did they think of his country now, the cradle of democracy, Lisa said they were sorry, they were *xenoi* and simply didn't know.

Once a policeman knocked on the door and said they were using a typewriter at forbidden hours during the afternoon. He could hear it from the street. He was polite and advised them not to do it again: how would they know it was a regulation since the Revolution?

They saw the tanks along Vasilissis Sofias Avenue, the soldiers with machine guns at the entrance to the Gardens behind Parliament. It was exhilarating but remote, as if they were children allowed to observe how grown-ups lived. Making love was more important to them than revolution. Fergus said with a sudden acuity Lisa was uncomfortable with, 'The whole point of travel anywhere is to define ourselves to advantage.' Yet how could they be anything but ignorant of what went on around them? They could not buy English papers for weeks. *Time* magazine had blocks of black ink obliterating any mention of Greece. The mothers and aunts in the houses where they taught did not discuss what dominated every conversation behind closed doors. They understood nothing of what they heard on the radio. Then the same man from the flat above their basement quietly asked again, he hoped it did not offend them that he asked, but please not to listen to the BBC on their transistor, it was sometimes difficult for those passing in the street to tell exactly where the sounds might come from. Another evening they were in a restaurant, a place rather more up-market than normally they would have eaten at, but it was Fergus's birthday. There was a sudden movement from a family eating at a table close to theirs, a group of several adults and a child. The mother quickly took her child with her, the father spoke to the waiter and another man who approached him. The men shook hands, the people left. It was nothing, a young waiter said, winking when his back was towards his boss. The child had been calling aloud the name of a fish that was only a letter different from the name of one of the Colonels. Such small things, an elderly man said to them, as the family left. A few minutes later the bouzouki player refused a polite American's request for music by a composer the regime had banned. That is how dictatorship works. It moves slowly, like a crab. We are here as voyeurs, Lisa began to think.

In the flat they took turns reading the *Odyssey* aloud to each other. They said to other young foreigners they casually met up with, that of course there was only one side one could believe. Did the friends they spoke with not know about New Zealand, Fergus sometimes said, its social experiments, its welfare state, its first giving women the vote? Where women, Lisa rephrased it, first *took* the vote. She was a little embarrassed by him. It was a short cut for Fergus to then claim a natural gift for fraternising with the poor, his insisting those who milled in the lavish lobbies of the hotels they could not afford to enter were indeed the enemy. He was good at the game. He had read a student guide to Marx, which was more than Lisa had, and so was armed with telling quotes. He knew the approved phrases to earn from a passing acquaintance in a bar the friendly tap of a glass against his own. If the other drinker was middle-aged, he would call Fergus *kalo pedi* and they would feel close to each other for as long as the bottle lasted. Lisa smiled and knew the older men liked her being there, even if she said little. Everything was something of a game in any case. When they walked in the big gardens behind Parliament, Fergus said, 'See those men flitting behind the bushes there? They come here to suck off.' She wondered if that was really true. She wanted him to tell her, even if it was not. She said to him one evening, when the weather suddenly became almost unbearably hot and they sat out late at pavement tables, 'You know we are all on a stage here, Fergus?'

'You mean pretending?' he said. 'But who's pretending?'

'The opposite to that. We believe every minute of it. Everyone believes it. History is performance. Acting up. We're excited because we're theatre.'

'Lost me!' Fergus had laughed at her. They liked life too much to argue. Lisa thought, without it bothering her, that the man she lived with for the moment did not care much about ideas that could not be seen in front of you, touched with your hand, tasted on the edge of a glass. But then didn't she do the same, or would do, once her own life took up again, as in a few months' time it would have to do? A doctor might be a philosopher, but not at the same time, she once joked with him. Stitches are what work for others, quotes for oneself. But as she thought it, admitted too what a fraud she was becoming, even putting it like that!

There were weeks in August when they had few classes. Several children went down with measles, many were on vacation, some set off to remote villages where families gathered for the Virgin's feast day. A flat malaise seemed to stall the city. The military looked back, indifferent, when you looked at them. If you glimpsed the Acropolis at the end of a street, from the window of a bus, even that was like a prop behind the wrong play. They lay on the beach at Phaleron, or sat under pines, Lisa reading de Beauvoir and Fergus underlining Orwell carefully enough to try writing like him in the *cahiers* he bought in a shop near the university. The French word on the covers made it seem more likely that these were the notebooks a writer would use. Neither for the moment thought too much about the inevitable fact of when they would need to leave. Take one day at a time. *Then barazi, pedaki mou.* The great seductive lie of the Mediterranean seeped into them. Then how quickly it was decided.

Although they might more cheaply buy in the market and eat at home, it seemed against the grain of things to do so. In the weeks when classes dropped off and money was tight, they went most evenings to a little place—even taverna was far too grand a name for it—a few streets from the flat, where the Maniatis, as his customers called out to him, stood behind the counter, above his trays of chopped onions and tomatoes, the pile of pita bread he attended to and slapped at, his large knife almost always in his hand, waiting to slice from the slowly turning *gyro* between its heated panels. There were four tin tables on the concrete floor, enough plates for a dozen customers, a wall of bottles and the long low refrigerator the Maniatis dipped across to draw out frosted beers. His business may be small but it was certain, mostly customers who waited and then carried their souvlaki with them, and the big man made no attempt to charm.

'Being a prick defines me,' Fergus joked as he watched his abruptness, his grunted response to questions, his handing back change as if he had taken offence. Yet he took to the young foreign couple who ordered bottles of cold beer and waited for the food he brought across to them on chipped white plates rather than placing it on the top of the counter for them to retrieve themselves. It seemed to have much to do with the fact that they were not Americans or British or Germans. As they came to know him a little more, they saw his contempt for most nationalities was a gift he cherished. An obligation, even. It amused Lisa when he showed her that if he turned a photograph of the King stuck with strips of sticky tape to the wall, it was attached to the back of a poster from before the coup, a party notice of some kind with the hammer and sickle large at the head of it. Such things of course had been put away with the assumption that their days would come again. The first rule of a changed regime is to lie with one's hand on one's heart. Above the King there were two crossed flags. But the man liked them enough to show how his heart for the time being was turned to the wall, and was patient as they spoke to him in their meagre Greek. He liked it that Lisa especially took such trouble to talk with him. At times his shoulders lifted with laughter, a tremor at his fat throat, his head slightly tilted back, these moments of solidarity that had no need to be spelled out. There would be times when Lisa thought yes, that is my happiest memory of Athens. The Maniatis. His poster. The shared quiet jokes. And that curious sad memory too which came back to her as though one story could not be in her mind without the other tangled with it.

Even the day of the week she remembered, Friday. There had been a sudden burst of rain. The air smelled of wet pine trees and the branches in the park they passed ran with bright fat drops as the sun again came out. They were walking back from checking their mail at Thomas Cook's. They passed the flower stalls in front of the high iron railings near the Gardens as the owners eased back the awnings drawn across when the quick storm pelted down. After rain the scent of flowers and wetness seemed almost thick enough to touch.

As they waited to cross the main street a convoy of army trucks drove past. They then climbed a side street towards the yellow-painted public hospital a few hundred yards from where they lived, where always there seemed to be groups of poorly dressed people gathered at the entrance, convalescing patients waiting to be collected, families arriving with children in their arms. If Fergus was alone he would walk further down Vasilissis Sofias to take another street back to the flat. He preferred not to see them. But Lisa insisted they walk this way when they were together.

It was hot again after the rain. The surface of the street steamed. The sun fragmented into shards and glitters on the trees above the pavement. As they looked from the brightness, the shadows were intense around an unmarked doorway and its shallow flight of steps. An old-model car was pulled in at the kerbside. Its boot was opened like a dark mouth, an elderly woman in black holding it high with one hand. Lisa and Fergus halted as two young men carried an unvarnished coffin from the doorway and down the flight of steps, and across the pavement to the waiting car. They were close to the raised boot when the man at the back of the coffin stumbled, and the plain wooden lid swivelled to one side. It seemed held by a single screw. For no more than a few seconds they glimpsed the suited figure packed inside. The head was concealed by the board that now slanted across the coffin. What they saw were two hands, one folded across the other. And the bare feet below the black trousers. The hands and the feet, for that instant, a glaring whiteness.

Lisa was shocked, more for the young men whose faces were distraught than for the sudden brute fact of death barring their path. She heard Fergus's sharp gasp as he felt the rush of blood to his head, the street swaying as if he were about to lose balance. But then it was the brilliance of the sun he was again aware of, the confused image of the shadow from the hospital wall cutting across the pavement, the angled unvarnished coffin, the now wailing woman who had let the boot of the car fall shut. Lisa at once went across to raise it. Another man, a stranger to the others, rushed forward from the door at the top of the steps and swung the pivoting lid back into place, concealing the man who lay beneath it. There was the strange sense as though something shameful had taken place. The two young men she thought the dead man's sons pushed past the old woman who continued to wail, leaning forward, unaware that a small group of people on the other side of the road had stopped and were looking towards her. Lisa continued to hold the raised metal flap while the coffin was placed sideways, awkward and suddenly grotesque, projecting to either side of the car. The sons did not speak to her as she stepped aside and they began to fix the box in place with ropes that passed around the boot and beneath the car. Lisa opened the back door of the car and helped the old woman get inside. The whole episode was quick, cluttered, somehow horribly attention-seeking. Then the car drove off with its crudely roped-in freight, people continued to walk on, the man who had rushed down the steps went back up and closed the door.

'You all right?' Lisa said.

'Fine,' Fergus told her. And then, 'You were great.'

They walked on towards the street and the corner where their laconic friend would be standing in his stained apron, his knife at the ready to carve from the slowly rotating pillar of meat. They were more disturbed than they would admit. For Fergus it had been a brushing against something he resented, almost as though a personal affront. The startling pale nakedness of the hands and feet. The grunting of the sons as they righted the balance of the tilting box. His sudden sense, so intense and yet not possible to speak of, of how closely death and poverty and shame so lay together.

He told Lisa again, 'You were great.'

She said, "The quickness of it all. It came as a surprise.'

Fergus put his arm across her shoulder, her bare skin so much warmer than his hand. A thin film of sweat. The faint lemony smell from her hair as his mouth brushed against it. 'I love you,' he told her, and she allowed her head to lean closer to his own. Poverty and shame in her own mind as well, closer than she had ever really been to them. She was conscious too of a reprimand to herself in the drama and crudeness of it, its jerk from how complacent her life had become. The stage effects of mere chance. She saw how rattled Fergus was, how he wanted her not to know. As if he apprehended that the surface of things had buckled. Without either deciding to, they passed their friend without stopping for a beer, as they would have any other afternoon. 'Later,' Lisa smiled at him. *'Apopsi.'*

They walked on through streets they were less familiar with. They found themselves trailing a group of tourists up to a square with a view across much of the city. The sky was hazed above the white glitter of the city. Neither wanted for the moment to go back to the dimness of the flat with its one iron-barred window, its feeling of looking up from a pit to the street and its passing cut-off figures. When they spoke, it was Lisa reminding them they must renew their permit again in the next ten days. If that was even possible. Since the coup it had become so much harder for foreigners to stay on. Fergus groaned at the thought of it, the hours waiting at the police station, the surly officials, their never quite knowing whether an assistant might help at the discreet slipping of a banknote or ostentatiously take offence. It was not a good time to talk about it. 'Must we?' Fergus said.

'We have to sometime,' she said. 'Even the lotus eating

came to an end.' They had put off raising it for days. When time ran out. Fergus's plan to go on to London, finding work with a paper. Lisa herself needing to go back, back to the studying, the 'hard yakka' she said, using the phrase that had always amused her, and her father as well, when Mr House the builder who lived further along the Crescent, with his team of blond-haired children, complained of what life added up to. Hard yakka and mouths to feed, and a fortune spent at chemist shops. Whoever makes iodine would close down if we weren't here, he told Stephen, close down like a bloody shot.

Fergus said, 'We'll leave talking about it, shall we, before we let the real world in?'

He was right; this wasn't the time. She saw that now. Leave it for a bit yet. So it was as though the dead man had not crossed their path, or the clock kept ticking. For the next ten days it was life again as it should always be: money enough to get by on, endless sun and beaches, retsina and olives and roast lamb. And fucking, as Fergus put it, to beat the band, and the band fucking knows what it's talking about.

Then it was September. Late September. They took a bus to Cape Sounion and found the column with the famous name carved into it, and swam in a rock pool a local directed them to, a basin of white rock and green gorgeous water. As they left the bus back in the city, their skin tingling with salt and the late afternoon sun, they were ravenous. They decided to eat wherever they came to first, an *estiatorio* with a smiling man flapping a cloth inviting them in. Its kitchen, as he told them from the door, was there to be inspected, how could they pass this for the expensive places closer to the centre, where tourists paid twice as much to eat half as well? He was glib and proud of his rapid ungrammatical English. Mistaking them for a moment, he told them he had worked with his brother in Austin, Texas, all Americans knew Austin? Ah, Auckland, he said as they corrected him, who does not know Auckland, thinking they had told him Oakland. But once they were at a table and gave their orders, he left them alone, conversing loudly, from the door where again he stood to entice, with his wife who busied herself at the pots of food above flaring gas rings. He brought them a dish of olives and ice-cold beers. He returned again with several magazines in English that he thought they might care to look at, implying he had read them himself and could recommend them, cosmopolitans together.

The most recent was several years old. A photograph of Gina Lollobrigida looked up at them. Apart from an air of calm which was part of her beauty, she looked natural and at ease and without the pert self-awareness of a star. Her dark sleeves came almost to her wrists, her neckline was high. Fergus recalled he had sometimes dropped in on a friend back in Grafton Road in a clapped-out wooden villa with damp-smelling carpet and worn lino where generations of students had laid one level of staleness upon another. 'Haven't thought about her since then,' he said, turning the magazine towards Lisa. There had been a massive blow-up of the actress on the sitting room wall, younger and more provocative than the woman who now looked up at them. He remembered a tight black swimsuit, her breasts drawn taut and scooped high. His friend would sometimes stand as though looking at an ikon and say more in reverence than in lechery, 'She's made for it, know that?'

Fergus said, 'If you'd asked us back then what Europe had that we didn't, we'd have pointed at her.'

An hour later they were sitting with their heads against the wall behind them, finishing their second bottle of Dias, the remains of their meal pushed to the side. There was that lovely sense of languor after the swimming, the hot brilliant afternoon, the temple like a postcard when they turned from the bus to look back on it. Lisa closed her eyes, the luxury of that too, as close as one might come to thinking about nothing. A red Porsche screeched into the kerb five yards from where they sat. Its canvas hood was drawn back and its driver crossed the pavement towards them, decked out in a lot of gold even for a Greek. He whirled his car key in front of him like a small propeller. He wore black slacks sharply creased enough to slice pizza, and a grey-ribbed sweater, the sleeves pulled back to give his bangles air. He was perhaps twenty, aware of how the world was made to look his way. He held Lisa's eye until she was the one who broke the gaze. He gave his takeaway order to the owner, who attended to it without speaking. He stood looking out to his car, whistling between his teeth, slapping his key back and forth across his fist. They had seen others identical to him parading in Kolonaki a dozen times. He probably spoke English with a fetching accent, and in the summer picked up easy New Zealanders or Australians at one beach or another.

'A car like that is a cock in any man's language,' Fergus said. He felt he had a duty to dislike him, although Lisa said nothing following his remark and flicked at the magazine. He knew that if he were a Greek himself he would detest him. His family would be royalists and discreetly accept the Colonels until democracy returned, when they would say that from the beginning they had been against the dictatorship, what Greek was not?

The owner arranged slices of tomato and onion on the meat he placed on circles of pita, and squirted dabs of garlic sauce from a plastic container. He rolled the bread into tubes, wrapped them in greaseproof paper and set them in a shallow cardboard box. He worked quickly, nonchalantly. Without a hint of courtesy, he said bluntly how much he was owed. As bluntly, the boy—he would have hated the description—handed over a note, shoved the change into his pocket without glancing at it. As if to rub salt, he looked up to the photograph of the man in uniform that hung above the door, and raised a thumb toward the tourists in the otherwise empty room. As he went out to the late dazzle of the sun he flipped his sunglasses from where they sat on his hair. He was back behind the wheel of his car when he took the note-wrapped coins from the pocket and smoothed the note on his knee. He flung back his door so it stayed opened as he rushed back into the restaurant, as angry now, Lisa thought, as he was handsome.

He started calling out as he entered, speaking quickly to the man who casually walked back from the kitchen, his contempt obvious and provoking. He rested his fists on the stack of paper squares below the slowly turning grill as the younger man shouted at him. He watched his rage without apparent concern. He then looked past the expensive clothes, the golden chains and the raised vein in the smooth young neck to hold Fergus's eye. In his maimed but fluent English he said, 'You musta see it, my friend? You sit this close you musta see the note this *malaka* give me?' This masturbator. There could not be more offensiveness in what he said.

102

He had not raised his voice, but the surprise of his word further enraged his customer, who turned to them and said, 'I gave this liar five hundred drachs and he gives me the change for one hundred. Did you see that, *despina*?', addressing himself not to the man the owner had appealed to but the woman who sat with him. His assumption that she would have been watching him, and would now speak on his behalf. She thought yes, I did see the note he passed across, and yet I scarcely took notice of it. I could be wrong. But for Fergus it was a moment of quick instinctive decision. He looked through the window to the car, to its sleek lines in their swathe of late reflecting light. Its driver stared at him, confident that he would come, of course he would come, to his defence. Instead of smoothly flicking his key as he had done a few minutes before, he now swung his tinted glasses in his hand. 'Yes,' he said, his tone now insolently patient, 'you must have seen?'

The owner too was looking at the foreigner, his eyebrows raised. The two Greeks vying for him in a frank theatrical way, a rapid moment of class war. He too was inextricably part of the performance. When he spoke he had the sensation of another speaking through him, words he had no choice but to say. 'I saw you give him a hundred. You were playing with it while you waited, that's how I know. I saw you give it to him.'

The young man stood for a moment as if deciding on what to do. He looked down at Fergus from where he stood on the raised step beside the counter. His expression had changed. Then with neither surprise nor anger but something the tourist did not expect, and that stung him as surely as if the Greek had covered the few paces between them and slapped him with his opened hand, he looked with such coldness that Fergus knew he understood perfectly the game that he was playing at, the working man against the rich boy, yet behind that, a deeper truth, the push-button foreign socialist lying because lying was his nature. The young man's rage gone as surely as if an ignition key had turned it off. It was no more than two or three seconds in which he looked at Fergus. He then turned and walked to the car, its door still open, and slid behind its wheel. He sat for a moment before driving off. It seemed to Fergus that the boy with his chains, his bracelets, his expensive toy, at the last was disappointed not that he had been stolen from, but lied against by a man he didn't know. What one person would do against another. Then Lisa stood up from the table and went to pay. She thanked the man who nodded to them as they left, but that was all.

Back at the flat they listened to a local radio station, the high insistent whining that Fergus dismissed as 'that half-Turkish stuff'. But Lisa enjoyed listening as she heated coffee, put two pieces of baklava on a plate and took two glasses of water from the fridge. She arranged the sweets and forks in the way Greek women did. She liked to copy them. There was not much then to say. They drank the coffee and sipped at the cheap Metaxa which only through the courtesy of labelling is related to anything called brandy elsewhere in the world. Lisa had grown to like that too, for all her saying the first time she tasted it that it was wrung through sacking.

'I'll have another,' Fergus said. 'That tells you how desperate.' Already he felt less shamed by what had happened an hour before. When they unfolded the bed they made love, and he put his hand across her mouth, which was a joke between them, 'the Colonels' ploy' as they called it, pretending neighbours would report erotic signals as they may have done the sound of typing in the afternoon's forbidden hours. She bit hard on the side of his hand, so that for days after she had left there was the tender purplish swelling from her bite.

Because that is when Lisa left, the next day, soon after noon. Fergus had gone to the baker's on the corner as on any other morning. When he returned the dish of honey was on the table, the mugs of black tea with the saucer of sliced lemon between them. While they broke chunks from the warm freshly baked rolls, she told him what she would do. He watched her finger scoop at the runnels of honey at the roll's edge. He supposed she had planned through the night what she needed to say to him. It was simpler, briefer, than he expected. She began, 'You lied about the money in the restaurant.'

As directly, Fergus said, 'Anyone would have.'

Then again as calmly as if they were discussing something so much less enduring, 'You play at everything, Fergus. It's turned you into a shit.'

There were times in their months together when they had argued and raised their voices at each other and each knew they enjoyed the drama of it. Not often, but a few times, about things they knew were not of great importance, about friends one wanted to visit and the other did not, once even about politics, when neither deeply accepted the point they defended, but they had been drinking, and there was the fun, for Fergus especially, of guessing what a real argument might be like. But this morning Lisa was practical and concise, saying that this must never be thought of as a 'misunderstanding'. It was more important than that. 'We are talking like this because we understand.'

Water suddenly cascaded down in front of their window and splashed to the concrete area beneath it, as the woman on the balcony above watered her stacked levels of pot plants. This happened every morning, and each time it startled them. They had never seen the woman who lived there, nor heard her at any other time. Water sparkled on the iron railings and on the pavement, and on the bars at the window. The sun already glared on the upper storeys of the building across the road, where the metal shutters were still down. The people there had moved away soon after the coup. Fergus held his mug of tea with both hands, looking at Lisa through the wisping steam. He asked her, 'Is that a reason to leave?'

'Yes it is.'

He began again. 'It's been nearly a year.'

'I know that.'

'If we're not together we'll be unhappy for a long time.'

'I know that too.' And then, reasonably, 'I was going back soon anyway. We knew that. Dunedin. Getting on with my degree. '

'And after that?'

'All this has been lovely. We both know that.'

'More than.'

They sat silently until Fergus went to the stove to top up his tea from the saucepan of boiling water. He looked back to Lisa, her head tilted slightly as she looked up to the street, to the fall of sun across the balconies on the other side of the road. The paleness of her arms, for all the Mediterranean sun, the massing of her tightly curled jet hair. He felt the prickling at his eyes, the tears that he

106

would have hated her seeing. He came back and sat close to her. He touched her wrist. He tried to make his voice sound jokey. 'It won't seem right, you know. Not being together.'

Again she said, 'I know that.' And then, accepting how it would hurt him, but there were more important things than that, she told him how she had no choice, not now. 'Otherwise I'll be corrupted too.'

1976

———

Miss McGovern said as she walked into the pharmacy, 'This is not a place to talk. This is a shop.'

She stood in front of Stephen, insistent, heavy, soft in that way he so disliked her for, as though melting towards something other than she was, this grotesque woman with her shiny lilac scarf. He thought resentfully of her jollity when she and Babcia were together, yet her facing him now, austere and demanding on the other side of the counter. She held in front of her the scuffed handbag with one corner of her Bible tilted too high for the zip to be drawn across it. Her eyes quivered oddly as she looked at him, instructing him, so Stephen thought, you do not rebuke me, you do not impress me.

'It is a shop because it is where I work.' He was not a man who raised his voice, who made an effort to impose on anyone. But he disliked her bowling in on him, her assumed right to disturb him. The shop fortunately was empty. He waited for whatever it was she might have to say to him. On that one day of the month when she visited her old friend, it was her habit each time, at four o'clock, to ask Eva to phone a taxi for her. 'Time to leave, I think.' Always the same phrase. Leave after the two hours in the sitting room with its tilted venetian blinds, the constant pouring of tea, the plate of *faworki* that Ruth had spent the previous day preparing. The two women talking quickly together, laughing, running through names, their leaning towards each other. And sooner or later during each visit, the mood changing between them, the torrent of their chatter running thin, their hands meeting, holding each other. A quiet settling in the shadowed room, the women content to speak sparingly, the air heavier now with the mix of talcum, the sachet of herbs Ruth at times turned absently in the hand lying against the sofa, the lingering sweetness from the plates on the small table in front of them.

Apart from bringing them a fresh pot of coffee as they sat together, Eva left them alone. There were repeated words they came back to, ones that carried special weight for them, phrases she partly grasped the meaning of, but she knew what she took in was so little of what passed between them. She knew at times her aunt spoke of the years before the camp, because the names of streets, of relatives, were there as well, but mostly it was of those years that could never be truly spoken of to others, in the language Eva poorly grasped at and quickly lost. 'The visit go all right?' Stephen asked each month, and Eva as briskly told him, 'As it always does.' An afternoon she meant of such ease, such contentment between two crazy women, the adjective Stephen reserved for his own thinking of them.

He guessed, without pressing his wife to say so, that she in some way envied them, those two old friends, so gifted with each other in God knows what place it was they met. But closer, as Eva sometimes thought, than she herself might be even to those she loved. Yet 'It does me good,' she would say to Stephen, 'just seeing them together.' And joke of it. 'So much life crammed in, along with all the cakes. Apart from what's already here.' For Miss McGovern arrived always with her own tribute, the brown paper bag with its smears from where the icing on the Sally Lunn stained through. The bag placed on the kitchen bench as she came in and then the little ritual, each visit, as she handed across a more enduring gift she brought each month, the cheap and trivial things she watched out for in the messy bric-a-brac shops along the stretch she walked from the top of Newton Road to Pitt Street. Stephen had bought a folding card-table Babcia placed beneath the window in her bedroom, where she arranged and rearranged the gifts each month as a child compulsively returns to displaying presents.

But today broke the pattern of many years. It was not a Thursday, for one thing. It was early afternoon. The time was wrong. Miss McGovern felt no compulsion to explain. She waited, as though the next move must come from him, from the reserved, cautiously hostile man she faced. Her thinking vaguely that if you witnessed, you were used to resentment. It was there since her first breaking in on him on the *Rangitata*, his impulse to speak coldly, to make little effort to conceal distaste. More than a quarter of a century. All of that. From the boat trip when Ruth had been with them for only months, Eva pregnant with Lisa although that was not yet known. He had been reading the H.G. Wells book Mr Golson had given him that last day in the shop in Finchley Road, the generous eccentric David whom Stephen's son would be named after, his quietly spoken and polite final telling him how he hoped Eva might one day come back to her people, *Baruch hashem*. 'Stranger things have happened, my young friend.' As more pragmatically Sam Abrams had tapped the rim of his schnapps against Stephen's glass, offering as his parting wisdom that whatever happens in the world, he said, good things or bad, he would tell him this, the world will always need windows that open and shut. That is a trade to keep in mind. Then Sam had cried. He always did this, he said. He was too soft-hearted for his own good. Memories coming to Stephen within seconds as he looked across the glass-topped counter and Miss McGovern then asking him, was that woman who comes in to help him the way Lisa did when she was a girl, was she with him now?

'Part-time,' Stephen said. 'Mrs Stoddart works part-time.'

'Today?'

'Do you need to speak with her?' How easily she irritated him.

'Then she can keep an eye on this while we walk.' She handed him the same shapeless bag she had been carrying that far back as well, as far as the ship drawing them all to what in time would be today, this minute, as she orders, 'Give her this to guard.' The quick drift of peppermint as she leaned closer to slide the bag across to him. She loosened the zip to set the Bible square. He glimpsed a hank of dull brown wool, the two stubby needles jabbed into its side.

'My earthly belongings,' she said, a surprising irony as

112

Stephen lifted the bag to take it through to behind the shop. Almost as if having him on.

'It will be safe enough here.'

'As anywhere.' Her eyes still holding him, unreadable. 'Another planet, it might as well be,' as he will write to Lisa, telling her of the unexpected visit, and what Miss McGovern will speak to him about. 'What no one much would want deliberately to remember. That's how distant she still seems to me.'

'Ready for the road then?' the old woman asked. Briskly, another unexpected word that came to him, the ease too of her movement beside him, for all the weight she carried. They crossed towards the house opposite where Doctor Satyanand's family lived behind the surgery, and turned to the gentle sloping of West End Road down to the tidal flat of Cox's Creek. Then as if they had spoken intimately for years, she began to tell him, in the harsh nasal accent that had always grated with him. Tell him of where he had always known she and Babcia had been together, and yet had no more spoken of till now than he had presumed to ask. 'But we are going to talk about it now, Stephen, although you would rather be anywhere with anyone else, I'm aware of that, having to listen to me.' A brief silence, the smell of mint on her breath, before she told him, matter-of-factly, 'But you have to forget about disliking me. This is about Ruth.' Her knowing as she began that her using his first name, even that, set his teeth on edge.

She began to speak as fluently as if she read from a script, her talk clear and precise yet from time to time steeped in the language and images of her beliefs. The feeling too that it was for his sake alone that she spoke, and not her own. It was important that he attend to her. It was because he was the man whose home protected the one other human being who mattered unreservedly to her. All the rest who mattered to her as God intended, but Ruth for her sake alone. And so begins to tell him of the place he knew little of apart from what he had read of it, the listings of statistics and abuses that he knew all women who were confined there must have shared. A place David of course made it his business to know more about than the rest of them, David with that judgement of his father Stephen patiently bore.

It was a small village until they were taken there, Miss McGovern said. Pretty in a way that brings tears to German eyes. There were—she supposed still were—black pines along the edge of a picture-book lake. The lies, she now repeated, the lies of the dark kingdom. They were almost the first to arrive, before it was even properly built, before it became the Gehenna which the world now knew it was. 'A place at first to correct us rather than punish us. Before the criminals and the others were brought in with their differently coloured triangles so you would not mistake those from one group for those from any other. Before the gypsies and the communists and the Jews and then so many Poles, who were parts of those other groups as well, but not always. The more women who came, the more severe it got.'

'I know all that,' Stephen said. 'I know that much.'

She said how she and her sister and others who witnessed worked at first in the sandpits at the edge of the lake, and unloaded barges that brought materials to build the camp, and believe it or not in the beginning those called to Jehovah embarrassed them. Those who held them captive. 'We were not political people like the communists and were not the unfortunates and the impure they rounded up or those they thought defiled by birth, who began to arrive soon after. They said to us, Sign this paper, cease to say what you say about the Führer, that he is the anti-Christ, and you are free to leave. But we refused to court damnation for so little a thing as release. We puzzled them and then they hated us even more. Then the more women who were brought for other reasons, the harder it became. There were more punishments. The guards became more severe. Evil for its own sake, but fortitude was still given us. We lived in barracks apart from the others but of course worked with them, stood next to them for hours in the *Appellplatz* when punishments occurred. You will know all that. Some fell and were beaten and some died and we prayed. The Lord was our citadel. And the hardest thing, I will tell you this Stephen, the greatest trial was to be hungry each minute of the day, the ravening beast it is. You think of that even more than fear of punishment. Hunger takes your mind as it does your body. Yet none of us would sign the paper. So of course they hated us. Some of the other women who suffered with us too. Some even of them. They hated us for being unbroken. But you know all that.'

Stephen felt a quick shame that she still so irritated him. Bluntly, he again said to her, 'Yes, I know that.'

They were now at the corner where the road angled down to the tide slapping at the stone wall, the rise of the yellow clay banks and the overhang of sloped dark trees. It irked him that she spoke so directly and lucidly, and the fact that for all her ungainliness she walked firmly beside him, as little bothered by the exercise as himself. The unexpected discomfort of it too, that she continued to speak of the vileness of back there as calmly as if such things were normal, privations to be expected, confirmations of her faith. Her steady insistent voice now recalling for him the pointlessly grotesque punishments, the delight of those inflicting them, as they walked on past the solid ordinary houses, the wooden verandas, the careful curtains, the neatly unimaginative gardens. And then, bizarrely, she was speaking of rabbits. The big well-fed angoras it had been her sister Irma's job to tend in their wood and wire hutches. Miss McGovern smiling at him, the absurdity of it striking her as well, the memory she said which was one of the few from the camp that filled her with joy as she thought of it, the one day when she walked to the hutches with her sister, and in a rare moment of their being unobserved, Irma handed her the warm placid weight of the creature she had picked up, for those few seconds, girls back on the farm together on the Stirling road. 'Not that we had rabbits then,' she said, 'it was calves we doted on.' At home before her sister married and chose to live in Germany with a man elected to spread their belief, and she had gone with her, they could not imagine life without each other, while yet another sister stayed at home until after the war. But the rabbit in that one fragment of time was passed between them, its long ears stroked, the quick pelt of its heart against her wrist, as they stood together in the blue smocks the prisoners wore, the white aprons, the violet triangles defining them.

It was a privileged assignment, as everybody knew, to care for those big timid animals. Irma was chosen, Miss McGovern guessed, not so much for her gentleness but because she had worked in Hamburg for a veterinary doctor. Even more, because those who organised the camp in its thousand aspects knew these women with their spotless barracks and their ridiculous beliefs would no more steal even the mash that was fed to the cages than they would fornicate or strike a fellow prisoner or so easily write a signature that would open for them the camp gates. But her sister's conscience defied the Beast in small things as in large. Even Miss McGovern had attempted to dissuade her. But no, Irma decided, the fur from her charges would become part of uniforms for the Reich. And so she refused the work that every other prisoner so envied her. It was February and the ice from the lake she was obliged to saw into blocks for punishment bit one hand so badly that two of her fingers were destroyed. She would be exhausted as she came back each evening but sang with the others because God was with us in the furnace. Sang without sound, as that was something they learned from the Poles, who moved their lips but made no sound, yet even that shaping of silence was forbidden.

Stephen interrupted her. He asked why it was important now for her to take him from the pharmacy, to speak this late of what for so long she had not thought he must know. 'I've read in any case what you and Babcia and those other women endured. Why come back to that now?'

They stopped at the white wooden railings of the zigzag that ascended from the footpath near the Sea Scout sheds. They turned and each held the iron rail above the slap of the tide against the sloped blue stones of the wall. The woman stood close enough for her shoulder to brush against his own as she faced out to the stretch of upper harbour and ignored his question. He thought, I might as well not be here, she is talking for herself. Yet later having to admit, no, it was not for her sake that she was telling him, not for some dark satisfaction in hauling at

117

such memories, any more than she spoke to inform him for his own sake. Yet for the moment his impulse was to turn from her and walk back alone, to abandon her with her hands holding the metal bar where the narrowing creek mouth surged beneath them. But he knew too that she compelled him, that his resistance to hearing her out was by comparison a feeble thing.

Miss McGovern picked up on his exasperation. Her hand touched briefly at his own. He moved his grasp further along the rail, away from her. She was speaking now, quietly still, but randomly, Stephen thought. About a Czech circus girl, a gypsy, who had defied as none other dared, who vaulted the wire and escaped and days later was brought back, thrashed and savaged by the dogs, no longer like a woman so much as a flayed carcass as she was flung in front of the assembled camp, the commandant shouting in his implacable rage at her presuming freedom was hers to choose. The prisoners had been herded together so quickly they stood with their different groupings mixed together, a jumble of triangles as one seldom saw. But rigid, not daring to move, each safe so long as the mutilated and barely moving woman absorbed the fury of a system provoked beyond endurance. For the first time Ruth stood next to Irma. After the Czech girl's pulped and disfigured limbs had been dragged away, the entire camp was obliged to stand for several hours. Snow had begun to drift then fall thickly on them. Their shoulders, their heads, whitened. If a woman fell from exhaustion she was left to lie, and if she died, discipline had been maintained.

Then Miss McGovern said, 'There is point to all this. No one will tell you if I don't. Even Ruth I think has forgotten the worst of it, her thoughts cleared of that at least.' And without reprimand, without changing her tone, she said, 'What you and Eva want to lie about to yourselves, that our darling's mind is gone far more than you admit. I thank God for that.' And then back to the day that remains so vivid for herself, and from now must become as much so for the man she tells. Telling him that when Irma fell the spread of snow around her brightened with the flow of blood not from the fall but the first sign of what she soon enough would die of, the haemorrhaging of her lungs. And again, the extraordinary fact so Stephen thinks of their standing in the utter ordinariness of a suburban street, above the grey-green harbour with its flecking from the slowly moving clouds, and the even tone in which she tells him of the day she wants him to know, speaking without distress or grief, for nothing now might change it by a jot. This was and is.

'It was done so quickly,' she said. Ruth knelt to help her sister. She had taken a rag from her smock and held it against the pulsing mouth. The blood showed on her hand. A female guard, who had been a housewife and a hairdresser in the local village until twelve months before, shouted and ran at her and kicked her hand from where it held the other woman's head. As Ruth lurched forward, spreading her hand to support her, the guard brought down the heel of her boot with such force, three, four times, the fingers buckling, the sound as if of snapped twigs, Miss McGovern said, like twigs, and silence oddly around all else apart from the shout, the stomping foot, the raking of the guard's breath at the exertion. Ruth sitting back, holding her hand, Irma now on her knees, stretching towards the guard who swung her crop across her, across Ruth's neck as well, and yelling now, the guard calling that she was being attacked, and one of the male guards who stood further back from the assembled women, their rifles at their shoulders, rushed to help, unslinging his rifle as he ran. By the time he arrived where the three women, the two prisoners and the guard with her long hair flaring back, her arm again upraised, grouped as if posing in some strange tableau, the guard's rifle had been turned so the butt was brought down with the precision of a man trained for such provocations, against Ruth's upper arm. Time and again. Her blood spreading almost black against the upper half of her blue smock.

Miss McGovern said, 'I stood with the others and watched her beaten and taken away to what was called the Block and some of us were told to take my sister back to our barracks. And Ruth I saw a week later, but her hand was wrecked and I became her friend. Irma was sent back to the ice. With her illness it could not be long. And somehow that we could not understand Ruth from time to time passed chunks of bread to one of our people that was brought back to Irma, who died that spring. After the linden trees at one end of the camp had broken into leaf, because she said that to me, that the cold would soon enough be past and we could walk where we would touch them as we had the year before.'

They were back on the rise towards the Terminus shops. What usefully might Stephen say to her? He understood the depth of what bound her to Babcia, that at least had come of it. Yet why wait so long, so many years, to let him know even that? And now another last weird telling, as if it was of some significance that he should know this too. 'There is an opera with a madwoman in it and there was a real madwoman among the politicals who sang that other woman's song over and over. Finally no one could bear it and at last she was shot, but when Ruth was put in the Block she was in the cell with that woman to punish her. But Ruth was the only one who calmed her. Who could get her to stop singing. I should have told you that.' And before they reached the corner back at Garnet Road, she had time to tell him that after her hand was broken Ruth could not return to the typing she had done in the transport block, work she so excelled at that the senior officer, a man more decent than the rest, now arranged for her to transfer to the clothing store where jobs were greatly prized. That she spoke German even better than Polish was in her favour. There was a place for her to go to because a woman who had been the lover of a guard who then reported her for theft had hanged herself. 'Things like that were not uncommon.'

The job she now went to was a simple one. When new prisoners arrived they handed across their clothes and were given those they would wear in the camp. Everything was orderly. What the women wore and what they might have carried with them was entered in a ledger and would be returned when they were freed. Even lockets, trinkets, religious things were entered too. The camps set great store on doing things the correct way. But of course there were things women did not admit to having, valuable things that they hid in the linings of jackets and sewed into hems—rolls of money, pieces of jewellery. Diamonds, even those. It was these that were searched for and it was Ruth's job to call out what was found, to tell the woman who sat at a table and typed the list, and the valuables were placed in cartons where a guard kept watch and sealed them when each was full. But some of the depraved prisoners and the *kapovas* too at times lied about the necklaces and earrings and bracelets found in the clothing, ones that were stolen and could buy favours from the guards. Such things could lead to privileges but also to savage beatings. Even worse. In the camp no certainty was fixed from day to day, even punishments. There was nothing, Miss McGovern said, that was spared in the evil kingdom.

Then silence, for the last few minutes of their walking back towards the Terminus, to the neat and almost toy-like row of shops, the bright advertising writing across the windows of Mr Cahill's the grocer, Mr Caddy's the butcher, the wooden toys in the shop on the corner. The big woman Stephen longed to be free of waited at the entrance to the shop while he entered, apologised to Mrs Stoddart for his time away, and came back to her with her bag. His assistant had looked at him, taking in his tenseness, his so unlikely curtness as he pointed to the bag behind her and told her, 'Give me that.' And then, 'You needn't stay any longer,' and waited until she had left, before going back to the woman who stood in the doorway, who moved aside but without greeting Mrs Stoddart as she passed.

She said, 'I will need to see you again.'

He knew without her having to spell it out that she had not come to the end of what she needed to say to him, yet he felt again the certainty that he himself was incidental to whatever she might have in mind; that the telling, the end point of it, was more her concern than his. He nodded rather than answered her.

'Next week, then,' she told him. 'I will telephone before I come,' and crossed to the waiting bus on the other side of the road.

From the shop he watched the trolley bus depart, heard

the stir of the overhead wires. He laid his hands on the top of the counter. He resented so much about the fanatical woman's visit, her raking over details he could see no point in imposing on him. Yet the distress at what must have been part of every day for Babcia. He hoped her friend was right at least about that, that so much had faded for the old lady he watched each day as she moved about the house, went about her routines in the kitchen, her sitting for hours with her good hand cradling the other in her lap, her laborious simple needlework, her speaking the handful of words Eva especially shared with her. But why that other woman speaking now of what she might have told him years before, yet had chosen not to? Details he hoped by now beyond the old woman's seemingly inane contentment. Miss McGovern would be right, surely, about that?

His mind leaped back to the woman in the room near Russell Square preparing them, warning them, 'It would be wrong to conceal that there will indeed be problems.' Yet her assuming what they shared as family would assist in difficult times, that surely? But neither Eva nor her husband at that moment realising how little that was to draw on, how in fact it could mean nothing to them, a past which was never theirs and was now imposed on them? It was something that had not occurred to them, not with the clarity so apparent now, how they were accepting the middle-aged woman with her awkward arm, her slab of close-cut grey hair, her languages they would never grasp, because they could not avoid doing so without an unspoken judgement against them. Against their humanity. They had accepted because there had been no choice. All that coming back. Miss McGovern had clawed at ancient regrets.

For one of the few times since he had bought the shop, six months after he and Eva and her aunt and their infant daughter moved into the Westmere house and the pharmacy with his name displayed in the identically styled gold print as had been there on Mr Golson's window, Stephen snibbed the lock early and turned the card informing the public it was Closed. He sat in the room off the dispensary, his elbow on the chequered cloth, his thumb and forefinger pinching at the bridge of his nose. How David would be so confirmed in what he thought! The boy was right. There was no atoning, even if one might reasonably insist there is nothing personally that needs atoning for. A loneliness that for the most part he adroitly kept at bay came down on him. He removed his glasses and rubbed his hands at the sudden feeling of exposure. The phone rang and it was Eva. She said the assistant in the grocer's next door had phoned to say a customer had asked why the chemist's shop was closed, she had prescriptions to be made up. Was something wrong?

Stephen lied to his wife for the first time in his life. He said Mrs Stoddart had been obliged to go home early and there was a sudden panic, he supposed you could call it that, when the Kempthorne Prosser man from pharmaceutical supplies had come in days earlier than expected. There was such confusion coping with him for a while, out the back there with invoices and catalogues, the front door must have blown to and locked. The notice? That must have swung around. And he asked, 'Is everything all right there? At home?'

Eva said, 'As it always is.'

'That's good then,' Stephen said. 'I'll see you before long.'

Next time Miss McGovern wrote first, which surprised him. She informed him she would come the following Tuesday afternoon, if Stephen kindly agreed? He had not seen her handwriting before. She did not sign cards with the little gifts she gave Babcia or send letters during the two times she was away, visiting a relative in Australia. And so the novelty of it now, the neat authoritative script of a woman who once had taught in schools, who on Sundays still stood in front of children, writing names from the Bible on a blackboard, instructing yet making a game of it as well, the way she looped and coloured them, the fruit she twined round the first letter of Eve, the bright ring of light setting the M of Moses. Even the A of Abraham could look like a curved knife.

This time Stephen walked along from the shop to the bus stop to help her descend, although she chose to grasp the brass rail as she lowered herself to stand beside him, and again handed across the scuffed heavy bag. 'Mrs Stoddart will keep an eye on it.'

She grunted rather than spoke in agreeing with him. Yet Miss McGovern assumed the closeness that had been established between them, that they would take up where a week before they left off. Stephen nodded to where clouds gathered heavily above the slate-grey harbour at the end of the sloping street. He said it looked as though the weather might turn at any moment, so they would drive across to Ponsonby. If she didn't mind. There was a tearoom they could go to and not have rain to worry them. A place he had heard Eva speak of.

'I like cakes,' Miss McGovern said, as if that were the purpose of his suggesting it. Stephen thought yet again how it was a challenge to warm to her, to comprehend her distance from anything he truly understood. Even that simple enough remark of hers just now, was it some kind of wryness? Or even teasing him, her knowing the distaste he felt for her, casting herself as glutton as well as stranger? They walked to the green Vauxhall parked in the lane behind the shop. He held the door open for her. She said, 'This smells different from other cars. I suppose it's the chemist stuff you have in it.'

'I suppose it is.'

He was right about the rain. By the time they turned to Jervois Road a wind swept up the streets rising from the harbour, wet dead leaves from the trees stuck like rags against picket fences. He surprised himself, although not it seemed the woman he spoke to, as he used her name for the first time. 'So you've come again to tell me something, Ellen, that you don't want my family to know what it is?'

'Important,' she said, 'that you know and they don't.' For the moment leaving it there, her implying she would tell him more as she decided, it was not for him to ask. Instead, 'This is nice,' she said, meaning the comfort of the car, how she had settled in the mock-leather seat beside him. He wondered what she might have been without the rest, all that? Without her kind of God. Without the camp. The absurdity of even thinking that. For she was speaking again, out of the blue, of her sister, Irma's asking that last night if Ruth would come to her and the danger of doing as she asked, and yet it was done. 'As if Ruth wouldn't have. She was young and tough and angry,' Miss McGovern said, 'you would not believe. Before other things were done as well.' And Stephen thinking, yet again, it is two lives we are always talking about, with everyone. And the impossibility of bringing them together, the frightened yet fearless young woman Miss McGovern recollected, the vacantly smiling, slow-moving aunt with her few dozen words, sitting hours at a time, as she liked to do in these colder months, on the sofa with its slanted stripes from the tilted blinds, her silence, her painful needlework. Then this unfathomable woman beside him laughing at something she did not explain to Stephen, the deep unexpected laughter Eva had told him of, when the two old women sat together in the sitting room. His thinking, as he turned to park in the street behind the block of shops at the Three Lamps, that there is a craziness through all this too, we are infected with it one way or another, all of us. We can no more follow them back there than they can get away to us.

Miss McGovern rubbed a fat pale knuckle against a leaking eye. Then as if linking her own thinking for a moment with his own, she told him, as she eased herself from the creaking leather seat to reach for the door handle, 'We were gifted with a kind of hysteria that helped us through. People hate us saying that, Stephen. Even those who share the truth. I say, God looks after us in different ways. It was not a place not to be mad, one way or another. How Daniel too must have thought that, as the beasts circled him.' They walked through to the main road, and waited until the traffic paused. He stepped a pace ahead of her to the tearooms near the disused cinema with its scrap of Californian façade.

It was a strangely old-fashioned place they entered, whose ageing owner had not kept up with the dark painted walls, the ceiling draped with nets and large glass floats of the smarter coffee shop a few doors further along. Towards the back of the long narrow room they took a table with pink brocaded chairs, a standard lamp throwing a cone of light from a tasselled shade. Stephen disliked everything it aspired to, a kind of crimped gentility, but his guest admired it. She sat with her fingers laced on the edge of the linen cloth. She nodded as she took in the room. He felt her steeping in the novelty of it. 'It's nice,' she told him. He was not an imaginative man. He disliked profanity, not for its offensiveness so much as not seeing the point of it, but as they waited he pressed his palms together, thinking, Christ, will she never get on with it! As he also thought, Whatever it is she has in mind, whatever it is she is convinced I must be told, I would prefer not to hear. And then an extraordinary discomfort he did not expect and so resented, as she untied the knot holding her scarf, and removed it from her head. It was the casual slight flick of her head, the loosening of her hair as he had never seen it revealed in the years he had known her, its glint in the sudden light across it. Almost an indecency that shocked him. It was the action of a young girl, a grotesqueness from this ageing mounded figure close enough beside him to again pick up that tang of mint that so accompanied her. He wanted her to remain as she had always been, a monument, a relic. And yet now that casual feminine flinging of her hair: this too is what I am.

A young woman then stood beside the table, an almost comic interruption. She wore jeans and a black-knit short-sleeved top, her casualness too at odds with the decor of where she worked. Without speaking she held a card towards Stephen, who told her, 'Whatever you have. What you have for afternoon tea.' The waitress said several things that this strange distant man—because that is what he is, the girl decided, even if he does not mean to be rude—seemed not to attend to. 'Yes,' he said, 'yes. What you have is fine.'

Miss McGovern had folded her scarf and placed it on a corner of the table, her fist lying across it. The light from the lamp softened her appearance, yet netted her too with a hatching of lines from the tasselled fringe. Get on with it. Then 'Listen,' she ordered him. And again, so it seemed to Stephen, her speaking at random, whatever it was she thought so important for him to know as yet elusive, distant. Her speaking first of the fights, the hatreds, that flared between the different groups of women, the betrayals and jealousies and indecent loves. Before coming back to Ruth, and to her own sister's death, always back to that. The prick of his own obtuseness also troubling him, his indifference, even that, to what he had thought of as garrulous and distant women caught up in their memories, their sentimental swathes of silence, but never this—the youthful and resurrected women younger than his own daughter now was, vital and determined to survive, elected 'to defy in their souls', in one of her redeeming phrases. 'So many of those too besides our own.'

She broke off as the returning girl placed patterned china cups in front of them, a matching teapot, and a few minutes later brought plates of neatly cornered sandwiches, scones which they were assured were fresh that moment, they couldn't have come at a better time. Miss McGovern waited, silent, as if accepting there was ceremony in how such things were done as she took the handle of the teapot and gently moved it from side to side. A pause again as she reached and took a scone from the stand and rearranged the dishes of cream and jam so they lay exactly between herself and the man who waited for her to speak. And then the first scone eaten and a second prepared, before her repeating, 'Listen.'

She talked of her transferral from her working in the camp laundry to the same unit, the same division. She said what the exact word was for it in English she couldn't say, but where the clothes taken from the new arrivals were gathered and placed on racks, where Ruth called out and set in place the things she took from them, and another woman typed up so order and detail in all things was maintained. Her own new job, she explained, after her sister died, was working in a nearby building with those who were on what she called 'the lists'. Towards the end, she said, when more women came each day, after the killing of the *Reichsprotektor* in Prague and the reparations for that, after the barracks were not sufficient and thousands were crammed in a great tent with only canvas between the dying and the weather. More and more women were taken away as well, not the ones railed east to other camps but the chosen who must be attended to at once. 'We did not have our own facilities. We were not one of those places. So they had to be taken to other places. When the transports began.' Those on the special lists, Miss McGovern said, her job to check as the women were brought out to board the trucks. These were women who did not get back the clothes they wore when they arrived, but were handed dresses, jackets, at random, no one bothering if the sizes were incorrect. The clothes they wore out in the morning would be returned sometimes later that evening, brought back from the range where the women were taken to be shot. Before they boarded the trucks and the metal gates clanged up, before the waving of some and the placid dullness of others, they were given the

130

drugged coffee the female guards told them was to warm them for their journey. To settle them. At times someone managed to conceal a stub of pencil, a scrap of paper, and notes came back and were taken from the pocket of a returned jacket before it was given to another woman on another day. The notes were brief and mostly said goodbye to a particular friend. A few confirmed that yes, what they feared would almost immediately take place.

Most days there was not the chance for her and Ruth to speak. But as the Russians crossed the great plains towards them the camp became more frantic. More of the Reich floated on drugs and drunkenness, yet even then as discipline slipped it became more savage. Typhoid raged in the tents. Some of the guards began to disappear. One was returned and punished as if she had been a prisoner on the *Appellplatz*. An officer killed himself in public, and more shameful than his death, the fact that it was done in front of Slavs. And so the details came, until Stephen said, 'I know that this must always come back to you. That there can be no end to it for you and Babcia. But to talk about it now. To insist on telling me. Is there point to that?'

Miss McGovern held his gaze until he lowered it. There must be an end, surely, to what she feels she has to say to him? And the thought too, as if any detail dredged and lingered over and handed on to him could matter a damn to the irretrievable wasting of the past, the iron fact of that coming in on him as they sat together now, as she instructed him in this absurd bloody room at the world's smug and inevitably forgetting end? He felt the pulse in his temple thicken and beat. He had hit the wall, wasn't that the phrase young Caddy in the butcher's shop had used, telling Stephen about one of the long races he ran

131

at weekends? It meant you had to stop because there is nowhere to go on to.

'Can we go now?' he broke in on her.

'No,' Miss McGovern said. 'I would like more tea.'

'The pharmacy,' he began to say, but left his sentence incomplete. He signalled to the waitress and when she came to the table he tapped the pot in front of him. 'Tea. Would you bring her more of that?'

He glanced across to the large man who sat at a table closer to the entrance, the length of dull glass confirming the drabness of the day outside, the continuing fall of rain. The woman with him examined a small diary for some time before placing it back in her purse. There was a surliness that seemed to emanate from them, Stephen thought, yet the absurdity of that too, imagining we can hazard anything about another mind. For the moment everything seemed touched with the insistence of the old woman beside him. The girl came back with the fresh tea, the charm-bracelet on her wrist tinkling close to Stephen's ear as she leaned forward to reposition things on the table. Again, his guest turning the teapot, pouring the tea, before commanding as she had before, *Now listen*. 'The family,' she said.

'Yes? The family?'

'She muddles it a little when she talks of it. Ruth. About Berlin. About before in Breslau. You must know that.'

'You forget you're the only one she talks with. Talks with properly. What we say with her is like children with a handful of words. Beyond that there is not even confusion. What can we talk of?'

'Not Eva's mother, you think?'

'Not even Eva's mother. Babcia at times may stroke my wife's cheek and touch her arm and say her sister's

132

name. Or their mother's. But what else is there to tell? A few threads. What they told us in London, which was little enough. Names of relatives. Where they died. The dates they sometimes knew but mostly didn't. At least there is comfort and safety for her as we live together. A bond between her and Eva which shouldn't surprise us. A closeness they don't need words for, is what I mean.' And the appalling emptiness of it all, that is what Stephen wanted to say. But instead, quietly, not wishing it to sound an accusation, 'That is why we wish you told us more. Those things you talk of and laugh about and must have in mind when you sit, even as you sit together in silence. That is what I wish you had said to us before. But there is always such a gap. With you and us. You know that too.'

Then the extraordinary truth that had never occurred to him, as Miss McGovern startled him with her insistent, 'Nothing.'

'Nothing?'

'That is what she remembers. Next to. Fragments. Next to nothing.'

'For how long?'

'A year at least,' she said. 'Nothing of importance. Yet of course it might come back. From time to time. I've read of that. A shock, say, raising it. Something might come back to her.'

Her words coming down on him as if a physical weight. He felt himself lean forward in the way men do when suddenly in pain. 'Perhaps as well,' he said, but not believing it. All that, and then its loss. Not the suffering, no, not that, but the courage that brought her through it, the simple yet implacable integrity of what she was. The cruelty of losing that.

It is then, surprisingly, Miss McGovern who looks at her watch. 'What you must know,' she said. At last.

'Yes?'

'This man from the other camp, close to our own. We were the women's camp, the one everyone knows of. There are people writing books about it. But there was a smaller place where only men were held, political people and the rest, the mix as there was with us. The ones who did the things we couldn't do, the builders, the electricians, ones who drove the trucks, took away the dead. Even bread. The bread, the scraps of it we lined up for, that was made there in the men's camp and driven across. I would see the bread truck on the road between the barracks and I would think this is like some dreadful pretence of what life was like in other places. Everyone I think had one thing like that at least, to remind them of somewhere else. Even for a few seconds.'

'This man?' Stephen prompted her.

'He was a political because his triangle told you that. He was taller than average height and fair and some of the women liked to look at him and at times he would come into where we worked because one of the female guards was a friend of his. The sister of the one who had been a hairdresser before we came. She was a stupid woman and she would sometimes give him things she had taken from the boxes where Ruth put what was found hidden in clothes when new intakes were brought in. Nothing was really secret in the camps. And once I saw him speak to Ruth as he passed and when she said nothing about it to me later I knew she must be afraid. But at other times the guard pretended not to notice as he passed the table Ruth stood at and would bend as though to ease his shoe or pick

134

up something he had dropped and later she would share with me the chunk of bread he had placed on the floor beneath the table. Share it with me, or if one of the women in her barracks was ill, conceal it and take it back for her. But even to me she said only that she had known the man in his own town and he had lived with a Jew, which he must have kept secret, to be here as one of the favoured prisoners. She said his giving her food was to keep her from recognising him, but she was in fear of him as well. We all feared those the guards took as lovers.'

'But why this now?' Stephen asked. 'Telling me about this now?'

'She must never be reminded of it.'

'She remembers next to nothing. You've told me that.'

'Either of them. Hear talk of that.'

'You mean Eva too?'

'We must look after them.'

Again, that surge of asperity as Stephen tells her, 'As if we never have.'

He moved his chair to distance himself from this soft watching woman. She put her hand on his sleeve to keep him still. She said, 'There is a man, an American, who is writing a book about them. About the male camp. Why you need to know.'

'A man who was there?'

'A relative of one. Some of them become obsessed. A little like your David but much more so. He is one of those. He goes to different countries, wanting to speak with people. Tracking down. He has written to me. He knows of the man who drove the bread truck. Whose lover was a guard and who stole things, and the American says there was a woman, a Jew, he had a child with before

135

the war. Other things he has found out. He knows where people are, the people he works for spend such money to find out. He is writing a history of the men's camp and every story he says is important to him.'

The point of it all at last, Stephen comprehends.

'I lied to him when I wrote back. I said I have no idea who the woman is that he gave food to, that I didn't know her name even.'

'He will want to talk with her?'

'With her. With Eva.'

She took up her scarf and tied it again about her head, the distanced incomprehensible believer he had always known, and yet now returned as something else, the breadth of a life spreading behind her, beyond her, that he honoured her for, and yet now feared as well.

'I'll make sure,' he said. 'I'll make sure that he doesn't.'

'I know that,' Miss McGovern said. She was the first to stand from the table. There was nothing more to say, once she had said, 'I would kill him first.' The same fervour in her eyes as she told him that, the same iron conviction, as if he had challenged her certainty in Christ, and what she would do to assert it. To give proof.

Some months later, after a summer's lucent evening when she sat as she so liked to do under the canvas awning at the side of the house, sipping at the fruit mix whose recipe she had kept with her from childhood and passed on to the house that became for so long her home in Westmere, Babcia died in her sleep.

David was more distressed than his parents. He flew up from his work in Wellington and was home by early afternoon. He had told his father when he phoned,

'You cannot stop this at least. The way it must be done.'
His friend Rabbi Liebermann arranged the burial, the
mourners who stood at the grave with the black-suited
family, the few neighbours who were not of the faith
standing respectfully back, Mr Cahill from the shop next
to the pharmacy awkwardly holding his hat in front of
him, moving its brim in circles, and Doctor Satyanand
whom Stephen had called the morning before, after he
entered the kitchen and for the first time had not seen his
wife's aunt already there at the bench, smiling, waiting for
him, the kettle boiled, the eggs poaching in the pan.

Rabbi Liebermann had said the prayers of the Kaddish,
some of which he repeated in English for the family, the
words whose timelessness and resonance neither Eva the
dead woman's niece, nor the husband devoted to her,
for all their affection comprehended as more than ritual
respect. David had spoken briefly and with deep feeling,
and quoted King Solomon, 'Greater is the day of death
than the day of birth,' and took a shovel to begin the
filling in of the grave. His parents left the opened scar of
earth hand in hand, Stephen on the point of saying, then
checking himself for what may have sounded trite, how
the woman they had buried was a life they had seen like a
shape through frosted glass, its reality quite other to what
they saw. 'Miss McGovern,' Eva said as they reached the
car, 'I suppose was not allowed? By her church?'

When the attending vehicles had turned and driven back,
a bulky woman stepped from the side of the crematorium
at some distance from the Jewish graves. She had made
the journey from the city in the Henderson bus, and now,
once the mourners were gone, she stood at the deep trench
the two workmen were already filling. The men stood and

walked back a little way until the woman in her dark scarf had looked down for several minutes. She placed a stone she took from her pocket at the foot of the grave. The earth already concealed the metal plaque that might have told her, 'Ruth Hannah Friedmann, 1903-1976.'

'A long wait till the next bus, lady,' the older workman said, but the woman passed him without speaking. She walked towards the cemetery gates and the steep hill where she would wait for the returning bus. The men went back to their work. 'Surly bitch.'

The other told him, 'Saw a woman once over that other section take her top off and start cutting herself with this broken shell thing.'

The older man looked at his watch. 'Two. Reckon that should do it. Two-twenty? Give or take?''

And the American did come, but not for some time. He had written to Eva a letter in which he said so many things had held up the book he wanted to write, but at last he had come to Australia, where several folk lived who could help with his research, and now would come on across to Mrs Ross's country. He had heard so many fine things about it, he looked forward to his visit quite apart from his project. Need he say, he would be in her debt should she agree to see him? And his sincerest sympathy might he offer for the loss of her aunt some way back now, a woman he would greatly have liked to interview, but time was the constant enemy if history was your passion, as it was his. A Jehovah's Witness woman who had been her aunt's great friend and now lived in the hills out of Sydney, she had written to him saying there was no point in his getting in touch with Mrs Ross, there was nothing to remember, nothing to tell, that language had always been a barrier, and then her relative's fading mind through several years. Yet even so, he repeated, he would be much in Mrs Ross's debt. 'Anything one retrieves about our people, we owe them that.'

Eva had written back. She did not tell Stephen, who for all his kindness could be overprotective. Stifling. As if certain decisions were out of her hands. Her tendency to worry, he would say. To get a little down to things. To veer in her moods. The things she knew he talked about with Doctor Satyanand. There's this and that, his friend would say, that might be worth thinking of? Some promising new medication? Eva always being able to joke about it when it was raised, so both men smiled back as she told them, 'I don't think so, Stephen,' or, 'No, I think we can put that on the back burner. Take a raincheck. Give it time to simmer down.' Phrases that amused him. Or these last couple of years in any case, that unexpected sense of lightening up. Just Babcia not being here, that of course she could never say, but the load that had lifted. The sense of freedom she was briefly reluctant to admit to herself, the elation of that. And yet a curious sense of being let down as well, all this freedom I had never expected to know, and yet what is there for me to do with it?

The American arrived in a rental car he hired at the airport. He had booked in at a hotel and then came straight to see her. 'I know, I know,' he said, raising both hands towards her, confessing to his obsession as she opened the front door to him. 'That's what we become,' meaning a little off-beam, a touch too hyped, as his forefinger twirled beside his temple. She liked him because he was so open, so boyish, though she guessed he could not be that much younger than herself. He showed her photos of his mother, his family, the twin boys wearing *kippahs*. Josh looked at the photo himself before returning it to his wallet. 'A big day, that,' he said. He explained his uncle had been in several camps, but mostly in the one he now researched. It was forgotten by most people that men had been there too. Or right next to it. His uncle had written an account and talked about this other man he had thought a friend and who had done some kind of deal then disappeared just before the Russians arrived and the liberation. 'I just want to know what kind of man he was.' And then he said, 'It is a matter of regret to me your aunt has passed away.'

'To be honest, we never talked of it. So much was lost. I mean from back then. And we knew so little. My son is the one in the family most interested, but most of that is from what he read. Or picked up from her friend, not from her. We are not close to it all in the way you are. I think I told you that when I wrote. My own background. My being English.'

She had no doubt the man talking to her would have disapproved, and was too kind to say so. Instead, he said, 'That Scottish woman who refused to see me. How odd all that is.'

Eva smiled. 'If you believe as someone like that believes there is nothing strange about anything.'

Josh opened his folder to take copied pages from a magazine. A student photo of some kind, he said, before any of the young people had any notion of what would happen in a few years' time. He pointed to the man in the second row. His hand on the shoulder of a girl in a white dress sitting in front of him. How carefree they looked, Eva thought, these young people, as Josh told her,

'Your aunt's sister, the clever one, which makes me think she could have told me something about him. All these young people. Socialists. Idealists. Jews among them as if that didn't matter. Leading them, even. These are the committee. They wrote in German but some published in Polish as well, to spread what they believed.'

'What was it called?' Eva asked him. 'Their magazine?'

'*Die Epoche.* Others too, of course. There was so much going on.'

The girl in white sat with her hands clasped on her knees, looking directly ahead. The man behind was turning slightly to the man next to him, his hair lifting in what must have been the moment's breeze. He looked nice, Eva thought. He looked nice. There were other photos, one of him in prison clothes, one standing in what looked like a fairground, a group of young men fooling about, arms round each other's shoulders, one holding the kind of toy bear to be won in a shooting gallery. 'Different names,' Josh said, 'different names at different times, but the one at the camp no doubt the right one. Fromm. Albrecht Fromm. But who knows now of course what was true and what was not? Journalists often used names all over the place.'

'But that photograph is early?'

'No names on the photograph you'll notice. It is meant to tell you not who is who but what fine young people communists could be! You could swap it with pictures in a right-wing student magazine and who would know? Cover the armbands and you'd never tell. Not now. All of them just one message really. This is us!'

'My aunt's family. Her family were hardly communists.'

'But her sister in Berlin. The one not traced anywhere.'

'They would hardly have known back home about her beliefs. One of the few things we do know is my grandfather was a businessman. Well off, we do know that.'

The American said again, 'I so regret I was not here earlier.'

Eva watched his fingers carefully return the papers to their clear folders, and snap them closed in his briefcase. She wished he would go. Her feeling towards him had swung within minutes. She disliked his so obvious disappointment, his loss of interest in her now his obsessive hunt had taken him no further. I can do nothing for him, and so I do not exist. He placed a card for her on the hallway table. 'Should anything occur.'

'Occur?'

'Come back to you. Something she may have said that escapes you now.' And condescendingly, oh there was even that, Eva thought, as he turned at the front door she held open for him, and he repeated to her, 'There is no such thing as an unimportant fact.'

She held the door until she heard the car reach the top of the slope and turn at the corner. She tore the card and placed its pieces in the kitchen bin, then went back to sit in the cool dim room. The goldfish Babcia so enjoyed watching glinting in their green corner behind the magnifying curve of the aquarium. The house creaked in the silence it now seemed steeped in. 'Stretching its bones,' her English mother used to say in the big wooden house where she grew up, when the small girl would ask, What's that, is that someone here? The kind quiet woman, who so often seemed unsure of what to say, but loved her, and told her how proud they were to have her. Strange, her now suddenly being so intensely there, and the thought which had not come back to Eva for an age, the sitting room with its horse brasses on leather strips, the shining copper pots with ferns so delicate you touched them and you scarcely felt their brushing. Mummy telling her how her other mother loved her just as much, but had died in another country when she was so little of course she'd not remember, and so it was her English father now who taught her to read, and this was Home. Good people in that other country had made sure she would get here safely where they expected her, she and Daddy waited for her.

Eva took a carton from the hallway cupboard. She had been meaning to do this for months. She placed it on Babcia's bed and cleared the card table of the little gifts and trinkets Miss McGovern over the years had given her. When one layer was complete, she laid sheets of tissue across them and began on the next, and so they were packed away, the miniature blue-and-white Dutch windmills, a brass Eiffel Tower, a small celluloid doll in Māori costume, the random chess pieces gifted one by one, a Viking knight, a pink soapstone queen, a bishop whose pointy hat was chipped before its mould was taken, the gifts the purer perhaps for her aunt's having no notion of the game they came from, the mystery of its pieces. A glass paperweight that flickered snow, a beetle caught in pale entombing gum, a little statuette of a flying horse. Once the table was cleared Eva swept her hand across the green velvet top, folded its narrow legs to slide behind the headboard of the bed. She then took the photographs from the bedside table and added them to the cardboard box, the gallery of the children in their school clothes, on the beach at Karekare even before Stephen had bought the bach out on the coast he loved and Eva, even on brilliant days, found oppressive, but for his sake, and the children's who loved it too, had never said so. The curious picture with the tear across it, beside the enlargement Stephen had the Kodak man make of it. A photo of Babcia and her friend on the deck of the *Rangitata*, the day they sailed into Auckland, to what each of them would refer to always as 'here' but not as 'home'. Two drab woman against a bulkhead. Eva had taken it with the box Brownie Stephen bought her the day before they sailed.

She carried the carton and returned it to the low shelf above the gumboots, the tennis shoes, the folded lolly-striped summer umbrella, the raincoats and what only she referred to as a mackintosh. On the floor there was a box of Lisa's textbooks from Dunedin that she had promised she would one day take with her. There was a cricket bat David used for one season and so hated the game he had never touched again but insisted that too be kept. There was a blue clear plastic coat that felt clammy against your skin if you put it on, and was used only if it rained when potatoes needed to be dug from the garden or the marrows lifted. For as long as she remembered she had intended tossing it out. But time for everything, she thought now, walking back to the sitting room. There was only so much you could do to fill in time. A week until Easter. Even until then.

1978

Most nights in London, in her room with its sloping ceiling, its third-floor window facing the brick side of a neighbouring house, above the upper branches of a tree she never learned the name for, Lisa listened to classical music on Radio Three as she worked at her desk. She was aware of the music only when she paused or stood to make herself a cup of instant coffee, or at the end of the evening, after she went to the shared bathroom on the floor beneath her and then lay in bed. At times as she sat working with her books spread in front of her, occasionally making notes in one of the small black-covered notebooks that would fit into the pocket of her smock at the hospital, she glanced up to her reflection in the window. Even in winter, she preferred seeing the reflection of her room ghosting behind her, rather than drawing the curtains patterned with their big sunflowers.

Against the wall a gas heater she fed with shillings and florins purred when the weather turned. Her room up here, beneath the gabled roof, was cosier than those of the two girls who rented below her. Often it was enough to sit with a blanket across her legs, the way the heater went through coins. As she wrote back home, 'If it's too warm I'm likely to nod off and get less done, so it's not as though I'm a stoic.' There was something of an irony in it, wasn't there, she wrote, her specialising in tropical medicine, with ice sometimes blurring the window panes as she woke. At times as she looked up from her reading she saw herself as though she were praying, her elbows on the desk, her hands clasped beneath her chin, the dark glint in her hair reflected back at her from the glass.

It was a guarded but satisfying life, hectic with travelling each day in the Tube, the bustle and excitement of the laboratories and lecture rooms, the quiet spells in the library, or alone at the microscope. She enjoyed what she supposed was the rhythm of it, the easy casual friendships through the days, the haven of the sober house in Drayton Gardens, the effortless and welcome privacy as she managed to keep up with both. She shared a kitchen with two other girls, one a reserved Iranian economist at the LSE, the other a chatty Canadian who worked on the cosmetic counter at John Lewis's, who sometimes passed on to her fellow tenants samples she had been given, until she realised neither showed interest in using them. The Canadian was seldom at home. She went to a sports club several evenings a week and saved each year for Wimbledon, when she took her annual leave. The Iranian girl surprised Lisa on a day that she said had significance for her by giving her a gold-rimmed ceramic vase. Then one day the girl was suddenly not there. It was mid-term, so she could not have finished her course. The landlady advertised and a week later a much older woman moved into the room, a librarian they seldom saw. 'A strange one that,' as the Canadian defined her. Like so much else over here, if you wanted her honest opinion.

Dad was good at writing regularly from home, letters he always signed 'from Eva' as well. He kept her up with what he called 'essential news', which was mostly about the family, the trials of Miss McGovern's visits, before Babcia died, details about elections and natural disasters, and what he picked up about 'life over there on your side'. Gossip she might like to hear from back there too. That Doctor Satyanand's boy had won a scholarship to Stanford. That the Sheridan girl, the one who had given her family such a runaround, Lisa would remember that all right, was now living with an Italian, which her mother took as a sign of settling down.

She tried to make her own letters cheery and interesting, knowing they would be read aloud in the sitting room. Occasionally, there would be a letter written from the shop, when Stephen spoke more frankly of David's moods and marriage and simmerings, and Eva's depression, which seemed a little harder to shake off each time a spell came back to her. The specialist changed her medication rather too often, that was his own opinion, and other than doing well in his job David had little interest apart from young Esther and reading about the Shoah, until Stephen had asked him not to talk of it when visiting home. 'His argument of course is that nothing comes from concealing things, although I tell him, and his mother too, not speaking of something is not at all the same thing as to conceal.' Then making the kind of joke his son would never forgive him for, 'He's angry at times I think because people are so nice to him!'

At least Lisa could write back about her courses, which Stephen liked to hear in detail, and the new medicines some of her colleagues were working on, and a paper she and one of her professors were publishing in the *Lancet*. 'I feel I'm not showing off too much to blow a trumpet about that! In any case, not a lot has been done on the area so we're scarcely scooping the pool.'

She sent him cards to the shop as well. The Wren churches she had taken a liking to, how cold their grandeur could seem, but consoling too in some odd way. 'I remember that phrase Mum used, about "letting the silence take you". She also went to galleries and envied people who were touched by paintings as she was not. But how true it was, and she knew Dad would understand exactly, the deepening satisfaction as she followed the details of a disease and the strategies for its defeat. 'Your mother was amused that you were disappointed when your yellow-fever suspect turned out to be something quite run of the mill.' Frail enough jokes to pass between them. And as her father told her again, the pleasure Eva took in hearing her letters read aloud. The simple details that caught her interest, and she liked repeating, when so much else in her life she seemed indifferent to. 'I liked hearing that.' Her mother was glad it was no more than ten minutes' walk from the station at Gloucester Road to where she lived, the big red house with its tree outside her window. 'I think I remember where that street is. Close to where my English mother had a friend and I was taken there as a child. She gave us seed cake for afternoon tea and I hated it. What people go through in other places, my

148

mother said, we are lucky to have cake at all.'

Once Stephen had folded each of Lisa's letters he placed it with others in a drawer in the sideboard, from which in those first few months Lisa was away, and towards the end of her own life, Babcia would sometimes take them, not to read, but to smooth her good hand across, to turn and raise to get whatever hint might be in their papery smell that she imagined took her for that moment closer to the girl she missed. Whose hair was too frizzy to brush.

The trail, as Lisa jokingly called it, though only for Stephen's ears, 'the trail' of what so bothered her brother and she herself accepted, was there one way or another, so important to other people once they thought they were onto it. As David of course so insisted that it was. But I refuse, Lisa thought, to be defined by what they imagine a Jew to be. Even the nicest of her friends coming at it, kind enough as they were. A shy Scottish boy called Alex, who worked close to her in the lab, who was mostly silent in the wards but cleverer than most of them, offered her an 'opening', she supposed that is what he intended. 'We outsiders,' he said once, after one of the senior consultants had spoken for several minutes to a confident, sporty young student, the only one of any of their year who drove a car, an Austin-Healey he dismissed as a 'rust bucket, never mind what they're cracked up to be'. And once he had left, the consultant becoming awkward, not knowing quite the tone to take to the quiet students also in the room.

'Outsiders?' Lisa repeated. 'You mean our accents?' Knowing that was not what her friend had meant.

'Well. Different,' Alex said.

'As we all are.'

'Some people are loners and some aren't,' Alex persisted.

'Background and stuff. You must know that.'

'Good try!' she laughed with him. She said she wouldn't have a pint after work but a coffee, yes, she was always on for a coffee. 'Outsider' got it right, was close enough as far as it went. But she was liked because she was generous and smart, among the quickest of them to pick up unlikely symptoms when they made their rounds of the wards. And as Alex was the first to admit, she's a bit too canny, that lass, for the likes of Aberdeen.

She knew Alex was hoping to put a label on her, that harmless enough assumption she sometimes found with others too, that if she admitted to the word they waited for, then presto, all mysteries were solved! She was more cautious with Harry Morris, the only one of their intake who spoke as a genuine Londoner, every word announcing, Look, I'm the scholarship boy who worked his way up. He was not, like Alex, drawn to her as a possible girlfriend— she was older than most of them, didn't that deter them? And whose mother, as he joked, would want her boy bringing home an older wife?

Lisa knew he watched her with a different kind of attention. He said to her one afternoon, as they shared a microscope and jotted notes, 'With my eyesight I'm likely to be wrong about the next person comes through that door, but I could have sworn I saw you Finchley way last weekend? You got people there?'

She was not to be drawn so clumsily. It would have been truthful enough, simple enough, to say her father had worked up that way just after the war, she was curious to see what it was like, if the shop was still there. Instead, 'I was looking for Keats's house,' she said. 'To send a card to my father.'

'You were well out then,' Harry said. 'That's right up the Heath end.'

'So I found out.'

'He's a teacher is he, your father?'

'A pharmacist. The way Keats was.'

'He wasn't, was he? The poet?'

'Halfway to being a doctor.'

'News to me,' Harry said.

'My dad hates scenes of London buses and the Royal Family. I thought I'd give him a surprise.'

Harry withdrew the slide they had shared, carefully read the label on another, and placed it beneath the glass. 'Must have been a walk,' he said. 'More Golders Green way, I thought I spotted you.'

'Oh, that.' She smiled as he moved aside for her to take her turn at the eyepiece. 'I don't know London the way you do, Harry. I was out by a few stops.'

'A long way from Keats then,' he said. They kept up the light tone between them. She told him, 'You've put that slide upside down.' Then she laughed, and looked at him directly, and was glad she had cornered him. 'You don't need to be so crafty, Harry,' she informed him. 'So *gunif*. Why not just ask me straight out?' It surprised her, how the word came to her. She would have liked to write about that to Dad, how she had dredged up this word that he used himself, that Sam Abrams so liked to use, and it amused him. She wanted to tell him. But Dad would have had to read it out, and Eva would not quite get the joke, and David would know it was one but not know why, and take offence.

Nor did she mention Murray to them, which would take more explaining. After the time with Fergus she

151

feared how easily mistakes are made. Not that Murray was one. But the fear there too of closing doors, of delivering herself to how others then define. When David had first discovered Sartre he was on about such things until she told him, Wait until you've lived, can you, before stressing about that one? Authenticity and the rest of it. Too big a word to be shackled to, she had said to him, the kind of teasing he expected from her. But knew it was real.

Murray, the reserved but entertaining Australian who worked in the School's medical library, who made a fuss of her. 'You mustn't take it as condescending,' he said, 'the fact that I am taller than you and reach the volumes down for you.' But politely distant too, as if biding his time. Then one morning he sat with her, as he sometimes did in the cafeteria, and laid his copy of the *New Statesman* on the table between them. He declared, 'Librarians and doctors, you might have noticed, are equally inept at social skills. I thought this leading story about Soviet policy might make us both feel at ease.'

'Murray, as if your Queensland charm isn't enough.'

He looked about him to the other tables. 'A club of two surrounded by natives,' he said. 'We need each other, Lisa.'

She knew he watched out for her. He tried to time it so there were only the two of them together. Murray stirring two sugars into his black tea, as Lisa held her coffee with both hands.

'Bad manners but comforting,' she said.

'It's that scent of formaldehyde that gets me,' he said. 'Librarians are too conservative to wear anything so arousing.'

'Female librarians?'

'Don't get me started,' he advised her. 'Harpic. Sheep

drench. The men can be impossible too.'

Then some weeks later he mentioned Paris in the mid-term break.

'Paris? It's a sweet life for some.'

'We could make it Berlin. Blackpool. You're the one to say.'

He expected her to say no, to keep up their easy banter. It was fun to see how an acceptance seemed to disconcert him. 'You're not accepting, are you?' His hand ruffling the side of his head.

They were four days as none other had been, she knew that for both of them. Their predictable enough strolling about the city neither had visited before, the things all tourists must do, the wine late at night with the swathes of light from the *bateaux mouches* shining out across the river, the trees and cafés on the quays catching the passing flare, the shadows again deepening as they passed.

'I've seen all this before,' Murray said. 'I've known this movie since I was fifteen.'

And the hours they spent in bed. They were hungry for the chance they had, they knew there would not be another time like this. 'But realists as we are,' Lisa said, insisting they get out early, back to their game of seeing what they could of the city. Murray telling her, 'But we can be tourists for the rest of our lives. All I want to be now is an antipodean sensualist. Camus would have understood me. He was a light and sand person the way we are.'

Lisa said, 'Isn't that a drink?' And an hour later he kissed her again, drawing her towards him on the bench where they sat in the garden behind Notre-Dame. She said, 'The whole world kisses here.'

'It'll do me,' Murray said. 'Bugger the rest of them.'

Then Lisa surprising him, and herself as well, by the quietness of how she spoke as much as the words that came to her. 'The biggest gift of all, Murray, saying "love" without *forever* coming into it.' Then that night, back in the hotel window that looked down on where they had eaten at a bistro called Le Buci, they held hands for a long time without needing to speak, and were sentimental, which they knew was the thing to be, that was part of what made it perfect. Then her standing behind him, her hands around his waist, feeling for the buckle of his belt, her head against the warmth of his back. Those at the tables on the corner beneath might almost have seen them standing naked had they looked up to the half-closed shutters. Her breasts pressed against his warmth, her tongue across his vertebrae. 'Christ, Lisa, I don't know if I can take much of that! How many bones are we supposed to have?'

'Takes a long time to count,' she said, 'even if one's trained.' And her knowing, as Murray did too, that their eroticism had become something lovely, something rare, the better for not being solemn. They then lay and talked half the night, so it seemed.

'How my sister in Toowomba, the one who doesn't believe in God so much, I think, as in sin with a big S, would envy us, don't you reckon, if she had an inkling of how nice it is?'

'That's what some of us miss out on,' Lisa said. 'Brought up without sin. It's getting things for free.'

She told him how hard her father had worked for them not to be swamped by the past. 'That's the word he used because you've no idea how he loved my mother, I think, in those early days. When he didn't want the past to own her in any way. And nor did she. Crossing the world back

154

to where he came from, he really believed you can get away from the rotten things that happen, that want to define us. He tried to bring us up without being ruled by a word like *transgress*.'

'I like the sound of him.'

'It was a fairy tale,' Lisa said. 'Everyone thinks they've got a better one than the other person, that you can make up your own.'

A plate—or several plates—broke on the pavement of the restaurant beneath them. That long second of silence, and then the sound of talk coming up to them again, even louder, and laughter.

'Hope he's not out of a job,' Murray said.

Lisa said, 'How can so many people want to sit out late when they can be home doing this?' Murray's hand raised to the tangle of her hair, her neck, his lips at her shoulder, drawing her to lie across him.

She locked her arms behind his head. To *make* love. She had never thought of it like this, something we construct, and cannot assume, and does not exist without our knowing that. The freedom to decide that is what it meant. Her fingers playing across his back. Her exulting in the luck of it. But her thinking, even now, her palms pressing down on his chest, why is it so hard to say *anything* and get it right?

The day was dull and scoured as they crossed the Channel, then the rain came in broad veiling sweeps across the countryside before the train reached London. Murray tapped the window at the diminishing colour, the sombre late afternoon light. 'See what I mean about Queensland?' he said. 'Why it ruins you forever?'

'The surfie librarian,' Lisa called him, looking at him against the late sky, now a drab rag.

'My female Schweitzer,' he came back at her. His hand rested quietly on her leg. Two older people opposite dozed against the padded headrest. An irritable-looking young man in the corner near the sliding door turned the pages of a magazine, slapping at each one as he decided he had read enough. They were again in the suburbs, the long uniform rows of houses ticking past, the streetlights hazed with rain. Then the moment when people stand to reach things down from the racks, and the rhythm on the rails slackens. When something ends and something else is about to begin. They were quiet as they walked the long platform, and held each other before Murray left the station to take a number 10. Lisa descended to the Tube.

It was dark once she left the station and passed the brick wall out into the night. Already, the time away refining down to the few images she knew would stay with her, so matter of fact, so special. Why is one memory so favoured, rather than another? A boy in a small restaurant, more a family room than the grander ones near their hotel, a young boy showing them a photograph of his brother holding a black goat between his knees. Her looking only yesterday morning, and yet already so much further than that, at a grey stone figure in the famous church, a woman with a child on her arm, the elegant curve of her body making Lisa think, absurd as it was, of the way tornadoes she had seen in news reports kink as they moved so gracefully towards one. She supposed the statue must have particular significance, the way people stopped at it, and some knelt in front of it. Or on the wooden bridge walking back the night before, and the buildings to either side rising against a sky that had the glow of distant fires. And now as she walked past the tall English houses into her own street, into the stillness of the shrubs and trees that spread their aura of calm, she knew that however fine the time with Murray had been, this sudden swelling sense of privacy, of total return to herself, was the central fact of her life. A thought that might have saddened her, and yet did not. Not what she had chosen, but what she was. She fitted her key to the front door's Yale lock. There is a limit, she told herself, to how useful introspection might be. You can love someone and yet think this as well.

The other women on the middle floor were not yet back from their break. Nor was there the light she expected to see from beneath the door to Mrs Beardsley's sitting room. The big house for the time being was her own. Now that she was back she knew how tired she was. Tired and contented. How her brother would have loathed the sloppiness, as he would call it, of how loosely you lot think, you scientists! Contented! It sounded like children settling down after a nice party. She supposed it was something like that in any case, home from a nice indulgent party with Murray. The nicest man she had known.

A light clicked on automatically as she took the last flight of stairs. She set her small suitcase down on the carpet outside her door, found the other key on her keyring, turned the porcelain knob with its flowery flecks. How so simple a thing as a doorknob could tell you so absolutely you are back in another country.

Someone had been in her room. Her chair, which always she set square against her desk, was at an angle. The two books at its centre had been moved aside. A piece of paper lay beside them, its edge held firm by the weight of *Clinical Tropical Diseases*. The note was signed by Mrs Beardsley. Lisa had not known until she read it that her landlady's first name was Iris. The note told her there had been a phone call from home. On Sunday, at eight in the morning. Her father would like her to ring back when she came in. Mrs Beardsley said she would not return from her sister's in Kingston until Wednesday, but Lisa must use the telephone in her sitting room, not the coin phone in the hallway. She had left the door unlocked.

Lisa removed her coat and the beige jacket she had bought only the week before. She thought, it can only be bad, whatever Dad has phoned about cannot be something I want to hear. She had called home on her mother's birthday two months ago, but that was the only time in the past year. We are hardly a family, as she told Murray less than a day before, to let emotion off its leash, feeling she had surely to tell him something after his own so warmly talking of his sisters, his father on his cane farm that was a shit of a life, at least to a librarian it was, and the family together, Jesus, it was like a rugby scrum, the amount of hugging and embracing it went in for. You had to go back to his grandparents before you'd hear a word of Italian, but it came through all right. Even his father.

'We don't like touching much,' Lisa had said. 'Our lot.'

She checked her watch, allowed for the twelve hours ahead it would be at home. She asked the exchange to put her through first to the shop, the surest lead she could have of something bad as she heard the ring keep on and on, in the dispensary she could have described in detail, shelf by shelf, drawer by drawer. It was almost as much that she meant by home as the white house with the dark red eaves, the matching front door, in the Crescent. Where he must be now. She imagined the burring—a different sound entirely from the shrill calling in the shop—of the phone at the end of the kitchen bench. After Babcia died, Dad had the ringing tone tamped down for Eva's sake. She said she hated the loudness of it.

And there was Daddy, as she called him at once when he raised the receiver, announcing as he always did, 'Ross speaking.'

'I'm just back, Daddy.' The line so clear they might have been calling from one house in the Crescent to another. 'Just back from Paris.'

He told her Eva had died on Friday, the funeral had been yesterday. 'At Waikumete,' he said. 'An inquest, yes, there'll be all that.'

'Your mother,' he kept calling her, although he had seldom spoken of her by anything but Eva, even to the children. His voice as level as though he spoke to a customer. She guessed what effort it must have taken him. He gave her the details, as far as they knew them. Dick Horgan, she'd remember him, the police sergeant who lived in Warnock Street, coming down to the house early Sunday morning, although of course he and David had sat up all night when they got home and her mother wasn't there. It was a matter of confirming what they knew.

'No,' he said. 'Your mother didn't leave a note.'

And then the long pause Lisa hated, and could do nothing about, because she no more than her father was up to clichés, to comforting when there was no room for comfort to take root. They respected each other too much to come at that. Nor did he say would she like to speak with David, and she did not ask if her brother was there.

She could come back, she said. Would he like that?

159

He insisted she was not to think of it. Then the longer pause when Lisa thought for a moment they had lost the line. Her realising he was crying in that arcing silence between where she stood in the English night and he would have been looking out to early light.

'In the kitchen,' Stephen said. 'I'm standing at the window.' As if it were important that his daughter could imagine that. To know where Dad was this very minute. At the window where between the house next door and the bare section behind that, there was the wedge of sea Eva liked so much to look out on. It would be blue and sparkling at the moment, because he had said to her, without being asked, 'It's a perfect day here, Lisa. The summer goes on and on.'

The story Lisa will hear fragments of at different times, but never all of it together, from her father later on and more from David, and Mrs Patterson who lives next door, and what that other woman told her, the neighbour who phoned the sergeant on his home number. At first she was not surprised to see the tall quiet woman who often walked alone, down the track to the beach when the weather was good, even at times when it was not. But on Friday it was fine. Down the grassy track in the dip behind the houses, Mrs Ross walking slowly enough at first the woman thought she must have lost something and was hoping to find it. First along the track and its verges tall with dry grass that was never mown, and on towards the little causeway you had to walk across to get down to the strip of sand, to the small beach below the shallow cliffs, a place so safe mothers could leave a child to potter there and lie back and close their eyes. So the woman in the highest house thought nothing of it until minutes later she again looked out from her window. It was early afternoon. Although schools had broken up for Easter, the beach was empty. There was no one else to see the tall woman in her blue plastic coat and her sandals hold a branch to balance her as she stepped down the last few feet of the track onto the sand. She removed her sandals and set them neatly side by side. 'I saw that,' the woman said. 'The way she took a few steps and then came back to make sure they were straight, one against the other.' She wore only her underclothes beneath the plastic coat, not that such a detail was available until later. She then began the long walk towards the black stretch of low volcanic reef a hundred yards out. The beach was famous for how gently it tilted, even at full tide. This afternoon it was quite some walk even to get to where the water began to lap, and Eva's feet splashed into the glassy shallows. Then another thirty yards perhaps—the woman said she was guessing now, the distance was not important to her, held as she was by what she now realised was taking place. Until the water was at Eva's waist, and the light sides of her unbuttoned coat rose to either side of her, floating beside her. She slipped her arms free from the coat that then drifted from her, you could hardly tell the colour of it from the sea. From the shore she would have seemed a woman in a bikini, willing to walk a long way to bathe. Then supposing—it is Lisa now supposing it, the picture unchanged from that first imagining—that when the water was high enough for her to cast herself forward to swim, Eva continued at the same slow and now impeded pace, until the tide was level with her throat, and her head there for several moments, as though floating on the utterly placid reach of the upper harbour, and then disappeared. The woman who knew

161

Mrs Patterson had rushed to the phone, and the sergeant had to tell her to say whatever it was again more slowly, and he had driven to Ross's Pharmacy, and arrangements were made to look for her.

'For your mother,' her father kept telling her. 'So many people came to help. When they found her on Saturday it was right across near Chelsea, near the Sugar Works.'

No, Lisa wrote to her brother, a few evenings before she left the room that had been home to her for the past three years, no, she had no expectations of any kind, regarding the place she was leaving for. 'So I can neither be pleased with what I find nor be disappointed. I am simply a doctor going to practise what I have some training for, and what goes on outside the surgery does not interest me as much as you might expect. Not even if the book you promise to send me turns up before I leave.'

One of David's heavy, condescending jokes. He wrote how he thought their father was having him on, announcing she was about to become a missionary! He said he would send her *Heart of Darkness* to while away the evenings, supposing the Tilley lamps burned that long, and the tom-toms did not disturb her. She wrote back, matching his weighty humour, 'I may be several hundred miles up-river, or a day's paddling by canoe from the nearest synagogue, but I shall make sure I recite the verses written in my heart.' Even in writing so much more easily to her father, there was really little enough to say. 'A year, Dad, pretending to be a *doctor,* rather than the researcher which of course I am, even in what we think of as a remote part of the globe (which is, I remind myself, right here and now for those who live there, we so easily forget that). And in a religious settlement at that. Which can't be a bad thing to broaden me a bit before I settle back to a life stuck to a microscope, and the rare stroll around a ward. I need to know a little more about people.' She then told Stephen what she thought might amuse him, recalling a student in her years in Dunedin after her time in Athens, the years when she 'straightened out'. There was a girl she knew, a dour netballer from Palmerston, who decided early on to specialise as an anaesthetist to be spared the fag of talking with patients. 'At times I feel a little like her, but without quite her degree of self-knowledge.'

She knew how deeply she would miss the library where she now sat, where she liked to spend evenings when the big handsome room often was almost empty, when the laboratories and the lecture rooms at the School of Tropical Medicine were closed for the day, the cafeteria below the grand marble entrance hall silent apart from the cleaners who quietly moved from floor to floor. In these months after her father's phone call, when she had stood in her landlady's sitting room with its heavy furniture, its aspidistras in their dull brass pots, the broad drooping leaves of one of them tapping at her arm as she spoke and listened, so much had changed. The image she could not dispel and that oppressed her, of her mother quietly borne by the harbour's currents, across the late summer tides she imagined in Auckland brightness, but more often their persistent threading beneath the darkness she looked out on from her bedroom window, the glint some nights of the seemingly still but always nudging sea.

She knew she had 'drawn into herself', that phrase she guessed her friends in the labs down here in Keppel Street, the staff from the wards in the great Victorian jumble across at St Pancras, were likely to be using of her. More and more she opted out from the Friday evening drinks round the corner in Store Street, and found excuses when her Scottish friend suggested some play he'd heard good things about, the sort of thing he knew she would like. Her friends understood and were too kindly to press her. More and more the library was where she preferred to sit alone. Her paper, she would say, her paper on something she worked up on epidemiology, was proving more of a struggle than she'd bargained for. There was truth of a sort in saying so. More accurate would have been to admit the rare contentment she felt in the long, high, elegant room, the gallery of shelves that ran three sides in front of the high handsome windows, the design of the 1920s metal rails and their now slightly embarrassing ornamental swastikas. From up here on the first floor she liked to look out to the massed exuberance of the summer trees, the backs of the tall brick Victorian houses, the slow fading of the evenings, the sky still clear and sharp above the streets when the library closed. She loved those occasional minutes when a gust rose and the trees stirred and thrashed in a sudden hurl of wind, the feeling of such rightness, such excitement. It was while she sat there one evening in August, a time when several of her acquaintances and friends at the School were off tramping in Norway, lolling in Greece, that her friend Professor Goldberg took a chair from the next table and placed it facing hers. He came quickly to the point. He made light of it, ironically using such quote-mark phrases as 'healing the ill' and 'succouring the afflicted' with dull professional ones, 'extending clinical competence', even 'going into the field for a spell'. He knew she intended to stay on at the School, that they would be glad to have her, 'to research as you so seem cut out for, rather than walk the wards'. She had worked with him on two publications; they had co-authored a paper on inoculation variants for a new Swedish journal, *Sub-Saharan Medicine*. She knew his respect for her, as she now guessed that although it might seem by chance, he had planned coming into the library when she was alone. 'You'll forgive my interfering, if it seems that.'

'It is never that, Leonard.'

The suggestion then, it was already there to be taken up. The professor had a friend, an old colleague, a serious Christian as it happened, which he mentioned only for its relevance to what he proposed. His friend would arrange it like a shot. A year at a hospital in Tanzania, say. That was a possibility. His friend was on more boards and committees than you had fingers to count on. They were always on the look-out for young people to spend time at hospitals, stations, missions, whatever you wanted to call them. There were choices enough. He said, 'Amazing how the human body surprises when it's not just under a microscope.' As if she had not already spent time in the tropical diseases wards, she reminded him.

'I'm overstating, of course.' His watching her, more concerned for her than actually found words. She might like to think about it? When he was her age a spell in Sierra Leone made all the difference. To him personally, he meant. Insect-transmitted encephalitis was his thing at the time. There was no marked decline in various problems once he left, he wasn't claiming that, but it gave him perspective. Served for a lifetime. The chance to see statistics as people. Hear case studies speak back. He apologised for going on. He stood as suddenly as he had sat with her. 'Let me know what you decide.'

'I have already,' she said. She laughed and for a moment she felt his awkwardness, as if he may have harried her a little strongly. Leonard, the one man she had ever known who wore spectacles without arms, a black ribbon falling to one side, as though he had stepped in from another century.

'Right then. I'll phone my friend in the morning.' He waited for her to collect her papers and settle them in the canvas shoulder bag that advertised a bookshop. She smiled to her elderly friend as they walked towards Tottenham Court Road. 'It might just be the making of me.' They walked on, as if once the important things were taken care of, there was little enough else to speak of. Close and yet curiously distant. Would she always feel that way with people who mattered to her? Then Leonard surprised her, suggesting he might buy her a glass of wine as they came to the pub on the corner. She was at a turning point, after all. Wasn't that something to celebrate?

He raised his glass of Bordeaux to her. A lozenge of orange light fell across his thinning hair. Lisa felt her friend's own shyness, that mystery of another person that sometimes strikes us so forcibly for no more than a few seconds, yet we feel we have seen more deeply than at other times, when he said, looking about the bar with its locals and regulars and the beat from a jukebox with the curved bright canopy that already looked from another era, 'They'll be no more strange to you out there, Lisa, than this lot is to me.'

As she later wrote of it to her father, 'People surprise you at times with their kindness.' She sealed both letters home and put her address and three small kisses on the flap of one of them, a childish habit she knew Dad would like. She imagined him with the big *Times World Atlas* on the table beside him as he read what she had written. She explained she would fly to the capital, change to a shorter flight, and travel by bus to where a man in a jeep would meet her and take her to the Mission. Everything arranged even down to that. A phrase came back to her that Stephen used to jolly them along as children when the thought of an afternoon drive to the fountain at St Heliers, or to a walk in the Waitakeres, bored her and David to tears. *Wot larks!* she now wrote, beneath the kisses. He would know exactly the tone of voice she used to mock him, knowing how his lips would part a little as he read, and laugh in that quiet way of his. I must have picked that up, he would say, from my boss in Finchley Road, who gave David his name.

She had promised that once she was there in 'the Compound', as she already knew the Mission called the enclosed space where the long low buildings of the hospital and school and dormitories stood on a gently sloping rise, she would keep him up with the play. How her father liked that phrase too. 'Wherever you are you must keep me up with the play.' But how hard that turned out to be, to find the sentences to carry across the world to him what her life became, once she was past the exotic details she so laboured to catch for him, the yawp and clamour of the bush, the trees whose names she would never learn, the harsh vividness of whatever caught her eye. 'The utter strangeness,' as she wanted to tell him, 'not so much of what I see or the work imposes on me, but what I have become in seeing them, and in so short a time.'

Sentences as she wrote them that struck her not as insincere, but as though she tried to write of someone else and not herself. She would tear up page after page, and wrote instead what she feared read baldly as an impersonal report. Names, timetables, occasionally of how much or little she could claim to understand. The merest sketch of a life, not the pulse and breath of it. She feared her father would be disappointed. How to tell Stephen he mattered too much to her for her to mock up travelogues, chatter, 'interesting things', when what she was most aware of was so much paring down in herself. Of wanting to get things right, vague as those words might seem even to herself. You wouldn't think it would be so hard to speak of. She did at least tell her father that, yet in a way that puzzled him, holding her letter as he looked out to the sea from the big window in the bach. 'So hard,' she wrote, 'to work out what is worth keeping, what is not.' She added, knowing it would amuse him, 'Don't let David read this. He is sure to misunderstand it.'

'I'm afraid you're too late for the good old days.' The first words from the large sweating man who seemed to lean over her as he took her hand to help her down from the jeep. 'No leprosy. No smallpox.' His own hand plump and damp. 'Lucky to see syphilis once in six months.' A man of fifty, sixty. As if his age mattered, yet curiously he bothered her. A long white robe that at least she knew from reading was called a soutane. Grey stubbled hair, the back of his neck pushed in a thick fold above the collar of the white shirt that showed above the gown. A quiet smile it was impossible to read. After the shock, the silliness, of his first remarks, his then telling her more formally,

168

'You're welcome, Doctor Ross. You must know you are very welcome.'

The young man in the promised jeep had picked her up, smiling at her after the bus had brought her several hours from a scrappy but busy town, to where she now stood. The bus driver had called 'Station One'. Or had she misheard? She had asked him and was still unsure, until the tall man tapped at her window and placed his two pink palms against the glass. He threw away a partly smoked cigarette which a boy dashed forward to retrieve. The heat and dazzle struck her, the strong smell of earth, the raw odours of drainage and the drift of cooking from a row of stalls beneath a spread canvas.

He sized her up, politely but directly. 'Doctor?' he said. Doctor *woman*, she understood. She knew how short she must seem among the people who gathered to look at her, but again *politely* was the word that came to her, their smiling yet standing at a distance. A small white woman with her frizzed hair that must surely have amused them. She was self-conscious as she had not been for a long time. In her tiredness, an absurd quick memory from so long before, a morning in her new white tennis frock at the club in West End Road, standing with a group of girls, while several boys on the edge of the clubhouse took them in, one of them especially looking at her, the warmth at the back of her neck as though a hand had been laid there. Her first moments in the part of a country where she had come as a scientist, as a doctor, and reverting to a teenager!

'I'm afraid I am,' she smiled at him, at those others who watched. How could she not disappoint them?

'Luke,' the young man introduced himself. He placed her suitcases in the back seat of the jeep, and the two

169

cartons of medical supplies she had been advised to bring as a gift, although the hospital she came to was known to be a good one. 'Post office,' he said, patting one of the packages.

A joke was it, she was not alert to? But before he walked to his side of the vehicle, 'You would like tea?' he asked. A woman indicated a space behind her where tables were placed beneath a strip of red cloth, and an array of plates, of cooking pots. 'I'm fine,' Lisa said.

'Tea?' he asked again. To be quite certain, was it? She wondered should she have accepted, was her refusal an unkindness? A rudeness, even?

She mimed her tiredness, her face against her opened hand. 'Thank you, no.' Smiling at the woman, at the others who looked at her with open curiosity. She took the handle at the side of the jeep and raised herself to the high front seat, Luke waiting until she was seated, closing her door and taking his place behind the wheel. Before he turned the jeep, the woman in the red gown who stood by the tables took a bottle she had lifted from a tub of water and handed it up to the doctor. Luke thanked the woman. 'Very good water,' he told Lisa, who thought, as she would continue to do for the months ahead, how does one ever break through, break down, this barrier that always seems to exist between ourselves and even those we like and care for? Away from the confining narrowness of ourselves, towards something more—not even sure what that 'more' might be. She felt the muddle in her thinking, but for the moment only her deep weariness compelling her, the grittiness of her eyelids, the effort to say so much as a few sentences to the man who drove her. Her fists clenched on her pale linen trousers. When she opened and moved her hands, she saw the dampness of where they had lain. Then as they took to the road people called out and waved. Luke laughed and said in English as good as her own, 'We like to stare at people. If we look at you we like you.'

The jeep picked up speed on an unsealed road. The dust rose and the road's corrugations swayed and knocked her against the driver, but it was easy to laugh with him. She grasped the bar running along the door. She looked out to the country they drove through, the vivid flatness, the lean of its trees, the gathering of huts, but little else came in on her from this fragment of the country she must try to make something of. 'Although one never does,' a new friend will say to her, months from now, 'not at least as we might hope.' He will tell her too that it will not be long before they won't need the likes of us. 'Which comes as an enormous surprise for us but not at all for them. We're not always too smart at seeing the obvious.'

There was a long stretch of road, more turbulent than the first half dozen miles. That wasn't the word, she knew, her exhaustion now a physical weight she had to force herself against, the accumulation of the long flights, the delays between them, the bus, now Luke talking to her in the leaping swaying jeep. Her mind ran with confused images, sudden starts. She closed her eyes. For several minutes she was back in a plane with its insistent humming in her ears. The jeep juddered again across the pitted road, her head jerking her awake, her mouth feeling as though it were packed with dust, and Luke assuring her, 'Fifteen minutes,' and surely teasing, even mocking her a little, grinning across at her, 'Fifteen minutes to civilisation.' But all that mattered to her was the desperate craving to have water falling across her from a shower, to be free of the clothes that stuck against her in the afternoon glare, to sleep no matter for how long. And then they were there. The fat man with a sweetish odour stepping close to her, surely some kind of sickness? His speaking through her tiredness as if drawing back veils, his stepping from the long low building to the side of the jeep and holding his hand towards her to help her down. 'You are welcome,' his saying the phrase Luke already had used, saying it over again, and the silly remarks that he supposed may have amused her but that she resented. About lepers. About what else was it?

'I must sleep,' she told him. 'Thank you.' Everything else could wait. Then for three days her temperature ran high and she was not sure when she slept and when she was awake, in the white room with nothing but a table and a carved figure on a kind of pedestal above the bed she lay in, and through the crumpling of time and troubling heat and the one sheet that covered her, into a massed and billowing confusion, a dark woman who spoke to her softly, and bathed her with wet towels, and the running and tangle of memories that came at her more vividly than her awareness of where she was.

At times she would open her eyes and imagine Eva sitting on the side of her bed, as if her not being there would have been the surprise; her mother close to her yet strangely distant, as she occasionally had been in dreams when Lisa lived near the Gloucester Road station, that would come again to her further on and, finally, in the confines of the truck, before fear set in. These quick and unsought images of the pale quiet woman with her hair almost to her waist, the hair the child so wanted to raise her hand to and run across the lovely fall of it. Her mother's face

172

calm as it had always been against the shaded light from the lamp in the hallway outside her room at home, 'plum-coloured' as was written on the tiny piece of paper glued beneath the base of the lamp, but 'rose' the young girl had thought, that should be the name of the colour, the rose-coloured shade. Her mother's hair so smooth it must have been brushed that minute, the girl used to think. And then asleep, and then awake. And now Babcia moving about the house before anyone else, and when Eva heard the old lady she would walk through to the kitchen in her black dressing gown with a yellow dragon on one sleeve. The women would say a few words and the aunt hand her tea, which Eva held on her lap. The mug was bright blue and made of tin, which later on the child knew was called enamel. Each morning was the same as the one before and after, although the light would alter at the kitchen windows as the seasons turned. When her mother had finished her tea and placed the mug on the table, Babcia stood behind her and ran the brush across her hair in long rhythmic sweeps. Her mother's head was tilted forward like the head of the woman in so many pictures Lisa would become familiar with at the Mission. The radio on the kitchen window sill on a station that played music and told the news, although neither woman seemed especially to listen. The brush moved on and on and Eva took little interest in the newspaper that Babcia brought in from the tin cylinder at the side of the letter box, as she did each morning, even before she took the dark cloth from the two canaries in their cage on the back porch in summer, in the wash-house from Easter on, until the winter months were run. Then once the brush had been placed back on a shelf beneath the telephone, Eva stood and called to the children from the doorway to their rooms. Or those rare days when she went and sat on her daughter's bed, and the girl woke to see her, as she did now through her fever.

'You never come into my room like that,' David complained to her. And his mother telling him, as she put her hands on his shoulders and explained what he knew was meant to be a joke, and yet for real as well, 'If my hair was touched any more the shine would wear off.' None of this strange to them as children, because that is what life was like. As it must be for any child, Lisa will think, watching the children at the Mission, every one of them thinking this is how things are meant to be. Then this first lucid morning after her brief illness, the blind raised and the sudden sense of clarity, as though the air was a kind of marvellous glass one took into oneself.

She sees for the first time with this same vivid perception the woman who had cared for her and bathed her and fed her broth with a spoon as though she were a child, a dark much older woman than herself, with hands as large as a man's, and dressed in a gown and veil and the sleeves of her tunic cut off at the elbow. Each smiled at the other before they spoke.

'Bernard,' the woman said, in an accent that was European. Each hour of the day would carry its surprise.

'A man's name?' Lisa said.

'A saint's name,' the nun said. And then, 'Sit here on the veranda and I will bring you tea. Before you meet them. The people you have come for.'

She sat in a cane chair that reminded her of the one Babcia for years claimed as her own in the glass conservatory at the side of the house. The old lady would sit for hours and look at the small backyard and the patch of vegetables

174

Stephen took pride in. Look at the drab sparrows and the piece of lawn, the rose bushes that followed the line of the driveway to the garage and never did well, and the grey boards of the neighbour's fence. The fingers on her good hand snipping at loose strands of cane in a constant monotonous click. Lisa remembering as she watched a brilliant bird flick through the branches of a tree a dozen yards from where she sat. The intense dreams, half-dreams, imaginings, of the past days now paling to the hard reality of what she looked at. And the strangeness of it coming to her yet again, how 'Eva' was how she thought of her almost always, more than 'Mother'. *Eva*. The certainty as she had wanted to reach out through her fever, through the silence of the imagined room at home, and touch again, touch over and over, the fall of shining hair, hoping the woman who sat in profile would turn towards her.

1979

———

The Compound. That was what a continent, a country, came down to, the buildings inside the cleared area between a slight elevation in the table-smooth land and the perhaps forty-foot rise that was grandly called 'The Hill'; the schoolrooms and the school's long low dormitories, the hospital with its wooden verandas, the house for the teachers and the priests, the blue-painted convent, each building with a name that meant nothing to her but something important to anyone but herself: St Jude's where patients convalesced, St Anne's for the women's ward, St John written in large ornamental script on the wall of the children's annexe. All within the boundaries of where the bush was cleared, and where a wire fence ran its line as if declaring, one world ends here, and beyond, another begins.

The fence with its double strands of wire was more a concept than a fact. No one expected a raid from any quarter, although the new doctor had not been long at the Mission before she heard stories of other places not far distant, the random angers, the occasional local disputes and tribal pride, a 'big man' staking a claim. A story even from 'over there', a piece of country which she later learned was in fact a hundred miles from where she lived, where the school of another religion had been burned and vehicles destroyed. The younger sisters liked to watch the doctor as they talked of it, guessing at a fear they did not expect to know themselves, but in the world to which their lives were dedicated, 'beyond the Compound' could be a phrase that conjured mystery for Europeans.

Three of the older nuns had trained in Europe; one even spoke of 'the Mother house' where she had spent several years, then come back to instruct the local girls whose vocation led them to the white smocks, the veils, their lives of service. They spoke English well, and Lisa felt she was the novice, the learner, the uninformed beginner, as they stood respectfully beside her, handing her instruments, following instructions, the thought inconceivable to them that their competence might indeed outrun the young white woman who so fascinated them. Yet it was with the younger sisters, who became friends as much as helpers, even more than with the French-speaking, splendidly professional Sister Bernard, that Lisa most felt the distance between herself and everything 'the Compound' must mean for them. Let alone what lay beyond, the minds, the languages, the thousand ways lives are led beyond our comprehension. They made jokes together, she and these ardent, humorous, kindly girls, with their metal crosses, their singing each evening coming down from the chapel up on the Hill, their gravity and eagerness to learn from whatever they saw her do or explained to them. She liked it when they unselfconsciously touched her hair that they were amused by, or placed their hands on her arm to claim how close they were. And yet lightyears away, wasn't that the expression her father used to use, when David pestered him about his time in London? No matter how much I know, she thought, I shall never know more than the merest surface of these people. Nor they of me. Lightyears.

In the letters she wrote home she felt the words came to her inadequately and slight. 'So that then dear Dad is what we call "the Compound" and what happens here. I am good with one body at a time, hopeless on anything else! Don't ask me what they think, or even what I think myself much of the time. If I'm not dog-tired at night, which I mostly am, I like to lie and think for a while about home, about the Crescent, about the lives we've all had there. My own people. This may all sound a simple life, which I suppose it is, and certainly a busy one, too busy for those old luxuries like wondering whether one is happy or not. What a pampered and distant question that even seems.' And at the end of her letters, often as an afterthought, she would put a sentence to be passed on to her brother, knowing her father would quietly enjoy her teasing him as she did. 'You might tell David that the women here feel a deep pity for me when they realise I don't simply not know the prayers they say but have no inkling of "the Faith". My young friend who helps me in the theatre says, with a certain tone that I think may even be a touch of irony, that the others pray for me. So I thought I might as well give them David's name while they were at it.'

She would have liked to tell Dad about the older friend who mattered too, but that was simply too hard. How to talk of that without misunderstanding. Instead, she told him that she had a two-roomed, neatly constructed home of her own, 'the Residency', that reminded her of the army huts some people had as baches on the road down to his beach house. It was here the visiting doctor lived in what was meant to be an assured privacy, not fifty yards from the buildings she walked to at six in the morning, and crossed back from in the evenings, back from the hospital, the wards, the clinic at their centre, the Admin Block with its two Imperial typewriters, its tin-sided cabinets and its perfectly kept files. Across a long space towards the rise of the bush, there was a group of make-do shelters where relatives of the ill slept overnight, where small fires burned at night and the odours of cooking came in layers on the warm still air.

Privacy, she quickly learned, was a flexible notion, something Europeans made so much of, something so much less to the local people, not held in the same webs of self, of isolation. For people to be so at ease among themselves—she was drawn to that, envied it, knew too it was not for her. People sometimes waited to talk with her for no other reason than herself; one of the sisters told her she was family to her. But she valued the gesture towards a life of her own, the two tiny rooms that would be hers and hers alone for the months she spent here in a place of utter strangeness. There was a small veranda on the side of the Residency that made her think of a doll's house, and a wire screen on the one door that led into it, a window with a dainty lace curtain to either side of the door. A small generator behind the hut mostly functioned but occasionally did not, and then there was the curious sense of sitting in a cave, the oil lamp settling to a pure comforting light, and even the pages of her reference books seeming oddly theatrical, with a hood of shadows above the shining circle. But how difficult to write of even these simplest things: 'The sky blazes most days, and the redness of the earth seems to take one over, so always there, always *foreign*,' did not come anywhere near what she wished to say.

'There is a strange thing I must tell you, Dad, but the more I feel the distance from almost everything that surrounds me, the look and sound of the people, the words I seldom comprehend, the way they live at such ease in a rigidity of custom and belief that I make so little sense of, the more I feel this particular kind of loneliness is something I would hate not to have had the chance to know. And this side by side with the deep reality of those I can assist and sometimes even cure! The marvellous enduring reality of *bodies*, where I am at home. Everything but that shades off into uncertainty. The extraordinary adventure of knowing so little about almost everything except the name of a condition, and what I can do about it. I wonder if you see what I mean? As I've told you before, being either happy or unhappy, those so over-used words, hardly come into it.'

Difficult to imagine, Lisa thought, as she sealed the envelope that Luke would take when he drove to the township the next day, how one's life ran so smoothly, quickly, in the satisfactions of routine, in not contradicting her friends the sisters when they spoke of God's will, but telling them that trying to do a job well, a day at a time, was really all she was up to. But an elation too, yes, it was actually that, at the words, the sentences even, she found she was now able to use with the patients, the women who walked such distances to her clinic, the ones who honoured her with such trust. She was diligent in entering onto index cards the details of conditions that were new to her, or puzzling, or contrary to what her training back at St Pancras may have led her to expect. She was glad that Bernard and her young assistant cared almost entirely for the pregnant women in the ward spoken of always as St Anne's, and delivered their children. It was work Lisa knew she had no natural gift for, and was apprehensive when her help was called on. She felt the apprentice at such times, admiring the hard, intelligent focus of the now elderly woman who for forty years had worked and comforted in these same few rooms, liking her blunt humour in the evenings as she ate the simple meal with the sisters in their 'refectory', as they called it, the bare room with two trestle tables and a religious picture on the wall of a woman clutching her chest with an opened palm and her eyes rolled back. 'Diagnose that one for me, Bernard,' Lisa irreverently thought. She walked back home, dog-tired, taking in the late hush that came down on the Mission, the sky seeping into darkness, yet light there still behind the black tracery of trees. She liked the taste of the cooling air, the plaiting of scents from the trees through the hospital odours that were always there, the drift too of food and burning dung and fuel from the flimsy shelters near the boundary, the earth smells the coming night brought out. The sweetish distant odour too that she picked up at times as Declan approached and before he spoke to her, the telltale carcinoma biding its time. Not that she referred to that. Silence on God and on his health stood as the unspoken courteous brackets of their friendship.

She liked the long, softly lit verandas of the schoolrooms as she glanced across to them. For a fraction they struck her as though she looked towards a lit-up riverboat, the wooden chapel too, with its small red light a mere speck through the mottled window, like some river craft as well. As if she had ever seen such a thing, apart from in movies at the Cameo, a childhood ago, at Surrey Crescent! 'To see things exactly as they are.' She had read that somewhere and written it as the motto on her homework books as a schoolgirl almost twenty years before. And here in Africa, a scientist, remembering an overblown old movie like *Showboat*! It amused her, lightened her, its ironic nudge. Declan laughed as she told him of it. He had dreams still, he told her, of winning games with sprightly back play, the most ungainly boy who ever pulled a rugby jersey on, even in jest. He had looked at her with an assessing sympathy. 'We're the sort,' he said, 'who finish up in places like this.'

There seemed nothing strange in the rapport she felt with this overweight, ailing man with his comforting book of ancient poetry, his puzzling accent that oddly moved her as he sometimes quoted lines to her that were important to him. She imagined that even with his own people he would seem eccentric. As so might she, she admitted to her friend who was the senior teacher in the school, the heavy man whose jokes she had hated as he helped her from the jeep, that fevered day of her arrival six months before. He carried a tin thermos with him it seemed at all times. Even as he sat at the edge of 'the playing field', that big white-outlined stretch of earth where he sat on the comic slenderness of the unfolded shooting stick that supported him, calling out to the boys, flinging his arms to urge their sweep towards the goal. As he walked the Compound, speaking to workmen who kept the buildings, the grounds, the service buildings, the sheds with their pumps and generators, in 'such grand shape there, men', as he complimented even the least impressive of them, he cradled a thermos in the scoop of his arm. It was there to be placed on the small table between them when he strolled at times to the Residence in the evening while the classrooms burned with their riverboat lights and the boys applied themselves until one of them emerged and swung the heavy hand-bell that rang over the buildings, and night after night set up a flock of roosted birds which seemed never to get used to it. 'Pavlov's birds,' Declan joked of them, 'and we flatter ourselves we're so very different, the way we obey the bell.'

He eased between the edge of the table and the rail of the veranda behind him. He placed the thermos between himself and his young doctor friend, who had set two mugs for him to half-fill with the cold, sweetly sugared lemon tea. It amused him, as it did Lisa, what a 'civilised world' might have made of their casual ease together, a fat ageing cleric, he joked, a Jewish doctor from 'the round earth's imagined corner', as he called her country. Our appearance, he assured her, too grotesque to give scandal even to the sharpest-eyed. Even to Father Ambrose.

'Give scandal,' she repeated, a mild mockery in her doing so. 'Those weird phrases of yours.'

'We are a religion of inflexible phrases.' His leaning forward a little, hands spread on his knees, to catch his breath.

'Surely all religions are? Don't they have to be?' But they leave it there. 'The imponderables', as Declan phrases it, batting them away. Often they might sit for five minutes, even ten, without feeling obliged to speak, then the metal side of the thermos tapping against their mugs as he again poured for them. 'If lemon tea were a vice,' he has told her, 'it would spell eternal doom for me.' He guessed at her smile, rather than seeing it against the dark. Two evenings a week, their sitting companionably. At times they tell each other about the country, the home, the families they come from. She will speak to him of Eva, her brother who seems always to crave what he feels eludes him, the quiet father she reveres. And Declan confessing, as he surprises himself by doing, that on his last trip home, six years back now, he was as ill at ease back there as ever he was out here. 'Nowhere that isn't foreign, that's the fact of it.' But she likes to imagine whatever it was, the 'back there' he speaks of. The big hills that frightened him as a boy and where he'd still not like to find himself alone, once the night was down. The wildness he told her where you step behind a rock, ten minutes from the house, and you are alone with Atlantic winds. 'I was never good at that,' he says, 'being alone like that. Then you give yourself to a place like this and it's the same again. Nothing like a community to bring that home.' But his tone hoping not too much of it, the sadness at the back of what he said.

She told him of Eva's walking towards the tide. The will, she said, a human being can find, courage surely the hardest thing to comprehend? But details too that came to her as they sat together, random memories that faintly shamed her. Those quiet, narrow, decent neighbours in the Crescent she had no right to think herself apart from, and yet the wall, she could think of it as nothing other than that, when she tried to understand them. The mystery indeed her family must have been to them, the damaged relative they called grandmother, whom the neighbours kindly excused on the strength of 'what she had been through', whom none of them could understand a word of any more than she a word of them, but their smiling towards each other as they passed, the odd ribbons of rumour and gossip that trailed her. 'The rotten times over there. We've no idea have we what she might have put up with.' The relative who one night while the street and its modest houses slept had left her room with its miniature menorah on her dressing table and the photograph of her sister Sarah, from when Eva was still unborn and a secret from the family for so long, for some forever, and the tear across the photo that left only a hand across her sister's shoulder. She left her room and went to the kitchen and turned the back-door key. Then once out into the night that was light enough to see one's way in, she took a spade from the unlocked garden shed and carried it the forty yards to the Stoddarts' white wooden state house on the other side of the street. Mr Stoddart who fancied himself as a gardener and planted wide beds of geraniums on either side of his short drive, and in a strip the length of the house below the bedroom windows. In the light from the moon the leaves of the plants were like dull metal and the heads of the flowers blackened fists. Babcia bashed at them and sliced against the stems and at three in the morning Mr Stoddart and the neighbour who first heard the noise ran across the street and belted with their opened palms on the glass panels of the front door.

The Crescent talked of it for weeks as the inexplicable thing it was, but considerately no one referred to it in the pharmacy, although it was in their minds as they watched the quiet courteous man and the pale teenage girl who was with him so often in the shop attending to them. Only Mr

Ross and the girl in fact comprehending what had taken place, and his deciding not to pass on to his wife, or to the boy who was so easily upset, what the strange heavy religious fanatic who was Babcia's only friend remembered and explained. When you first arrived at the camp, she said, and the cunning of its first deception, the rows of neat barrack buildings, the carefully tended paths, the sense that here you would find discipline, of course, but hygiene too, and even pleasantness, for outside each of the buildings the already planted and cheerful swathes of red geraniums. That first lie, Miss McGovern said, in so simple a thing as that.

'My aunt was ill by that time,' Lisa said. '*Quietly* mad, and so it was easy to pretend she was simply elderly and forgetful and since she only spoke properly in any case with that one friend, we could keep the fantasy up. That we were more or less normal, which of course we never were.'

She hears the subdued rasp of his breath a few feet from across the table. 'So there you are, Declan,' she tells him, 'that's where I am from.' He poured the last of the sweetened tea. He says, with the wry sardonic tone he reserved for the Mission's superior, 'I see our preserving angel makes his rounds.'

The glimmer of Father Ambrose's robe as he came towards them. The unexpected memory of the darkroom off one of the laboratories where her Scottish friend carried out his photographic work, that strange shaking of the solution in a shallow dish as he held with tweezers the corner of a sheet of paper, and the slow, slightly creepy emerging of the shapes it released. The priest's long garment suddenly so close to them, a few feet from where

187

they sat. The silence of his approach, his head invisible against the night, his folded hands a dark stain against the fall of his white soutane.

'A pleasant evening, doctor.'

'An evening for human fellowship, Father,' Declan's voice a shade this side of provocation.

'You're very welcome to join us,' Lisa said.

He bowed slightly towards her, 'a fierce one for a touch of ceremony', as Declan once said of him. She felt the inflexibility that chilled most of those he spoke with. She knew the boys feared him; the younger nuns preferred not to meet his glance, their answers timid should he speak to them.

'Thank you,' he said. 'Another time. We all have duties.' He turned and the night took his walking towards the workmen's area of the Compound. The men would stand from their sitting at the edge of the fire in their cooking hut, speak quietly and thank him for his visit, grateful for his attention to them, his asking was there anything he might do for them? And their respectful silence as he left them, their prodding at the fire until he must be some way off. Their knowing their good fortune, as he reminded them, to have work here at the Mission. Yes, Father. Lisa liked their singing that at times came across to the Residence later in the evenings. The warmth it conveyed, rather than any pleasure she might take from the music, where she knew her ear was at fault. Just tired men at the end of the day, content to sing together. The loveliness of wanting that. The freedom to do so.

Declan broke in on what she knew was her too easy sentiment. 'It is possible to be a good person and a bastard, you know that, don't you, Lisa? It does not happen often but we are privileged with Ambrose to see a rare instance of the phenomenon.'

They laughed as he stood and shook the empty thermos against his ear. He assured her, in what she presumed was a take-off of something likely to be heard in the hills back home, 'When the drink's gone entirely now there's nothing for it but a man getting along back home.' Then he too was gone into the night, his fading from her as Ambrose had done a few minutes before. She sat on at the table, holding her empty mug. The patterning of trees, still faintly darker against the dark. The dynamo behind the wards jerking as it sometimes did, the quick flickering of the lights. Then the silence, but not really that at all, the click and chirr and the high yelped scaling of an animal's alarm. The trailing ropes and nets of stars as she looked up. So easy to take them for granted, then to be startled as one attended to their vast haul. One of them falling, scoring like a pen tip. The delight in simply taking them in.

She urged herself to stand, to enter the small room whose walls leaped startlingly white as she touched the switch inside the door. The sisters' rooms could not have been simpler than her own, the single bed with its furled netting, the desk with the bright slashes of her stacked books against the wall, the few cards she had pinned above them, the childish scrawl of a crayon drawing that amused her. David's daughter had sent it with the words dictated for her mother to write, saying this was the picture of a tent Daddy had put up for her in the backyard because Sukos was a fun time and this was how their people had lived for so long but it had rained and the tent had leaned over and they had to come inside the house to sleep. And a big leaned-over upside-down V, meant to be a sagging tent, that Esther wanted her to see. Lisa easily imagined her niece's father insisting as ever that his child be brought up with customs and celebrations he had been deprived of, his irritation at the elements thwarting his being the father he was determined to be. The comic little drawing bringing the family even to here, as she had written back, saying how people here lived in huts that looked a little bit like the one in the picture, but theirs stayed up even when it rained.

She took off her smock and placed it on one of the hooks set on the wall by her bed. The freedom to stand in her underwear, with the chug of the wooden-bladed fan taking up its soothing beat as that too she turned on, and the small lamp on her desk, with her medical texts arranged between the bookends one of the workmen had made for her. She took a bottle of boiled water from what was called the ice cupboard, although the ice placed there by one of the house girls hours before had melted in the broad dish below the shelf. There was a small area where a bench held a paraffin stove which she seldom used, and the tin of biscuits with the swirled lettering of Huntley and Palmers on its tin lid.

A bright cloth with a red and yellow pattern lay across the small table beside her bed. She disliked its garishness in the otherwise almost clinically simple room, but she knew it had been placed there as a gift when she arrived. To remove it would have been ungrateful. At first she thought there must be some local craft in the weaving of it, but a sister told her how Europeans began to crave things to remind them of where they came from, and this was from Italy, she would see that on the little label on the other side. She had felt a prickle of irritation she was assumed to be a home-sick foreigner, that any scrap of Europe somehow would soothe her. As she had told herself before she arrived, and said over and over after her first days of fever, whether she liked the place or not was not the point. But by now she accepted the arrogance even of that, of thinking one knows exactly what is right for one. As Declan had put it to her, in his ironic, good-humoured way, telling her as he sat with his broad white sleeves pulled back and rubbing at the rash that troubled his wrist, 'We're inclined to go off, you know, in a place like this. Not spectacular Joseph Conrad stuff, I don't mean that. But gently, like mushy fruit. Yet there's a certainty we can find here as well. Of another kind.' She had laughed and told him he had lost her again.

She undressed completely and stood in the tin trough beneath the shower. She reached up to the lever that, once moved, dumped water from the cistern across her rather than allowing it to run down smoothly. Although the water was never cold, that sense of mild shock all the same as it broke across her. It had become something she looked forward to at the end of each day. Its quick battering lifted her mood and calmed her. She raised her arms to let a loose-fitting slip drop across her head, before sitting at her desk. She reached for her *Adams & Maegraith*, a volume bristling with yellow strips of paper to mark pages she returned to. It was a time she looked forward to each evening before she went to bed, her mind focused on finding what might be of use for the next day's clinic. There was usually something she felt unsure of, some ailment she had not treated for maybe months, or not at all, and would be there waiting for her in ten hours' time. She found what she was after, the Neil Mooser reaction that took her back to her friend in the lab holding up a guinea pig, noting the scrotal swelling, the name not too far from that of a colleague they both disliked. A disease, she now reread, 'of poverty, human distress, and overcrowding'. Mild in children, increases in severity with rising age. An elderly man, unsure of his years, had come to the clinic that morning, and would be there again tomorrow. One of the sisters translated for her. He lived in a hut two hours' walk away, with other elderly men who, she guessed, were outcasts of some kind. She read again the notes she had made once she examined him, and the few details he offered were written down. A recrudescence, from the symptoms she had noted. She had been too cautious in isolating him until she might feel more confident. His temperature was high; he had rubbed his thighs and upper arms to indicate the soreness in his muscles. She listened to the bronchial rasp of his chest. The sister had to raise her voice when she spoke to him, but his deafness would have been from quite another cause.

She read and added notes to the card. This is what gave her most satisfaction, the tracking down, the fact that she might be of use to those who trusted her. Why deny the reward of feeling that? But she recalled the South African specialist who once had lectured her on the kind of diseases she now saw almost daily, a clever sensitive man who told his students, almost as a refrain, that it is your intellect that will save the lives of those who come to you, not the nice feelings you may have about them. Although adding what at the time she did not appreciate as now she did, 'to keep those for when they may be of use, of course'. Meaning at the end, when that was all there was, little else left to offer. But this morning's patient was nowhere near that. Chloramphenicol. She was pleased she already had guessed what to recommend. Of course the old man would go back to conditions that were prime for contracting the cycle over again. But never think of the big picture, the same teacher had surprised his class by saying, or you will throw up your hands in horror and become a missionary. It was one of his curious attempts at humour. But his message was clear. To take one instance at a time was what you were trained to do. The patient under your hands is not a statistic. Otherwise you despair. That, or fall back on the kind of faith she supposed her colleagues here must be sustained by.

Lisa placed the textbook back with the other volumes arranged between their metal bookends. In the front was a postcard she had kept with her from Athens, and looked at often in those years as she worked in her room in London, a black-and-white photograph of a young woman's marble head. Hygeia, explained a note on the other side. Another gesture she supposed to sentimentality. She had bought it that week she decided that yes, this is what she would do, she would leave Fergus and the flat in Ravini Street, she would go back to Dunedin, and after that specialise as she had done. And try to speak the truth, always. How simple and grand it had all been, to think of that as she walked through the museum along from Omonoia Square. She had bought the card as she left the museum. In fact, had bought two of them, and posted one back home, telling them what she had decided to do, telling her parents and David, who was still at school, and Babcia, busy at her baking, at her needlework, although it is the old lady in repose Lisa likes to think of, her sitting in the sun in the conservatory for long hours at a time; or when the sun failed to come out, in the sitting room with the wall heater turned on, her hands resting in the lap of the apron she insisted now on wearing at all times, and watched—or so the others in the family assumed—watched always with a curiously attentive interest the glint and poise and sudden flicker of the goldfish in the tank between the bookshelves, with its constant rise of bubbles from between the miniature rocks. Eva would say she hated the sight of the thing, but smiled as she said it. At times she sat beside her aunt and let her own hand rest on those folded on the apron. All this coming to her as she glances at the photograph of the marvellous stone head.

Lisa's mind felt cleared, rested even, by her reading, by her looking last thing over the typed sheet on its clipboard one of the sisters gave her each evening as she left the 'office', the spotless room where the medical records were kept, the schedules for the next day prepared. She took the bottle of water from its shelf in the ice cupboard and swallowed the tablets, the last thing she did each night, the capsule for malaria, the mild sedative which she had added only in these past few weeks as the boy came into her mind once the light on her desk was turned off, and she lay beneath the one sheet that covered her. More and more, it seemed his life was for her to decide on. It was a weight she knew was illogical and, more than that, absurd. She had seen a play once with her friend Alex, who liked to talk about choice and other words that he said were the things we must think about, the play would say it so much better than he could put it. She was tired the evening they went, and was irritated by the talk, by how little story there was to what they sat through, but *absurd*, Alex kept returning to that as he enthused, and she told him could they move on to something else? She had never much enjoyed talk like that for its own sake. She lay in the dark, the fan's chug so insistent now there was nothing to distract from it. She waited for the sedative to work its course. She heard the movement outside, as she did now each evening. The sound of the chair moved on the veranda where he would have been sitting until he knew she slept, the brush of his opened hand moving across the door, a slow circular sweeping repeated each evening, as if some kind of ritual before the day was truly night. And then his moving away. She lay in the dark and her eyes grew heavy and her friend's repeated word after the play circling in her mind as well, beating as if an insect that had lain until now to clip monotonously against the walls.

She quite knew what Declan hinted at. As she knew he did not for a minute give credence to it, yet felt he must raise it with her. What the ageing, compassionate Bernard had heard talk of as well, and also disbelieved. But as her friend had told her, one must never forget we are among remote and tired and anxious people, we missionaries, where goodwill may surprisingly run thin, where rumour easily flares, where local superstitions feed on little enough. We all have our mantras to keep so much at bay.

The boy, as the Compound said, had come out of the night, where else could he have come from? One day no one has heard of him or seen him, a day later he is standing in the early yellow light, ten yards from the veranda of the clinic, unaware what building it is he waits at. He wears a white shirt, a pair of black trousers folded up at the cuffs, a leather strip for a belt. He is bare-footed, bare-headed. He is neither short nor tall. No one thought of him as a child, no one thought of him as yet a man. His cheeks are smooth, his skin is a little lighter than that of most of those who look at him, but there is disagreement even on that. So much depends on where he stands, on how he looks back at you. He is there facing the building when one of the young sisters first comes down to unlock the theatre, the admin office, the room for patients. The figure is not standing as most strangers do, with a relative or friend who has come with them, but with a solitariness that at once defines him; and even more, the sister will say, not just standing there but giving the impression that he has been set down and placed rather than arrived. As no one quite puts it, but as fact bears out, if nothing is known about a person, then anything is possible. If anything is possible, there is no guessing with substance.

The English doctor had beckoned him to come across. The boy watched her, allowed her first to touch his hand and then his arms, to place her stethoscope on his chest and on his back, to tap his knees for reflexes, to shine a light in his eyes, and then to touch the scar from a long time ago that ran from the hairline at the back of his neck across his shoulder and sloped towards his chest, like a piece of pale twisted cord. His eyes followed her quiet speaking to him; his head turned sharply when Luke revved the engine of his jeep outside the hospital, waiting to drive a patient and her child out to her village. He can hear all right, the young sister said, but is silent as a lizard.

When Lisa coaxed him to the office and sat him at the desk with a piece of paper in front of him, and gave him a pencil to hold, he turned the pencil between his fingers but that was all, although she showed him how to mark with it. It was also clear that apart from the doctor he did not like people coming close to him. He ate food that was left on a bench for him outside the kitchen where meals were made for the school. He would not go inside a classroom, or into the chapel. A workman set a thin mattress for him in a lean-to behind the shed where the jeep and a tractor and several mopeds were kept. The Mission quickly became used to him. But as Bernard was the one to say, he was on the other side of the Compound, even when you were standing beside him.

And as everyone saw, he followed the doctor at a distance, and liked to stand where he might see her, even from a long way off. Yet Lisa no more than the others truly knew how much he comprehended, apart from his trust in her. He was given the name Francis, although she thought, That is not his name, that is nothing like whatever name he has, and referred to him only as the boy, as if there were no other he might be confused with. He walked the Compound and watched and took things in. If the workmen were not close to him, he shifted timber and sand for them, moved buckets of water to where he knew they were needed. He carried plastic baskets of laundry for the sisters. But he was quick to move should they seem too close, and when Father Ambrose called to him he did not approach, as though he felt the suspicion the tall man held for him. The boy's strange self-possession even as he withdrew seemed to irk him. As Declan repeated, if we don't know the truth of something, there's no shortage of something else to fill the gap.

Lisa watched the women who were her colleagues, the local women who cleaned and helped in the wards, the kitchens, the school. There was nothing in their way of relating to her that seemed different, and yet she felt some change in the currents of the air, in the glances she was alert to. Even when Sister Bernard joked to her, 'He is like a carving, that boy who follows you like a dog,' it was said lightly, as if the older woman was amused by it, and yet hinting, was it, at something left unsaid? This boy who had come from nowhere and could tell them nothing of himself, neither a child nor a man, but drawing attention by his sense of mystery that shaded towards something inexplicable, even sinister, as others observed the grace of his movements, the silence that surrounded him almost as if a physical barrier, his following the frizzy-haired doctor with her paleness that sometimes startled those who saw her for the first time.

The boy who now each evening leaned against a tree trunk twenty yards from the Residency, waiting on Lisa's return from her last tasks at the hospital, or from the evening meal. Sometimes she left the outer door open, in front of the wire screen the curious might look through into the room where she sat late and worked until the door was closed and the lights turned off, the boy's white shirt showing out in the night against the tree he leaned against in the clicking, busy darkness. Of course it is innocent, Bernard said with her humorous directness to the younger sisters, no woman she had ever heard of needed to travel to a place like this if behaviour of that kind was what she had in mind! Yet her wisely knowing too, and hinting as much to 'the girls' as she thought of them, that once a story was given a bone to feed on, rumour ran loose like fire in the scrub at the edge of a village. Hadn't Father Declan told her how the boys in the senior classes already joked about it? And the workmen. 'The ghost,' they called him, never Francis. The ghost who haunts the doctor.

There was little that was vicious in their chatter, but

their ribald amusement at the boy's dogged attendance carried the suspicion that was always there of a foreign woman who had no husband, even one whose paleness was unattractive, whose figure was meagre, one a speechless teenage boy, perhaps under an enchantment of some kind, might become obsessed with? Bernard was alert to the hurt that lay behind such talk, running her hand along her friend's arm, but laughing with her too, advising how for a woman not given to prayer, surely mocking nonsense was the best defence? But alone, Lisa more convinced it was for her to protect him. The thought coming to preoccupy her, her writing to Murray in the library in Keppel Street, asking that he send her, urgently, anything he might have on autism, on related conditions, on trauma, whatever might give her some insight to a mind beyond her comprehending. In a rare flare of bitterness, she said during one of her evenings talking with Declan, 'I do everything I can to help him, and what comes across most is that I'm somehow unnatural. Resented.'

'Few enough think that,' Declan said. 'Very few.'

'Your superior,' she said. 'Isn't that enough?'

'Ambrose has a natural calling as a vigilante.'

For the only time, Lisa was angered by her friend's knack for deflecting, his deference to some code he adjusted to that was beyond her. 'You joke about it, Declan, but you are subservient too.'

His looking at her frankly, his admitting, 'As if, my dear friend, I'm not aware of that,' and her quick regret that she may have hurt him. But 'Don't,' he anticipated her. 'Don't regret your saying what you think to be the case.'

They sat on, contented enough with the long silence between them. Her briefly touching his warm, plump

199

hand. And her not being sure that she understood him, as he stood a few minutes later, screwing the top down on the thermos, the warmth and distance in his voice that moved and saddened her as he said, 'So much for all of us. To keep at bay.'

At the moment of his saying it, the realisation not so much coming in on her as seeming to arise from what was deepest in her, the fact of quite how intense it was, her dislike of the tall dark cleric who so resented the boy's presence in the Compound, and yet held back from compelling him to leave. There would be too much feeling against his doing that. Declan's now saying as he stood, replacing his chair against the small table there between them, speaking as if from the blue and yet how pertinent to what she thought, 'They may think they prevail, men like that. And we say to ourselves, "They don't, they don't," we say that, even as they do.'

Then how quickly matters changed. 'A few problems sorted out,' as she wrote the next week, imagining her father as he read her pages, lifting his head to catch his reflection in the expanse of plate glass in the house out on the coast. Across to the big lift of the rock with its own distant clinging history. To the sea whose breaking he seemed never to weary of looking out to. It was comforting to think of him like that. His hair of course much greyer, thinner, she knew that, than it was as she liked to imagine him. The man in the dispensary at the back of the shop. The man happy enough to be bewildered, a little, by what he loved, and what love had brought with it.

These last few evenings Lisa had stayed on in the clinic and the admin room and sent her assistant off early, to her prayers, her reading, whatever it was they did in those last hours before bedtime in their quarters up on the rise beside the chapel. Not even Eugene, the twenty-year-old who looked five years younger, could have brought more sparkle to the chromium surfaces, more neatness to the theatre she would be back in the following morning, for the hernia she saw at the top of the schedule's typed list. A blue vase of flowers placed there on the desk. Not even that, she thought, I have been here nine months, and not even knowing the name of the spiky blooms in front of her. Flowers. People. How much we cram into simple elusive words.

She ran boiling water across the teabag in the mug she held beneath it. The quick tang of the cinnamon rising to her above the pervading disinfectant. 'What a sensualist I've become,' she said to the empty office, the delight she found in so simple a thing as this. She read over the details for the next day, the timetable as familiar to her as her own pulse. The mornings in theatre, the clinics in the afternoon, occasionally with Luke, and one of the sisters as translator, driving into the open country that was still startling to her, to follow up on some request, some report, of a person too ill to make the journey by foot to the promise of whatever 'the Mission' must mean to them. The infections, the diseases, that could still surprise her, the shock that never left her, of how little it might take to save a life, or lose one.

There was an asterisk beside one of the names on the list, which told her the patient had been treated before. The writing on the card was in a hand she did not recognise, which told her, surely, the patient by now must be older than most. The neat fountain-penned script she assumed

201

from a sister now beneath one of the wooden crosses on the further side of the church. She had walked up there soon after she arrived, when she sought out details to tell her something of the community she would work with. She disliked the too easy melancholy of standing before the graves of strangers, the limiting clichés of what might come to mind. Even at home, on the trip back the year after Babcia's death, in the section of cemetery where the old lady lay among her own people. She had gone because of David's insistence—chilled, if she was honest, by the headstones, the lettering she could not read, as well as the words there in English, the conventional comforting scraps imploring God to keep in mind his daughter, his faithful ones. The strangeness of her relative's name, spelled out there in full, as she realised she had never until then seen it. As she thought again now, this trying to make a person out of the scraps we're given to put together!

She returned the card to its file, and carried the narrow drawer across to its cabinet. She came back to sit with her head leaned against the wall, her chair tilted back, her eyes closed, her hands circling the mug she had taken up again from the table. The luxury of simply this. She opened her eyes to Ambrose standing at the doorway, watching her.

'You should have spoken,' she said to him. But she smiled, telling him, 'You surprised me avoiding work!'

'I know how tired the doctor gets.' His stillness part of what unsettled her. Whenever he stood and spoke, not only to her but to the sisters, to his fellow teachers, to the students who were in awe of him and feared not any punishment he might inflict but simply his presence, there was this sense Lisa experienced now, his looking not directly at but above her. As though this was not the talking of one person with another, but an announcement that went beyond. The fall of his robe from his shoulders to his sandals, the neatness of its folds, the immobility of his features—as if everything about him, all that one saw, was an act of will. He made her think of a man who was carved. Who had carved himself. As she looked up to him now, determining not to stand although he had entered the room.

'May I offer you a cup?' She hoped he might unbend. From his hesitation she thought he might accept. But his answer was more like the beginning of something he had prepared. 'Francis,' he said. The fingers of one hand moved against a pleat in his gown. 'He has become a problem for us. For us all.'

She continued to look at him, at the light sliding on his glasses. The tiny blank ovals. That was it. Like the Beatle. 'We know little about him,' Ambrose went on. 'He arrived at the Mission and, as you know, is unwilling to tell us anything.'

Lisa felt the pulse in her neck throb, but she spoke calmly. 'His silence is not by choice, we all know that.'

Ambrose then saying carefully what she knew was meant to tell her more than the words themselves declared. He explained, as he might to a child, to a foreigner who failed to know these things, that for those who lived here, those who knew this country, the boy was from another place entirely. Had she noticed how people here observed him? Had it occurred to her he did not speak because he did not understand the language, that he had nothing to say in return when he was addressed?

The priest took her silence for agreement. His tone altered slightly, as if he meant to compliment her that she was wise to attend as she did. There is nothing remarkable, you may think to yourself, Doctor, that a boy walks into the Mission, 'a boy from the bush', a phrase he knew ironically carried more than it simply said. He knew he spoke English with a subtlety that might surprise her. He repeated, 'There is nothing remarkable in that.' People of all kinds, of different ages, as she of course well knew, came to take their turn at the clinic, arriving with hope, perhaps because God had moved them, it is not for us to ask such things. He paused, giving her a chance to speak, and then went on, 'But the boy is not like the others. We have given him a name and a place to sleep, but you must have noticed, Doctor, people look at him because his strangeness strikes them. His silence, his scrutiny, discomforts them. The handsomeness even of his features, which you must be aware of? The sense of such distance from the rest of us? People are afraid of him.'

'There is no reason to be, surely?' Lisa said. 'The boy is either sick, or afflicted in some way we are not yet quite sure of.'

'Which is what I mean,' Ambrose said. 'Perhaps even reasons we are right to fear?'

And then the tall commanding man changed tack again. She felt his distaste at having to speak with her, even that. He said, choosing his word precisely, and the choice not lost on her, 'The boy is possessed with you.'

'He trusts me. That is fairly obvious and simple.'

'As he does no one else. But then they are not his people either. Which is why he must leave.' And after a pause which he knew disconcerted her, 'His safety cannot be guaranteed.'

'You cannot say that, Father,' Lisa said, the first and

only time she addressed him as others did.

'You might ask your friend,' he said, 'the friend you drink tea with. He has been here a long time.'

'Longer than any, I believe. Apart from Bernard.'

'Sister Bernard,' he said.

His glasses again bright glints as his head tilted. Then the man taking her by surprise. Without alteration in his tone or emphasis, his telling her, 'I can help you.'

'Yes?'

'In a few weeks your time here comes to an end. Your contract.'

'My volunteering.'

'Francis. He might even leave with you. You would not be deserting him. You could save him.' For the one time, his smiling slightly, as if the word he chose should amuse her as well. His too obviously enjoying the irony of it.

How matter-of-factly it was done. How neatly choice was taken from her. And then, a brisk phrase cutting across his usual formality. A sigh, was it, of relief? 'Right, then.' They would work together. In confidence.

'You mean Declan?'

'Father Declan need not be told.'

Lisa felt the sense of relief that flowed from him. His surprising her yet again as he removed his glasses, holding them for a moment in his opened palm, a folded wire insect. The tiredness of his eyes one noticed at no other time.

'You of course will need to attend to matters as well.'

'Of course.'

'At that end.'

'You mean what we're doing is illegal.'

He corrected her. 'Unauthorised.' And then, 'I expect it is a little like being a doctor. There are times when necessity suggests its own rules.' He then explained, almost condescendingly, that she must not expect things to be done everywhere as they were in England. But yes, he would arrange travel in one continent, while she took care of whatever might need to be attended to in another. When such things were arranged, Luke would drive them to the airport for the capital, from there a flight to a country further north. There were trucks one might make deals with, 'people deals', on crossings that every day of the week carried legitimate cargoes to and from Italian ports. Legitimate cargoes and sometimes people. 'There will be no difficulties with that. Not on this side.'

'And then?'

'Then, Doctor Ross, you are more or less with your own people. You will be back in Europe.'

Strange, how so suddenly clear it was, what she might do to begin. She had not thought of Fergus for an age, not in any serious way. His charm, his impulsive vanity, his untroubled lack of principle. His desire for her, oh that, certainly, which she knew might still be appealed to, for the reason he had not put an end to it himself. The cards they sent to each other at the end of each year. The pretence of a surviving thread. The cold thought coming to her that she was prepared to lie, to him, to anyone. The fact striking her with an insistent force, as she watched the tall dark man who had now unfolded the glasses lying in his hand, and replaced them, their wire again finding the thin indentations where their arms fitted at the side of his face. At last there is a commitment I cannot avoid.

Lisa said, 'I will need to use the telephone in the teachers' common room. There are several calls I will need to make.'

'The one in my office. You will find that more private.'

Within a day of their speaking, then. While Father Ambrose stood at the front of a morning class, teaching the clever senior boys mathematics with a clarity they admired yet found intimidating, she sat in a wooden chair in his office. A row of folders along the wall faced him when he worked at the dark polished desk, a heavy slab of nineteenth-century furniture from a disestablished German mission fifty miles away. She arranged a call to London first, unsure of the exact time, but finding her professor on the point of leaving for a grandson's birthday party. Leonard was cordial, he understood quickly what she explained to him, he did not question the decision she had taken. He told her, 'As if there is any choice.' He would get in touch at once with his Italian friend. 'They are more imaginative in dealing with the unexpected,' he said. Lisa easily imagined his quiet smile as he wryly avoided other words for the strings that would be pulled, the possible favours to be returned, the network of possibilities as a suitable institution was sought. Of course, he assured her. He would be in touch at once with what he called 'my contacts'. And with another word that seemed so appropriate to him, proposed a week's time, that would be sufficient for what they planned between them, their 'co-ordinates'.

She was moved, holding the black heavy telephone in her sweating hand, by how her friend and teacher so immediately accepted what she asked of him, his agreeing without questioning her in detail. Her story must have sounded absurd—to smuggle a boy without papers into another country, breaking immigration laws, risking prosecution, a thought that came to her only as she spoke, and listened to the precise voice answering her from the room she imagined so clearly, the faded Persian rugs on the polished floor, the old-fashioned bookshelves with broad wire meshing, the small Chagall, an animal's blue head with a small inverted figure drifting in its mirroring eye, that he had showed her with such pride. A handicapped boy, she said. A child who would be at great risk, and Leonard telling her further details could wait, for the moment. His assuring her, 'I do,' when she said, 'You must take so much on trust.' Then the dead tone of the disconnected line.

Her next call was the more difficult. She was glad it would be late at night, that it was the answering machine she would speak to in her brother's office. The dark slice as it would be at this hour, the wedge of harbour between the dull concrete sides of the commercial blocks he looked out on. The room where they had argued together last time she was back. But now, the easier part first. To transfer money at once to her bank in Gloucester Road. She would explain all that to him later, as she paid it back. Perhaps for three months. 'So much up in the air,' she said, 'quite a few things to be sorted out.' She knew David would do this for her at once. He did not need details. A sister who was sensible at least in things like this, to do with money, unlike wives who had no more conception than a child of how it must be worked for, how it might strike them as a boring thing to observe, as a tiresome reminder, but money, no, even though you are a wife, it does not grow on trees. Scraps of his confiding curiously coming to mind even as she left her message for him. Then she needed to ring back, when the recording loop came to an end. The hardest part, not because it would puzzle him, but because what she asked would hurt him even more than anger him. He would think she had not been straight with him. She asked would he walk the hundred or so yards in the Crescent, from the home where their father now lived alone, to the Costellos' plain brick state house. He must ask Fergus's parents how he might get in touch with him, urgently. An address, a telephone, whatever. Tell them what story he liked, she said. She realised how much it was, to ask her brother to do this. But she must know. She would explain another time. You must do this for me, David. A life may depend on it. There is nothing I have done so important as this.

The phrase which her niece would hear in twenty years' time when she talked with the prematurely aged and agitated man Esther's father loathed and yet encouraged her to visit, whom she sat with beneath a scab-trunked plane tree in a wire-enclosed garden, the harbour on that first visit blue as cobalt in the distance. Sat flattering him, drawing his story. His telling the young woman on the institutional bench facing him, whose similarity to the woman he spoke of both placated and disturbed. That is exactly, he will tell her several times, exactly what she fucking said, what I fucking fell for. *There was nothing she had done so important as this.*

2001

———

He tells her again, he doesn't give a monkey's stuff for why she is there, why she wants to know, if it's sentiment she's hoping for she can forget it now. You won't get him playing that line, girl, when you've seen as much of the fucking world as he has.

Esther holds his eye, letting him know she is no more offended by what he says or how he says it than she is intimidated by his age, his illness, the bully she guesses is there in the petulant and decaying man sitting opposite her, his hunching forward in his chair, one hand clasping tightly on each knee. Epi the Tongan security guard walks up and down on the path outside the visitor's lounge they sit in, snooping, that's what they're paid to do, the man tells her, he has to put up with that every fucking hour of the day. She'll have to wear it too for the time she's there. If she doesn't know what pissed off is like then hang round here for a bit. She smiles at him. She knows he is desperate for her to listen to him. He might dismiss her but he wants that too. He wants to talk. Wants that most of all.

She turns on the tape recorder. 'It wasn't posh,' she prompts him. The last words from the week before. To take him back to that. He does not answer but looks at her. Fascinated as she knows he is by how similar she looks. To what her aunt must have been at the same age as herself. The deceptive petite demureness. The iron you might as well call it beneath the looks. The head of tight black curls. A way of looking so you felt you were held in place by it. You can look at someone so they're the fly and amber settles round them, he had told her that, so far back. Before Athens even. Hard as rock when it suited her.

'We don't need to go on,' Esther says. She knows the conditions she is under, the supervisor telling her, remember it is always up to him if he wants to talk with you. If he wants to call it off. She knows she is there under sufferance, you could call it that. Only because her professor had cleared it along the line. Only because the old man agreed. 'We can stop any time you like.'

'Who's talking of stopping?' The flattery, she had to play on that. His wanting her to attend even if his swerves of mood turn against his keeping on. 'I'd be disappointed but of course it is up to you. Up to you, Fergus. It always is.'

So he starts again. It wasn't posh, he says, the London he went to and hawked himself round as a teacher, supply teaching they called it, shoving you in front of animals who'd rather eat a book or even defecate on it, anything but read one. But after Corinth it was a breeze. There's no prick he tells her who'll fleece you like a Greek will, months of picking their fucking oranges, lying like the bastards they were when it came to pay. Then Turkey would you believe it writing ads for travel magazines, for desperadoes who'd make a Greek look honest, no wonder people want to kill them. 'The way I wrote about those shithole resorts of theirs you'd think I was Lawrence Durrell. I made them sound like paradise.' She had picked that up already, how proud he was of what he wrote.

'Yes,' she would tell him. 'When you talk about those places I can see them.' Shameless, but it drew him out. Bait, how the word came back to her. But he talked, and that was what she wanted of him. Her own deceit did not come into it. So a year after she had left him, he said— it was always 'she' he spoke of, as if Lisa's name tasted bitter to him. A year to the day in fact since she had shot through and he was there in London. That's how time goes. Notting Hill in those days was black enough to think you were in another country they'd called England by mistake. Lefties of course loved them. If there was one woman I knew in those days must have been half a dozen, couldn't get themselves a black length quick enough. Then another year I might as well have been Epi out there the way he watches us, me walking up and down classroom aisles at a school in Kilburn Park, every second one of them a mick I can tell you that, their old men truckies and their mums scrubbing offices so there's no one there when the kids get out of bed to make my day. I wasn't a teacher, I was a fucking warder.

He laughs as he thinks of it, kids with their flick knives brought back from pilgrimages to Lourdes, the side stories there was no point trying to bring him back from, Esther thinks, you just wait until he starts again on what you want to hear. The story she will never get from anyone else and maybe not from him but tries to find a way to, the researcher who convinces him he is the one, the only one, to tell it. Sympathy like the great lie it is. Her knowing he wants to look at her as well, although there's no ill intent in that. Mad more than bad, her grandfather says, not that David will hear a word of that. The stories he thinks make him cut a figure, the saddest bits. The Latvian woman he'd shacked up with for a while, her dreaming of Riga like a retard schoolgirl dreaming of being a pop star, no more chance of her getting where she had never been but accepted was paradise because her parents told her Latvia means 'to believe'. Half the women he ever met, anything rather than facing fucking life the way it is. The Scottish woman after her. A Latin teacher who had been a novice in a convent when she fell for a carpenter brought in to build hencoops. Her first experience of sex on the cleared floor in the back of his van with a hundred chooks clucking and shitting a few feet beneath them. The tradesman's legs so long the van's back door wouldn't close. The woman Fergus said had told him that as they themselves made love on the floor in her Streatham flat, after she had made him an omelette. He wanted Esther to think him entertaining. No idea of his grotesqueness. A man more sinned against than sinning, she must know that? Even if he said it about himself. She must know the quote.

Esther breaking in, 'But you still wrote to her? After Athens?'

'We didn't hate each other. Just because she left.'

'Of course you didn't.'

'She still mattered.'

'Of course she did,' Esther says. She knows early on that placating, flattery, will be part of what he demands.

'Of course she fucking did. That's what I'm saying.'

214

He would send a card a couple of times a year. She sometimes sent one back. He knew she'd feel obliged to. 'That was us all over. Everything I did was impulse and on the spur. Everything from her was calculation.' His old man's self-regard. 'She hadn't lost interest just because she'd left.'

'Italy, though,' the young woman says. 'Can we move on to Italy?'

If that's what you're waiting for, he thinks, I'll give you fucking Italy. He undoes the button of his shirt cuff, folding it back to scratch at the patch of raw skin that bothers him. 'Paper. At this age we're made of paper.' The skin had begun to bleed. He dabs at it with a handkerchief. Pleased even with that, she guesses. Something more to make one attend. Then the frankness he hopes will shock her, set the young bitch back a bit at any rate. Because of a man, he said, that's why I was there in the first place. Another story but one she needs to know. A soft pampered Italian who admired him and he knew would serve a turn. 'He thought it friendship but now we're talking together, Esther, we can call things their right names. We both did all right out of it.'

He looks out from the window, across the sloping lawns of 'the Home'. How it amuses him as he calls it that. *Te Hokinga Mai*. As full of shit as we are, he tells her. But back now to what he wants to talk of as much as she is obliged to hear. Years of that teaching racket. And what's the one step you can go down to from teaching? he asks her. I'll tell you what it is. Journalism. The sort of stuff I did that they call journalism at any rate. Local news, police reports in Scarborough, social notes in a twice-weekly Tory rag in Surrey. But never church news. Never dog shows. He never sank so low as that. A quid, though, he will tell her this, a quid for every pub he stood in long enough to be asked to leave and he could buy this place twice over and afford to burn it down. Chess clubs. He didn't mind chess clubs. Nor school prizegivings. Must have touched the soft side of him. And on one big break, working for a sod of an editor in Hastings, would you believe it, he covered the Queen? 'There's a phrase to make the heart beat faster.'

Esther looks from the big window to the workman seated on a mower near the distant trees. The old man at his inflamed forearm, his intense blue eyes watching her, the curious impression they give of still being young, their body too old for them. Fascinating even, she thinks, an absurd word and yet a just one, for her sitting here with her pad, her tape recorder, paying him the regard he craved, in this yellow room with its bright red couches. Her waiting for a disturbed 'patient', as the language of the institution insisted he be called, to indulge her, indulge himself, with the story she must listen to 'objectively'. The lie of that as well. Her Honours paper required an interview as a 'case study' and he had jumped at it when she wrote to him. Up front and honest and saying who she was and she knew the man the public read of years back when the story was news was not the man she felt he truly was. Everything would be in confidence and she signed a form to say she would publish nothing he did not approve of, but the privilege too should he agree. She said she knew of her aunt's affection for him. She knew of their time in Greece, years before she herself was even born. She so wanted the end of the story as only he would know it. Her thinking again, not proud of herself yet realistic, When he looks at me, he will want to talk. He will not be able to resist it.

Fergus coming back to his Italian friend. 'At least places I saw with him I'd not have seen by myself. Berlin. Prague. I drove and he sat beside me. He was devoted to me. He cried at operas and called me an ingrate when I once said I should look for work. So I stayed and travelled with him and refused to admit even as I thought it that I was a cross between a gigolo and an indentured serf.' Esther picking up the satisfaction as he demeaned himself. From time to time they would return for several weeks to stay high up among the rich houses, the secluded properties, above Genoa. He said he had tried to write but what might she expect, the shit of someone who pretended to more talent than he had? 'But the notebooks I used had *prendere nota di vita* written on them so that at least was literary.'

They stayed up there in La Fonte Clara as it was grandly called, huge and ugly and as you drove towards it, the building like a rotten old tooth you saw through trees. Alfonso's mother was English and wore wispy chiffon scarves and flirted in her geriatric way and hated and loved her flaccid son in pretty much equal proportions. She went to bed incoherent after the long summer dinners that were made and served by a graceless woman with a cloudy eye, it was as if Hammer Films had made a movie about high bourgeois decay. While she and her son bickered and again made up, until her head drooped and at times Alfonso would lean forward and say *Scusi, mamma* and take the cigarette from her fingers before they burned. She would tease her son about not being a real man and he would place his hand in his friend's, and there were occasions when they sat there quietly and the swallows dipped and cavorted only feet away, and the evening drew back, and Fergus held the hands of mother and son to either side of him. A mosaic of perfect boredom. When the old lady went to bed they would go into a spacious room referred to as the library in honour of the two glass-fronted cases of mostly English detective stories no one read, Edmund Crispin and Edgar Wallace and Dorothy L. Sayers, and older soft-covered French novels with deckled edges whose authors' names meant nothing. A yellow kayak lay along one wall. One night as they sat there and Alfonso sighing like an emperor among his ruins, Fergus felt a flake fall on his wrist from the dim painted ceiling, from its gambolling shepherds, its maidens trailing ribbons, high kitsch from another time. 'If you're looking for symbols,' telling Esther, 'then I'm your man.'

He wanted her to know the enchantment of it. Hate her to miss out on that. Alfonso telling him at times, half-pissed and easily moved, aristocratic and vain, how he envied his young friend, a mind unhampered by anything but what it sees, that history left unmarred. A mind pure and simple. Then one morning Alfonso tapped at his door. (Mamma at least alert to what rooms people woke in.) He wore a powder-blue robe he had taken years ago from a hotel in Cairo. He said his mother could no longer extend the hospitality she had until now been so pleased to offer him, and that he himself, as an only child, in deference to her years and her ailments, regretted but must accept her wish. 'He bloody talked like that. Christ knows how that particular family story ended but it could hardly be a good one.' But that morning, Fergus said. The gown his friend wore swinging loose as he stood beside the bed with his apologetic news. Fergus raised his hand and put it on his friend and sucked him off by way of *arrivederci*. It was the least he could do.

218

Etsi ketsi, he said now. That's what they say in Greece. It means *so it goes*. Fuck all you can do about it. And so it was back to earning a living and the train to Rome. Something generally turns up. You have to believe that. His saying so almost as if this was advice he was offering the young woman who watched and listened to him, rather than a credo he had lived by. But that is enough, he now bluntly decides. If she thinks he is going to wear himself out rattling on for her sake she can think again. The next bit is too big to start on anyway. Next week, if he is up to it. The bit he knows she is waiting for. As if he can't see through that.

He has shaved, and wears a tie he may have borrowed, sprinkled with what looks like army insignia and badges. He nods rather than speaks, and sits with his fingers laced on his knees, while she adjusts the machine that will hold his story for her to go over and hear again, would want to hear again, or why want to capture it? But his unexpected calm is soon enough dispelled. His first words when Esther nods at him that they are set to go, 'Carol Sheridan then, Jesus!'

The past as if rising like reflux from his stomach, tasted in his mouth, the funnelling together of his jokes, the fear behind their bravado, even the tennis club, those years again at West End Road. Carol back then and as much as when he sees her again, her glamour, her blazing hair, as if as the Stoddarts said she was a barn on fire, she'd singe your arse a hundred yards off. The way she'd stare back at you, certain of herself as stone. You said hello and looked at her, a minute later sport, if you weren't cut down to size then there was no size to begin with. As if this pale slip

219

of a girl he spoke to would have an inkling, how fucking could she, but he'd tell for all that. That slow curve of Carol's mouth that was not a smile and not contempt any more than any other word would serve for it, although the image was there perfectly in Athens, he remembered that, in the big museum, those huge carved figures from before the beginning, before the later sculptors smoothed things out and made bodies look like the rest of us, give or take, figures with one leg stepping out from whatever past it was they had but did not let on, their hands held as fists beside them, male and yet oddly not male too, an excitement in that even. But their lips, that was the thing. Broad and beginning *just* to smile, yet the curve there too of indifference, cruelty if there had to be, a distance you would never cross. Esther thinking he must have loved her to talk like this. But the shock of it as he guesses at what is in her mind, and disabuses her. 'I fucking hated her.' His laugh then as he puts her right. His so apparent satisfaction that he disgusts her.

Then the rambling account begins of Carol before that, before they met up by chance. Esther had picked up some of it from her father, and more from Stephen on those weekends when she stayed with him out at the bach, as they walked at that time of day he loved when the tide drew back and the wet sand stretched out shining as a dance floor. Carol whose havoc placid Westmere so remembered her for. David's contempt as details came back to him, but her grandfather trying to speak of her without rancour. Some people are born wild, he said, you cannot change that. And Fergus now traversing it again, the running off with Mr Taylor when she was eighteen, the chaos trailing behind her, so Esther thinks randomly of those scenes

220

you see in movies, an invader running through wheat fields with a burning flare, a city torched for the fun of it. The reckless and bizarre comedy of it too, the way the elopers were sprung by a woman from Richmond Road spotting as her holiday photos were developed back home the figures she hadn't picked up at the time in the crush and clamour of the leather market in Florence, Mr Taylor there, middle-aged, grinning among the hanging racks of handbags, the girl who had babysat the young Taylors for years, looking up to him as she stroked the bronze nose of the famous touristy pig. But that was years back. Years.

Fergus off again on his own tack. The dreariness of before that, he is telling her, before fate hurling him and Carol together and everything changing forever. After those easy months with Alfonso and then straight into working for this shithouse paper in Rome, an English-language giveaway for foreigners to pick up in railway stations, in the lobbies of hotels, in budget restaurants that took out advertising. The inane fatuous stories he wrote to keep the Roman wolf from the door. It would have been gutter journalism if the paper's sights had been higher. His self-contempt taking off as he speaks of it, of the scum-arse editor, the innate Italian genius for making a balls-up of anything they touch. Read Italian history half an hour, he challenges her, find me five years, five *months*, since Julius Caesar the arsehole, they didn't make a hash of?

She reins him back. 'But meeting her?'

For the moment he has simmered down. He tells her, a routine assignment for the crap he was underpaid to churn out for them. That's the scenario. To travel with a coachload of dyed-in-the-wool Australian pilgrims, a mob not content to gnaw on what Rome could throw at them, the cathedrals and catacombs and human remains galore in their vaults and boxes, as if that's not enough and now this drive to Castel Gandolfo, an indulgence was it for gawping at where il Papa takes his collar off for the summer break, stretches out in the sun for all we know about it behind the walls, martinis from Mary Magdalen at the end of the day? So he's in this smart hotel with his well-heeled Aussies, accountants from Hobart, Canberra civil servants, the missus in tow with most of them. The odd widow on the prowl. Not that they didn't slop the house bar until the small hours, don't think that. The tour leader was a famous tennis player so everything they could dream of, the inside story on the Australian Open and incense thrown in as a package deal. His brief was to spend two days with them and write it up, and another feature on the town itself, on Lake Albina, the usual tourist shite, the rowing course for the Rome Olympics, who the hell cares—who even remembers that far back? The first night he's there he drinks himself to floor level with a dwarf Neapolitan who works at the summer residence. He laughs thinking of it. 'One of my scoops. That's how I angle it. The inside story as an outsider invents it.'

Then the next evening there she is, across the marble lobby with its tricksy mirrors, her hair scorching the whole place, reflected over and over. Skin that startling white you don't see that much of over there. Anywhere. Tits there should be a blast of trumpets for. All that dirty kid talk from West End just flooding back, Fergus says, I have to remind myself I'm grown up. I even think there for a moment how Lisa would have laughed at it, we used to joke about her. About the Sheridan sisters. Back home. Then Athens. Never mind all that. Carol had come up to him as if it was only days since they'd talked at the bus stop as now and again they did, not much, but sometimes they had. Everyone had wanted to. Just to be seen talking with her. So there was that between them right away. Everyone else so suddenly strangers and remote, you know that way when you meet someone from home? That was the trouble. The appeal. They saw through each other for what they were. Carol said she had come in for a friend of hers, an interpreter who had taken ill, so she was filling in with the Aussies. Quick to tell him she didn't do this sort of thing for a living, she didn't want him thinking that. Pouting her lips to show what she thought of all this, the hotel, the tourists' voices. Her leaning towards him, confiding. 'Things we do for a crust,' Fergus had said. Or don't do, she came back at him.

Like that then from the start. Bullshit, but my God was it well cooked. They sit up late in the bar after her charges, and his copy, have gone to bed. She says she has an Italian boyfriend, an older man. She at once revises that, a sort of boyfriend. A man who likes to look after her and she works for his business. She seems eager to let him know. She knows about importing and transport and Franco, that's her good friend's name, even has government contracts, food deliveries from other countries, trucks at times as far as Russia. His big warehouse, his *capannone*, out at Monterondo in the shit industrial zone with other haulage depots, twelve miles from the centre but near the Tiber still, if you think polluted rivers give a touch of glamour. This and that on the side. Under the radar, she says. She pulls down one lower eyelid with her forefinger, making him laugh at it, the game they play together, his too talking up the kind of writing he does. Sitting up there at the bar on tall black stools. While he talks she watches him, her lips in that faint curve.

They order another glass. 'The pilgrims' tab'll pick it up.' She wants him to know she is at home here. She notes his own Italian isn't up to much. She is talking again about her work. About his too, in a way. It's a fine line, she is saying. She means between what people back home would solemnly call above board, between that and knowing life here is 'a little more flexible'. Fergus likes it that she uses the phrase. As if, he says. As if he hasn't picked that much up.

Amazing, how quickly they felt at ease. He knew they were showing off, tilting their lives so the light would slip across them as kids at school turned their shiny rulers to skid reflections till they were whacked for it. A game they were good at. He supposed she had done it a hundred times, a thousand, since she was back there knowing the boys on the bus were unaware of anything but her, her laughing at innuendo, her throwing glamour at each as though for *him*. As Fergus knows now she must have liked him, the ease as the evening went on, their performance together. *Christ, are we a team!*

Their affair began from there, in their fabrications about the past, their exaggerations, their seeing each other for what they were, one mirror to the other. Weeks later Carol said, of the way they'd taken to each other, 'It's like wearing clothes when we're naked, running round starkers when we're dressed.' Laughing at the sheer extravagance of it, yet how it rang like truth. You had to lie to get to bedrock. And that *frisson* when each knew the other was speaking the same, her secretive smile, her hair as he ran his hand across it, her raised eyebrow in cine noir coolness as she quizzes him, 'No shit, Sherlock?'

The play acting, he will tell this younger woman, Lisa's dead spit as he thinks of Esther decades further on. Their exciting each other, he and Carol, with the fact of this is how we are, but not exactly. Fergus with his quick bland images that amused her, the sex lit between them like a bonfire in a paddock, he tells her, his constant talking through their love-making, Carol's rapid coarse commands.

The months then that followed their meeting in the town where, as his article had put it, 'even pontiffs earn their spell of R and R'. They spent every hour together they could wangle from the assignments Fergus worked on for the readers he despised, Carol away from co-ordinating timetables and routes in the office above the big yard where the trucks pulled in after turning from the ring road, her efficiency in moving the coloured magnets about on the wall maps of where the shipments moved, the cargoes were delivered. Franco was proud of her. The drivers liked the amusing foreign woman in her black skirts that swung like a bell and the tight pale sweaters she wore with them because she knew men didn't mind being given instructions, filling in schedules and flowcharts, if it was for someone like that, a woman who could banter back and match them if a bit of spice was called for. *Mio tesoro*, no wonder Franco called her that, telling her their being lovers was everything to him and more than that, she stroked his very soul. He joined the tips of his fingers and kissed them when his foreman Ricardo said, 'She is a wonder, Franco, what she does for you. For the business. For those who see her.'

Ricardo who was Franco's uncle and loved the truckyard and the warehouse and the offices above the loading docks as he would have loved the family he had not got round to having. One damned thing, he would say, there is one damned thing and then another, and you get to where I am now, an old man who is still young. Before he worked for Franco he had been for twenty years the chauffeur for politicians, he knew what he called 'the moving world', the connections, the levers, a man in this line of work must know. He meant the intricate connections and conflicting interests, the numbers to call, the men to avoid, in this universe of camions and long-haul vehicles, the web of a thousand strands that ran the length of Italy, that linked with Spain and African ports and as far as the Ukraine. You sit at this desk, Ricardo said, and you feel it. He was Franco's man to ask favours from, who handled the delicate placement of *tangenti*, that word which crude translations, 'bribe' or '*pot-de-vin*' or 'graft', did such injustice to. For Ricardo would also say, to the few he might trust, that Franco his nephew was a good and straightforward man who asked no more than to be judged by his girlfriend's tits, but leave the business side of things to him. He told Carol she was indispensable to both of them. 'Success is using the gifts God bestows on us,' Fergus tells her. She touches his leg beside her as she drives him back to Trastevere. *We are so alike.*

Carol turns from a busy road into a dull street of post-war flats. Not your tourist Roma by a long shot. She pulls into a strictly no-stopping zone fifty yards from the building he will walk to when she leaves.

'She puts up with your nights being somewhere else?'

'As if she has the choice.' It is not as though commitment has ever been raised. He is the woman's boarder, the rent a little less than if he kept to his own room, but there is no deceit about it. If there was no understanding how could there be? He says simply, 'We needn't think of that.' Think of Angela with her dry-cleaning shop beneath the flat, a handsome good-natured woman too young to fear death which is not a problem but her anxiety at signs of age, her angling the bathroom's magnifying mirror to catch the first etchings of time at the corner of her mouth, the spoke-lines from her eyes. And the unspoken question which she supposes is natural enough, should she lose this kindly enough stranger, whose work so demands his time away, might there be another with the same care for her? Her daughter who hugs her and assures her, But Mamma you are younger than any mothers who come to school! As if a child knows how to look at other mothers! In one of his notebooks Fergus had begun to write a story about her.

He and Carol sit in the car. Neither wants to leave. But Franco has a dinner tonight with other business friends where she will be an ornament. Thank Christ there is a family across on the other side of the city so calls like this on her are few enough. Business trips, she jokes, oddly that's when Franco needs me most. Men can be such bastards, he jokes back to her. Why we ever get caught up with foreigners! A new sharpness in their playing with each other.

'Trying to make me feel bad?'

'Just feel at all.'

'Then we'd have nothing to share.'

Yet no more than momentary, these quick jabs. Part surely of why they so get on. Who ever said love wasn't given a nudge by the occasional sharp edge? That too becoming a joke between them. Feed me another haunch between the bars. The zoo, they had begun to call it. Her bedroom. The bed they shared several times a week. Franco part of the menagerie, but held fortunately on his family leash. No one gets their own way all the time. Fergus likes to hear her run through them, 'the other cages', he says. The Spaniard he likes, especially, that was years back but never mind, the motor mechanic for Formula One who spoke marvellous things in rotten English, who said her snatch was Compostela, men walked barefoot for weeks just to arrive. The lovers, the places, as she too asks him, tell me more about Alfonso? About the one who was a nun? Only once she teases him about his 'missionary'. Her sister had mentioned it in a letter, the woman in the bakery telling Mum about it, the weirdest thing, all that study to be a doctor then haring off to Africa! The swotty girl from the chemist shop he couldn't see past in those days back then, pedalling his bike round with her father's name on it, wasn't she a Jew as well? Did that make so much difference?

'You've been in Italy too long,' he accuses her.

Carol quickly dropping to the fact that this was out of bounds. *Verboten?* she said, running her finger along his cheek. Leaving Lisa there until he was the one to mention her. As he did, but not for months. The timing strange, she thought. Early July, which can be so lovely. One of their rare quiet days together, a Sunday, when they played at tourists. They walked to a museum she had been to once, the week she first arrived, that's how far back, but something there she would like to see again. That mad compelling woman turning into a tree, even her fingers in the first delicate thrusts to another life, her marvellous body turned and writing into the bark she longed to become. To escape into. Carol unsure why the grotesque yet beautiful thing so held her.

Fergus stood beside her, a little bored, she guessed, with these rooms of canvases and plinths. Her asking him, as if matter-of-factly and his seeming to accept it as that as well, 'What do you think will happen? Once we're burned up?' Something was it in the strangeness of the room, the fact they were speaking in lowered voices, although no one else was there? A guided party had moved through, moved on, in a flicker of cameras, an urging from the woman who led them, tapping at her watch. The sense of being alone in a way that was seldom theirs. Fergus saying, 'We'll be the same as months ago, before we met.' Not sure quite of why he said it, of what he meant. Carol smiling at him, the expression he was used to. 'The born romantic,' she told him.

In the park outside she took his arm. They walked towards a man selling gelati from a wheeled cart like a big fringed pram. People sat on the benches, others walked the paths diverging from the main walkway, called out to children and laughed together, or ambled in silent couples. 'I can't get enough of it, can you? The *glut* of things.' Saying the word so her mouth sounded crammed with it. And it's then he tells her, as if it is an ordinary thing he speaks of, no great deal. He says he has heard from her. A letter. He will show it to her. Saving a child, that was the gist of it. Luckily, the kind of thing they could help with. He told her the little Lisa had passed on. Carol laughed, 'Is that all?' And then, 'Franco will like the joke of it. It's not gun-running but it could be fun. Helping out the Church.'

It was several days, and then more than a week, as the chance to see each other eluded them. It was the beginning of high season for the tourists. Fergus's editor had plans for a special supplement, extra advertising, an arty piece on

Keats, a discreet guide to porno cinemas, a schedule of opening times for the catacombs. He had two weeks to get the whole thing together. His boss sitting there with proofs streamered out from his desk, his green eyeshade as if he thought he was editing *La Stampa,* his ridiculous belief he carried a torch for the free press. Fergus angry at it again as he thinks of it, this much later, telling the girl there with her bloody machine listening in on them that if there's one thing they can do, those Italianos, it's exploit a foreigner. Fucking brilliant at it. He had sat there in the office space you wouldn't keep a dog in, slaving over his Brother portable, wonder the prick of a thing didn't melt. Then Carol away in Volterra, don't ask him where Volterra was, but Franco chose places where he could give *la famiglia* the slip. And so devoted to her, Carol said, he might as well have worn a blindfold.

He had met Fergus and liked him. He bought the story that he was Carol's cousin from the same town, it amused him to hear them talk about the people there they knew, the past they shared together. That he knew treasure when he saw it, pointing to the signed Number 10 Azzurri shirt framed above Franco's desk, even knowing the name, the year. He liked it too that her friend was literary and a journalist, you had to remember further back than they could go, he said, to appreciate how freedom of expression was what civilised values were built on. Not that he personally had time to read. *Amico,* Franco liked to call him when they met up, it is important that someone does our reading for us. Then at the town where Franco said he would buy Carol alabaster but her skin was too pure for it, and settled for a red gem that she wore back to Rome burning at her throat, they had stood on a high wall and

Franco out of the blue checked with her, 'So it is planned, once she is here? That friend of Fergus we are helping?'

'We just pick her up and take her there. To where she is going. Take two people there. And then come back.'

'As quick as that?'

'A hospital. An institution. San Spirito. Not even a hundred ks.'

As she knew he would be, Franco amused at that, the idea of illegal 'cargo', the Church in it up to their soutane sleeves. But his saying sharply, when Carol supposed Ricardo would help her with the details, '*I* will help you. The van. The route. We shall plan all that together. Such things take care.' As he early on had said to her, not with vanity so much as a simple assuring fact, 'You would not believe it, how many men like to say if someone speaks of me, You know Franco? *That* Franco? He is the one to get things done.'

Then in the last weeks before the rendezvous Carol and Fergus seemed to speak of little else. Although without apparent fuss, Franco took care of things in his office above the yard. As though no more than some routine consignment. They would take a van with tinted windows, they would act like friends driving about as tourists, they would be meticulous in the last part of the event, that most of all: to meet the truck driven up from the port at Bari that would have dropped off its apparent cargo earlier that day, and then on to where they would meet. To do such things discreetly, one of Franco's favourite words. The day they left he would tell them exactly. The meeting point. All that in good time. He has all that in hand. You must book somewhere close enough, he told Carol, so there is not far to drive next day. At least that he could leave to her.

They played it up to each other, 'the rescue'. Nine years, Fergus said, yes, nine years since he had seen her. The smart of it still there, her walking out on him from the tiny flat in Ravini Street. The trailing green tendrils from the plants on the balcony above, the splashing down on the barred window when the woman up there watered them. Moments coming back to him of such immediacy it hurt to think of them. The mistake now of trying to speak of it. Probity, he said, you had to use a word like that when you thought of her. Not that he ever had for anyone else. And yet a gift for wildness in her too, an iron recklessness once she made up her mind. Like when they had taken off for Greece, back then. The way she told her father as frankly, as calmly, as if they were going to Ruapehu for the weekend. The amazement too, looking back on it, that her family seemingly had taken it as calmly as they were informed. From the little she had told him of it anyway. She wasn't one to rattle on.

'Smitten,' Carol said, a shade from mocking him.

'Not as simple as that,' he said. 'Just knocked me when she left me.'

'Black condoms for a year in mourning after that then, was it?'

His quick anger at her shallowness, but he left it there, and Carol unbuttoning his shirt, commanding him, 'Lighten up!'

Next day as she leafed through a file of manifests a call came through and Franco, at his desk a few feet from hers, spoke quickly in dialect, losing her completely. 'How was I supposed to follow that?' Teasing him, as she knew he liked. 'Was that a woman?'

'These Southerners,' he said, hunching his shoulders,

spreading his hands. Mocking her a little, she knew that. He said, 'Remember these. Don't write them down.' He gave her the time, the name to look for on the truck, the fact there was other cargo as well. Cover one delivery with another, there was nothing unusual in that. The quick throb of excitement now it was next thing to here. The Rescue. This as well as the rest of it. She said to Fergus later in the day, 'I'll be with Franco tonight. His mother-in-law has taken ill so his wife's away. That's the way it is.' But Fergus too on edge now everything was in place. He surprised his landlady by asking would she like to have dinner at the *trattoria* along from the dry-cleaners. Angela kissed his cheek, wore the new navy top she had been saving, told her twelve-year-old to get on with her homework, she would know if she touched the television. Anything, Fergus thought, to take his mind off what was almost here. More troubling than he had expected, the thought of what it would be like. To see her. The condescension she would no doubt have for Carol, as she had back then, at the tennis courts. So much still that wasn't clear. Whatever the story was, about the illegal native she hauled along with her. He is glad to be distracted. He amuses Angela with the stories he tells her. It is weeks since he has taken her out like this. And when she asks him, is he happy though, is he content the way things are between them, he asks, Who can ever answer that, on a particular day, in a world like ours?

'It isn't so difficult,' Angela said. But writers like Fergus, she supposes, people who think more deeply about things, you cannot expect them to quite see things the way others of us do. She stretches out her hand to put it across his.

'Take it a day at a time,' he says. He sees the crinkling at the corner of her eyes. 'We can't do more than that.'

They set out towards Bari, leaving a day to spare. An afternoon's drive, had they gone directly, but Franco advised, 'Enjoy the travelling, there is so much on the way.' He told Fergus, There is more to this country than Rome, my friend. It is always beautiful, Carol added, even if driving through it can be hell. She knew the roads well, the pull-over areas, the likely trickier sections, where the traffic build-ups would be, the best stops for coffee. There was almost the feeling of holiday, of adventure, as the van drew out from the yard to the Via Salaria and headed for the autostrada. She switched on the radio and tapped the steering wheel as Lucio Battisti blared out his recent hit. Between the flow of pop songs the chatter was too fast, too laden with expressions he had never heard, for Fergus to pick up more than the name of the next number. He said, 'I'd rather just look out at what we're passing, do you mind?' Carol pressed the control, and for several minutes, through the silence, only the burr of the tyres on the road. She asked him to light a cigarette for her. Then, 'A law-abiding one, I mean.'

'As if there's the choice.'

She laughed that he had taken her half-seriously. 'Can you imagine foreigners like us pulled up with a joint by some small-town *poliziotti*?'

How she talked like that to impress him, even now, months after they took up—Carol who knew the ropes, was up on the street lingo, got her way with most things, she said, because she did her homework. As if quoting from a B-grade movie, which very likely she was. She had told him early on, 'It's rattlesnake country out there. You've got to draw fast.' They were on to that again now. Survivor tactics. Turn the other cheek in this world, she said, next thing you find you don't have one to turn. The nine-pin element, she liked to call it. Bowl before you're bowled. He wanted to tell her, Don't try so hard. I wouldn't use that even for the rag I'm underpaid to write for.

He liked this though, taking in the country sliding past. Franco was right. How little he had seen, apart from the big city, apart from the climb into the hills above Genoa, the haze that so often softened the stretch of coast. But all this was new to him, vivid and set out there as though waiting on a million cameras, many of the names spelled out on the signs they passed ones he had known since he was a kid, scraps from those memories of sitting at the kitchen table as a boy and his mother's sister from Australia handing round the photos, snaps that had her in tears, the grave of their brother dead in a place called Sangro. Not that they were anywhere near that now. But other names, strange how they lay like seeds inside you, blooming for the few minutes as you saw the places themselves far off against a hillside, across a flat stretch of land, then out of sight. Even Monte Cassino that he had heard of since he was a boy, the monastery he craned to look up to. He wondered at why we can be so touched by it. Drawing threads together as he was doing now, simply sitting here, the flowing hills, the towns, the bigger ones Carol took circuitous roads to avoid, the spread of farms and the ochre angular farmhouses, the nostalgia that rose in us for what was it, quite? The dullness of back there coming at him too, the placid yet smothering streets where he and Carol had lived within a stone's throw of each other, she especially so desperate to 'break out', as she put it, but to what, exactly? Was this it? Then for a long time they drove without speaking.

They stopped once for coffee, once to look at a famous church, huge against the small buildings surrounding it. Pictures and statues much as in any other they might have gone into. A dead man behind a pane of glass stuck there beneath an altar, a mask across his face, his hands brown and frail as leaves. At one point she told him the country round here was once famous for witches, he might have tasted Strega, had he, the liqueur made over here? Then an hour further on, Carol said, 'We'll stop soon. I've booked a place. Go over things.' The mood between them changed. Efficiency. Care. She was good at those. Somewhere in the middle of a town, she said, the more people there are the fewer who bother to take notice of you. And how much better than to pull in at one of the big areas where truckies parked, where drivers grabbed a rest at quick turnaround routiers, where there was the chance of someone recognising her, the woman who worked for Franco. Not that everything wasn't above board. But caution, there was no need to spell that out. Another lesson she said she had learned early on. Why ever make public what you have the chance to keep to yourself?

This sense now of on the verge. Carol's alertness, her own excitement as if crafting herself to something new, the adventure of discovering a fresh aspect of herself. Even to her telling him, soon after they had set out from the depot in Rome, that Franco always insisted that there was 'protection' when she drove, a gun in the glovebox in front of her, beneath the manuals, the maps. 'Decoration,' she joked to Fergus, 'but you better know it's there.' She joked she was glad to hear he wasn't frightened by it. It was routine. Like carrying a jack in the boot, a spanner for the wheel. They were back at games together. He knew

236

when they stopped and he took their two light overnight bags from the back seat that she had transferred it to her shoulder bag. He pretended not to notice, and so each kept up the adventure of it. The fun of blurring lines.

Carol had booked two rooms in a pink stucco hotel favoured by tourists who arrived by car, rather than the big coaches. Middle-aged people whose licence plates gave them away as mostly Spanish. The kinds of guests who liked to look at art and history during the day, and spend long late evenings in the dining room with its welcoming red and yellow flag and reproductions of paintings they would recognise. Not the kind of place Fergus would have expected her to choose. She surprised him again, having asked for separate rooms on different floors. As she told him now, Franco trusted her with his life, but if he should ever check, he would know he was right to trust her.

After dinner they sat, like a holiday couple themselves, in the hotel's lounge. They sipped at glasses of limoncello. Carol placed on the small table between them her opened book of maps for the region they were in. She knew the way all right, she said, she wasn't worried about that, but the pick-up was a place she needed to check on. Her finger touched first on the port and worked back to where the truck would leave the autostrada and turn towards the network of minor roads, towards the farm where they would meet. She had once been close enough to the rendezvous, back in her early months with Franco. That time though it was a delivery, 'medical stuff' for some bigwig in Africa, the kind of thing only the rich could afford and not a chance of getting hold of any other way. Sounds dubious, Carol said, but apparently it wasn't. 'In this line you're paid by someone because questions don't occur to you. One of the reasons Franco finds me irresistable.' But the joke falling flat. Better just to be quiet, Fergus thought. Does that not occur to her?

She came back to tomorrow's schedule. He realised how little she had really told him until now. As Franco would say, Whoever these people are, they know what they are doing. The long difficult name of a foreign haulage company along the vehicle's high side, local people were unlikely to remember it if they saw it on one of the smaller roads. The driver who had brought it across on the ferry would leave the truck at the port, another would get behind the wheel and drop off the official freight before driving through to the meeting point, the farmhouse discreetly deserted for the afternoon. The fewer people who saw each other, the simpler such things were done. Her fingernail tapped at a junction on the map. Then an hour's drive, at most, through to the hospital, the institution, whatever it was, to drop off what she called their consignment.

Fergus said, 'Her name's Lisa. The patient's name is Francis. They both have names.'

Carol smiled, ignored the reprimand. 'God folk, anyway. You can't ask for a better cover than that.'

And God knows, now he was brought into it, what it would be like. The thought keeping on at him. Seeing her again. Hearing her. The weirdness of it. But Carol breaking in, his having to ask her what was that, he was miles away, so she repeated, 'We should be back by evening. Back home.' She would drop him off first then get the van back to the depot. Franco would be waiting for her. She touched his hand. They could have the weekend together, though. 'Seems ages since we had one.'

'A fortnight.'

'That's what I said.' She closed the maps. The woman behind the bar came back to them. Carol smiled up at her, charming her, Fergus thought, as she can anyone when she sets her mind to it. 'How can we not have another?' The woman said it was made locally. And Carol, 'As if one couldn't tell?'

When the woman brought fresh glasses she and Fergus tapped them lightly together. 'These taste like that cough stuff my mother used to get from Mr Ross's. If I tell the truth.'

Two older couples came into the lounge. One woman carried a cat which she had brought with her from wherever home was. Again, Carol was back in Westmere. 'My mother was like that, anything rather than humans.' She liked watching the woman stroke the creature's back and dabble her fingers beneath its throat. 'I wouldn't mind one myself one day. Does that surprise you?'

Fergus raised his own glass, avoiding answering her.

Carol laughed. 'It surprises me.'

They met again at breakfast. Carol said she had been reading, it was so unusual to lie in bed awake, but she did not say what, and Fergus did not ask her. They sat at the same table as the evening before, now reset for breakfast, with its fresh white diagonal cloth. Through the window he watched the Spaniards loading their car, a family taking a photograph of themselves outside the hotel, a man kicking at a front tyre. As they walked to the van he and Carol shared a cigarette. It delayed needing to talk. Their van with its shaded windows that reflected like black mirrors was the single vehicle still in the yard.

Fergus noticed how she was dressed, as though wanting to seem subdued, conventional, in a dark business skirt,

239

a green high-throated blouse, dull housewife shoes. She had said to him once how in work like hers, with men to placate and deal with and give instructions to as she checked fuel consumption and toll charges, confirmed deliveries and timetables, approved or queried invoices and dockets, you wouldn't believe how a brassy touch did wonders. It had amused him, as it did her too, her using that word, *brassy*. The kind of thing his mother might have said quite seriously, Carol though sending herself up. Catch their eye, she had meant, lean towards them as you spoke, smile as you questioned. Top buttons of a blouse never done up. No, not cynical she had said, just a happier world all round. Fergus now struck again by her craft, her thinking of the day ahead. Her appearance of sober middle-class respectability, the kind of woman an enquirer might expect, should she tell them yes, she was driving friends to a religious home, where Doctor Bosco was expecting them. San Spirito, did they know it?

She arranged the inside of the car. The map in the door pocket beside Fergus, her replacing the gun beneath the papers. 'A Beretta. That's the name.'

'I know that at least,' Fergus came back to her.

'Sorry. Of course you do.' Then, Routine, she said again, simply part of Franco's insistence, his liking to tell her, 'It is not always nice out there, *cara*.'

Fergus made light of it. 'I was a dab hand with stuff like that in school cadets.' A lie he almost believed.

She stretched her arm through the lowered window to adjust the outside mirror, then tilted slightly the one above her to watch the road behind. 'Right,' she said, 'all in hand.' Fergus more anxious than he would admit even to himself. He too had woken before six, lying there in the strangely single bedroom, the print of a Madonna looking out at him from the further wall, the kind of look he supposed was meant to make you think of spiritual things. The cheeks, the woman's plump dimpled hands, in fact looked overfed. Going over what it would be like, why was it so hard to imagine that? What Lisa would say to him in a few hours' time, what he might say to her? The madness of it. Why telling her in the first place he would look after things at this end? Would meet her truck? Would take her to where she needed to be? Fucking simple, he had said to Carol, right back when he first heard from her.

'Anything for a laugh,' she had said. Fucking Carol Sheridan.

'I didn't know,' the old man saying, so much later, so much further on. His sleeve rolled back, worrying still at the eczema weals on his forearms. That girl there watching him like he's some kind of freak who will disappear if she takes her eyes from him. While Esther is thinking, He is almost there, God knows what it must be like for him, amazed that he agrees to talk of it at all. Yet knowing too he cannot stop himself, that she is the last rapt listener he will ever have. His knowing that.

She presses her hands together on the folder she holds, as if she is the one who is nervous at the story she knows and has known for years, the one her father is obsessed with, the one in the folder with its photocopies from Italian papers, the legal documents, the inaccuracies that came into the retellings of it in papers back home. The man draws his lower lip together between his forefinger and thumb, pressing until the wedge of wet flesh turns dark. Then his living it again, the van turning to a side road, and another smaller one again, the fine crooked line on the map he has on his knees that is the small almost waterless river the road rose across, then again flattened out. His admitting, although more in the voice of one speaking to himself than to anyone who might attend, 'Being so close, I was shit-scared after that.' His agitation as he now speaks of it, the quivering of one hand that he attempts to subdue with the other. For a moment she fears that his arm will sweep across the table and send her recorder flying, that the security man will rush in and sort things out. But Fergus himself knows the threat of that and even smiles as he draws himself together. 'You're getting me on a good day,' he says. 'I'm medicated up to here.' He taps his throat above his opened shirt. 'You'd better listen.'

'So we got there.' He is back now. Back beside Carol who is quiet and alert, hunched forward a little over the wheel. A car travelling fast as it approaches them, blasts its horn and swerves on the narrow road. A few minutes when nothing was said. Carol's eyes flick up to check the road behind, the dust now settled behind the vanished car. He does not quite comprehend what she means, as she says simply, 'The driver.' She means from the truck they are on their way to meet, although he will understand that only later. That the Polish driver has left his truck as instructed, he will return—that will be the plan—when the consignment has been transferred, the details he is better not to know.

The fields they are driving past are empty, the neat rows of a crop he cannot name. There is a single farmhouse coming up on their left, a large square ochre-coloured building well back from the road, a sloping slab of vines across a framework at one side. The charm of such places, that striking him, he remembers. Wondering what it would be like to live in a place like this. The same hankering to get out, he supposed, as you'd find any place else.

'Did you check in there?' Carol nods to the glove compartment. He tells her, 'I know where it is if I need to know.'

'Of course you do.'

Their speed now reduced. They hear the swish of a bush along the panels of the van. A blue tractor marks the driveway they wait for. The big truck then visible, at the far side of the house. Carol follows instructions she had not spelled out to him. She stops the van, walks the few paces to the tractor, runs her hand beneath the sacking covering its metal seat, returns with the keys she expected to find. She tells him one is for the cab of the truck. The other will open the less obviously noticed entry to the space between the driver's cab and the cavernous area for whatever its official load might be. A neatly crafted place to hide. To conceal. So many trucks these days had ones like that built in. No shortage of custom. He'd read that too. One in ten ever caught. Less than. The space with its false panelling where two or three humans might travel concealed for days and pay to be taken across borders, delivered as the contraband they were. Risky but what's the choice? Fergus assumes the girl he is talking to now must know all that, the details that came out in the hearings, the appeals, the legal tangles, before he was allowed back home. Being found crazy helped. The law his friend, can you imagine that? Twenty years back and immediate to him as he tells of it quickly, simply, now they are there. The van already placed to face the road, to move at speed as soon as. As soon as the day turns to something else. His voice surprising Esther with its almost gentle confiding.

243

The last minutes of his life before it fell apart.

Then the first thrust of something unexpected into what he had believed was so carefully planned. Like the sudden belt of something heavy against one. Like that, he says, this shove into a different world. Carol walks ahead of him but does not stop at the back of the truck where the big bolts have been slid across and the metal bars lifted, the courtesy he takes it of those who have helped them until now. Laddered steps lowered even, the great doors drawn back enough for the long slot of darkness from the depth inside. In his ignorance thinking it would be merely a matter of climbing the steps, entering the empty vault of the truck, finding the concealed apartment at the back. He smells the tang of something dry and pungent, the grain he supposes that must have been the official cargo dropped off before the vehicle came on to here. A distant meaty sweetness somewhere in it too. But Carol must have had her reasons for passing the partly opened doors and heading for the high gleaming front of the vehicle. He called to her but she gave no answer. He turns the towering corner of the truck to see her mounted at the metal steps to where a driver would take his place, the swinging out of the cab's heavy door beyond her. At that point, he says. The intensity now as he recalls it, the frantic scrabbling and agitation in the cab. He thinks for a fraction that she is fighting with someone who has been concealed, then sees her agitation, her turmoil, whatever word one used, is in herself, her dragging at papers from the leather pockets, wrenching back the doors of the small compartments behind the driver's seat, clawing from them whatever they contained, something in her hand then ripping at the leather coverings across the cab's metal frame. Her

244

leaning forward to find a lever was it, a catch of some kind, concealed beneath the dashboard? He had no idea of what she felt for until he hears the click, the released door he now saw opening above him from the side of the truck, not a door so much as a concealed fragment of wall there was no indication of from the vehicle's smooth outside. The fear and certainty that at that moment gripped him, the fact that he and Carol were now in different stories.

The phrase he used for it. 'In different stories.' The conviction he was now part of some overarching fraudulence, some lie too big for him to comprehend. At that instant the door swung fully open, its lower edge level with his head, so it seemed he looked into a room he entered at floor level as if from a trapdoor. The stench came at him more like a solid cloth pressed against his face than the mere impact of stalled air. The space he looked into for no more than seconds deeply shadowed, yet what he saw vivid and sustained as if the glare of lights exposed it to him. A quick column of bile rose in his throat, its force splashed back against him from the side of the truck he leaned towards. The body of a woman, her white blouse suddenly and grotesquely brilliant as the light moved on it, slumped across a dark leather couch. Her legs and feet were bare. Her head tilted forward so that all Fergus saw of it was the black tangle of her hair. Another body, darker, as small as her own, looked as though it slept on her lap. The quick pinpointed glint from the fixed opened eyes. And again the hauling of his guts as he looked to the confusion and mess on the floor of the tiny space, the torn plastic bags of food, the tipped and strewn bottles of water, the gaping haversack from which clothes and books and medical stuff had been pulled and tossed aside as though in some desperate search. Beside one of the dead woman's naked feet the glitter of a broken phial he did not for the moment take in for what it was.

And then the curtain. The red curtain Esther will hear him repeat, her not understanding at first that it is not reality out there he speaks of but is describing something in his mind. Knowing it was God, something that hated God, as if he gave a fuck he said what you wanted to call it, it was the red blinding hood that comes on a man when he is lifted further than he has ever been, what Homer means when he tells you of the insane possessing rage of battle. Like that, Fergus says, the ancient image as seemingly his own as the leap of spit from the side of his mouth as he recounts it now, as he listens to Carol through the narrow wall between the bodies and where she continues to ransack the truck's elevated and now ripped-at cab, that he and Carol are in different worlds—again his putting it like that. *There is something so much more important to her than us.* For that is all he was thinking, Fergus says. Lisa and myself. As if his saying it like that, saying *us*, made sense, yet under the red hood there was nothing else but rage at what had been defiled.

Carol has now jumped down from the cab. Not descended fully by the metal steps but thrown herself towards the ground, half-sprawled there, jerking herself back up, running her hands along and beneath the great silver fender and metal guards at the front of the truck. It so immediately obvious to him that Fergus hears his own raking burst of laughter, even that. He held the gun in his hand, unaware of having taken it from his jacket. As if at that moment it had become an actual part of his body, as natural to his hand as the thumb he ran along the butt warm from his pocket, and found the nub his finger craved.

Justice, you must remember that, as he will later explain to those who question him. The police. The psychologists. The *authorities*. The level certainty of his voice as he told them, 'My saving grace,' putting it as clearly, as perversely, as that. Not an excuse. You do not offer excuses for justice. He turns at the front of the truck to see her kneeling as if before some huge altar, both her hands now at whatever it is they seek beneath the curved shining metal strip. Her dark shirt has come loose and the whiteness of her skin shows where the cloth has rucked up against her back. The dark skirt covers her crouching so she is shaped like a bell. And then the weight of the gun so suddenly apparent to him as he raises his arm, as Carol flings back several feet from her crouching at the front of the truck. He sees the quick movement at the window on the upper floor of the farmhouse, the tilt of a rifle barrel, a black sleeve, and that is all. All too rapid to even think of as a blur. There and not there. Before and after and between. He looks at Carol, her skirt hauled back by her fall, immodest. The awful calm that descends on him. Then the stillness as big as the sky, the stretch of empty fields.

It not occurring to him that the figure at the window might have shot at him as well. His attention entirely on the woman lying in front of him, the dark stain spreading across the fabric of her blouse. For no reason he could later explain, and yet as obvious to him as the surge of satisfaction it carried with it, he fires twice into the dry earth beside her, 'the pointless malice' as the court would hear it described, and yet finally the telling plea as well for the insanity that drove him. A desecration, for the woman

247

already was dead. His second bullet smashed into the palm of Carol's outflung hand. One of the police who helped remove her two hours later said it was like a photo he had seen of Padre Pio with his stigmatist's bandage unwrapped. The same officer who gave the simple evidence of time and place and the anonymous phone call that directed them to the farmhouse, to the foreigner who had simply sat there at the table beneath the framework meshed with vines, who had taken a pot of purple flowers from the porch at the back door and set it at the entrance to the fetid space where the other woman and the African boy lay dead. After the injections she had given them. The morphine she carried for emergency. Her believing that with the truck delayed at the docks for several days at the North African port, in implacable and unbearable heat, they had been abandoned. But the foreigner had touched nothing, just set the clay pot near the woman's feet and gone and waited for the *Polizia* to arrive. Yes, the officer confirmed, the *straniero* leaning back against a post, his eyes closed even when spoken to, as if resting until the heat of the afternoon had passed. As if merely that.

2002

———

It was a fact of life, she one day will explain to Milan, that Stephen seemed the important one, the presence between her father and herself. 'As though he were as close to me as a father should be, and David the distant one, too far to understand.'

So her grandfather was the one who waited for her in the carpark the afternoon of her last interview with the frail, disturbed man. She had said to Stephen on the phone the night before, 'I don't know how I can face it, really. Tomorrow's session.' She would take the bus for once: she knew she would not want to drive. 'If you can meet me after? Can you do that for me?' And so he was there waiting for her, an old man with his new black-framed glasses and his white hair trimly cut, ten years younger perhaps to a stranger's eyes than to the family who knew his age. And yet still, at times, with the hesitancy almost of a boy, not certain that what he says will be the thing to say.

Yet so certain for her, Esther thinks. She cannot

remember a time when he was not there to say what needed to be said, as silent at those other times when there was little useful to be drawn from talk. When her mother had died and she was at boarding school and they had not lived with her father for nearly as long as she remembered. David, a father of holidays and sudden kindness and carefully punctual presents, yet his saying, back home after the funeral, 'You'll understand. This isn't a good time for us to live together *permanently.*' As though the emphasis somehow explained whatever it was he failed to say. 'Keep on at school and then there's the summer break. We can be together then or you can be at the beach with Stephen. You love it there. Just it's more than I can cope with right now. You must see that? My real marriage could not accommodate that.' How he always called it that—not my second or my next, but the one that qualified as real. 'We are not people who condone divorce, everyone knows that.' And the phrase he then chose to tell his grown daughter, a disappointment too in that what should be her faith meant so little to her. 'Things with Rachel,' he said, 'things are folding there, I'm afraid.'

'Like a camp bed,' Esther later had said, and Stephen smiling, indulging her. If she needed to say childish things then say them. The old man's rare gift of knowing when to choose silence. Yet David keen enough to tell her, several times, 'You have no idea how *weak* that kind of tolerance is. His gentleness, as you take it for. The way so much can be shelved off hiding behind it.' His meaning how Stephen might, not might but *should,* have done so much more when Eva was ill, and been aware of how severe it was; and before that again, not left Babcia in isolation all those years, as good as a prisoner with her own. And Esther, by

250

then in her first year at university, defending him. 'The old lady wanted to be as she was. Lisa thought that too. To be with us. The family. That's all that mattered to her. And that friend of hers. There was nothing else she wanted.'

'He tried to deny her past. Thinking the present could make up for it.' Esther knew he meant, 'She was a Jew. And Stephen wanted her to forget.'

She said, 'She didn't think of things that way,' and her father demanded of her, quite rightly, 'What could you know of that?' The pity she felt for him. David who as a teenager, without saying a word to the family, going to the big white synagogue in Princes Street, knowing the minute he sat through the first and bewildering service that this was home. Telling himself there was something beneath the incomprehensible words that nevertheless was his, his loving from the start the uplifting space, the patterned windows, the intricate designs along the walls. The formality. The rituals he watched so avidly. *They are mine as well.* After a few weeks a boy his own age had spoken to him, and Rabbi Liebermann, and soon he joined a youth group, aware he was on the edge of so much yet believing himself at its centre.

'This is where I want to be,' as he told the family in the sitting room one Sunday evening as they listened to the 1YA music programme his parents liked, as Babcia worked at one of her cloths, its German words spelled out in red thread, and his sister sat with a textbook she looked up from as he told them, 'I've come back.' So much later, decades later, telling his daughter his feeling of disappointment, of so being let down, as his mother said in her calm and kindly way, that if that was what he wanted, then of course they were happy for him. He had wanted to shock them, even anger them. But his father too simply nodding, pressing his shoulder as he walked through to the kitchen to put on the kettle for the supper they always had when the radio programme came to an end. David said after his mother's death, 'I had sort of hoped it would mean so much more to all of you. That we could really be ourselves. Well, my mother could and Lisa. But that just didn't happen. I thought I had done it for all of us.'

Another memory that sometimes comes back to her. She was older. She was working at the *Herald* for a holiday job over the summer. It was after her father's real marriage too had ended, and she had called around to see him. In the house above the bright sheet of the harbour stretching out to Rangitoto that he loved to look at but his wife had said made her uneasy with its precision, its too-insistent symmetry. Esther cannot recall what set her father off, some reminiscence she supposed from the Westmere house and disagreeing with his father before he left home and went south to Wellington for his degree. His raised voice as he spoke of it, the phrase that stayed with her, *We were His bloody people after all!* She saw he was appalled at what he said. He raised his hands against his face as if in the action of washing it, then lowering them and looking at her with the stone-grey eyes his mother's family had passed on to him, as he had to her.

He then sat quietly beside her and the girl said, quite without calculation, 'Why don't you go to Israel, Dad? For a trip? There are tours all the time. You'd be bound to know someone? ' Implying, she later supposed, now that you're free. Again unmarried. His answer staying with her, making so clear what she had misunderstood about him for so long, 'And be more out of place than I am here?'

His at once laughing, passing it off lightly, attempting to cover the rawness of what he had said, saying if he was young enough for military service he'd be off like a shot, he'd always fancied himself in fatigues and camouflage. He looked at his watch and walked towards the drinks cabinet with its strips of bevelled mirror. 'Leave it there, Esther, shall we?' Our people don't divorce. He might have said that too, for she knew how that troubled him as well.

She waited until he brought her a glass of weakly poured gin before she said, 'It's not only us. What happens to people.'

'But it's us especially. You must know that.'

'I would see it as you do if I could, Dad. But I can't. If we're crushed by it that's defeat again.'

He quoted to her lines she had heard him use before, how God's will has no obligation to coincide with ours.

She said, 'There's more to it than quotes.' Then she had gone across the room to hug him. 'You're not into big displays but I insist!'

David said, 'You could stay over maybe? Tomorrow's Saturday. It would be nice to have you here. And Judith.' It was the first time he had spoken directly of his new friend. 'Judith will be here for Shabbat.'

'If it means so much,' Esther told him,

'So much? *Everything.*'

'One of those Polish novelists I wish you'd read but you won't. It was a sentence I underlined twice. Once for me. Once for you.'

'Oh yes?' David humoured her.

'"In families of special closeness, blackmail sits quietly in several chairs."'

'Why I don't like fiction,' David said. He took her glass. 'I know,' he said, 'less light-handed than the last one.'

Stephen waited until she felt like telling him. He had been in the carpark when she left the room she would never need to see again. The man looking up at her as she left. His last audience. Loss. Contempt. His stare might mean anything. Imploring, even.

'Home?' Stephen said.

'Wherever.'

He drove towards Mount Eden, where she rented the back flat in a wooden villa, on the slopes of a blunt volcanic cone. (Milan would be amused at that, to her saying, in furthest SW6, 'When I lived on the volcano.') Then, 'No,' Esther said, as they stopped at the lights at Hall Corner in Point Chev. 'Let's go to your place, Granddad. For a cup of tea.'

Not often she called him that. He liked it that since she first talked she had called him directly by his name, almost a prank between them at first, the mop-haired child back then, this quiet handsome young woman who so reminded him of Lisa. Still there were times when he could enter a room and be surprised. That fraction that disturbed, elated. Similar to himself too, he supposed, in some way. How at ease they had always felt together in any case, across a lifetime, if you could say that of one so young. His thinking of David and her mother breaking up when the girl was scarcely old enough for school. When mother and daughter took off to Australia, their visits back once or twice a year. Then Auckland again once her mother died, the years that didn't work, Stephen supposed that was a neutral way to speak of it, with her father and his second wife, a woman no better suited to him than the first, or he to her, synagogue wedding notwithstanding. Yet David telling his father, enjoying his edge of righteousness, how his marriage was something his mother would have understood, and Babcia of course. But then that wife too leaving him, without acrimony. 'These things can be done in a decent way,' David had said, and Stephen thought but did not insist, without a child to make divorce the savagery it is?

They sat at the kitchen table in the Crescent while they talked. Esther liked the old-fashioned feeling of the house, the same unfussy and dated furniture her grandfather and Eva had bought when they first came back, so young, soon after they married, and Babcia with them in a way even six months before they would not have dreamed of. There was still the framed poster in what had once been David's bedroom, one of those bright old Railways advertisements with a pretty woman bang in front of the Southern Alps. An assistant in New Zealand House had given it to Eva to let her know what it was like, the lovely place where she would make her life. It had stood rolled in a cupboard until only a few years before she died. Stephen said, 'Eva had a sense of humour some people didn't quite catch on to. Mount Cook as never seen from the other end of the country.'

'She might have wanted to go there?' Esther said. 'Mightn't she?'

He used to ask her, but she had no hankering to go past Wellington. She told him often enough, 'I knew what you were bringing me to, Stevie. I'm not desperate for other places.' It was a sort of joke between them. Her putting the poster up all those years later. When Esther was a girl and

255

stayed overnight she liked to lie in bed and look at it, at the mountains drawn in chunky blocks, and the woman who wore clothes like she had never seen, and wonder if it was meant to be her grandmother before she had met Stephen. She had liked too, although she could never understand them, the bits of sewing the so-far-back old aunt she heard her father talk about had made, writing that told you things Babcia must have seen a long time back when she was a girl in Poland. Or Germany as it was when she was there. A place that was both. Esther chattered on about how mysterious all that had seemed to her as a girl, Eva as she imagined her, the auntie who could not speak English, the framed embroidery that told you what you couldn't guess at, the funny shapes of the letters, the words long and too hard to read. And the secrets about it all as well, back then. Her father telling her some things, while she knew there were others he kept to himself. 'In any case,' she said, 'children actually love not knowing things. Half-knowing them. The mystery of it.'

It was only then, as she talked on while Stephen placed the pot and the cups on the table, that Esther, beneath the framed sewing spelling out its wisdom of *Sauberkeit ist des Hauses Schmuck*, began to cry. These were not the ready tears that her father so easily came to. But her crying now quickly becoming a sobbing that she hated. Stephen crossed to a drawer to take a packet of tissues he placed beside her and then sat again facing her, patient, knowing in time she would say whatever needed to be said. He lightly tapped her hand. 'Whenever.' He raised his cup in both hands and blew on it as he had done as a boy. 'Too late to learn manners now.'

Esther smiled and crushed the tissues against her eyes.

She breathed deeply and told him, 'There!' She sipped at her own tea. 'The stupidest,' she said, 'the stupidest thing in my life, probably.' She meant that she had ever thought there was any useful purpose to it, to have sat for those hours of taped attention with the man who told her the story she had waited for. 'No matter how deranged, he will be fascinating at least.' She had thought even that, ashamed now at the condescension of it, the vanity of fooling herself that she could draw from him more than was already known. Her trickery of tarting it all up as 'academic', as part of a thesis! 'The Unreliability of Evidence: The Telling of a Family Event.' This sense now of so much less, the blank space of egotism playing over itself, over and over. As if she hadn't read enough to have expected it. His banality. The wounding scar of that across other lives, yet still banal.

'The worst thing,' Esther began, and stopped. She balled another wad of tissues and pressed them hard against her eyes. 'I'd make a great war correspondent, wouldn't I just? Great when the heat is on.'

Stephen left it a minute before bringing her back. 'The worst?'

'Oh, that.'

'Whatever it was he told you.'

'No, it wasn't even that. The details, I mean. I don't mind those. It's more than that.' She held out her hand. 'I hate these tissue things. I'd rather have your hankie.' Their managing now to laugh together, at least to pretend to laugh, between the tears and snot, her eyelids puffed as though bitten by insects. But her voice level now. She was ready to tell him. 'No, what I hated about it. My thinking I'd get a "special angle". As if such a phrase even makes sense. I pretended I was doing this for Lisa and of course I was using her.'

'Don't think that,' Stephen said.

'Kidding myself I'd be closer to her. If he talked to me. All that stuff I'd read, the transcripts, the trial, the rest of it. Hearing *him* tell me. It would make *her* closer. I really did believe that. The dreadful shit of thinking that!'

Her grandfather turned his cup in its saucer. 'I had thought that too. I'd hoped for that.'

'Both of us, then.'

'Details, I suppose,' he said. 'A few little things we didn't know that it would be good to have.'

Esther shook her head. 'Bits about the smuggling. The double-cross business he and that other woman were caught up in. The way Lisa and the boy were cover for the gems, diamonds, whatever, that are smuggled north from South Africa like that all the time, across one border and then another, all the stuff Carol Sheridan was wise to and Fergus was not. But her Italian lover had seen through her as well. It was payback time. And the change of drivers and the truck left standing for days in heat in the African port as one game followed another. As if it matters now, the details of that. Their thinking how the smuggled strangers would distract from what was going on. As if he told us one more thing we are better for knowing.' The *littleness* of him, she thought. That Lisa could ever have cared for him. The fact of that. The end of life that must be there in the beginning, somehow, surely? *Oh Lisa.*

It surprising her, shocking her even, the swerve Stephen's thinking then took. His voice as matter-of-fact as if he spoke of weather, of something read in the paper. 'The Sheridan girl. I remember her coming into the pharmacy. Overdressed. Tarty, as we used to say back then. People making fun of her behind her back. As if she had a chance.' His having no idea of how extraordinary Esther found it. That his kindness might stretch even to her. To the woman Fergus would have killed, had he not been beaten to it.

Stephen took the cups and rinsed them at the sink. He stood looking through the window, at the strip of sea visible between the neighbours' houses. The water brightening as the sun came from between the trail of clouds, the recent rain. With the breeze in that direction the afternoon would go on like that, clear, shadowed, mottled, the light changing within minutes. Scooting clouds. David used to call them that as a child. Babcia not having a word for it, or not one she was able to share, but fascinated too at the sudden changes.

'A stroll to the beach? Feel like that?' Stephen asked. 'Blow the cobwebs.'

'I'd rather the cobwebs than down there. A day like this.' Esther guessing at what might have been going through his mind. Or was bound to, if they followed the track between the houses to the little beach. No, she wanted to spare him that, at least today. The past like an avalanche. The past always waiting to happen. Whoever it was said that. Then a few minutes later her telling him, 'There, wasn't I right?', the blobs of rain landing against the windows, persisting briefly until another slab of sun fell across the yard.

'Up to the Terminus then,' he said. 'Seeing you don't fancy the beach.'

'It's still going to rain.'

'We'll outsmart it.' He left the kitchen and at once came

back, handing her one of the coats that had hung there in the hall cupboard since David and his sister were still at home.

'Talk about high fashion,' Esther said. 'This should be in a museum.'

'It fitted Lisa so it will be right for you.'

The rain's tinny needling against the plastic hoods as they stepped from the porch. She took Stephen's arm as they turned into the rise of the street. The slightness of his forearm as her hand closed on it. 'We must look like twins in these ridiculous things. If anyone walks up here behind us.'

'After fifty yards they'd know who the fit one is.' He talked about the street as they walked on. They were shadowy things to her, the names, the people he referred to. He told her the Pattersons, who had been there next door from the start, were both in a retirement home across at the Point. 'Pushing a hundred, they must be.' Then, 'Know what it's called, that place they're in? *Hillary Heights*, can you credit that? *Forget-me-slowly*, they never come at names do they that tell the truth.'

She liked his rare sardonic remarks. 'You're supposed to be nice at your age, Granddad.'

Their walking now even more leisurely. A chance for Stephen to remark on who else had been there in the early days, although few enough of those families were still here. The Laverys who were Catholic, whose boy went off to become a monk, if that was the word, the ones anyway who didn't speak, who lived on farms and he supposed were like farmers in a silent movie apart from when they prayed. Or sang. They were allowed to sing. And the Stoddarts around the corner, the tribe of them, Esther hearing again but liking the repetition, the story of Babcia walking across into the night with her spade, wrecking the geranium bushes under a late moon, and her never right after that, not really, as we say at some point, don't we, about quietly crazy people? Quiet enough not to be remarked on. Not until someone else first says so out loud. Geoff Stoddart had caged her there in the bright ring of his torchlight, this crouching fearless old lady looking up at him in her sandshoes and her nightgown. Stephen said, 'I remember the way he looked and Alan McIntyre from the house next door, as though she was something they feared to touch. Like something you get in ghost stories.'

'And the Peacheys,' he said, making a story of his memories, as they came up towards the house with its deep concrete base and the gratings that for years David as a boy had thought were the grilled windows where people hid. One of the Stoddarts had told him that. 'Kids like you. They took their pants down, the ones who were after them, so they could tell you were one of the ones they were looking for so of course they had to hide. It's dark as all buggery under there.'

Esther saying, 'Is it any wonder my dad has hang-ups? He mentioned that a couple of times. It must have sunk in.'

'He never told me that,' Stephen said. 'Even then we weren't that close.'

So she tried to make light of it. 'See, I do know something about the Crescent that even you don't know.' Yet knowing she somehow had hurt him, and wished she could take it back.

Stephen doing his best to cover it as well, nodding at the windows at the side of the house, saying, 'The Peachey girls. They were very striking and never quite had the blinds down and Dick Horgan who was the local policeman had to call round one night and tell Wes Peachey, who was a schoolteacher, to do something about the blinds.' But then he came back to his own story about David, as they crossed the street at the top of the Crescent and said about the house facing them, a faded blue that hadn't changed in all the years they were there, 'There was an unpleasant young fellow in that house. He did the lawns along the strip there on the footpaths and one day out there with his mower he called David over, David who was about ten at the time, and said could he give him a hand, would he touch one of those little white porcelain spark-plugs for a moment just to check it was OK? So David who liked to be asked by one of the bigger kids to do something grown-up touched the plug and of course got this one heck of a belt from the shock. At least that time I was able to talk with him. It was only brainless sort of stuff but damaging enough. I suppose we were lucky that's all there was.' But Esther knowing the old man walking with her did not mean 'lucky'.

They kept on as far as the shops and then turned back. 'See, what did I tell you?' The sun had broken through again. They were high enough to see the black bar of the reef lying along the strip of water, bright in the late slant of light.

'It still feels like winter anyway,' Esther said. 'Whatever it looks like.'

Back home Stephen insisted they sit in what used to be the sitting room but everyone now called the lounge. Where a long time ago the aquarium had stood that Babcia took such delight in watching there was now the big television set he was rather proud of but felt he should say, in an off-handed way, 'I've taken to watching it a bit more in my dotage.' The overseas news channels you could now get. Eva would have been a starter for those. 'I'll watch anything if I'm honest about it except motor racing.'

He took two small glasses from a cupboard beneath the TV, and a bottle he said a former customer regularly gave him, would you believe that, all these years he'd been out of the shop? Every year the same present. 'He runs half-marathons to this day and thanks me for prescribing him fairly useless vitamins thirty years ago. He still takes them and still runs so who am I to deny science?' He showed her the bottle with a cord around its waist. 'My reason for drinking it is medicinal as well. To be taken especially after rain.' He handed Esther a glass that she held between herself and the bar heater to catch its glint. 'You're warm enough there?'

'I was having you on about the weather,' she said. 'It's hardly cold.'

'The young need pampering.' Then he said, 'I won't put the light on yet.'

'No, don't. I love it like this too.' The steeping of the room into that last hour before dark. The fat red coils of the heater. The soothing burn of the liqueur. Each of them at ease with long spells of silence. Until Stephen asked, 'And so what now?'

'My life?'

'Now your degree's knocked off.'

'I've applied for a few things. A magazine in Wellington I'm not hanging my hopes on.' She crinkled her face. 'PR stuff for a while, if it has to be. There's even an advertisement I answered in Australia. Slightly mad but I liked the sound of it. "An almost serious and soon to be mature person", fancy saying that in an advertisement, "to assist an elderly long-retired ballet dancer with semi-fictional memoir." It's not as if I'm educated—how can you be with sociology, a bit of literature, a dollop of French, for a degree? Dad of course only believes commerce halfway counts. He'd probably accept Polish for genetic reasons but no one teaches it. But in the long run—'

'What in the long run?'

'Well, a decent job obviously. But time too to work all that out about us. Ourselves. Why we're the mess we are.' But laughing, as Stephen did. He knew what she meant. To understand something of it at least.

'Go easy on your grandfather,' he said.

The glow of the heater was brighter, the windows now almost dark. 'You'll be right,' Esther said. 'You're the straight man. And so much of what I know comes from you anyway.'

He blocked out the orange bars for a moment as he stood in front of her and tilted the corded bottle. He said, 'Reminds me of an old man who was half my age when I thought him that, who had little glasses like these and thought your grandmother was going to live on a desert island.'

'But not with her own people?'

'Have I told you this before?'

'Well that, or I'm better at making things up than I thought.'

A few minutes later Stephen said, 'You must go to Australia. Of course you must,' when Esther told him, 'I feel I'm marking time.'

'Such a good phrase that,' Stephen said, 'when you think of it. Marking time.' And after another pause, he reminded her, 'Eva was glad we were set on coming here.

I know I've told you that, but it's good to know.' His hand lifted from his knee and moved slightly to indicate the room, the house, the street where he had brought her. All this. In spite of everything. Glad.

They were like a parody of the short stories she had read in a literature course at university, lectured by a woman who was sharp and vivid in her first lectures and a few weeks later seemed opinionated and without great substance, and by the end of the term, once Esther had read in the library beyond the set books, was admired still but for her deftness in taking from other scholars the colours she flew as her own. When she mentioned it to David, he good-naturedly instructed her, 'You must realise scholarship is authority. It does not mean being the first to get there.'

'Well, thank goodness for Henry Lawson. He made up for her.' Those droll and probing stories flitting back to her now as she stepped from the interminably slow train taking the gradient of the hills, and saw three men in their slouched hats, their dungarees, who leaned against an iron railing, nonchalantly eying the few passengers who left the train. Yet how lovely the country had seemed, once the train left the sprawling flatness of the city's suburbs, their stretching out in haze and glitter like great sheets of heated tin. Then the train's rise through cuttings of ochre rock, bush-concealed villages, through the repetitive and speckled screens of gums, their grey and almost white-limbed reach towards a sky so intensely blue it seemed like overdone advertising. Then half an hour before she read the name on the wooden station telling her this was the place to get off, a storm had blackened above the bush and heavy rain slid against the window she sat at. The deluge though had passed when she stood and took her shoulder bag from the empty seat beside her, and the platform and the road beyond it steamed as she stepped down from the carriage. The air smelled of lush wetness, the sudden tang of eucalypts, as if she had broken brittle leaves and rubbed them against her palms. She glanced again towards the men leaning at the rail. One of them dropped a cigarette and ground it beneath his boot. A shorter, younger man, his hair shiny as straw as he removed his hat, came towards her. The Lawson vignette fell apart as he addressed her in a polite voice from the other side of the world. 'Milan,' he said. 'I'm sort of English.' As she would joke with him much later, 'Here was I expecting a stockman and found I was in the next thing to *Coro Street*,' and he will tell her back, 'If you'd played your hand right with the bloke next to me you might have got yourself a geologist. He only looked like a shearer for the easily taken-in.'

As she walked through a stile into the street, she saw the two other men lifting a heavy piece of equipment from the van at the back of the train. Only when they had crossed to a ute with a crumpled mudguard the man who led her flicked his head, suggesting someone, somewhere, they would drive to. 'He said you're sort of Polish. Not that you sound it.'

Esther laughed, thinking he referred to something she was not quite onto.

'Just saying what he said.' And clarifying that at least, 'The man you've come up here to see. Letting me know you're not from here.'

She remembered the word from her time years ago at school in Melbourne, at 'the Ladies' College' as its notepaper claimed, which her father for no more than a

266

year thank God had paid to refine her. The hard time two foreign girls had had of it, the favourite term to remind them there was a price for open skies, for the privilege of singing the anthem with others young and free. 'Well,' she said, 'I do have a touch of wog in me, way back. Perhaps he was thinking that. The man who told you.'

The man David had insisted she must visit. All right, it was in the mountains, it was hours away from the city, but there were debts one paid with a few hours' courtesy, she might at least see that? David's voice insisting across the phone line, reminding her yet again of the old lady who had been their aunt's one consolation for years. All right, his saying again, so she was an oddball, Miss McGovern, she was as far from us as they're likely to get, but they were close as that, closer than sisters, she and Babcia. You don't forget that. She had been kind to David too because he was the only one who gave a damn about it, about back then, and she understood him. The way even his mother didn't, let alone. He meant let alone his father, who thought the world began and ended at Surrey Crescent, maybe Newton Road if he thought expansively. And once Babcia her great friend died she went within a month to her relatives in Sydney, then on to a nephew on a scrap of land in the hills, as mad probably as she was when it came to whatever the stuff was they believed. As if that came into it. So his daughter could at least do that for the family, what was left of it. And it doesn't matter, David said, if he really knows who you are or not. 'It's something I want you to do.'

She understood him more than her father had thought likely. Not the details of his reasoning or what particularly led to it but the general drift it took. It was a duty. A covenant, even that. 'Of course I'll go, Dad,' she told him.

'If he's still there. You know he's there?'

'I wrote to him, the nephew.'

'Back then?'

'This month.' He described the reply. It was not illiterate, but clearly from a man who would prefer not to write. Square firm letters, one sentence to a line, on ruled paper. The first line said, 'She can come.' The second, 'My aunt died earlier this year, when she was very old.' Then the last, 'Tell the girl to write and I will have her met.'

David had said when he and Esther talked of it, 'I had no idea she lived so long.'

And as Esther told it now to the man driving her, 'I'm the sort of end to a long story I don't even know. If you're wondering why I'm here. I wouldn't know how to tell it even if I knew what it was.'

She was glad the young man did not quiz her as she expected he might. Instead he told her, perhaps by way of preparing her, 'The man I work for sometimes talks about God as if he holds the mortgage on the farm and other times as if he's an employee he's disappointed in. He never talks to me directly about it but when I overhear him around the place I know he's got God's ear. Either thanking him or slightly ticking him off. Rain not delivered in time. A disease one of the cattle has got. When God's around all the time I suppose you tend to get a bit casual.'

She liked the way he spoke of the man he worked for. Making fun of him, but a warmth there too, a tolerance for something slightly crazed. Which Esther understood at once as he stood on the veranda waiting to greet her, a tall spare man whose features might have been chipped from weathered wood, but who extended his hand towards her in an almost delicate arc. He introduced himself by saying

268

his name was Cameron, but he was comfortable with Charles, he would find acceptable whichever she chose. He turned and walked ahead to a sunless kitchen with deeply stained rough walls, its white plates set along a rack, white moons in the gloom after the brightness of outside. Where he then told her again, 'Cameron. The nephew. You are far too young to remember her? Ellen?'

'My family. They owed her a great deal.' She added, not sure why it must be said, 'My grandfather who disliked her for a long time then came to respect her. But my father was the one who wanted me to come.'

'David,' the man said. 'The one who kept his faith.'

Why be embarrassed by that, and yet she was. Then the man said, 'She died soon after my labourer here'—his turning slightly to Milan who still stood at the doorway to the kitchen—'soon after he arrived to help keep this place together.' Was that a smile even, she wondered? The younger man raised his eyebrows as she looked to him beyond the other, who now kicked at the grating of a range that flared to life. He threw a length of wood through the metal door he yanked at with its wire handle. A sharp waft of burning gum filled the room. The man turned to look at her again. Strange that she thought of him as that already, 'the man', as a couple of times on the drive from the station Milan had called him. As though the vagueness of it nevertheless defined him. He told her she must not believe the country looked like this all the time. A few months ago, had she seen it, she might think it was ready to burn. But a month of rain. So green it might well surprise her.

Then the strangeness of it, their sitting in silence in the darkened kitchen, the heavy breathing of the man now that she was aware of it, while Milan's thumbnail tapped at his mug. A plate of biscuits was moved towards her. 'They are not things I crave,' he said, 'but because of you, these were brought from the village.' And another pause, before his announcing, 'Women say they make such things for men, but it is their own inclination, I think.' And, of all things, smiling at her as though in the midst of some solemnity. 'Although it is not as if I am expert on such matters. Is that right, Milan?' The young man whom he liked because he was good for the farm. Because he did not talk unless addressed. And for that other reason too he would tell the girl. 'And because he is a Czech,' he said. 'My aunt knew Czechs where she also knew your aunt, and said she liked them.'

'Great-aunt,' Esther said.

She expected he might ask Milan to explain to her, but instead they sat quietly until he said, 'Ellen was with me here almost until the end. When she left Auckland she came to me. We followed different truths but she respected mine.' He said he was not a man at ease with writing letters but Esther might assure her father, her grandfather as well, that she was contented in those last years on the farm. He told how his aunt read aloud in the evenings yet spoke sparingly through the day, and laughed at times so that he too laughed, for the joy she found in life. And the rare gift she had, he explained, for what he called her curious grace with the hives, and the combs covered with damp cloths on the ute as they drove to Sydney a few times a year, and she attended meetings with those of a like mind to herself. So long as she was at the farm she seldom wore her scarf in those last years and her hair falling loose as it might have been as a young girl. He said she would listen to the wireless so long as there was music even of a modern kind, but felt to listen to voices talking contravened her precepts, and so they knew little of what some think of as indispensable news, or of the world much beyond the line of trees she would watch from a chair on the veranda on clear evenings. The man saying how the stars first pricking out against the dark was something she loved as she did few other things. He said again how in her last months she had been with her own Witness people in the city. A short time before Milan came to work for him.

Then the man stopped and stood abruptly. He told her again he appreciated her coming. 'The boy will drive you back,' he said. 'The train leaves Lithgow at 15.25. It is here at 16.32.' He waited on the veranda until Milan had stopped at the wire gate, opened it, driven through to the road and again fixed it with a loop of chain, before he turned to walk back inside.

'And so it goes,' Esther said, settling again in the ute, placing her shoulder bag between her feet. 'Now I know why prophets are so scary.'

'I've forgotten what the sane world's like,' Milan said. He let out a whoop as he turned from the farm gate, into the corridor of trees on the drive back to station. 'I feel light-headed with release.' They began singing a Beatles song, 'You say goodbye, I say hello', like kids coming back from a party, away from the world of adults and admonitory quotes. She liked his voice, his easy fun. The ute veered to the edge of the road to avoid a deep rut, a branch clawed across the windows. They slewed against each other, laughing.

'The man,' Milan said. 'Didn't I tell you?'

'I liked him. Oddball as he is.'

'Oh, it's not a question of liking him. I just don't want to be with him a hundred years.'

'And that Czech riff? What was that?'

'My dad's family was from a place in the country. A man from there took care of Heydrich, you must have heard of him? The top Nazi dog in Prague?'

'Of him. Not of the town.'

'So they rounded up the whole place. There's books about it. The women finished up where your own relative was. The women's camp.'

'So your family too, then?'

'They had a knack for getting out of most things.'

Quiet now, as they covered the last mile before the houses of the village half-hidden behind stands of trees and ragged bush. Then schoolkids shyacking near some kind of monument, a truck towing off a damaged car.

'Small world,' Esther said. Not minding how banal she might sound. A heavy dullness suddenly, after the fun and shouting ten minutes before.

As he pulled in at the station Milan said, 'I won't wait. The train's here any minute.'

'No, don't,' Esther said. 'Thanks for all this running round.'

'Take one of the back carriages. More likely to be empty.'

'It's three hours back?'

'A couple anyway.'

She took her canvas bag from the cab. He said he hoped she had something good to read.

'It's all new to me. All this. I'll enjoy just looking at it.'

'It could be just about dark before you're there.'

'Then plenty to think of,' she said. She hitched the

272

strap across her shoulder. She just wanted to be on the train. God, she thought, do we never get away from it? One way or another? She reached to shut the door and Milan leaned across from behind the wheel, stretching out his hand to stop its closing. He tilted close towards her. His hair was darker now, not such pale straw, in the later light. 'I can get down to the city on Saturday. Shall we see each other?'

She took a folded square of paper from the pocket of her shirt. 'I knew you'd ask so I wrote it down when I went to the bathroom. And my number.'

Their grinning at each other, open, complicit, for the first time.

'We've a lot to thank the man for,' Esther said. She liked it when the Englishman, the Czech, whatever, said, 'Better wait and see.' Not trying too hard about anything.

Days later she met him at Central as his train pulled in and the doors flung loose a swarm of teenagers come down to the city for a pop concert.

'You don't look like a farmer anymore.'

'Does that let you down?'

She walked him through the few parts of the city she knew well, across the big park, past the tall brown cathedral, down to the quays and the ferries, then across the harbour to where they stood together on sandstone cliffs and neither said this playing at tourists did not greatly interest them, but each thought it pleased the other. So they said the expected things about the bridge and the Opera House and the glittering expensive inlets and bays that Milan said made him think the shoreline of the harbour was like a huge scribble some child had made, supposing it wasn't sure what a harbour was and was told to draw one. He liked it when she told him more about herself, and about the vain ageing woman she was helping to make a fairly ordinary career as a dancer come across as more thrilling than it might have been. 'Yet I like that about her,' Esther said, 'a life delighting in itself. Her father was a railway driver who had been devoted to her and she would grow up to be for three entire seasons, and an American tour as well, one of those quivering disciplined swans who danced behind Fonteyn. Why shouldn't she be a little vain?'

On the ferry back across the harbour, the charm and shine of the afternoon suddenly gone as the wind clipped at the waves and the sky clouded. They spoke of seeing a movie. Milan said it must be six months since he had been to one, but by the time they walked through the long shed back to the fringe of the city, he said, 'We could give it a miss, you know. Now that we've started talking.'

'Ten minutes in the bus,' she said. 'It's what my friend calls a scungy neighbourhood but I envy her. If you saw the room I rent further out you'd know why all right.'

When they stood in front of a yellow door up three shallow steps and Esther took a key from her jeans, she explained she had the place for a fortnight while her friend Gail and her husband were across in Bali. 'Every Australian's dream,' she said, 'the way New Zealanders' is the Gold Coast.'

'I'm a foreigner to everything,' Milan told her. 'My mum's dream is Eastbourne.'

'Not that it's my taste exactly,' Esther said, as she opened the darkened apartment, and crossed to tilt the blinds and the afternoon flooded in.

'People only say that when they disapprove.'

'I prefer my taste to theirs, that's all I'm saying.' But then shrugging at how grandly that might come across. 'There was a short story I read a week ago. "Two kopecks looks down on one and a half." Only you can put a string of noughts behind Gail's kopecks and cut mine down to half.'

Milan said, 'An American I worked with used to say that about rich people. "They've got a lot of zeroes." Took me ages to work it out.'

'Well, we'll pretend for a bit,' Esther told him. 'Just don't look at the paintings.' At the big dark imitations of what Gail's husband believed distant and fabled New York thirty years ago had defined as where art was at. 'Sorry. I'm not half the bitchy person I sound.' There were also bright prints framed in aluminium strips, and hung diamond-shaped rather than square. 'It's the kindest thing for my friends to let me have the place. There's plenty of places round here we can eat at later on.'

He must sit down, anyway, Milan was instructed. A long red leather couch, a plain varnished wooden floor, a deep white flokati rug, an intricate lampshade that swung slightly as the door was opened. Milan said, 'I like the way you can feel a personality in a place, even if you don't know the people.' He looked at the bookshelf with its tall catalogues and volumes about photography. 'Everyone always seems to know so much about things you know nothing about yourself.'

Esther opened a bottle of wine from the fridge, and carried the two glasses to the couch where Milan sat. His asking her, 'Have you ever thought how the things we surround ourselves with, what we like on our walls, the books we keep, they're kind of emblems for a gene pool? Just how much is us, how much is *them*. The before people. No one ever quite works out the mix.' He raised his hand to take the glass from her, as though in the falling of late afternoon light she was passing him a strip of gold.

'Romance wouldn't last a week if anyone believed that.'

'Just a random thought.'

'It makes all of us like a ghost story. I'm starting to half-believe you.'

They sat at either end of the deep comfortable couch, Esther's right leg tucked back beneath her, Milan with one arm spread along the couch's back. He said, 'It's nice sitting here. Like back to normal life. I think I've been up there in the hills too long. Always just the two of us. He hardly ever goes into the village so that intensifies it.'

'The loneliness?'

'Not for him. Others don't exist the way they do for most of us.'

And then it was her father they were speaking about, something more even than loneliness, Esther said, something sadder. What you wanted always somewhere else. Not the place you were in, not the person you were with. Lonely before the reason for it even happens.

Milan regretting he had made life sound quite so programmed as he had. 'I say all sorts of things that don't stack up. An indulgent parent would call it imaginative but my mum simply puts it down to not getting things straight.' His smiling at Esther and her smiling back, each of them veering from being too solemn about things. He was telling her now about his PhD supervisor back in London, his most frequent comment on anything his student wrote. 'Just the capitals BS with a question mark.

'Does this Bear Scrutiny?' He's an old pedant of course so it makes it all the worse when I know he's spot on. No wonder I took a break to sort myself out and then ended up working for the man in the mountains. If you call that a break.' He set his glass on the low table beside his end of the couch. 'And don't go saying I'm just unsettled the way *my* father was or my mother would agree with you. I don't know if I could cope with that.' He reached out his hand and placed it on her bent knee.

For a while neither spoke. Through the big window a high pink swathe of sky. The frames of the prints caught in the reflection. Then the glare of the light diminished. Soon the room seemed oddly sullen. If you can say that, Esther thought, can you say that about where light has been? The dark floor still gleamed faintly, a polished black. The Greek rug a hollow pale slab. She had known he wanted to put his hand on her knee like that from the moment she sat down facing him. Its lightness more confident than if he had grasped at her. Her stillness telling him that she too had expected it. But he was talking now, back to talking again about the farm. The weirdly story he now was telling her. And that too striking her, why that word *weirdly* had come to her, not even grammatical, why not just weird?

'I'd heard about it,' he was saying to her, 'about telling the bees of a death. Had you?'

'No,' Esther said, 'never. I don't know what it means.'

He had heard his mother say something of it once. It was a belief, a superstition, that had been around for centuries. When someone close died, the family told the bees. Her parents were country people for ages back, before her father had gone to work in Cowley, before the land was sold off and tenants had no choice. He had forgotten about her even talking of it, the bee thing, until he had been up there on the farm with its distant blue escarpments, its jagged sloped horizons, for only a couple of weeks. Cameron had no telephone let alone a cellphone but a letter had come to tell him that his aunt had died. He had driven into the village that morning and returned with the groceries he bought each week, and the white envelope stood against the milk jug when Milan came in from clearing understory near the creek.

It was summer, Milan said, he hadn't believed there was heat like this, he was whacked when they broke for lunch and he would sit on the veranda after lunch until three o'clock. The man had explained to him when he arrived, 'We break the day in two so it's like we have two days.' Milan said that after his life in libraries and behind desks and working in a bicycle shop in the vacations, that was about as physical as his life had got. 'It's not true that hard work means you don't think, as people like us are brought up to hear. To flatter ourselves. You just think about different things. So *today* matters more immediately than it ever mostly seems to do. But I'm supposed to be telling you about something else.' About the way he was sitting at the top of the wooden steps leading up to the veranda, holding his cold sweet tea between his palms, when the man stood tall and quiet beside him. Milan turned to look up at him and was instructed, 'Stay here until I've told them. Told them she's dead.'

It was then that what his mother once had said came back to him. *You have to tell them. It goes badly unless they're told.* 'But it was more than just that now, this was something else as well to what I'd heard about. As if a

278

kind of ceremony he made up himself.'

So he had sat and watched the man cross the scuff of what was called the home paddock towards the wall of the eucalypts at its far boundary, to where in the angle of the meeting wire fences, the hives like unpainted oblong boxes placed on end. He stopped several yards from the hives. I should have said, Milan told her, he wore the same jeans he wore each day I had been there, a white shirt as he did at times for 'special occasions' as he called them, without explaining. The sleeves now rolled down and buttoned at their cuffs, a curious mix of casualness and almost formality, that's the effect it made, his calf-high boots, his broad-brimmed leather hat tipped slightly to shade his eyes. With his height and spareness and sense always of calm possession, the man of God walking his earthly acres. None of the gear you might expect to see a man wear if it's dealing with hives he has in mind. And although Milan could not hear the words he knew the man spoke to them as he stepped in closer, as though he feared they might not hear what he had come to tell them. And so Milan described it for her as they sat in the darkening room, the unsettling vividness as she imagined it, the tall man and the burring hives and the grey and dappled barrier of the bush in front of him, the glare of his shirt in what seemed the afternoon's hot empty pause.

He had now removed his hat and placed it on one of the iron spikes that supported the wire-stranded fence, where he crouched for a moment, lit a match which he placed against what seemed, from where Milan sat, a kind of small funnelled can, and that the man then held as he approached one of the hives and took a covering board from the top, which he laid on the ground. Drifting billows of smoke came from the contraption in his hand which he then set down as well, before he then took the top level, like a broad deep tray, and placed that too on the ground. He removed another level and then a third. Already there was the rising blur of the smoked bees darting, flickering, as if the weave of a fiercely thickening veil, through which the man now knelt on one knee to put his hand into the hive's lower level on its shallow platform. Milan watched in his ignorance what seemed both methodical and crazed. The man standing again and placing what the farmhand only later learned was the queen against his forehead, her hive responding in a gusted whirl about the stolid figure. And the man speaking, as if addressing them. 'It was too far off for me to hear, but I could tell that was what he did. There was a sense almost of reverence in the way he stood stock-still with his hands now held in front of him, the way you see men standing at the side of a grave.' The strange stalling formality of that as the dark fluent stain as it seemed on the shoulder of his shirt swelled, the bees compacting and spreading down his sleeve and across his back. Milan, standing now on the veranda and appalled, compelled, by what he witnessed, the blurred seething fabric of the air, and heard the sound like some distant implacable machinery as the only thought that came to him, a mad enough thought in itself, *The man is dressed in bees, it is his sound as well as theirs.* And then the man stooped again and rebuilt the storeys of the hive and it was as if an apparition had been withdrawn. The extraordinariness of what he witnessed remaining with him still, an occurrence seemingly cut off from any notion of time. For he had no idea of how long all this had taken, or how brief it may have been. It was something discrete, entire, apart from anything else he knew or might imagine. He did not expect Esther, expect anyone, to believe it was quite as he had said, a standing living pillar that was both calm and fury, and then later, the man walking back across the paddock, the burr of the bees behind him returning and settling to their hive. Yet so simple too, if you wanted to think of it like that, merely countless bees clotting about a figure they knew, then returning to where they had been about their business until he went down to talk to them. Milan saying now, 'I doubted I'd ever mention it to anyone. One madman's enough.'

Esther imagining it so vividly its strangeness excited her, the seeping across the man's back like a frothing lung, and yet the stillness somehow of it too, even beautiful to think of, even that. The making and unpicking of a living shroud. She said, 'I don't know if I can take it in. Make sense of it.' As if another story went on within it that eluded her. An awful exhilaration as she thought of it. And yet what a shonky phrase that was, as she knew the second it came to her.

'Oh, to hell with it!' she said. Laughing, not wanting to laugh. She took Milan's hand from her knee and knelt on the warm leather of the couch and moved towards him, *coming to get him*. God, she thought, if only it wasn't bloody words we have to work through all the time! Her fingers found the buttons of his shirt and touched the warmth of his throat. *Fucking bees*, she said, pressing her mouth against his ear.

2004

——

It was Hitler's fortress, Milan tells her. *Festung Breslau.* His last-ditch stand. His sea wall against the Russian tide. Or that was the idea. If Breslau held, so would Berlin. 'Neither did,' Milan said, who knew so much more about history than Esther. About the city now with its Polish name that her forebears could never have guessed at. Milan knew where borders had shifted in the past, just as he might guess at where the boundaries would move again. It was what he was good at, the kind of thing he was trained for. He was what his mother called a barrel of opinions.

'Not opinions, Debbie,' he corrected her. 'Facts.'

'What I said,' his mother told him. 'A doctorate is enough opinions to know where other ones are coming from.'

'Well, that's my job.' As a journalist, he meant. As a scholar. He was writing a book on political borders, on borders of imagination. He reviewed for the *New Statesman.* The BBC sometimes asked him what he thought. He worried about the present. He called history 'toothache without a qualified dentist'. But as Esther seemed surprised to say, he was not a pessimist. He was fun to live with, and was busy enough for two lives. He patiently stood on High Street corners collecting for Oxfam, he helped at book stalls to raise funds, he read one evening a week for an old man in the shadow of the stadium at Stamford Bridge. A blue-and-white Chelsea scarf stretched across the wall in the man's bedsit, a querulous old man who at times would break in, 'Why do they bother to write if they can't make things clear!', and Milan knew it was the cue to stop reading from the papers and pick up a war book, which was always preferred. Old Jack pretended it was the politics that held him while in fact it was tunnelling and escapes and dam-busting and decisions before dawn that he waited to get back to. He would fetch a bottle of beer and two glasses and settle in against the wall beneath the scarf he could see only dimly.

Some evenings when Esther carried a coffee through to Milan's desk and asked hadn't he done enough for one day, surely, he grinned and leaned back and let his hand rest on her thigh, as she bent forward to press her lips against his forehead. 'I can *taste* your thinking.' And she sometimes thought, without telling him even as a joke, that she could see an elderly woman with both hands carefully balancing a cup, bringing coffee to a balding scholar at his desk, whose book on borders was almost finished. It's so hard to keep up with them, she imagines the old man saying, they keep outsmarting you. Wars. Boundaries. But the young man says, 'You're right, this is ridiculous.'

He neatens the papers in front of him and says, 'Shouldn't we be in bed? Like normal people?' There are moments when he wonders at how casually he can say such a thing, how after two years she is contented still to be with him. Everything in life seeming so ordinary, and then here she is, living with him. Thanks to the bush, as he still calls it, the scrap of farm high in the blue hills, in that other world. He tells her so, and she makes light of it. She tells him back, 'You English think "exotic" where we'd say "run-of-the-mill".' And the long silences they both revel in. The closeness, he would not have believed it, of how saying little can so suffice. Yet the utter frankness, when they choose it.

He holds her hand in the dark. He sometimes thinks she is asleep but she is wide awake. He likes to tell her, 'I don't know if deep down you really approve of us.'

'Us?'

'*Us*, I mean. Brits. Not one of *you*. From over there.' When she tells him things he is surprised to hear her say.

She leans against him. She says, 'Complaints should be submitted in writing.'

'That's the book after this.'

'*Us*,' she says again. 'The things you come out with. You're only half-Brit anyway.'

Esther thinks about it now. About the man she lives with. She admires the way his writing so comprehends duplicity, and yet at times there is such innocence as well. His believing that given a choice, people will act for the best. His commitment once he believes a thing to be true. Her own wanting to tell him far more often than she does, 'You're so certain others aren't necessarily worse than yourself!' She knows she hurts him when she says, 'If I wrote down all these pronouncements I could set up as a moral guide.' He says, his fingers stroking her arm, 'They're simply possibilities. Things worth giving a chance.'

She remembers her father, his heavy dismissive shrug that anything might be taken on trust. *As if we haven't reason enough to doubt that.* Milan's hand dabs at her throat, he brushes at the tight black mass of curls. She turns her head for his mouth to graze at the beat of a vein. The smell of his skin comforts her. She thinks of him as she walks in the city that she has come to, the third in line: after Lisa, after Eva. She likes thinking that. Likes it that Milan belongs here without having to consider it the way she does. 'He gets on with things,' as Debbie likes to say of him. His mother who works in a café in Camden Market, with its plain wooden tables, its mix of students and locals and tourists who are a little off the track. No one would be there for the food alone, the scones and the no-nonsense sandwiches that she prepares out back. The place ringing with voices and orders called through and the clatter of the Jamaican kitchen-hand who scours dishes as though he has it in for them. It does not bother Milan that his mother works at something so unassuming. He laughs with her, 'You *work*. It's not a word a lot of people are proud of but I am. The place would close without you.' Her slapping lightly at his arm. 'You needn't condescend to me, lad. You might even try it on yourself some day.' The closeness between them Esther likes to watch and envies, thinking as she does so of her father in the big house he had always wanted and at last comes to own, on its cliff looking out to sea. As good an address, he reminds her, as any woman could wish for. Tell him one that was better? Yet her father, she guesses, as on most days of his life, wanting to declare, We are born to be uneasy. It goes with who we are. 'Your gift for misery on behalf of the world!' she had shouted at him as a teenager, and regretting it before the sentence is even out. Daddy saying nothing as he looked at her. His turning then so she would not see how he had been stung. Now for his sake as much as any she would go. She would have to go. That certainty coming to her so intensely she feels it almost as though she were physically shoved. Milan says to her, blurred from waking, 'Is anything wrong?'

At breakfast she tells him she has decided. 'Don't press me too much on why.'

'And it never occurred before?'

'Not the way it does now.'

'A voice from a cloud?' And then, 'That's not much of a joke.'

'I won't be making you wear your hair in long curls.' She twists a finger at the side of his ear. She wants him to take it lightly. 'But it's not a whim.' She wants him to know that too.

She phones a travel agent in the King's Road. By lunchtime she has the ticket in her hand. 'I agree,' the direct young man who attended to her nods when she remarks on how reasonable the price of the flight was. As though he intends a career somewhere other than in travel, he says, 'Ryanair are cattle trucks but they'll get you there in one piece.' Then 'Oops,' he says, his hand across his mouth.

'And back, I hope,' Esther says.

That evening Milan tells her about what Wrocław used to be. *Festung Breslau*. About when the borders changed. How one people become another. 'We're before all that,' she says. 'Mind you, that's about all I know. Out of a vague Eastern village I sentimentally imagine every time I look at Chagall, how's that for avoiding fact? But always on the rise. David always insisted on that. There was nowhere for a Jew to go but up. As if that isn't true of most people, most of the time.'

'Not that I know much more about my lot,' Milan says. 'We're a gritty social-realist movie.'

Debbie had 'filled Esther in', as she said, with the few details that seemed important. 'Married when we were twenty, would you believe it.' Milan's father was a Czech, they both worked at a Butlin's holiday camp. 'He was the camp electrician and I looked after what they called a crèche which meant the snottiest kids in England could run amok.' Milan apart she had never seen a baby in her life she'd give you the time of day for. But his father liked the trade he had learned from his father in another country that was no longer the same country and they fell for each other and it was goodnight nurse from then on. And there were perks. Debbie said she must have been one of the last girls in England to see George Formby alive. Not on stage, she wasn't wanting to make too grand a claim. He had come into the big room where dozens of children shouted and yelped and had looked at them and said to her, with honest to God the biggest teeth you'd ever seen, pictures gave you no idea, 'Only a lion-tamer should be in with this lot, love,' and gone out again, grinning all the time so you wondered if it was actually a grin or just the way his face was. It was a story she liked to tell. So she and Milan's father married, didn't they, as she said, and that was that, married in a church with bells galore, prayers you couldn't understand, oh no, the English version not good enough for Czechs. Then after a few years Bruno ups and goes east, that's how

288

he used to put it, going east. Sent money back, never a problem with that. Never said he wasn't coming back but never said he was either. Then his brother writes to say he had died and Milan eight years old. 'And that's that. Not such an interesting story,' Milan says, 'but the only one we had.'

'All lives are interesting if we know enough about them,' Esther tells him. 'Virginia Woolf's father said that.' She takes hold of Milan's wrist. 'Keep your hand quiet until you've stopped telling me.'

'And Debbie had the house not far from the Market. That was something. Why she still thinks of him as a good provider.'

'As he was.'

'She's still got photos of him everywhere. Pity I didn't know him.'

Their lying there, the radio beside the bed playing quietly. Until Esther adds, 'I'd like to know more about our lot. I know the end but more than that.'

'There's always something. Enough to start from.'

'But it's never right. Not exactly.'

'What we don't know, then,' Milan says. 'We at least know that.'

She leans across and kisses him, his hand runs along her side. 'That doesn't make sense,' she tells him.

No more than a week then, until she leaves. 'About time,' Milan says. He has been to a conference in Ghent and is home again. He talked with a German publisher from Frankfurt who liked the borders book, as much of it as he has done. She tells him an American journal has taken a piece she sent without letting on to him that she had. She said they had thought it was autobiography but she doesn't mind that. 'If they believe that they'll believe anything.'

'What fiction means,' Milan says. And then he tells her, 'They get along quite nicely living together, don't they? Scholars and writers?'

'Early days yet.'

She doesn't mind that he thinks there was something more considered to her deciding on Wrocław than was actually so. She thinks again how it had been Daddy's obsession, and yet one he did nothing more about than talk and write his querying letters. Stephen telling him, 'You've got as much as you're likely ever to get, David. Names. A few addresses. There's walls you have to stop at.' She thought of his desk drawers, the correspondence that went on for years, the organisations that helped when they could, the queries that came up with nothing new. Stephen repeating to him, 'They were as good almost at destroying records towards the end as they were at keeping them beforehand.' Her father insisting he would go there one day, already knowing he never would. His bitterness at himself when there was no one left to blame. Wives. Business commitments. Inertia. Stephen cited for not getting more from Babcia, and the old man mildly explaining, yet again, 'It wasn't possible. Not the way you think it was.' David telling her when there was no one else to tell, 'If I went there it might pull the threads together.'

That hard last year before she came away, the months when his speech was difficult and there was his relentless and implacable glare for whatever came into his sight, at existence itself and its goads that seemed directed at him. She had sat and read to him from the Psalms, finding beforehand the ones that might carry consolation. She had phoned his friend Harry Liebermann, whose father had kindly brought the teenage David back to faith. 'If you'd come and read to him from the book he's marked in lots of places,' she'd asked. Her knowing how awkwardly, how laboriously, her father had learned to spell out the words he was never at ease with, which even when not understood consoled him. She thought of him leaning back against the stacked pillows, Harry Liebermann's voice softly reciting to him, his friend's hand resting on his. She had left the men together in the hospital room and sat on a bench in the carpark and thought, What if this is the end? But the miracle, as we blithely say, his recovery against the odds, his happiness now with Judith, the discipline of his no longer drinking, his exercise, his seeming not to fret. 'His third marriage,' Stephen said to her, smiling, gently sardonic, can one say that? 'Practice presumably does make perfect.'

She liked to talk of Stephen as Milan liked to listen. 'We'll go there anyway one day,' she said. The bach, she meant, the beach, the waterfall she thought of as her own, because her grandfather had told her that so often as a child when they walked there, 'Esther's stairs, see?', and they would stand after the heavy rains and the spray laid veils on their faces. And her laughing, 'God, this is the way old people natter on. Before they're locked up!' But her lover knows enough by now for details to find their place, with the grandmother too whose photographs on the mantelpiece Esther loved to look at as a child. She would stand and touch their frames and turn them, trying to make the features move, the always unsmiling, directly gazing woman who was young enough to be a girl, for none of the photos were of Eva once her children were too old to sit on her lap, or lean against her knees. Who had died before Esther could remember her. And her Aunt Lisa who looked so like herself that even Milan for a moment had mistaken her in the snapshots she kept in the drawer of her desk. She had tried to tell him how the mad bastard she spent time talking with and recording would look at her when she sat with him. The regret and sorrow, she supposed, to give him the benefit of that. The one time she had ever used *appalling* for the grief she guessed at behind the eyes, their intense attention. What she guessed they saw and returned to and no end to their regret.

But the only photographs Esther takes with her, once her passport is on the desk with her tickets, are the copies she had made years back, that Stephen said were handed to them fifty years before. They had not been married more than a few months before the official letter came to Eva. The stocky, bewildered woman who waited for them, whose age as he had then thought might be anything up to sixty, but decades younger, the woman who had proved her strength simply by surviving and whose body seemed—yes, he had thought this, Stephen said, absurd as it was—seemed as if that of another person, this woman who looked at them with neither apprehension nor at first any hint of pleasure, who waited until the translating woman beside her moved her hand to indicate they might come together, she and the tall young woman who was her flesh and blood. Each stepping across the carpet between them as if in some strangely scripted drama, the tall vase of spiky flowers on a table behind them, it was like that, Stephen remembered, like a play that he watched and neither actor knew her lines, nor even the language she should speak in. He saw his wife's hands clasped in front of her as she had never held them before, a schoolgirl covering her nervousness. The older woman's eyes that made him think, as she moved forward, that what she looked at was not in fact what she believed she saw. And then her features crumpled as if actually distorted, quite beyond her will, and she raised her damaged hand, a crushed half-opened fist sliding down the fall of Eva's hair. There was another photograph of the woman, much younger than when Stephen had first seen her. She was smiling slightly, her hair cut short, standing on the step of a building, a door with a heavy ornamental handle behind her. Esther now placed it in a compartment of her purse. That, and the head-and-shoulders photograph of the woman looking directly to whoever may have taken it, the rusted indent of a paper clip marking an upper corner. 'They were all my old aunt brought with her,' Esther said as Milan held them for a moment, then placed them down. 'That and the list of relatives who didn't have her luck. The address in the street I hope to find. That's about as close I guess as the rest of us will ever get.'

She had hoped the flight from Stanstead might be clear all the way. The weather was good, after a week of indeterminate English grey. The look of lovely summer. The trees across from the terminal's parking area the gorgeous July as one always hoped for, then the spill of handsome countryside, hazed as it rose towards a wooded skyline.

Esther asked for a window seat. The plane crossed the long sandy sickles before the Dutch coast and the neatness, the packaging, the intricacy of European farmland that enchanted her. Then soon enough the more expansive reach of Germany beneath her, and the excitement she did not expect, the thought of how at last it would come to her, the city she had always heard of, yet as remote as if its reality was in stories heard and repeated rather than in streets, in people, in ordinary things, as of course every place became once one was there. The woman in the seat beside her spoke to her, thinking perhaps she was a young woman coming back from holidays. But the language sprang between them, and they smiled at each other, and Esther turned again to look from the window. The captain made an announcement in English, then told his passengers again in Polish, they would soon begin their descent, and when they might expect to arrive. But a sudden canopy of cloud opened beneath them, a great swathe dull as canvas. Only for the last few minutes they emerged, the flow beneath them of fields that seemed larger, less chequered, than those earlier on. She looked down to the quick frothiness of clumped trees, the dull strip of a river, a distant tilting rake of spires and immediately beneath, the white blocks and orange roofs of farmhouses.

The terminal was much as any other, the movement through Customs brisk and impersonal. The man in his peaked cap looked at her twice, back to the page of her passport, handed it to her without speaking. An incommunicative driver on the taxi ride to the city. The farmhouses she had seen from the plane and now glanced up to with their gabled roofs. Why was this, she wondered, her quick stab of disappointment. At what, she thought? How dare she? From the cab radio the long tolling of a bell, the sound of what may have been a recited prayer. She thought the driver spoke to her. She asked, Excuse me, what was that? Then asking again, in French. The driver glanced up at her in his mirror but made no attempt at courtesy, simply tapping the clock in front of him showing midday. And the sentence repeating itself in her mind, *I am back where we came from. This is where we're from.* How she would like writing that to David. To phone him, even better. That odd pause whenever he took up the phone, a hesitancy she noticed nowhere else. To say simply to him, 'Breslau, Daddy!' And it coming to her more strongly than ever, how he might have so easily have come here himself, on one of his business trips to England. How he met with people from one of the German companies he dealt with. 'Pfizer', a word that puzzled her when she first learned to read and saw it on an ornament on his desk, and her mother saying, 'You must ask Daddy why it's spelled like that.' It would not have been so hard, even in those days. Or perhaps it may have been. The days of East and West, of blocs and serious borders. Daddy so blustering to the world and afraid of it too. She felt the prickling of her eyes as she thought of how for all his talk, his sentimentality, his obsession with what he called—he must have taken the phrase from somewhere—'history's implacable erasing', he could have done as she did now, for all of them.

'Here,' the driver curtly tells her, but carries her bag across the pavement to the address she had written out for him, close to Dominikanski, a church that to her untrained eye is like a huge dark brick barn, with a steeply angled roof. He thanks her with no more than a nod when she hands across her notes, making it clear she does not expect the change. She rings the bell beside the 'Boransky' label to the side of a wooden door. She thinks as she waits how it would have been nice for Milan to be with her, but he was right, she knew that, insisting this was something she should do by herself. She feels alone, as she had not done for years, but so I should, she thinks, so I should. She presses the brass button a second time, she hears its burr from deep in the apartment. A cough before the door swings back, the middle-aged woman smiles warmly at her, tells her she is welcome, and takes her bag from her. Is good to get here? she asks in careful, heavily leaned-on English. She says her name is Vera. She is handsome, perhaps fifty, she wears a ring on her left hand, but in the days her guest will be with her, no mention is made of a husband, and there is no sign of a man's presence. She leads through to a sitting room, sweeping her hand as if to introduce her home, the plush magenta chairs set against the dark table, the vase in its centre stacked with artificial flowers, the long settee with buttoned leather cushions, and above it two big tinted photographs in oval frames, from a time when men wore whiskers and a woman's bosom swelled beneath a black tightly drawn bodice. There is a smaller table that holds brochures and folded maps for guests. And what clearly is an item of pride, a sideboard carved to match the ornate legs of the dining table, its shelves bright with sets of coloured flutes and glasses, and photographs in ornamental metal frames, and in the centre, the statuette of a dancer, her arms flung behind her head, her hair falling loose and long as her spine arcs back.

Esther smiles to let Vera knows how she admires her home, that this is what she had hoped for.

'All good?' Mrs Boransky asks. She leads Esther to the bedroom with its wide bed, a blue rucked quilt, small crossed flags on one wall, on another what must be a religious picture, a man in a long robe holding his own heart as though he has caught a cricket ball. She is anxious that her guest feels at ease. She offers to make her coffee. She places a plate of biscuits on the table back in the dining room, and says the name for them, says them again, smiles at Esther's first Polish word, as she takes it to be. She places a fan of brochures for her to look at. 'So much to see.' Her hand circling again, this time to the city she so obviously is proud of. She assumes this is what the pretty pale woman with her mass of hair has come for, the handsome square, the famous town hall, the steep-roofed churches, the sunbursts of baroque. There are boats that make excursions on the river. There are islands you cross to on iron bridges. There is so much here to see.

Esther walks slowly through the town, one of whose names she has known since she was a child, but not the other as Mrs Boransky pronounces it, that is written there on the guidebook she carries with her. But it is the earlier name that means where the family began, and her great-grandfather, and the list of names in her father's desk. The old aunt whom for some reason they had called 'Grandmother' in Polish, but who had spoken to the family in German that only Eva understood a little; and somewhere in the story as David told it, another language too Babcia heard as a girl with old people who were not as well-off as her own family, people from distant places.

Those few words Esther liked repeating as a child when her father said them and 'Remember these,' he would tell his daughter, as if he gave her something precious. But Esther guessing, even by the time she was eleven or twelve, that the story was not as David told it, that the old woman Stephen spoke about more frankly, with her increasing quietness, her obsession with a few ornaments and photographs, her methodical routines and the delight she took in her one friend from the worst of times, had a life already more diminished than they could know. Stephen had taken her to a specialist, one of the few in Auckland at the time with any training of the kind that was called for, an Austrian who spoke with her and told him, more as a human fact than a medical diagnosis, 'You should be grateful for how much she has forgotten, how marvellous it might be to sit in a room and to have the children liking to sit there even in silence with her, the gift of getting beyond language altogether.' But Daddy convinced until the end they might all somehow have done much more. A row she remembered at the bach when she walked in from the beach and heard her father shouting, heard her grandfather saying in his measured considerate way, 'But we gave Babcia more peace than she ever would have known had she not been with us,' and Daddy shouting back, 'But on your own terms, wasn't it, always yours!' She had felt grief for both men but mostly for her father, with that narrow valley he lived his life in, between his easy tears and an equally ready fretfulness. But at least the streets. Esther could walk them now for all of them.

She decides though she will walk about the town as a stranger might, before looking for more, before finding the special scraps of it she has come so far for. She stands at the corner of Rynek, the great square with its high coloured houses, its ornate facades, the dozens of restaurants extending in front of them, the sound of music coming from a group that plays further along.

She has taken the street from Mrs Boransky's and the church whose roof strikes her as like a deep upturned keel. At a corner of the square she looks up to the tower of another church with its handsome tower, its copper dome. This too is part of what she must do. Odd that she should want to, but that is important too. Those who watched what had happened. They were part of Breslau. She stands in its porch, one of a group most of whom enter the church a few yards ahead of her with their hands raised as if in some parodic salute, their cellphones held high to bring down the great arched vaults to fit into their pockets, the brilliant slits of light from the tall shafting windows at the nave's further end. The irony coming in on her, as she thinks of how she will speak of it in a few days' time to Milan, in the flat that at this moment seems another world. None of them, none of her people, she supposes, have ever stood here, not exactly here. The oddness of her being the first to do that! But so many of those who knew them, neighbours and friends perhaps and those they spoke with through business and casual greetings in the street, they must have, surely; all were part of that, the community of what so many must have shared. When the city had its other name. Before the borders moved.

As she turns and goes back out to the summer light and the bright facades and the rising restored extravagance of the Town Hall facing her from the middle of the square, its ornate gilded clock and its medieval figures, its ironwork and high orange roof, Esther thinks, *I am as much a facade as all this is, there is nothing but the moment we are in. I can no more be them than they are me.* For those moments, minutes, whatever they are, she feels a surge, a panic, the taste of it in her mouth. *You cannot do this for other people! Not for Daddy or Eva or Babcia, not in any way that matters for them. Let alone the ones before.* She finds a table beneath a canvas awning and orders coffee. A tall elderly man brings it to her without saying a word.

299

She thinks it a mistake not to stay at a hotel. If only there was a room she could return to and be alone in and not have to speak, not go through the game of making out this is an authentic thing, to sit in someone else's home, to watch as though kindly Mrs Boransky has been caged for her to gawp at, the meals she feels obliged to praise, the pictures on the wall, the meaningless television. As if she has the right! She begins to walk at random. Her resentment but with no clear idea at what. She knows had she seen a woman like herself at that moment, and bothered to guess at what distressed her, she would despise her slightly. Why expect things to be other than they are?

She follows the streets towards the river and, because there seems nothing else she might do, buys a ticket and walks up the tilted gangway to the wooden benches on a small river cruiser. Making no more conscious effort than if she were observing a screen that pretended this indeed was life, she watches a group of young Americans hand around among themselves a carton of sliced pizza, and the boat pulls out into the river, and the grandness she supposes of the city's architecture slips past, until the town is left and she watches the shallow banks of the river turn to countryside. There are solitary men fishing from the edge of the fields, a few families camping, which makes her think of the few times back home when she was first at school and her father had said they must do more of this, live as their country gave them the rare opportunity to live. But he found they had no gift for the outdoors, and her mother hated it enough to throw a Primus stove into a lake when their food was stolen at a camping ground, and from then on they stayed at motels, and her mother read, and David watched the clock until it was time to drive back home. It lightens her mood a little, thinking back to that. Even a warmth for her parents in remembering how awful the holiday had been!

There are swathes of reeds further along the river, a group of young boys in yellow vests in a huddle of kayaks, a landing where people lolled in canvas chairs and drink at rustic tables. Then the small river boat turns in a broad sweep and plies back towards the towers and the high-roofed churches and the picture-book quays. Already life does not seem quite so grim. She would like to phone Milan but they talked about this only a few nights ago. She has to do this by herself.

Through the night there is rain that makes her think again of back home, its soft beating against the window in her room, the runnels of water on the pane when she draws back the curtain and the street light level with her wobbles behind the moving glass. In the morning the rain is light, almost a kind of veiling Englishness. Then later the sky clears, the heat is sudden, the streets steam: it is summer again of the kind that tourists travel for.

Esther checks her maps, the notes she carries in her folder, and in twenty minutes she has crossed Rynek and the smaller square that leads from it with banks of flowers outside shops, restaurants as everywhere, groups of young people here for a youth conference assembling under flags. She takes a narrow alley and is away from the tourist centre. She follows a broad road and crosses tramlines, finds other names she checks on her maps, is struck by the occasional ornate and grimed old commercial buildings, among the drab post-war office blocks, much as they might be in any city. Soon she stands before a high tiled building in quiet curving Włodkowica Street. She recognises it from the photograph in her guidebook. She passes through a short vaulted archway and finds herself in a large courtyard, the windows of several storeys rising on three sides, and facing her on the fourth, the facade of the synagogue, the tall flat white columns against painted stone, classical Greek detail flowering at their tops. She feels a quick stab of disappointment. There is nothing obviously religious, Jewish, about the building she looks at. It is like a concert hall, what she has waited to see.

The White Stork, that oddest of names for a synagogue, a long time back the name of a drinking house that stood there first, so there is no surprise in that. A pub, a place to stay, nothing to do with them, until the families of whom her own must have been one were rich enough to buy the land, to build in a style that showed their wealth, their education, their being like anyone else apart from this, apart from their wanting their God to have a place that no one would doubt belonged to them. To decorate it with fine galleries, with the white-and-gold patterns and designs and elegance that made it worthy of Him, and themselves worthy of it. This was the nineteenth century, this was Germany, the people she came from were part of what sustained the fineness of both. This was not a place where peasants, where mutterers in Yiddish or local dialects came to declare descent, but an educated people were proud to be seen. She had heard as much for years from David and now saw why his version was another world. But the building is a shell of what it may have been, expanses of raw distempered walls as she enters its big spaces, the derelict rooms, where workmen seem in the process of attempting to bring them back from their general sense of neglect, loss, decay. The rough concrete tubs, the tangle of pipes, as she walks down to the female baths. Back on ground level she makes out the dim high gallery where the women would have sat, the glaring emptiness of the windows whose patterned glass they would have faced. But the stairs she might take up to it are closed off with wooden barriers. The dull reality that this is what the past must first journey through, before it is retrieved. And her accepting too as she reads a summary account of where she stands, the further scouring disappointment that her family, those at least that she knows the names for, would not have attended services here in any case but have gone to the larger Reformed synagogue streets away, so grand and handsome, so certain and established, destroyed the night of the other Jewish fires across the country they once were part of. Yet to say so much as 'was' is surely to say it in the present: the past is here or not at all.

'They were significant people.' How she remembered her father saying that. And the quick snap of her irritation as a teenager, her demanding why he had to drag his bourgeois snobbery even into this, as if it mattered a damn whether a great-uncle as he claimed was a famous scholar? She had shouted, What difference would it make if he couldn't read a word or was fucking Einstein? When they came to get him? When he died wherever it was they decided he would die? The hurt in David's eyes as he took in what she said, and the words she chose to say it, and his own shame, the shame finally of *everything*. But telling her only, 'You disappoint me, Esther.' And the worst then she could think of to hurl at him, that *he* must disappoint *them*, did he ever think of that?

303

She walks out again into the open air, to the walls rising on three sides of her, the lift of the synagogue across from where she stands. It no longer bothers her, the confusion of one imagined building in mind, the reality of another in front of her. Her *accepting*, she thinks, that is what must define me. The mess of it all is what I am. To be here now, in the square of the courtyard that struck her as so like the bottom of a well, rising several storeys to that other square of now sharp blue sky. Where they had been instructed to assemble, those who in absurd optimism, in incomprehension, still remained in the city to be rounded up. They most certainly were here for that. To stand for further instructions and watch the faces of the those they had known for a lifetime, their standing against the ones who mattered to them most, the comforted, the comforting, as they waited. *For orders.* How that word mines beneath all others, hollows the pit where everything in its implacable force descends. She looks at the overlap of one cobblestone against another, the window ledges exactly as they must have seen them, the rise of the flat pillars against the painted wall. *They*, the family, their hands holding, touching, comforting, she supposes. Or perhaps not. She had read how the older ones at times like this, the devout, the ones with certainty of more than fear, already would be moving their lips, speaking the words louder even than that, and the guards amused at their presumption, the joke that prayer might slow so much as a child's shuffle on the march that would soon begin to the rail lines and the station. Once the timetables were set in stone. Esther's own lips move as she says the names. *Chaim. Lisabet. Sarah. Hannah. Ephraim. Sol.* She closes her eyes, leans her head back against the wall. Like saying a line of poetry. A prayer. She says them over again. There is nothing more she can do. The closest she will be with them.

It is a short walk, once she is through the archway back to the curving street, from there to a broad pathway beneath a canopy of trees, and a few yards to her left a long expanse of water that at first you may mistake for a river, with a narrow wooden bridge glimpsed through the foliage, spanning it a hundred or so yards away. But you notice the water has no more movement than a pond, that leaves and detritus and an abandoned toy boat lie as still on its surface as if placed on a table. This, as a placard behind a sheet of protecting glass informs you, is what remains of the old moat that once protected the city, which over the centuries one invading army and then another coveted. The long handsome wooded promenade, should you see it in a movie, or walk there in a novel, may strike you as a place for trysts and confidences and the haul of nostalgia. *Europe*. She was amused at how she so fell for stereotypes, how easily the sludge of teenage reading and the thrall of films so survived in her! She watches an old-fashioned pram with a big cane hood being pushed by a mother in fishnet stockings, a leather skirt, shoes blood-bright as a wicked stepmother's. But mostly elderly couples, an occasional single person like herself, on the benches at intervals along the path. On a seat close enough for her to hear their breathing, a young man and an older woman were talking very seriously. She strokes his bare arm with a leaf.

Esther again unfolds her map of the city. She finds exactly where she is sitting, runs a fingernail towards the bridge she can see from where she sits, as she can the street across the moat, its buildings flecked and concealed by trees. The day has grown warmer, the tunnel of trees 'as still as candles', wasn't that too a phrase David used because his mother was amused by it, when Babcia said how quietly Lisa sat as she read?

She walks with the water glinting beside her, like a stretch of stalled river, she thought, if one can say such a thing. The brighter now for the sun angling on it more sharply. She puts her hands on the railing of the narrow bridge, looks down at the sprinkling of fragments and twigs on the metallic surface. A single leaf drifts too gently to think of it as *falling*. To the water like a stretch of silk. She stands aside for others to pass her on the bridge. A child heaves a toy saw from the side of his pushchair, which the mother stoops to retrieve, and the child lets go of it again. This time she places it in the bag that hangs from the back of the pram.

Once on the moat's other side, Esther steps through patches of light falling through the trees, flecking the shoulders of the cyclists who ride on the roadway beside her. Everything seems still to demand of her, *Attend to this*. Another child, rocking unsteadily as he stoops to touch the shifting patterns which he finds are not there to pick up on the rise above the moat. A middle-aged man speaks to her. He wears a Tahitian shirt, which seems an oddity. She smiles, shakes her head, he moves on without nodding. Was it the time he asked her for? A direction? She has no idea. She stops and touches the iron railing that runs beside her, above the sloping bank to the water. For a moment she closes her eyes; the light shows red inside the screen of her eyelids. The hiss of bicycle tyres the louder for her not seeing them. A girl laughing from the bridge she was at a few minutes before. She crosses the street to the deeply shadowed footpath on the other side, beneath the cliff-like rise of drab unlived-in buildings, the decay of what once, as the ornamentations, the fine bay windows tell, were gracious apartment blocks. She leans back to read the street sign attached to the wall above her, the word filmed with dirt, the letters hard to make out. Although she knows already what it will be. *Ozcrim.* She says it aloud, as she heard Mrs Boronsky pronounce it for her, when she showed it to her on the map. And the name her landlady would not have heard, the only one that matters to herself. It was not a number she looked for then, but the building, the scrap of building, in the photograph she had known since as a child she stood on tiptoes to look at it on Daddy's desk, Babcia when she was young. A bigger word too he had said, the one the old lady had told him the house was called, and the child's mother, the first wife who so disappointed him, saying again, 'You'll only confuse her, David, using words like that.' The steps of the building Esther now stands at, beneath the projecting ornamental windows, the deeply scalloped stone panels to either side. A building similar but not identical is beside it to the right, a vacant weed-strewn scrap of raw earth to its left. The panes of glass in the different windows on several floors are smeared with grime. Remnants of curtains hang at some of them. The effect is dismal, charmless, the hollowed shell of what she would like to imagine, the impossibility of anything but what this minute they are. The summoned dead refuse to assist. The glamour of the street as David had always thought of it, the colourless shell she now stares up to. She walks up the broad curved steps to stand in the cavern

307

of the high porch, its smell of damp and powdery stone. She touches the black ornamental iron knocker, a beast of some kind with a heavy ring through its mouth that moves stiffly as she grasps at it. The dead fall of its knock against the wood. As close as one comes.

Esther descends the steps and looks back along the pavement. The street is empty. The laughing of the schoolgirls still there, but distant now, until hushing into the tunnel beneath the trees. She crosses the road to stand again beside the rail above the water, the slant of afternoon light. She looks for the last time at the high grey building, the embrasures of empty windows, the shreds of curtain. She then walks back, past the wooden bridge, further on again, taking in across the street another group of buildings, these ones lived in, two children at a window on the second floor, a small dog with its paws against the glass of another, its head jerking with the yelps that cannot be heard. She walks to where the width of water ends in a sudden abutment, and wide roads curve and meet beyond it. She is at a huge memorial, its stone vigilant lions too tall for children to be able to clamber, a huge sculpted naked man, his legs braced, his back arched, his posture the grand defiance victors assume, high above her. She begins to read but does not understand its inscription, something she assumes about victory and defeat, the dates of one inevitably the date of the other, before the century even that concerns her. It may as well be the hieroglyphs of an Egyptian monument. For a moment Esther feels not oppressed by all this, but liberated. It is not her quarrel, not her triumph. There is nowhere to fit, ever, but where one is. Milan would mark that as another of her clichés.

Mrs Boransky smiles and is glad when her young visitor, who must be worn out she supposes with galleries and churches and whatever serious young foreigners find of interest to them, says yes, she would love some soup, and then coffee and cake, she would be so grateful. She had not felt like eating as she passed the rows of restaurants on the way back. Music had come from groups playing at different places, string quartets and jazz groups and occasionally soloists who struck her as heroic, gifted cellists, saxophonists, musicians her own age, who busked for casually attending tourists, offering the classics they once presumably had thought it was their gift to serve, now watching the opened cases of their instruments as coins rattled into them, or where occasionally a person who had attended to them longer leaned forward and placed a note. The gift at least of attention. Paying that.

Mrs Boransky laughs as she tilts a slender bottle and pours wine into a blue flute for the girl, and into another for herself. Once poured, the wine looks as though they are drinking ink. They touch glasses. Mrs Boransky says, '*Na zdrowie.*' Laughing, Esther repeats it after her. Later the older woman pours another glass, glad to have the occasion to allow it. They chat easily together. She asks what the girl has done all day, and is amused when she answers, 'Looking for history.'

'Did you see so much?'

'It seemed to know I was coming so we couldn't see each other.' It's good, being like this, as if knowing exactly what the other says is unimportant. Mrs Boransky asks, 'Our university, you must have seen that?'

'I don't think so,' Esther says.

'Seven Nobel Prizes. A town so small as this.' Three was

it?—four?—were Jews. The man who invented chlorine gas for the Germans. Whose wife was also a scientist and killed herself when the gas was used. Another fact. Another pebble fallen down a well. Esther again touches the rim of her glass against the landlady's, who cannot believe she likes her young English visitor so much. She says the words again that say more or less what they intend, 'welcome' and 'this is to your future, your happiness', for only those who are content together would want to say it, '*Twoje zdrowie*'. She then looks at Esther, not remembering quite what it was they spoke of.

'Seven at least,' Esther reminds her.

She comes back to the dinner Debbie has prepared for them that afternoon, a stew that isn't English, as Milan's mother likes to say, something from foreign parts she supposes but one of the good things her husband has left her that didn't wear off over the years, the recipes he picked up in one place or another in his years knocking about. She says as Esther opens the door to the flat, 'No woman wants to come home to cook for herself first night back.'

Debbie has set views on how people should live together, a checklist of protocols she draws on as occasion calls for them. 'Especially,' she says, 'back from a place like that. You need something that's good for you.' Milan tried to tell her the trip to Poland was a kind of homecoming in its way, but it cut no ice. That Esther wouldn't like what she was forced to eat there was to be assumed. 'Well, apart from where I stayed you're right about that. Dull food. Rude waiters. Now I've found what my heritage is.'

'Proves my point.' Debbie takes her jacket from the peg behind the door. As if she'd think of hanging around to share the meal with them on the girl's first night back! She'd be home in half an hour, after the worst of the traffic, and watch television that meant something, as she always put it. Another of her certainties is that what Milan chose will be unwatchable. But then again, as she also likes to point out, if they weren't so different the three of them mightn't get on so well, might they? Esther is not always sure where Deb's utter certainty ends and pretence begins. As Milan says, 'If mum wasn't convinced education separates families, she wouldn't be English.' But they all hug at the doorway, there is a warmth there is no call to explain. Esther follows her down to the car. She presses her arm, leans down and kisses the older woman's cheek through the lowered window.

'That's all very well,' Debbie says by way of thanking her.

'She loves it,' Milan tells Esther, 'loves it I didn't end up with the kind of trashy local girls she warned me about since the time I was ten.'

Once back in the flat they embrace, kiss properly as they've wanted to do since she came back. 'Can I have my tongue back?' Esther says.

The table is already set. A clump of pansies flare in a small glass vase in the centre. Milan picks up an oven-mitt and takes his mother's stew from the oven. He places it on the tile they bought last year in Avignon, a medieval drawing of a skinny clawing cat. The suddenly opened oven door steams his glasses to white discs. He swears and bumps at a chair and Esther says, 'The blind feeding the hungry. See, I do know your Bible.'

'Pity Deb went home. She'd have been proud of you.'

'Smells divine anyway.'

'To the lot of us,' Milan says.

Esther tells him, 'I seem to have been drinking toasts for days.'

An hour later they sit on the battered sofa that came with the flat, when they took it over from a friend who had gone to Stanford. To the privileged world of the elite, Milan had teased him, and their friend, a physicist, told him, 'Journalism's envy of the higher callings.'

Milan empties the last of the wine into their glasses. Esther leans against him. She says, 'I sound like your socialist mates when I say I detest those pits of seduction at airport Duty Frees. Every bottle I buy adds to the argument.'

They are quiet, as he runs his hand along her leg. He asks, 'So you're back another person, are you? Now you've been?'

She had told him the obvious things over dinner, how the rebuilt city centre had struck her as impressive and vibrant and yet sad too, the replica that becomes the real thing, defeat turning into something else one has to believe in. How she admired the whole country for that. But the older parts that survived, the few bits of it in the streets away from the centre, were where she had felt more at ease, where she could say, 'At last I've been here.'

Milan stood to turn off the lights, apart from leaving the candle burning low on the table next to Deb's bowl of pansies. He came back to sit with his arm across Esther's shoulders. 'Glad you've come back anyway,' and she said, 'A good place to come back to.' She laughed, brushing his cheek. 'I'm at my best when I'm trite. My father used to say that about his business partner. For a long time I thought it was saying something nice.'

'Well it can be,' Milan told her. 'Both at once I mean.'

His face pressed against her hair. 'We don't have to talk.'

She closes her eyes and must have dropped off at once. The candle that much lower when she opens them. A flicker now as it burned near the rim of the candlestick that held it. She says, 'Your arm must be killing you?'

'Now that you mention it.' Then 'Here,' he says, standing, drawing her up beside him.

Esther says, 'Your mother would think I'm a slattern, leaving the kitchen like that until the morning.'

He takes her hand and raises it towards the wall, now a fall of deep shadow. He tells her, 'I got a sort of present for you. I'm dead scared now it might be one of the silliest things I've ever done.' It surprises her, his saying that, quiet, confident Milan. He is talking now to cover his awkwardness. He says he asked his friend Siggy at the Institute, a tough New Yorker so he knew he'd be straight with him, who had told him, Sure, you're not breaking any rules, but what the hell? Siggy had even gone with him to a place in Cricklewood, a room of antiques and such, if it was nineteenth-century he was after, this was the place. He even came back and advised Milan how to fix it, 'If it means as much as you want it to mean.'

Milan raises her finger and places it against a small metal strip at the side of the door. He said, 'Just to make it more like home for you. That's what I had in mind.'

Esther is glad that what light there is conceals the rush of blood to her throat, her cheeks, as if she was blushing, which she has never done, as if she might be angered even, but she could not be further from that. Milan lets go her hand, as her fingers spread against the metal case. He feels her tenseness as his own hand falls to her shoulder. He assures her, 'The design when you see it properly is from back then. It's the right kind. From the right place, I mean. Genuine.'

She presses her face against his woollen jersey. Merino. She had made a point of that, ordering it online from a factory in Dunedin last Christmas. Possum and merino, the label confirming it.

It is so vivid to her, the memory of her father coming to her, her mother too, when she was small, the way he touched the *mezuzah* as they came into the house, and her mother picking her up, her parents laughing as the child insisted she touch it too, and her somehow realising even then, how her mother so wanted it to please her father, the little girl asking to be lifted to do as Daddy did, to touch whatever it was. David's solemn explanation to her years later no doubt, why it was there, the tiny words on the scroll inside their metal case, declaring the room, the house, a special place.

She put her arms round Milan. She raised the wool at the back of his jersey, felt the warmth of his skin through his shirt as her palms spread across him. 'I can't believe,' she begins to tell him, 'can't believe you thought of it. It's a bit mad and mixed up and I've never had anyone do anything near so kind for me. So important.'

'That's all right then,' Milan says. 'Just glad you're home.'

1938

What Mother liked best was the family in what she called 'full flight', meaning the dining table in the room with the big embrasure windows laden with good things to please her guests. The number who might sit there varied from week to week, travelling relatives on their way through to Berlin or even further, occasionally slightly awkward but still welcome *Ostjuden*, when Father deliberately embarrassed her a little with the halting Yiddish he drew up from his youth, teasing Lisabet even more by translating for her. But he delighted in seeing how the Shabbat dinners so enlivened her. And whatever the number that sat there, always those who lived at the handsome residence in Schweidnitzerstrasse, Chaim and Lisabet of course, and old uncle Sol, with his sentimental addiction to operettas, his self-flattering belief he had spent a life working hard in the bank where yet another relative had kindly kept him on; Mother's sister Hannah, with her journals, her novels, the packets delivered each month with their Berlin postmarks; Father's less than brilliant brother Ephraim, a mild accountant who disliked argument, whose saving phrase was 'the worst has passed, surely?', whom Hannah quickly grew impatient with and would at times go so far as telling him, 'We are a people afflicted with paralysis, does that occur to you?' Mother then taken by embarrassment of another kind, by any challenge to her certainty that the family was an example to all, that harmony was yet another approving seal to what they had all become, in the generations from the *shetl*—not that she would ever have put it so starkly—to the handsome city they were part of. She liked repeating that. Not lived in but were *part of*. But Vati's deep satisfaction too, that he could provide all this for those who mattered to him, a deep quiet pleasure his daughter Ruth more than any of the others was aware of, as he encouraged the harmless fantasy of those he housed and fed that they contributed in some substantial way to the life they shared. His insistence from the end of the table, holding the long thin bottle of Gewürtz, 'You're not stinting yourself there, Sol?', or 'Eat up there, Hannah, we owe it to ourselves.' The Friday evenings especially he looked forward to, his agnosticism notwithstanding—the feeling of timelessness as the bread was uncovered and his uncle intoned the verses that bound them, his catching Ruth's eye through the meal and winking at her. Dear Ruth, so solemn and competent and kindly, but would to God, he thinks, that there might be some young man, even one of the older earnest students from the seminary across from the synagogue, whose eye she might catch? So unlike her sister there in distant Berlin for years, with her politics, her clever writing, the rest of her life that he and Ruth might at least protect the family from being

316

distressed by. He sighs and puts the thought to one side, and says when the talk comes back, as inevitably it must, to the bad things that each week get worse, 'There is so much to put our minds to.' The streets even here they already make a point of avoiding, the careful recent awkwardness with neighbours they have spoken with for years. The friends who are one day not there, who sensibly moved on. The Blumhardts from the pastry shop gone this week. They are fortunate with relatives in England, which is not so far. But Mrs Blumhardt, a nervy, garrulous woman, Lisabet says, why be surprised at the suddenness of it? One must think about these things more rationally.

'Bad times,' Ephraim mildly supports her. 'When have we not had bad times?' The Hirshfelds, Vati tells them, whom he heard about only today, that humourless family who have sailed for Australia! How would they go down there, Chaim wonders, the boys with their long curled locks, their hats, the father with his chest-length beard! How his own family's certainty of their being Germans after all, say what you like, and whatever fanatics might be shouting at the moment, closing on them like a door, as only Ruth comprehends. A door they cannot imagine seeing through.

Father's friend Doctor Guzmann, who is often their guest, begins, 'Should you ask my opinion,' at which Lisabet leans to touch his sleeve, 'Whose else would we ask for, Herr Doktor?' Her sister Hannah nods agreement. And so he tells them, 'If my wife was not so confined by illness, as you know she has been in recent years, I would now be in practice in Main Street, Bronx.' The doctor likes to be precise, informed. He uses the address of a cousin, who married into real estate.

'I have things in hand,' Father tells the table. 'Each week I am attending to it. Ruth knows that.' He feels more determined by being able to say so. Sentiment too has its part in firm intentions. It is Ruth though who says, as Doctor Guzmann nods in agreement, 'Nothing will improve. The sooner one plans the better.'

'But the turmoil of it,' her mother says. 'Can't you imagine the sheer *business* of it all.'

'Others manage,' Doctor Guzmann says, and Uncle Sol nods. 'Times change.'

Ephraim folds and unfolds his napkin, turns its pewter ring as he has done since he was a boy. He is glad he had never married. He will read late, which always comforts him. But one stays alert, of course. One does not cope with things the way the family is coping without staying alert. He looks across to his brother, smart practical Chaim, and thinks warmly of how much he owes him. A good man, praise God for him.

'Yes,' Father assures them, 'Ruth and I keep our eye on things, believe me.' Ruth who sometimes thinks, have we left it too late as it is? There are so many more like ourselves, Mother reminds them, who are not to be panicked. As were the Blumhardts, the pastry people.

Then one Friday Doctor Guzmann does not arrive for Shabbat dinner. He has sent a note apologising, there are unforeseen problems. Father too comes in later from work than usual, but in time to light the candles. He asks Uncle Sol to say the *kiddush*. The old man's voice takes on a richer tone as he holds the cup of wine and begins, '*Barukh atah Adonai . . .*' But the evening is already sombre. There is silence until Maria the Polish maid has left the room, and he tells the news. That Guzmann and his wife are in Riga.

318

The doctor had permission to attend a medical conference, and his invalid wife surprised neighbours a few days before as she walked towards the car that she steps into as any other woman may have, not even a stick to aid her. They had spoken of it to no one.

It is the deep hurt of his friend not confiding in him that so brings it home. Father says to Ruth that he could have been so—but leaves his sentence in the air.

'Words run out,' Ruth says. They are sitting in the office before walking home. How he has depended on her for years, yet looks at her now, this solid, reserved young woman, as if there is so much he has been too occupied to take in. He had never thought of her as clever. Not as her younger sister is. Sarah who so easily learned things, who at fourteen won a city prize for an essay on Goethe that was published in a newspaper. Sarah with her golden hair as if she stepped from a storybook. But it was Ruth who now took the two folders from the safe, the letters and details from shipping lines that he had left it to her to assemble, to have on hand, 'in case', as he had been inclined to say. 'To have on hand.' In case. With things so different now, quite suddenly. As if Guzmann leaving like that, without confiding, was a blind sprung up and the room quite changed. Back home he would stand at the big bay window and look down on the shining trees, the stretch of water, a boy breaking its surface with his skidded stones. He would turn and light the candles and take his *kippah* from the sideboard and nod towards Sol, and smile at Lisabet and sit beside her. A little later, after the news of Guzmann, he tells the family again it is as well to be prepared.

It was a dull, almost silent weekend. The weather was broken. No one suggested a walk even across the little bridge and along the promenade. Mother lay in bed until late, Hannah read a novel, Sol played his gramophone in his room so it sounded as though Vienna may have been at the far end of the house. No one enquired about Ephraim when he did not show up for lunch. On Monday morning Father joked, as he and Ruth had breakfast together, and Maria remarked they had scarcely touched the cheese or the dark bread, 'We might see an accident later in the day to cheer us all up.' And as he took his black hat from the antlered hatstand in the hallway, and Ruth lifted an umbrella from a deep porcelain vase, he said so they both smiled, 'And so the workers go off, to support the bourgeoisie.' Downstairs, he pulled at the ring in the lion's mouth to click the heavy outer door.

'You and Sarah have more in common than you think, talking like that,' Ruth told him. And so they spoke of her as they often did, as they walked towards the office and its workroom in the dull street near the Bahnhof, but seldom spoke of her at home. Vati liked remembering what a delight it had been when she was there with them, Sarah his favoured one, which of course a father never said. Smart as a monkey, hadn't his own mother said that when the old lady was still with them, the child hopping round, reciting rhymes she seemed to learn out of the air? Lisabet saying the child was spoiled beyond belief, closing her eyes in frustration as she used words copied from her grandmother, expressions used by villagers, some of them uncouth. But Sarah making from cardboard a little hand with a pointing finger that fitted over the end of a pencil so Lisabet could run it along the lines of her book, the way the Rabbi did with his scrolls, and winning her over. 'Yet broke her mother's heart, I make no apology for saying that,' Lisabet repeats, 'I make no apology for saying that.' The girl with her political notions and going off to Berlin, writing for papers it was not sensible to write for, but at least she changes her name and spares her family shame. Doctor Guzmann would sometimes defend her, 'Her views may be extreme but they are correct much of the time.' Sarah who now had not been back home for three years, and only then for an uneasy few days, when she had said to the whole family, 'Most people I respect no longer believe in marriage. There are so many more important things than labels others put on us.'

As she spoke, her sister had watched her admiringly. The courage to say such a thing as that, at the long table that since childhood had been the centre of their world. Later in their bedroom she laments to Ruth, 'They are living in an old world there is no room for.' And with what is both sadness and scorn, 'They are still proud of what they think their country is.'

'You can't tell them that though.'

The sisters looked at each other. Ruth says, 'You have no idea how bewildered they are. Uncle Sol with the music he believes is his Germanic soul. His war medal to prove it over again. Our aunt still reading *Jugendstil* to show she is modern.'

Sarah laughs, 'You could write a satire page for us if you only believed how sharp you are!' There is a minute when they joke again and reminisce. Does her sister remember, she asks, when she can have been no more than four, and had run off to find Uncle Sol in the bank in distant Albrechtstrasse, run across the bridge and past the bookshops near the White Stork and further on, crossing the tram tracks and through the little square that opened into the great square itself? When it was known she had run off Mother had telephoned their father and Aunt Hannah who hated the embarrassment of a family that could not watch its children, the neighbours too, the friends from the garment shop, all running about, imagining—well, whatever it was they imagined—that the Hungarian gypsies had inveigled her, the Cossacks had arrived expressly to hunt her out, the stories that had scared their own childhoods! Neither sister wanting the spell to break, this casting back together, 'And you were the one who found me. You coming up to me by the statue of the bear outside the Town Hall.'

'You were trying to feed it one of the chocolates Mrs Rosenheim gave you as you passed her shop. You had asked her to give you one for Uncle Sol and one for the bear that had stood there forever and no one had ever given him one.'

They lay in beds on opposite sides of the room. Once the light was off Sarah sat up on her bed, drew the heavy velvet curtain back from the window beside her. 'The sky, and silence at the same time. You forget in a place like the capital what that is like.'

Then they spoke of course of the child. There were too many uncertainties to keep her with them, she and the girl's father quite knew that. Once Sarah had thought there was nothing she would so much want Mother to know, to know her grandchild's name was her own. But can you imagine if I had? That kind of shame that would destroy her. Vati thought that too.

Ruth heard her sister slap her pillow, in irritation was it? Perhaps not. She said, 'What different worlds we live in,

Sarah. I can't even guess at yours.'

'The communists are the only ones who will stop them,' Sarah said. 'Everyone else accepts.'

'There's so little I know of anything,' Ruth said. 'A handful of people who matter to me. A few ideas I am easily muddled with. Beyond that so much becomes a blur.'

'Which is the thinking we must destroy,' Sarah said. 'Think clearly and everything follows from that.'

Last thing before they slept, Ruth said, 'When we get up I must brush your hair. I can't imagine how you ever get on without me there to brush it.' She had wanted to cry, but laughed to cover it. Sarah saw through her at once. She stretched out her hand in the dark, to touch Ruth's that was there to meet it. 'Even Marx admitted Jews are sentimentalists. We have to work on that too.'

They walked together to the station. Other passengers leaned from the windows, but Sarah stood back behind the glass as two uniformed men walked the platform until the train pulled out. Last thing, before she had stepped up into the carriage, she pressed her sister against her and said, 'You mustn't worry about young Lisabet at least. Her father is as devoted to her as I am. It's the best we could do for her.'

'I wish you'd told me more.'

'She's safe where she is. They'll look after her.'

And now three years further on. 'Almost four,' Father corrected her. It was late in the day. He locked the office door before bringing the folders to the desk. He had told the foreman from the workroom to leave them for an hour, make sure they weren't disturbed. A good decent man, Palachek. He worried for the workers, Chaim knew that. Orders had fallen this last year, but he was determined not to lay men off. What sort of people would we be? Orders from Berlin, for the crafted furniture that was still in fact so in favour, the *völkisch* designs people seemed to believe appealed to their earthy patriotic hearts. Chaim not unaware of the irony of it, nor Palachek either, who joked with him, 'I hear people in uniforms like to stack their homes with it?' And Chaim and his foreman close enough to smile, as they understood, without needing to declare it, there must be another reason for the orders dropping off. Zimmer, of course, Zimmer with his handsome house in the Bayerisches Viertel, a man cannot do better than that; who had taken the furniture for years for his chain of stores in several cities, taken the tables, the carved-back chairs, the sideboards, as much as they could send him, things he praised for their workmanship and craft from the workshop behind the office where Ruth and her father now sat. But in this past year Zimmer's name gone from his stores, the friendship and business of years brought to an end with a brief letter explaining nothing, beyond 'We regret . . .' The new owners regretted too, there were commercial demands more in tune with the times. The first time Chaim had seen a business letter ending with a salute.

Ruth sees how her father, within these last few days, has become more obviously dependent on her. Since Doctor Guzmann's letter, delivered by hand by another medical friend. Not excusing himself, but explaining his leaving as he did without a word. He said for his wife's sake, but also his own, he could not risk telling even Chaim, his dear friend. Things were worse than they had tended to think, bad enough as that was. He knew from a patient of his, a high-ranking officer but a decent enough man, that things soon would become much worse for them. He implored his dear friend to decide at once. He gave him the name of an agent who would most certainly do what he could, if he used Guzmann's name. That was all. A simple S at the letter's end, as if already Shalom might not be written. Destroy the letter when it had been read.

'We will destroy these too,' Chaim said. The folders of private correspondence, the letters from old friends in America, in France. As if, Ruth thought, Vati thinks by rushing now, he makes up for the time we have lost. She bundled the answers from cursory queries about shipping lines and sailing schedules, and more personal letters, a postcard that amused her, of a giant head at a kind of fun park, a brief note on its back from a distant cousin, saying 'This is at the end of a street where the *konditorei* would make you think you were at home and not in Melbourne.' Letters with postmarks from Manchester, the Bronx, Argentina. For years it seems Chaim had written asking questions, and filed the answers away until the day they might be useful. 'Better to get rid of them all,' he said, and Ruth assures him, 'We are not being searched you know, Vati.'

'You read Guzmann's letter,' he said. 'Nothing is safe.' She sees his hands move nervously. This is not like her father at all. And before he unlocks the office door—it has never been locked so far as she remembers—knowing she watches his hands, he tells her, 'Don't be disconcerted by that, Ruth love. My head has never been more clear.' He has already telephoned the number to the agent, as his friend advised. He will hear back for certain within a few days. In the meantime she will go to Berlin. She will take a bank draft for her sister. This is not the time to talk of it now, but he knows more of Sarah's life in the capital than Ruth might think. The draft is on an English bank. 'It will provide for them,' he says. 'You must do everything to urge her.'

It is arranged as simply as that. She would take the Berlin train as Sarah had last taken it three years before. Father holding his daughter's secret, as Ruth too has guarded it. And her thinking now, the tragedy of that, how we are the only ones to speak of it, Mutti having no idea. Was that perhaps too why her father had so delayed, not wanting to leave Sarah? It is too bewildering a fact to think of clearly. The dreadful muddle we are in. The fear, even from yesterday, that rises about them like a tide.

It is so much later than usual when they begin to walk back home. The workmen had left hours before. It worries Chaim what will happen to them. He will leave all that to Palachek, whom he knows he can rely on. By the time she is back, in a few days' time, he says to Ruth. As soon as that, they will know what they are to do. It will not be an easy time. He will have told the family. At least she will be spared that. 'The wailing,' he says, with heavy irony.

His daughter takes his arm, his hand comes across to rest on hers. She tells him, 'It's cold enough for gloves. You should know that by now.'

'Shh!' Vati says. 'How often can we listen to quiet like this?'

Uncertain times, the inspector on the train complains as he goes through the carriage, explaining passengers must change at Guben, nothing is as it should be. Ruth sits in a waiting room where an elderly woman next to her, who wears a brooch with its small hooked cross set between silver leaves, says the delay is a small price to pay to be prepared. A freight train rumbles through the station without stopping, its covered wagons stretching on and on. The woman says she regrets her husband passed away the year before, he would feel as she did the exuberance of watching their country rise to its appointed task. She mouths 'exuberance' as though it were a word she heard another person say and had been excited by. Her face took pride in sharing it. She offers Ruth a section of the apple she placed on a white square of cloth and cut neatly with a pearl-handled knife. Ruth accepted the small gift. She says it was early in the year for such fruit? She encouraged the woman to talk about herself. When asked herself was she visiting relatives, as the woman was, she says it was work she was coming to the capital for. An interview for a government agency. 'They have encouraged me to apply.' There will be work enough for all, the woman confidently says. Where there is order there is work.

Once the train arrived they mounted separately. Ruth took care that they sat apart. But the woman smiled across the distance between them, and a young man in uniform raised her suitcase to the netting above her seat. Ruth watched the broad flat passing country, the fields ploughed and misty, the early November trees sketched against the sombre spaces between the tidy villages, the towns. It surprising her how frequently the red flags, with their white circle and broken lines, were draped at windows, on buildings, bright static flares. Yes, it had been too easy at home to watch the changes in the streets, to hear the way people spoke differently and raised their voices or quietly said little, minding their own business. To repeat, as Vati's brother Ephraim did, that things surely would pass. As if

327

repetition made it more likely to be true.

It was late afternoon when they arrived at the great station with its echoing spaces, the hiss and clamour of the trains, the slanting lights and the press of passengers leaving platforms, pushing towards them, the growl, as it came in on her, of a great city about its business. How timid, almost, how distant, Breslau seemed! Far more men in uniform too than she had expected to see—police, army, costumes that told her nothing but authority, watchfulness, there to protect. The gleam of leather, tilted cap-brims, boots, as if so much was smeared with oil, light skidding from them. She supposed it must be like this every day, every evening. Again, so sharply her sense of what a backwater they were in at home. How much you believed might be kept at bay once you closed the door in Schweidnitzerstrasse! It is all so like a performance that surrounds her, that one was caught up in. But the laughter too, her surprise at how many people laughed and called to each other, embraced as they met, held their hands high to departing trains. As she moved from the concourse she heard a band playing on the wide street, a procession of some kind, was it? But then as Sarah had written to inform her, in a note without an address or a name signed to it, there would be a friend to meet her, a friend who had seen her photograph, who would know the colour of her scarf to watch for, the coat too with its astrakhan lapels, its curved half-moon brooch.

A woman now touching her sleeve, saying 'Take my arm,' as she stood by the glassed panels displaying timetables for the eastern lines. Saying her name is Carla. The woman so heavily made up, her mouth so vulgar and bright, it is difficult to guess her age. But the shock of more than that. A tart. One who so obviously stood out.

328

Her perfume. The sense she gave of display. She smiles to a group of military men at the wide entrance to the station, they grin back, the first time Ruth has seen such a thing, how to smile with contempt. Arseholes, Carla said.

Sarah, in one of her rare light moments, will tell her a little later, 'The perfect way to not draw notice to a stranger, a whore with a female friend on her arm.' The shop owners might take them in with middle-class contempt, but not the police, not those who stand with their thumbs in their belts and display their armbands. They take their cut. They know who to leave alone. Carla is invaluable. 'They cannot conceive that a woman like that might have subversive thoughts, cannot at some time be used to inform.'

The woman led her across tramlines and between the heavy swinging trams, across to the side of the huge square towards crammed shabby streets. Crowds milled in the big open space with what seemed a vague intent but no immediate focus. A sense of life on edge. Most of the men seemed poorly dressed, restless and alert. Some spoke to Carla, amused by the dull woman who held her arm. 'Auntie come to town?' 'Two for the price of one?' Carla said the city was like a fuse, who knows when it might flare? But oddly it was music she then talked about, her friends in some of the clubs that were being closed down, the musicians no longer allowed to play. She mentioned names as though naturally the woman she walked with would know who she meant, and Ruth felt her remoteness from so much, how like a kind of dark carnival all this was, a world in which Sarah surely must be at risk? 'She moves often,' Carla said. 'Luckily this time she is close to Alexanderplatz so we are almost there. The papers she wrote for of course have been shut down. So much comes and goes.' Then Carla laughed, not unkindly, but her words stinging for all that as she tells Ruth she so looked the kind of harmless woman from outside the city, as if nothing apart from groceries would occur to her, she would make the perfect cover. Yet provincial as she might be, Ruth picks up from Carla's constant looking about, the pressure of her arm, that her guide is anxious too, but brave for whatever was required, and would get on with it. Then she is left at a door that Carla taps at and walks away before it is opened, and her sister is in the unlit hall, waiting for her.

She had always known that comfort was not of great importance to Sarah, that so much of it at home had irked her as a teenager. As Vati joked about it, the girl was a cradle Marxist without needing to read Marx. But the raw dampness of the apartment, its lino-covered floors and cheap furniture, repels her. Sarah takes in her glance. 'Come on,' she says, 'there are worse things. At least your bed is fine.'

She leads through to the kitchen with its table, its two chairs, its books and papers neatly piled on the floor. A small kerosene heater glows like a red fist against one wall. 'Better to keep your coat on,' Sarah says. Only now do they embrace. Ruth runs her fingers on her sister's cheek, feels the thinness of her through the cardigan she wears. Again Sarah spells out what her sister thinks. 'You don't come to Berlin to be another plump Aunt Hannah.'

'That's as well,' Ruth laughs with her.

Sarah takes a plate from a cupboard, and two cups for coffee from a pot that simmers on a burner. Slices of sausage, a square of cheese, two slabs of bread. 'Looks like breakfast I know, but if you're hungry.'

330

Ruth tells her, after that train journey it's *Die Silbergrotte,* a favourite place when they were children and were taken for a special treat. The man behind the counter with one arm stumped from the same war as Uncle Sol's, his suit sleeve folded back and held against his shoulder with an ornamental pin, an injury that so fascinated them as girls, and Mother instructing them to stare at something different about someone was not what polite people did.

They drink more coffee, and when the heater flickers out Sarah brings blankets to wrap around them. So much to speak of, to catch up on. Sarah tells her what of course could not have been said in letters home. That Albert through some church group had heard word of Lisabet, whose name had changed even before she was taken there. She would be a schoolgirl speaking English, what turns history takes! 'As if you need ask,' she says, to Ruth's 'You must miss her.'

It was beyond her sister's comprehending, the belief Sarah so held to, the belief one gave up everything for or betrayed one's soul. It was almost ten years now since the baby was adopted out. One could not work as a journalist for the party, as an organiser, a courier, and expect a family life. 'We will win, you know,' Sarah had said. That time back home a few years before. 'There's an imperative larger than our own designs.' Words that meant so little to her sibling, who had known since they were at school Sarah's certainty that the future was their own to make.

'They must be after you, then,' Ruth says. 'All the time.' She means those she had seen at the station, the uniforms, the slogans. Their cold strutting excitement at dressing up.

Sarah shrugs, as if too weary to agree. She says, rubbing her wrists as though they ached, 'We should talk about Vati.

331

What he plans.' And so Ruth tells her of the arrangements he was making even now, the quick leaving he had in mind that of course would distress their mother and the others, but at least their father saw at last nothing could be delayed. 'We must work out a way to let you know. Once we are there. Wherever we get to.'

'I move about,' Sarah says. 'But we'll find a way. Albert will help.' Albert whom she is no longer with, who moved in some years back with a comrade from Bremen, but the personal must be put aside, she implies. This is not the old world we live in now. But of course they saw each other still. Never forget he was the one who arranged little Lisabet's new life. She was insistent that Ruth knew that. It would be impossible had they left things until now. The comrades had seen what was coming so much more clearly than most. The one important thing he might do, he had done. 'Whatever else.' They sat on in the cold kitchen, talking until late, until Ruth touched her sister's arm and told her, 'You're exhausted. We must go to bed.'

When they stand Sarah picks up from the table the bank draft their father had sent Ruth expressly to give her. Enough there for England. America. Wherever she chose.

'You'll use it? You'll arrange things too? You must.'

'Of course,' Sarah says. But almost indifferently, it seems to Ruth. As if weary even about herself. She takes the manila envelope, raises the corner of the lino at the side of the room to slip it beneath. Nothing more is said of it.

For a few moments, then, a reaching back in both their minds to the big bedroom years ago at home, as they now go to the freezing room across the corridor. 'Don't undress,' Sarah tells her, assuming there is no reason to spell out something so obvious. One never knows. This is

332

the way things are. She lies beside her sister in the narrow bed. Their hands meet, and at once her breathing alters, and she is asleep. Ruth presses close to her, thinking back to then.

When she wakes, Ruth is in bed alone and hears voices from the kitchen. She stands at the door, to see Sarah sitting at the table, her chin on her closed fist, her hair falling to one side, curtaining her face. A man stands leaning against the wall by the unlit heater. Ruth shivers at the heavy chill. She has seen the man before, but only in photographs when Sarah was back home years before. He is tall and fair-haired, his arms folded, his head tilted forward as he speaks quietly, then stops and turns as she enters. He nods as though they might have known each other for years. There is a scar across one eyebrow like a tiny track.

'I'm sorry,' Ruth says. 'I overslept.' She senses an urgency that places them beyond normal courtesies, even that of saying who they are. Sarah says simply, 'It is better, Ruth, if you leave at once.'

Albert explains in a few sentences. The growing unrest these last weeks. The rabid, brawling marches, the daubed yellow stars. The humiliations, the confiscated shops. There are rumours of worse to come and very soon, today even. Tonight. Although one scarcely needs the rumours, there is the stink of it already in the streets, in the air one breathes. Sarah looks at her sister. 'I want you to go right away.'

That is what she and Albert have been speaking of. Even if it means travelling north, then connecting back to Breslau in a roundabout way. This morning, she says. Right away. Her friend will walk with her to the station. She herself will move out after they have gone. Not that there are guaranteed safe places, but some are safer than others, one has faith in that. Albert watches both women as they walk to the small hallway. 'Better not to take that,' he advises, and Ruth puts down the small valise she had carried with her the night before.

The sisters embrace. 'You must eat more,' Ruth says, smiling at how inane she must sound to clever Sarah, who says only, 'You will let me know? About everything?'

Walking here last night with Clara it had seemed as if they were in some kind of fairground, the moving shadows, the groups of men in cafés, the seethe of pedestrians that moved more as though circling itself than with direction, the sense of being on the verge of more than was taking place. How different, the feeling that came to her this morning. The grey light washing across the facades of buildings, the apparent ordinariness of a city's day beginning, and yet it was more than that, as if the dregs of last night's anticipation lay there still.

'Walk as though you are used to all this,' Albert says, as they cross in front of the huge Bahnhof, into the ringing hall, the announcements, the long drifting banners, the echoed shouting she could see no source for, the presence yet again of military figures. That sense always, so it seemed to her, of performance, of display; and yet behind them, through them, the newspaper kiosks, the food stalls, the tables where already foaming glasses are placed by waitresses with puffed homely sleeves, the haste and loitering of travellers. The life of ordinary things.

Ruth asks, 'Will there even be trains? The ones we need, I mean?'

Albert laughs. He assures her, 'There are always trains.' He hands her the ticket he has ready for her. They stand back as a man with a barrel-accordion is ushered through from a platform, four uniformed men accompanying him, and a woman who screams at them until she too is taken with them. 'So much for music,' Albert says. Yet it is strange, Ruth thinks, how little she feels for the man who is helping her, her niece's father. The oddness of thinking of him as that. Who at least had got the girl away.

There is an unreality about all that she now looks at, walks through, towards the *Wartezimmer für Frauen* for those with first-class tickets. Albert holds back the door for her, and then he is gone. She sees him walk towards a man in uniform. He is lost in the crowd.